The Purity Pledge

KJ Quinn

Published by New Generation Publishing in 2022

Copyright © KJ Quinn 2022

First Edition

The author asserts the moral right under the Copyright, Designs and Patents Act 1988 to be identified as the author of this work.

All Rights reserved. No part of this publication may be reproduced, stored in a retrieval system or transmitted, in any form or by any means without the prior consent of the author, nor be otherwise circulated in any form of binding or cover other than that which it is published and without a similar condition being imposed on the subsequent purchaser.

ISBN
        Paperback   978-1-80369-323-1
        Ebook   978-1-80369-324-8

www.newgeneration-publishing.com

WHAT'S YOUR STORY?

This book was published through
The Book Challenge Competition part of
The London Borough of Barking and Dagenham
Pen to Print Creative Writing Programme.

Pen to Print is funded by Arts Council, England
as a National Portfolio Organisation.

Connect with Pen to Print
Email: pentoprint@lbbd.gov.uk
Web: pentoprint.org

Barking & Dagenham

June
2018

Cars cruise the rows of the conference center parking lot, which is rapidly filling. At the far end of the last row, surrounded by concrete shimmering with heat, the door to a silver Porsche 911 Carerra swings open. A slim woman wearing a black jumpsuit with spaghetti straps emerges, dark hair and Gucci sunglasses piled on top of her head. She wipes her palms on her pants and grips the gold chain of a black handbag, walking past the empty spaces.

Her mother had told her not to come – "Why bring up the past, hon? When you're doing so well?" – but it's been ten years. *Ten years.*

Her heels click past cars and vans with baby seats and bumper stickers.

My son is an honor roll student!
Christ is Life – the rest is just details
Gun control means using both hands

Cars pass her, their occupants staring. She pulls down her sunglasses and focuses on the breathing exercises her therapist recommended. *In for four counts … hold for four counts … out for six counts …*

She approaches the clusters of green and gold balloons swaying in the breeze. A forest green banner spells out **Welcome Class of '08!** in gold lettering above the entrance. She becomes surrounded by couples merging and accumulating until the entrance is a mass of exclamations, laughter, hugs.

Her heart beats a fierce tattoo against her ribs.

She takes one more breath and walks through the throng under the banner.

It's been ten years.

It's time for some fucking answers.

August
2007

"He that walketh with wise men shall be wise: but a companion of fools shall be destroyed."

PROVERBS 13:20

ONE

"Well, honey, I think this is so exciting," Molly's mom widened her eyes and grinned.

Molly stared out the passenger window, picking at the skin around her nails.

"And I think it's wonderful you're dressing up a little for your first day. Senior year. This is the year that really counts." Molly's mom glanced over at her as they pulled up at an intersection. "Why wear jeans? You look great!"

Molly wasn't wearing jeans because she couldn't fit into them. A summer of watching soaps and working at McDonalds had resulted in Molly gaining about twenty pounds. And she wasn't wearing her shorts even though it was about 90 degrees because her legs were pale, fat and disgusting. So she was wearing the only pants she could still fit into. Molly was wearing her frigging McDonalds pants to school.

"Can you let me out? I'll walk from here," Molly said.

"What? Molly, hon, it's another two blocks."

"Mom, let me out. I want to walk."

"Molly, I have to drive right past it to get to work. It's hot out there, just hang on."

"*Mom.* Let. Me. *Out.*"

Molly's mom sighed and pulled over. She turned to look at Molly. "I know you're nervous, sweetheart. Maybe a little walk will do you good." She reached over and patted Molly's thigh. "But if you just keep doing what you're doing, you'll have a fantastic year. Just keep getting those grades, and you'll be able to go to any college you want."

Molly could feel her mother willing her to make eye contact and kept looking straight ahead.

"I'm so proud of you. Have a good day, chicken, and I'll see you back at the house, okay?" She released the door locks.

Molly grabbed her bookbag and climbed out of the car. "See you later," she muttered.

"I love you!" her mom sang as Molly slammed the car door, rolling her eyes.

Molly trudged towards the school, cars and buses full of students passing her. She had walked past two houses when the friction of her rubbing thighs began to burn. The polyester pants seemed to be soaking up the heat. She pulled at her t-shirt to get some air circulating around her chest but it settled back on her damp skin instantaneously. There was still another block to go and the straps from her book bag were digging into her shoulders.

She should have stayed in the car.

TWO

Lauren applied another coat of mascara and couldn't stop Proverb 11.22 popping into her head. *As a jewel of gold in a swine's snout, so is a fair woman which is without discretion.* She felt the usual pang of guilt, but the men who wrote the Bible never went to high school.

She hid the tube of mascara at the bottom of a half unpacked box and crept down the stairs, wincing as a step creaked. She made it to the pile of bubble wrap by the front door when she heard her dad call out from his study.

"Lauren, is that you?"

She hesitated, her hand on the door handle.

"Lauren?"

Lauren looked at her reflection in a mirror balanced on a stack of books. She saw mascara, blush and lip gloss.

"Lauren. Come here."

The words were becoming more clipped. Lauren quietly opened the door and heard his chair scrape across the wooden floor.

"*Lauren.*"

"Sorry, I'm late!" she called.

For the first time in her life, Lauren disobeyed her father. She jogged out of the house, pulling the door shut with a slam. She scrambled into her car, notebooks tumbling out as she threw her bag onto the passenger seat. As she reversed out of the driveway, narrowly avoiding the mailbox, she glimpsed her father's furious face peering out of the study window. She'd pay for this later.

THREE

Jason paused to wipe the sweat from his face and heard the school beginning to come to life. Muted conversations and giggles and shouts drifted into the gym, reminding him that he had fifteen minutes before homeroom.

Jason threw down the towel, picked up a ball and dribbled it along the court for one last three-pointer. The ball swished through the hoop, barely touching the sides.

"Good shot, Myers," Coach Wilkins clapped.

Jason jumped, unaware he was being watched.

"You've worked hard this summer. You still have a shot at playing college ball," Coach nodded, satisfied.

"I'll think about it, Coach," Jason lied. He ran to the edge of the gym to start collecting the balls rolling around.

"Leave it, Myers, I'll get them." Coach Wilkins picked up a ball and shot it into the ball cage. "Have a good first day back."

"Thanks, Coach."

No excuses left for procrastination, Jason jogged to the locker room, limbs flailing as they always did without something to hold onto, a basket to aim for. He'd miss the last few weeks, when most days the gym was his alone. Coach had even given him a key to let himself come and go as he pleased, the first student he'd ever done that for.

But part of him was impatient to get the year over

with. Jason stared in the mirror, rivulets of sweat running down his face. Ten more months, 292 days, 180 school days, and he'd be free to go and start a new life.

FOUR

Lauren's escape from home had been an effective distraction from the butterflies in her stomach, but they had now returned in full force. She walked down the empty hallway, looking for her homeroom. She'd had to wait for her schedule from the secretary, who had been busy answering one phone call after another. The bell had rung as a freshman had entered in tears, which took up another five minutes of the secretary's time. Now Lauren was ten minutes late for homeroom – so much for making a discreet entrance.

She found Room 24 and looked through the narrow window in the door. A grey-haired man with glasses was standing in front of the chalkboard talking with wild gestures, telling some kind of story. He grinned and laughter erupted from unseen students. Lauren tucked her hair behind her ears, pulled her shoulders back, and opened the door.

"Sorry I'm late," she said, relieved her voice wasn't shaky.

"Welcome! You must be ..." The teacher consulted a list. "Lauren Davis?"

"Yup," Lauren gave him a small smile.

"Hi Lauren, I'm Mr. Keating. Welcome to your homeroom." He was overly hearty. "Why don't you sit at the back there, next to Tiffany? Tiffany, give Lauren a wave."

In the last row of chairs, a pretty, tanned girl with blonde hair in a bun raised her arm, expressionless.

Cheeks burning, Lauren walked down the row of desks, watching out for chair legs or rogue feet ready to trip her up. Unscathed, she sank into her chair and turned to give Tiffany a grateful smile, but Tiffany was staring out the window, chewing gum.

"So Lauren, you're from – where is it now? Idaho?" Mr. Keating asked. The students craned around in their seats, waiting for her answer.

"Iowa," Lauren's voice trembled and she cleared her throat. "Des Moines, Iowa."

"Well, yes – Iowa. That's right. Idaho, now, there's a beautiful state. But, Iowa ... yes, well ... a lovely place, I'm sure."

Lauren gazed at him, avoiding the curious stares of her classmates.

"Well. Anyway, welcome to Hanwell High." He paused, then did exactly what Lauren was dreading. "And let's all be welcoming to Lauren, and help her settle in. It can't be easy moving right before senior year."

Lauren felt tears spring into her eyes and stared down at her desk, hating her dad with every ounce of her being. She could feel the students looking at her, judging her. Deciding whether she'd be worth talking to, or making fun of, or – worse – not worth anything at all. She envisaged class after class of sitting by herself, lunchtimes spent eating alone, a prom night she wouldn't have a date for. She blinked back tears. If her mascara ran then they'd have a reason for making fun of her.

A small hand with chipped pink nail polish placed a pack of gum on top of her notebook. Lauren looked up and Tiffany grinned. Lauren smiled in surprise. Tiffany was probably one of the beautiful, popular girls that everyone wanted to be friends with – and now, it seemed, she wanted to be friends with Lauren. Lauren unwrapped a piece of gum and popped it in her mouth, savoring the minty flavor. Maybe things wouldn't be so bad after all.

And Lauren was right. In fact, her day actually got better. When the bell rang at the end of homeroom, Tiffany asked Lauren if she wanted to eat lunch with her later. Lauren was pleased but cautious – she'd seen enough movies to know the new girl was always lulled into a false sense of security before the popular kids took her down. But as it turned out, it really was an invitation to eat lunch with Tiffany and her friends. As they sat in the crowded cafeteria, sharing a table with several girls on Tiffany's cheerleading squad, Tiffany explained that her boyfriend had moved a million times.

"He says moving is just the worst thing," Tiffany said cheerfully. "Says it totally blows. Apparently he and his mom moved all the time – California, Texas and everywhere – until his mom got a job here. Which is crap for him, cause California would have been amazing to live in, but worked out well for me, huh?" She looked smug and Lauren laughed. She had already heard, several times, how cute and talented Jason was, but hadn't seen him yet so she could only use her imagination.

"Why'd he move so much? What does his mom do?" Too late, Lauren realized she shouldn't have asked.

"Some boring accountancy thing. I dunno." Tiffany crunched a carrot. "What about your parents?"

"Er, yeah," Lauren busied herself with her baked potato, picking off bits of tuna. "So when do I get to meet your boyfriend?"

"Well, how about right now?" Tiffany looked past Lauren's shoulder and beamed. "Hey, baby!"

Lauren turned around and saw a tall, mixed race boy arriving behind her. For some reason, her first thought was how difficult it must be for Tiffany and Jason to kiss, given the contrast in their respective heights. But wow, what an attractive couple they were.

Jason squatted down next to them and gave Tiffany's hand a quick squeeze. "Hey, yourself."

"Jase, this is Lauren. She's new." Tiffany nodded towards Lauren.

"Hey, how you doing?" Jason asked, his eyes flickering across her face.

"Hi, nice to meet you," Lauren wondered about extending her hand but Jason had already turned back to Tiffany.

"So I have to go, just wanted to say hi." He stood up.

"Jason, don't be rude, sit down with us," Tiffany said.

"Oh, I can't. I want to practice some lay ups. But nice to meet you."

Jason smiled at Lauren and shifted his bag onto his other shoulder. He squeezed Tiffany's hand again and walked off in the direction of the gym. Lauren smiled to herself. He clearly wanted to kiss Tiffany, but in a crowded cafeteria, there was no privacy.

"God, sorry about him," Tiffany said but she was grinning as he walked away. "He's always playing basketball, or thinking about playing basketball, or *dreaming* about it or whatever." She rolled her eyes. "So what do your parents do, again?"

"Oh, you know. Boring stuff, too," Lauren blushed.

"What's his name again? He seems nice."

"Jason. Yeah, he is." Tiffany beamed. "So like, what kind of boring stuff?"

Jeez, she was like a dog with a bone.

"Um, well, my mom doesn't work. She takes care of the house and my two little brothers. And one of my brothers was sick for a while, a few years ago, so she looked after him. Which was pretty much a full-time job, you know – because, yeah, that took a lot of time." Lauren heard herself yammering on and finally paused for breath.

"Your brother was sick?" Tiffany looked intrigued. "Like, really sick?"

"Yeah," Lauren nodded. "He had leukemia."

"Oh my God."

"But he's okay now, he's fine. Yeah, like, completely fine."

"Wow. That's crazy." Tiffany's brown eyes widened. "Could he have died?"

"Well ..." Lauren always tried not to dwell too much on that. "I guess, but –"

"Because I was watching this show the other day – about this kid, and he got really sick? I can't remember what now, but they made a whole documentary about how much it messed up his family, especially his sister. And his parents got divorced and everything. Oh my God, it was so sad," Tiffany looked anguished. "The kid died in it. I mean, he *actually* died. Like, for real." She stared at Lauren meaningfully.

"It was so sad," agreed Jessica, who was sitting next to Tiffany.

"But then, the sister ended up having a whole episode just about her. Like, about her going back to school and stuff after the funeral. She basically ended up having her own TV show." Tiffany finished her Diet Coke and crumpled the can. "On MTV! I mean, how lucky is that?"

Lauren blinked.

"I mean," Tiffany's cheeks turned a pretty shade of pink. "You know ... obviously not about the dying stuff."

Thankfully, the warning bell rang and the cheerleaders got up to throw away their half-eaten salads. Lauren wished she hadn't chosen a jacket potato. She felt bloated and anxious as they left the cafeteria to go to their Biology class. But at least Tiffany hadn't asked her about her dad's job.

"Oh, yeah." Tiffany turned to her. "What does your dad do?"

Lauren sighed. The truth was going to come out anyway, so it might as well be now.

"He's a minister," she admitted.

"What?" Tiffany frowned. "What do you mean?"

"Like, he's a minister. In a church. On Sundays. He's the guy giving the sermon." When Lauren was younger, she had thought her dad was amazing, standing up in the front of a church and speaking to a congregation. Now Lauren just wanted to curl up and die whenever she watched him preach. Or told anyone about his job. Or any time she thought about him at all. "So, yeah. That's his job ..." she trailed off lamely.

Tiffany stared at her, oblivious to the ringing bell signalling they were late. This is it, thought Lauren. Friendship already finished on day one. Thanks a lot, Dad.

"Oh, Lauren." Tiffany grabbed her arm.

"Yeah, I know." Lauren nodded. She had been so stupid to think cheerleaders would really be friends with her, or that wearing makeup would somehow make her popular. "It's okay. We don't have to –"

"This is amazing," Tiffany grinned. "My parents keep telling me to hang out with a nice, sensible girl, and now here you are. It's fate!"

"It is?"

"Yes. Of course!" Tiffany's enthusiasm was infectious. "Now I can say I'm with you and they'll have nothing to worry about. I'm so happy we're friends."

Tiffany linked her arm through Lauren's and marched her into the Biology Lab. Lauren smiled, aware of the other students' envious glances. She wasn't sure what had just happened, but it had definitely worked out better than expected.

In Computer Science, Tiffany ignored the classwork entirely and helped Lauren set up a Facebook account. She uploaded and tagged a photo of her and Lauren standing in the hallway, their arms around each other's shoulders, captioned 'We survived Day 1! Only 179 days to go LOL.' Tiffany had undone two buttons on Lauren's polo shirt before their photo ("You don't want to really *look* like a minister's daughter, do you?" she'd snorted before applying blusher and shiny lip gloss onto Lauren).

Lauren received twelve friend requests, mostly from the girls at lunch, but a few from people she didn't even know. She looked around the lab, wondering if anyone was doing the classwork at all.

When the final bell rang, Tiffany invited Lauren to the mall with Jessica and Brianna, who had sat with them at lunch. Lauren instantly said yes, buoyed up by the unexpected success of her first day. She sent her mom a text to let her know she'd be home late. As Tiffany drove them to the mall, windows down, singing along to the radio, Lauren realized she was looking forward to her senior year for the first time since her parents had told her they were moving. In the excitement of trying on the makeup testers, helping Tiffany choose new jeans, and buying some denim shorts for herself, chosen by Tiffany and much shorter than what she would usually wear ("to make you look, you know – normal," Tiffany had said), Lauren lost track of time. It was suddenly 6 p.m. when she checked her phone. She had three missed calls and a message from her mom.

Are you ok? Pls come home now. Your father is worried. Love you.

She had quickly tapped in a message *Sorry! At mall, heading home now, Luv u 2 x*

Lauren had wanted to leave immediately, but the other girls weren't finished looking around and Lauren needed a ride back to her car at school. They had started teasing her, singing *Son of a Preacher Man* and changing the lyrics, and Lauren laughed in spite of herself. As Tiffany pointed out, they might as well be at the mall because they had no homework and they were buying clothes, not crack (which had made Lauren laugh even more). Lauren sent her mom another message and resigned herself to staying until they were finished, pushing down her nervousness.

When she was finally on her way home, Lauren got lost and started feeling nervous. All the houses looked the same and she spent ten minutes circling around looking for her street before realizing that her neighborhood was a half mile south. As she pulled into the driveway, almost two hours after responding to her mother's text, Lauren's stomach contracted.

She opened the front door as quietly as she could, but as soon as she softly closed it behind her, she heard her dad's voice calling out from his study.

"Lauren, come in here. Now."

"Just a minute," Lauren called out as she headed towards the stairs.

"I said *now*." His voice thundered.

Her brothers' faces peered over the banister, their eyes wide. She gave them a grimace and turned around. She entered the study, her hand shaking as she turned the door handle. Her dad was sitting behind his mahogany desk at the computer, books lining the wall behind him. He was holding his 'Blessed Dad' mug and the smell of coffee permeated the room.

His eyes ran over her bare legs, the new shorts hugging her hips, across the open buttons on her polo shirt, and came to rest on her eyes, covered in glitter eyeshadow and mascara. He placed the mug on a coaster.

Why, *why* hadn't she thought to change and wipe off her makeup in the car?

"I don't know why you think it's acceptable to be coming home at this hour, dressed like a –" he clenched his jaw and cleared his throat. "I don't like your attitude, young lady, and I am not impressed with your behavior. Your mother tried to convince me this is normal for a teenage girl. It is not."

"I'm sorry. I was just trying to make new fri–"

"*Don't* backtalk me." His voice trembled with fury. Lauren felt a rush of fear despite her father not raising a hand to her for years. "If this high school is the kind of place where this behavior is normal then we need to change it." He steepled his fingers together. "I'm organizing a purity pledge for the high school seniors at church before you all head to college. Temptations there will be even greater."

Lauren was devastated. Her dad had mentioned a purity pledge last year, but she had hoped he would forget in the chaos of moving. Lauren tried to picture someone like Tiffany still wanting to hang out with her when she'd publicly committed to years of virginity. It would send Lauren into exile – she'd spend the last year of school miserable and alone.

"Dad, I really don't think –"

"*I am not finished speaking.*"

Lauren's heart pounded.

"You will take part in the ceremony. You will commit yourself to purity and chastity and behave in the way a young woman should. Someone that your mother and I can be proud of." He glanced at her shorts. "Unless, of course, it's too late?"

"Wh – what?" Lauren stuttered. She felt sweaty, shaky.

"Have you been a young woman of God?"

"I – what?" she repeated helplessly. She felt tears building up in her eyes, threatening to roll out and send dark stripes down her cheeks. She imagined her dad's disdain and blinked frantically. "No, Dad, please. I mean, of course I have. I wouldn't ever –" she struggled for the words as her dad sat gazing at her in silence, almost as though he was enjoying her suffering.

"I'm, I'm waiting until I get married." Lauren didn't know what other words to use and felt herself flush with embarrassment. She looked at the photo on her dad's desk, the five of them at a church picnic, years ago, smiling at the camera.

Her dad stood and Lauren involuntarily took a step back. He stared at her, eyes narrowed. Please God, let this be over. She would never come home late again. She would stop wearing makeup. She would stop wearing stupid, slutty clothes.

"Go to your room," her dad snapped. "And remove that muck on your face. Your mother doesn't need to see you looking like a whore."

Lauren backed towards the door to hide her shorts riding over the curve of her backside. She slipped out of the office and closed the door behind her, relieved to see her brothers had disappeared. She could hear Michael excitedly chattering about a class guinea pig from the kitchen at the end of the hallway, her mom making encouraging noises. Tears streamed down Lauren's face in dirty streaks as she silently padded upstairs to her room, wishing she was still small enough to curl up in bed next to her mother.

FIVE

The beeping noises began as Jason was running down the court, about to pass the ball to line up a shot. He was confused, hearing the harsh bleeps over the shouts of his teammates. Was it a fire alarm? A tornado drill? But no one else seemed to hear, they were just shouting his name over and over because he was taking too long to make a decision. He panicked and passed the ball to the defense. He realized his mistake as soon as the ball left his hands and groaned, but his teammates were shaking him, furious. He'd let down his friends, his school, his parents. Again.

"I'm sorry, I'm sorry," he implored at the sea of angry faces, desperate to find some sympathy. "It was a mistake, I –"

His eyes flew open and he was staring into his mother's face as she stood over his bed, her hand on his shoulder. Her dark eyes were barely visible in the gloom.

"Jason, your alarm's been going off for ages."

Jason blinked, struggling to emerge from the depths of sleep. The alarm beeped incessantly. Jason reached for the button on the bedside clock and knocked over a glass of water.

"Sorry," he murmured, his voice husky.

"It's just water." His mother turned on the light by the door. "I'll get a towel. You need to get up."

Jason watched the puddle of water spread across the carpet and shivered. Maybe he should skip this morning's training. It had been past 2 a.m. when he'd finally fallen asleep last night. He needed to increase his dose, like Dr. Schaffer had offered. But then Dr. Schaffer would ask why. And his mom would notice the prescription had changed. But maybe it would be worth it?

He brushed his teeth and dressed quickly, pulling on the shorts and t-shirt that were folded up on his chair, and made his way to the kitchen with his bookbag.

"Mom?"

"Mm-hmm?" she stared at her laptop and clicked the mousepad. A mug of steaming coffee and an empty bowl were next to her.

"I was wondering something." He sat across from her at the table.

"Make sure you eat breakfast. We're leaving in five minutes," she said, her eyes flickering across the screen.

Jason got up to pour cereal and milk into a bowl and sat back down.

He cleared his throat. "Do you remember, er, a while ago –"

"Hmm?" she scribbled something in her day planner.

"When I started, er, seeing Dr. Schaffer?" Jason heard his voice breaking.

His mom lifted her head. "Yes?"

Jason opened his mouth but a cough emerged instead of words. He circled his spoon around the bowl.

"Jason, what is it?" His mom closed the laptop and leaned forward, like a detective ready to catch out a criminal on a minor detail during an interrogation.

"I was just wondering if maybe, if – if um," he scooped up a huge mouthful of cereal, and chewed slowly. His mom tapped her shiny red nails on the table. He forced himself to swallow down the cornflakes, which tasted like cardboard. "Um, I was wondering, if, if we could change the time? Of the appointment?"

"Oh." She sat back in her chair. "I'm sure we could ask." She put her laptop and day planner in her bag. "What time were you thinking?" She drained her coffee.

"Just by like, fifteen minutes. So there's not so much of a rush?"

"I'll call his secretary later, I'm sure that'll be fine." She stood and took her bowl and coffee cup to the sink.

Jason stared at her. The fitted skirt suit and high heels looked so uncomfortable. For the hundredth time, he wondered if she really had to dress like that for work or if she chose to spend her days in physical pain to prove a point.

"Jason?" She rinsed the dishes in the sink.

"Mmm?" He chewed another mouthful of cereal, cramming down the urge to ask – no, beg – for something that would give him just one night of pure, unbroken sleep.

"You do find the sessions helpful?" She kept her back turned.

Jason concentrated on capturing the last flakes of cereal in his spoon. "Sure. I guess. I mean, I don't, you know. Yes. Dr. Schaffer's nice."

He tipped the bowl to his mouth to get the last of the milk as his mom turned around.

"Jason, that's uncouth –"

She was interrupted by the beep of his cell phone. Jason glanced down and saw a message from Tiffany and his stomach contracted. He pressed open.

Morning! How r u?
I'm good, kinda tired. You free later on?
Yes come over xoxo!!

Jason exhaled with relief. After Monday's disastrous afternoon, he hadn't been sure she'd want to see him again, or even if she was still his girlfriend anymore. He smiled to himself and glanced up. His mom was gazing at him curiously.

"Sorry," he said.

His mom turned around and clipped across the kitchen tiles to the hallway. "Let's go," she called.

He sighed and picked up his bookbag. When he was eighteen, he'd get a prescription for the strongest sleeping pills in the world and it would be no one's business but his.

Jason survived hours of classes with the help of Pepsi and numerous bad jokes from his best friend Calum about what he or may not do with Tiffany that evening. Now he just had one more hour to go.

"So, Jason." Dr. Schaffer rested his large hands on a file and looked across the desk. His bulky frame, shaggy beard and slightly mournful expression reminded Jason of Winston, the St Bernard dog his family used to own. "Ready for the new school year?"

"Yes, thank you. Looking forward to it," Jason nodded his head and suppressed a yawn. Talking about the future always made appointments go smoothly.

"Good. Glad to hear it."

Dr. Schaffer shuffled through some papers in the file for an interminable amount of time. Jason swallowed and shifted in his seat. Five pencils and only two pens were in the holder on the desk but otherwise the office was the same as always. Dr. Schaffer read through some notes and raised his head, his eyes invisible behind the light reflected on his glasses.

"And you'll be playing basketball again?"

"For sure. Yes, on Varsity again. Shooting guard."

Dr. Schaffer smiled blankly.

"Offense," Jason offered. "It's a good position."

He knew Dr. Schaffer didn't give a crap about basketball but he had spent entire sessions talking about games, tactics and techniques. Dr. Schaffer seemed content to sit nodding his head or jotting down notes. It was better than it used to be when Jason had filled the gaping silence with whatever came into his head, like what he had eaten for dinner or watched on TV. And the more Jason talked about basketball, the better prepared he was for his next game. His playing improved and he scored more points with each session.

In June, after Jason had spent over forty-five minutes explaining the complexities of man defense plays, using diagrams to illustrate various outcomes, Dr. Schaffer had suggested that their sessions be reduced to 30 minute 'check-in's' once a month. Jason's mom had been thrilled at this development. Jason's new goal was to get his sessions down to fifteen minutes.

"Shooting guard. Well done," Dr. Schaffer congratulated him. "Exercise is very helpful for mood elevation. And sleep."

Jason nodded, resisting the urge to turn around and look at the clock on the wall behind him.

"And how are you sleeping now?"

Jason hesitated. "Better. Yes, much better. Really well." He sat back in his chair and forced his hands to rest casually on his knees.

"Hmm." Dr. Schaffer stroked his beard and jotted something down in the file.

Jason wondered if beards were prerequisites for becoming a shrink because all the male ones he'd met had them. He preferred female psychiatrists. They kept things tidier.

"So," Dr. Schaffer put down his pen. "Anything else you want to talk about?"

"No, thanks." Jason couldn't believe how easy this session had been. Definite progress. He stood up.

"I think we have a few more minutes."

Jason sat back down.

"So, how are your symptoms? The counting?"

"Non-existent."

Dr. Schaffer raised his eyebrows.

"Almost." Jason clarified. "Almost non-existent."

"Huh. And now that you're sleeping better, no memories coming back?" Dr. Schaffer leafed through the papers in the file.

"No."

"Nothing playing on your mind?"

"No."

Dr. Schaffer tilted his chair back and nodded slowly.

Jason's legs were jiggling up and down. He pushed his knees down with his hands and willed himself to stay in the chair instead of running out of the room.

"Well, then," Dr. Schaffer said. "I'll tell Penny to make the next appointment for September."

"Great." Jason jumped up. "See you then, thanks."

At the end of one of the longest days of his life, Jason lay still, listening to Tiffany's breathing, astounded that he was really – finally – here. In her bed. Naked. He glanced down at her. Her closed eyelids flickered and a thin line of drool made its way slowly from her mouth down her chin and onto Jason's bare arm. He had never expected Tiffany Vanderkamp to drool. It was gross.

At least their second attempt at sex had gone more smoothly. The first time, on Monday, had been so terrible he hadn't been sure he'd get another chance. He burned with embarrassment as he remembered it. Tiffany had been stretched on her bed, wearing only red lacy underwear. When he had fumbled with her bra hooks, she had snapped, "Careful, it's Victoria's Secret!" like it made some kind of difference.

He had panicked and torn the sheer fabric as he pulled his hand away. She had rolled her eyes and wriggled around, unhooking the bra herself. Jason had watched her, arms awkwardly by his sides, his legs dangling off the side of the bed, unsure whether to help. What would his teammates say if they knew he was screwing up his first time with Tiffany?

Things had gone from bad to worse when they were both naked. After trying not to react to the sight of Tiffany's pubic hair (there was so much! Was that normal?) Jason had been physically unable to find the right location to make losing his virginity a viable option. Was he too tall? Was his dick too big? Tiffany was pretty small though – was it her? After she had said "Not *there*," three times, she had pushed him away and muttered "You have to go. My mom will be home soon."

He had left without being sure whether they had

done it or not. But this time had been much better. He grinned. Finally, he wasn't a virgin any more. Definitely. But still, the whole sex thing seemed to be … kind of awkward. He closed his eyes and tried to take his mind off his arm, which was aching and trapped under Tiffany's head. He thought about Tiffany's new friend, Lauren. They had History together in the mornings so after meeting her at lunch, he'd smiled at her when she walked into the classroom the next day. She apparently took this as an invitation to come and sit next to him and had done the same every day since. He spent most of class watching her neat handwriting spread across her notebook as she wrote down everything the teacher was saying. Her nails were short and neat, free from nail polish and not bitten to the quick like Tiffany's.

Jason wondered what sex would be like with Lauren. She would have white cotton underwear, not little scraps of fabric that tore as soon as he touched them. She would just laugh gently if he struggled with her bra, or caught his fingers in her hair. Lauren would smell like fabric softener and keep her eyes open the whole time.

Jason felt the tingle of an erection begin and willed it away. Why was he thinking about some random girl when he had the most beautiful one right here? Tiffany shifted, and the pain in his arm intensified as she began to snore.

SIX

Molly's pants had been digging into her waist all morning and now she was getting a stomach ache. There were another three hours to go before her shift ended. She rolled back and forth on the balls of her feet, which were already aching and sweating inside her black Wal-Mart tennis shoes. She rested her belly against the cash register and watched yet another customer approach.

"Welcome to McDonald's, can I help you?" Molly asked mechanically before realizing that her customer was, in fact, Tiffany Vanderkamp.

Her heart sank. Seeing Tiffany always made Molly feel like a disgusting piece of lard. She watched Tiffany delicately nibbling her fingernails while pondering the menu above Molly's head. Tiffany's white shorts hugged her slim hips perfectly, and she was enveloped in an oversized black t-shirt with a diamante D&G logo across the swell of her breasts. It probably cost more than all the clothes Molly owned. It was about half the size of Molly's clothes too. Molly knew she was getting bigger, and the seams on her pants also knew – and they were dangerously close to losing the battle with her thighs. Yet somehow, every weekend, she managed to defy physics and squeeze herself into the brown polyester trousers and mustard yellow polo shirt that always had a lingering scent of grease, no matter how often her mom washed them. Molly hadn't been able to do up the button of her pants for the past two weeks, but skillfully concealed this by untucking her polo shirt a few inches so that it hung just over the waistband. No one had noticed and anyway, she would lose weight soon. Definitely. She would diet and go running and do sit-ups, or whatever didn't cost any money. By college she would be thin, and pretty, and wearing diamante t-shirts too. Maybe her pimples would have disappeared by then as well, but she didn't want to be too hopeful.

Tiffany was still standing before her, silently mouthing the options on the menu to herself.

"*Can I help you?*" Molly found herself shouting.

Tiffany started and looked at Molly with wide eyes, like Bambi caught in headlights. Molly pointedly looked at the line forming behind her.

"Sorry, I just can't decide!" Tiffany giggled.

The man behind Tiffany smiled forgivingly as he ran his eyes over her curved behind. No one ever looked at Molly like that.

"I guess I'll go ahead and have the chicken wrap, no dressing and a coke. To go." She looked at Molly properly for the first time. "Molly! I didn't know you worked here. Hi!"

"Yeah, hi," Molly punched in the order. She hated kids from school seeing her here.

"Wait. Make that a Diet Coke."

"Sure." Molly hit the amend key.

"No, wait," Tiffany interrupted. "I don't know. Do *you* think the chicken wrap is good?" she enquired.

Molly waited, her hand poised over the register. "It's McDonald's," she pointed out.

"You're right, it's all good," Tiffany agreed, opening her Gucci wallet to pay.

"Is that everything? You don't want fries?"

"Well, I do but, no. Thanks."

Molly felt strangely shy. She and Tiffany had known each other since sixth grade and this was the longest conversation they had ever had. She finished placing the order, giving Tiffany change from a twenty-dollar bill without making eye contact.

"Enjoy your meal," Molly said loudly as she handed over the small paper bag, aware that her manager, Darryl, was in earshot.

"Thank you, you too!" Tiffany smiled at Molly before sauntering to the door, already rooting through the bag and oblivious to every guy's eyes following her across the restaurant.

What an idiot. *'You too!'* Jesus Christ. Whatever. Molly turned her attention to the next customer, who was gazing out the window at Tiffany's backside as she wandered to her car.

"Welcome to McDonald's, can I help you?" she snarled.

Three tortuous hours later, Darryl spoke to her for the first time that day.

"Hey, Molly. Can I talk to you for a second?" he asked from behind the counter.

Molly looked up cautiously from the seat by the window where she was keeping watch for her mom's car and picking at the spots on her chin. "Sure, Darryl."

Molly stood up and pulled off her cap. She let down her ponytail and fluffed up her shoulder-length brown hair. She followed Darryl into what passed for an office. It was so small that with both of them in there, it was uncomfortably close, especially after Darryl closed the door. As they both perched awkwardly on opposite ends of the desk, Molly found herself getting nervous. Was this going to be the moment when Darryl would make unwanted sexual advances and she'd refuse, and then he'd fire her? Or he'd say she could become assistant manager, but only if she let him put his hand in her pants? Or maybe he'd be more refined – and slowly reach over, resting one hand lightly on her thigh, gently cupping her face with the other...

Molly felt her face flush red, while Darryl seemed increasingly fidgety and nervous. Oh God, this was it. This was totally happening. She *knew* he had a thing for her. Ever since he'd told her she was the only person he could trust to open up at 5 a.m. on a Saturday morning. The way he'd looked at her then said it all. And now, now –

"Molly would you like a new uniform?" Darryl blurted, his words falling over each other. He stared at her, a wild-eyed look on his face.

" ... What?" Molly squeezed her cap with both hands.

Darryl took a deep breath. "I was wondering if, if you wanted a new uniform," he said carefully, looking at a point over her shoulder.

"Er, no?" Molly looked down to examine her clothes, which were pristine considering she worked in a fast food restaurant. "We just got these uniforms a few weeks ago. Are they changing them again?"

Darryl cleared his throat. "I just thought you may be more ... well, more comfortable. In a new one. A new uniform. If you want one, I mean." Tiny beads of sweat formed on Darryl's forehead. "I mean, I remember being a teenager," he continued, now examining the ceiling. "Growth spurts, hormones ...

ha!" He picked up a McDonald's napkin from the centre of the desk and wiped it across his brow. A dark stain was spread across his armpit.

Molly clenched her jaw, putting her whole being into not bursting into tears. They listened to the wall clock ticking and the muffled clamour of the kitchen. Seven seconds passed before Darryl glanced up at the clock, opened his mouth and then closed it. He dropped his head and cleared his throat, and started picking apart the scrunched up napkin.

"Well," Darryl told her feet. "I guess, er, if you're comfortable, I mean, happy – then it's fine." He paused. "Good ... great!" He reached across her to pull open the door, his arm lightly brushing momentarily against her breasts.

Molly nearly collapsed.

"Okay then, thanks Molly. See you next time!"

Molly stepped from the office into the steamy, clattering kitchen and through the window saw her mom's Ford LTD waiting outside. She hesitated and then headed for the disabled bathroom across the restaurant. There was no way she could sit next to her mom being all skinny and perky, asking how her day was. Molly shut and locked the door behind her just before hot tears spilled from her eyes.

After an excruciating journey home ("Molly? Are you okay? No, but really – are you okay?" over and over and *over*), Molly went straight into her bedroom and slammed the door behind her. She unzipped her pants and groaned with the luxury of being able to breathe normally again. She pulled off her shirt, stinking as usual of grease, and threw it in the laundry basket. Before she put on her pyjamas, she stood in her bra and panties in front of the mirror.

Disgusting. Just disgusting. What if she couldn't fit into the dress she was planning on wearing to church tomorrow? Her mom had bought it for her a few weeks ago. In the clearance sale. With her staff discount. As usual. But at least it wasn't from the stupid Salvation Army and it might be floaty enough to look halfway decent. Navy blue and covered in small white flowers, Molly had shoved it in the back of her closet, dismissing it as too large and too ugly to bother with. She rooted around until she found it crumpled under some t-shirts she'd grown out of. She pulled the dress over her head and pushed her arms through the sleeves. She managed to get it over her shoulders and chest, but pulling it down past her stomach and hips was impossible. She tugged again and heard a small tearing noise but the dress didn't budge. Molly raised her head and gazed at herself in the mirror. Her greying underpants looked about to burst. Bunched up above her hips, with her cleavage spilling out of the v-shaped neck, the dress was a pervert's dream. There was no way she could wear this. Damn.

The floorboards outside Molly's room creaked. She looked at the door. *Don't come in, don't come in,* she prayed.

"Dinner's ready, hon!" her mom called.

"In a minute," Molly yelled. Why didn't the damn door have a lock?

Her mom's footsteps retreated and Molly started to pull the dress off, lifting her arms. But after sliding up over her face, the polyester came to an abrupt stop. The waist of the dress dug into the side of her ribcage, struggling to overcome the mounds of her breasts. Her head was stuck between her arms and she could smell her own sweat layered with the hamburger grease in her hair.

She wrinkled her nose and waved her arms, attempting to wriggle the dress up her torso. Nothing. Crap.

Bending forwards, Molly waved her arms more frantically. Heat travelled down into her face. The waistband popped up over one breast only to dig more sharply into the other. She blindly grabbed one sleeve with her other hand and tugged as hard as she could, ignoring the pain in her left breast. With a tearing noise, the dress finally squeezed over her armpits and head, catching her hair in a few buttons. She was red faced and sweating, holding the fabric over her head, yanking at her hair, when the door burst open.

"*Mom!*"

"Molly, come on! Your dinner's getting cold –" her mom stopped short. "Oh hon, let me help you with that, you're going to pull your hair out –"

"Just go away. Please!"

"Molly, don't be silly – I've seen you naked plenty of times." She reached towards Molly's hair.

"*No!*" Molly smacked mom's hand away and yanked the dress free, clumps of hair tangled up in it.

Her mom clutched her hand to her chest, looking at Molly as though she'd shot her.

"Sorry," Molly muttered, grabbling an oversized t-shirt from her bed.

Her mom opened her mouth and inhaled – was she going to shout? – but seemed to change her mind. She bent down to pick up the dress from the floor. "I'll just hang this so it doesn't get all creased," she said quietly.

"Just leave it. Christ, Mom." Molly pulled on a pair of sweatpants.

"It's fine, it'll just take a second –" she reached for a hanger.

"Mom. *Leave it.*" Molly pulled on her sweatpants.

"And don't take the Lord's name in – oh!" Her mom held up the dress, a gaping hole in its side staring out at them.

Molly pushed past her and went into the kitchen, her mom right behind her.

"Hey, hon, it's no big deal. I can sew it right up, no problem."

"No, it's okay. Don't worry about it." Molly slumped in her chair.

"I'll do it tonight, so you can wear it to church." She started spooning mashed potato onto their plates.

"Mom, please don't. I can't – I'll wear something else."

Her mom layered broccoli and chicken onto Molly's plate and handed it to her.

"It's no problem, you know me – I like to keep myself entertained when I'm watching TV and you've got all your homework," she burbled cheerfully.

She poured a drop of gravy over her meal and tipped the rest onto Molly's plate. Molly frowned. Why was her mom so skinny and Molly so fat when they ate the same meals? Did her mom seriously not see how huge Molly was getting? Or was she doing this on purpose? Making it appear they ate the same meals but serving Molly bigger portions to make herself even slimmer while Molly got larger and larger?

Her mom glanced up. "Eat up, hon. It'll get cold."

Molly watched as her mom carefully cut a miniscule sliver of chicken and placed a piece of broccoli on her fork. Her mom looked at her again.

"Molly? Are you okay? You seem ..."

She put her fork down on the plate, untouched. Amazing. Somehow her mom had made it *seem* like she was eating – waving utensils around, moving food to different places – but she was not *actually* eating. Her mom always ate slowly, but Molly had never considered that perhaps she wasn't eating at all. Was this how skinny people did it? Some kind of pretend eating method?

Molly looked down. The gravy-soaked mashed potatoes looked particularly appealing, but she speared a piece of broccoli with her fork instead.

"Molly, I'm going to ask you something and please answer honestly, okay?"

"Okay." Molly moved her fork from her right to her left hand and picked up her knife. She would eat the British way of holding the knife and fork at the same time. British people were skinny.

"Do you want me to exchange that dress for a different one?" her mom asked. "If you don't like it, just tell me. The label's still attached. I can sew that tear up at the seam, and they won't even notice," her mom said. "We can exchange it for a different one, I saw a red one the other day that would be nice on you. Was it the flowers? I did think maybe it was a little *too* feminine."

She *still* hadn't taken a bite of food.

"Just let me know what size to get, I wasn't sure," her mom shrugged, "Maybe I wasn't paying attention."

"Huh?" The broccoli plopped off Molly's fork into the potato. "The same size, Mom. You know my size."

"Well, you know. The way they make clothes now, it's all different, isn't it?"

"Not really. We only ever buy clothes from one place." Molly was so irritated she accidentally shovelled a load of potato into her mouth and was already swallowing it before she noticed.

"But you know, the different brands. It's just ..."

her mom finally – finally! – placed food in her mouth.

"It's just what?" Molly demanded.

Her mom chewed her food a while before swallowing. "Maybe come with me. To the store. Then you can try it on before we buy it. Just to make sure."

"To make sure *what?*"

"Well, you've got some beautiful curves, hon, and I just want to make sure I buy the right size." Her mom busied herself stacking chicken on top of more broccoli.

"You know what?" Molly threw her fork onto her plate and pushed back her chair. It scraped loudly across the floor. Her mom looked up in surprise. "The diet starts now. So screw the new dress and *screw you.*"

September
2007

"Children, obey your parents in the Lord, for this is right."

EPHESIANS 6:1

SEVEN

Lauren pulled into Tiffany's driveway and let the tears run down her cheeks, relieved not to be driving anymore.

"Oh my goodness. Your house is huge." Why hadn't she said *God*? Or even better, *holy fuck* – her favorite expression of Tiffany's but one she couldn't quite bring herself to say aloud.

"Your dad sounds like a nightmare, babe. A purity pledge. Like, whatever. 'True Love Waits' my ass." Tiffany rooted around in her bookbag and pulled out a tissue covered in lip gloss. "Come in a while, pretend you're helping me with homework." She patted Lauren's cheeks with the sticky tissue.

"That's disgusting, Tiff."

"What, homework? I know."

Lauren smiled and sniffed. "No, the tissue. And I can't stay." Her voice broke. "I'm grounded forever."

"Whatever. Come in, and I'll do your makeup. Take some photos for your Facebook profile picture? I could make your eyes really pop, you know. And!" Tiffany clutched Lauren's arm. "I have something that'll make you feel better, I promise!"

Lauren took the tissue and blew her nose. "I don't know. My dad said he's staying late at church tonight planning for the ceremony ... but I'm in enough trouble as it is."

"Say you're trying to convince me to do the purity thing, he'll love that. And I guarantee I'll make you feel better."

"Well, let me call my mom. I think she feels kind of sorry for me." Lauren wiped her tears and pulled her cell phone out of her bookbag.

"Hurry. The fun begins in exactly two minutes." Tiffany slammed the car door and skipped up to the house. She opened one of the double doors and disappeared from view.

Lauren's mom was thrilled she might convince Tiffany to take part in the ceremony (*"You're such a great influence, honey. Of course you can stay!"*). Lauren didn't feel as guilty as she expected to. She walked up to the house, which looked so much like the one in *Home Alone* she half expected Kevin to appear.

"Hello?" Lauren called out as she walked in the front door. "Mrs. Vanderkamp? It's Lauren, Tiffany's friend."

She stood on the white marbled floor in the vast entryway and looked around. A staircase curved along the right leading up to a balcony where she could see two doors. A cream armchair sat in the staircase recess, even though there was a huge sitting room with two white sofas and light beige carpets on the left. Maybe it was exhausting walking from the living room to the foyer and people needed to sit down. On the other side of the foyer, a cream marbled table with chrome legs held a large white vase of fresh lilies under a chrome mirror. Lauren had never seen so much white, cream and beige in her life.

"Hello? Mrs. Vanderkamp?"

"Don't bother. She's asleep. Or out. Whatever."

Lauren rubbed her puffy eyes and followed Tiffany's voice down the hallway and into a kitchen where she was peering into an enormous refrigerator. The kitchen was covered in stainless steel surfaces and black glossy cabinets as though making up for all the whiteness earlier.

"Mrs. Vanderkamp is out."

Lauren jumped at the voice which came from behind her. A Hispanic woman wearing a maid's uniform was loading a dishwasher.

"I'm just finishing here. You girls behave yourselves, yes?" The woman winked at Lauren.

Tiffany retrieved two Diet Cokes and bumped the fridge door shut with her hip. "Of course we will, Maria. You know me." She grinned and widened her eyes.

"Ay, yai yai, Miss Tiffany. I do know you. I've marked those bottles." Maria turned on the dishwasher and slammed it shut. "I see *everything*."

She left the kitchen and Tiffany rolled her eyes.

"You guys have a maid?" Lauren was even more impressed.

Tiffany shrugged. "Only on Tuesdays and Fridays." She opened a cabinet door, pulled out several bottles and placed them on the island in the centre of the kitchen. She crouched down so the bottles were eye-level and spun each one around. "I knew she was lying. Look – no lines. Just trying to scare me. *She's* probably drinking out of them, anyway. I would, if cleaning up after my mom was my actual job." Tiffany got two glasses out of the cabinet, filled them with ice from the ice dispenser, and opened a bottle of vodka.

Lauren watched, wide-eyed, as she sloshed vodka into each glass. "Oh my gosh. Isn't your mom home?"

"I don't think so." Tiffany put the bottle back in the cupboard and opened a can of Diet Coke. "Besides, we're just drinking soda, right?" She topped up the glasses with Diet Coke and handed one to

Lauren. "Let's go upstairs."

Lauren felt like she was holding an unexploded bomb as they walked up the staircase and into Tiffany's room.

"Wow, your room is so big. And your bed! Is that a queen?" Lauren couldn't see a coaster, so she put her glass down carefully on top of a textbook on Tiffany's bedside table.

"Um, I dunno. I think it's a king?" Tiffany sat on her bed, sipped her drink and started tapping away at her cell phone.

Lauren wandered around the room. Makeup was piled on a dresser next to several bottles of perfume. A corkboard surrounded by fairy lights was covered in photos – Tiffany cheering at football and basketball games, sitting on Jason's lap, and there was a younger Tiffany, probably around thirteen or fourteen, grinning with her arms thrown round a middle-aged man who had his head thrown back in laughter. It was like looking at a collage of the perfect teenage life.

"Is this your dad?" Lauren touched a corner of the photo. "He looks really laid back."

"Yeah, he's great." Tiffany sipped her drink. "Makes up for my mom being a total space cadet, right? So, make yourself at home." She put down her phone and patted the bed. Lauren sat opposite her, leaning her back against the footboard. Tiffany threw her a pillow and handed her the glass she had put down. "It's not usually this tidy, it's just because Maria was here. Don't expect this every time you come over," Tiffany said.

Lauren was thrilled to think she might be here regularly. She hoped Tiffany's car would take a while to be fixed, and then she could keep offering her rides home, even if it meant having to study at the library while Tiffany was at cheering practice. She lifted the glass to her lips but couldn't bring herself to swallow.

"If you don't like vodka you can have something else," Tiffany offered, taking another sip of her drink.

"I, um. No, I like vodka."

"You are a really bad liar!" Tiffany giggled. "Seriously, you don't have to drink it."

Lauren felt relieved.

"There's gin or whisky, although your parents will probably be able to smell the whisky so maybe not."

Was drinking a sin? Lauren was pretty sure it wasn't. Jesus turned water into wine, so it couldn't be.

"I just remembered, I can't drink. I'm driving," Lauren said.

"You can have a little bit. And you're not really driving for a few hours, right?"

Lauren studied her drink. It looked just like a regular Diet Coke. "Um, I guess not."

"It'll make you feel better, trust me. I always have this when I'm sad. Drink up, and then I'll do your makeup." Tiffany was almost finished with her drink.

Lauren couldn't imagine Tiffany ever being sad. "When do you –"

"You have tried alcohol before, right?" Tiffany asked.

Lauren had never tasted alcohol. She had literally never had the opportunity. Is this what high school was like for normal kids? They had cheerleading practice and drank vodka after school and went on dates with their gorgeous, basketball playing boyfriends? She thought back to her life in Iowa, and how rebellious she and her best friend Shelby thought they were when they had toilet papered the awful Mr.

Greenway's tree at Halloween. And even then she'd prayed for forgiveness afterwards. How sheltered her life had been!

"Well, I –" Lauren sighed. "No."

"You are *adorable*."

"I am?"

"Yes! You're like, like that girl – what was her name? The one who lived in a cabin?"

"Walt Whitman lived in a cabin?" Lauren offered.

"No, you must know! That girl. We learned about it in middle school." Tiffany finished her drink. "And there's a TV show."

"Oh, right. Laura Ingalls Wilder?"

"Yes! You're so cute. You're like her."

Lauren was so embarrassed. She'd read all the books and watched all the episodes – one of the few series her parents allowed her and her brothers to watch. Tiffany was right, she *was* like a pioneer girl. She didn't drink, smoke, or make out with boys. The worst thing she'd ever done in her whole life was ignore her dad once (once!) and put on some makeup (*makeup*! Like trying to look a little better was some terrible thing!).

"Now I feel kind of bad." Tiffany tilted her head, considering. "It's okay, I'll drink it. Don't worry." She reached over and took the glass from Lauren's hand.

"What? No. Screw that!" Lauren snatched the glass from Tiffany's hand and took a glug. The fizzy liquid burned her throat and she burst out coughing.

"Oh wow, prairie girl. I'm proud of you!" Tiffany clapped her hands gleefully. "Do you like it?"

"It's disgusting." Lauren swallowed the rest of the glass in five gulps so she couldn't change her mind.

Tiffany raised her eyebrows. "Want another one?"

Lauren's eyes watered and her throat was burning. "Yes." She belched and Tiffany let out a whoop of joy.

An hour later Lauren flopped onto the bed. "I can't dance anymore!"

Tiffany lowered the volume on the stereo and *I Kissed a Girl* softened. She sashayed up to the bed and pulled at Lauren's hands until she was sitting up, swaying gently. "Feel better now?"

"Yes. Much better," Lauren nodded vigorously. She felt the best she'd ever felt. Ever! How had she not known about this before? She'd missed out on so much fun! And why didn't her parents drink? Maybe they'd loosen up and enjoy life more, especially her dad. That's what he needed. A very large vodka and Diet Coke. Or two. The second one helped more than the first.

"Now it's makeup time. I'll get you looking sexy, Laura Ingalls!" Tiffany sounded very authoritative and Lauren grinned. "Not that you need much help, anyway. I think a couple of Jason's friends might be interested in you, by the way."

Lauren shook her head. Tiffany was sweet but deluded.

Tiffany rummaged around the makeup on the dresser. "Hmm, should we use blue eyeshadow, to bring out the blue of your gorgeous eyes? Or maybe reddish gold, for contrast?"

"You better tell Jason's friends to be careful. My dad will probably shoot them." Lauren laughed. "Or, or, hit them with a Bible or something!" She giggled hysterically and felt a tear run down her cheek.

"Hey, no crying!" Tiffany sat down on the bed with a pile of compacts, tubes and lipsticks. "Don't be sad.

We're having fun, and I'm going to make you look amazing!"

"I'm never going to be able to date anyone. So there's no point in anyone even being interested. That's the whole reason my dad's doing the stupid ceremony thing. It's so embarrassing. I hate being his daughter and I hate him." Lauren thumped her hand on the bed. "I *fucking* hate him," she corrected herself. It was very satisfying. No wonder Tiffany used that word so much. "*Fuck* him!" Yes, an excellent word.

"Yes, fuck him. And anyway, it's just a ceremony. It doesn't matter." Tiffany cupped Lauren's chin firmly and started rubbing something onto Lauren's face. "This is primer, by the way."

"I've never heard of it, and of course it matters!"

"Why?" Tiffany picked up a small bottle of foundation and pumped some onto a makeup sponge. "I don't think God gives a shit what I do."

"Tiffany!" Lauren had never heard anyone say anything like that in her life. The room was actually spinning.

"I'm sure God is great and all, I just don't think he cares about what some seventeen-year-old is doing with her boyfriend." Lauren felt like a child as Tiffany patted the sponge around her face. "He's got a lot of other things to worry about, like earthquakes and stuff, ya know?"

"Of course He cares." Lauren was scandalized. "He – He *always* cares!"

Tiffany put down the sponge and held onto Lauren's arms. "No, Lauren. He doesn't. You're, like, the closest thing to a saint I've ever met, and your dad is horrible to you and *works* for God. So, I just don't see the point. I mean, I'll do the ceremony and everything, but just because it'll make our parents happy."

Lauren couldn't keep up. "Wait, what? You *are* doing the ceremony? But you don't believe in it?"

"Yes, prairie girl, exactly." Tiffany picked up a thin tube. "Now stop talking and close your eyes."

Tiffany's breath warmed Lauren's face as she drew liner onto her eyelids. Lauren felt eyeshadow being spread across her lids, and smelled Tiffany's perfume. She felt like an actress sitting in a makeup chair.

"Ok, now open your eyes a little bit and blink," Tiffany instructed.

Lauren was startled to see a mascara brush right in front of her eyes and jerked her head back.

"I'll be careful, I promise," Tiffany said.

Lauren leaned forward and fluttered her eyelashes obediently.

"Perfect. Now, let's fix your hair." Tiffany twirled a lock of Lauren's hair thoughtfully. "It's long enough to go up, right? And we can have some wispy bits floating around your face. It'll look sexy." She opened a drawer and pulled out hair curlers and clips.

"You remember I have literally nowhere to go, right?"

"This is nothing. Just imagine how much I would have done if you'd been able to go to the Homecoming Dance!" Tiffany plugged in the straighteners and walked around, examining Lauren from various angles, like an art critic examining a sculpture.

"It's really not worth this much trouble."

"It *totally* is. Your profile picture needs some help, sweetie. And you've really got to stop wearing your hair down in this bob type thing all the time. Wearing it up will bring out your cheekbones, make your face look – oh, I can't remember the word. But it's good." Tiffany started brushing her hair. "Your hair is *gorgeous*. Properly golden blonde," she chattered away as she worked.

Lauren enjoyed feeling Tiffany's fingers on her scalp, and didn't even care when she was briefly burnt by the straighteners. Was this how Tiffany felt when Jason ran his fingers through her hair when they were – well, whatever it was they did?

"Tiffany?"

"Yeah?"

"Do you and Jason – so, after the ceremony. I mean, you and Jason are like, well. You don't have to tell me or anything, but do you guys –"

"Mm-hmm?" Tiffany clipped Lauren's hair up with several small clips.

The words Lauren wanted to use slipped away every time she opened her mouth. She wasn't even sure what she wanted to know. Did they do things? On this bed? What things? When? What did it feel like? Could she even ask these questions? Her mom had told her it was a private, sacred act. But from the way Tiffany talked, it didn't seem sacred or particularly private at all.

"Lauren, just ask whatever you want, okay?"

"Do your parents care that Jason's black?" Lauren wasn't sure where that question had come from.

"God, of course not. My dad doesn't anyway, and my mom probably hasn't noticed. Why? Would your parents care? Oh shit, are they racist?" Tiffany stopped playing with Lauren's hair and looked horrified.

Lauren was certain her parents would have a problem with it, but wasn't sure why. Her friend in elementary school had been black, and she'd stayed over at Lauren's house a few times, but for some reason that seemed different. Lauren *knew* they'd have a problem with a boyfriend being black. "I don't know."

"Do you like Calum? Is that why you're asking?" Tiffany glanced at her as she picked up a compact and brush from the bed.

"What? No! No, I was just wondering."

"Calum's a nice guy. Just saying." Tiffany expertly brushed some rouge onto Lauren's cheeks and smeared a heavy coat of sparkly pink gloss across her lips. She stood up and stared down at Lauren. "You know what? I've outdone myself. Don't look yet." Tiffany walked to her closet, riffling through her tops. She pulled out a plain black v-necked t-shirt and threw it at Lauren. "Put that on and don't mess up your hair."

Lauren held it up and snorted. "There is no way this will fit me. I'm taller than you."

"Just put it on, prairie girl."

Lauren took off her polo shirt and pulled on the top as quickly as possible, loosening some of her hair from the clips.

Lauren looked down at the cleavage spilling out the neckline. "I can't wear this."

Tiffany nodded and pulled open a drawer. "You're right. Put this on," she tossed a piece of pink fabric towards Lauren.

Lauren held up a padded bra. "Oh my goodness!"

"I know, right? It'll make you look great."

Lauren fumbled to remove her plain white cotton bra still wearing the t-shirt, feeling herself getting sweaty. She never got undressed in front of anyone, ever. And here Tiffany was, yanking up her t-shirt, removing her bra and fastening the new one on like it was nothing!

Tiffany pulled the t-shirt down and walked to stand in front of Lauren. "You look *hot*. Go see."

Lauren stood up and stumbled. The floor seemed to sway under her. She walked towards the mirror.

"Hey, look at me!" Tiffany called out.

Lauren turned. Tiffany was holding up her phone. She tapped it a few times and scrolled through the images.

"This photo is beautiful. You look like a model, Lauren. We should send this to a modelling agency!" Tiffany handed her the phone. "You're tall enough, I think."

Lauren studied the photo. Tendrils of hair framed her face. Her eyes, surrounded by eyeliner and dark shadow, looked enormous. Her slightly parted lips were wet with gloss and seemed fuller. Cleavage was spilling out of the t-shirt and the fabric of the pink bra was just peeking out, teasingly. If her dad saw it, he would say she looked like a whore.

"I don't feel very good," Lauren said.

"Let's take a few more. I think agencies like a full body shot as well."

A wave of dizziness overcame her. "I really, I don't – I think I need to sit down."

Lauren staggered to the bed and sank down, putting her face in her hands. Her chest felt tight and painful.

Tiffany was back at the closet, rummaging through the clothes again, pulling out dresses and skirts. "So now you need to wear something that shows off your legs. Shorts, or a skirt?" She turned around. "Oh, shit. You're really not okay, are you?"

Lauren fell back onto the bed and shut her eyes against the rocking of the room. It made her feel even worse, so she opened them again. Something was crushing her chest and she couldn't breathe. She moaned.

Tiffany rushed into action, pulling her up and supporting her weight into the bathroom next door. She made Lauren kneel on the floor, encouraging her to throw up and "get it out of her system." Lauren stared miserably at the toilet while Tiffany rubbed her back. "This happens every time someone tries drinking the first time."

Lauren was never, ever drinking again, whatever Tiffany said about making the drinks weaker next time. Eventually, Tiffany agreed Lauren couldn't drive home and called her mom to collect her. She rubbed off Lauren's makeup, splashed water on her face and brushed out her hair. Lauren felt strangely detached, like a rag doll being jostled around by a sloppy child. She didn't even care when Tiffany took off the top and bra she'd been wearing, replacing them with Lauren's demure ones. Lauren's mom hooted the horn as she pulled into the drive and Tiffany opened the front door. Lauren's mom hurried to the doorway, leaving her brothers sitting in the car.

"Oh, bless you both. Tiffany, it's so good to meet you but I'm sorry it's like this."

"Hi, Mrs. Davis, it's so good to meet you." Tiffany rubbed her stomach and clutched at the door frame. "I knew there was something wrong with the cafeteria's spaghetti, Mrs. Davis. But Lauren just kept eating it!"

Tiffany didn't care that lying was a sin, either.

"You poor things!" Lauren's mom put her arm around her. "Let's get you home, honey. Are you sure you don't mind Lauren's car sitting in your driveway tonight?"

"It's fine, mine's in the shop anyway. It was so kind

of Lauren to give me a ride home."

"Well, thank you so much for looking after her. Now, who's going to look after *you?*"

"You're welcome, Mrs. Davis, and don't worry about me, I'll be fine." Tiffany lowered her chin and looked up at Lauren's mom through her eyelashes, the picture of innocence. She winked at Lauren as her mom turned towards the car. "Oh! And Mrs. Davis?"

Lauren's mom turned around. "Yes, sweetheart?"

"I just wanted to say, I can't wait to do the purity pledge. I think it's a *great* idea."

Lauren groaned softly.

"I'm so glad you've made a friend so fast. She seems so sweet. And that house. Wow!" Lauren's mom put a glass of water on the bedside table and pulled the curtains closed. "I'll talk to your father about your grounding. I think perhaps two weeks is long enough. You won't really be able to make friends if you can't go anywhere, huh?"

"Really? Thanks, Mom." Lauren curled up under the covers. Her dad wouldn't agree to it, but it was nice of her mom to try. She must look pathetic right now – her mom never contradicted her dad.

"I'll bring up some dry toast in a little bit, just try and get some sleep now, ok?"

"Mom? Can you just stay here for a little bit? Just until I fall asleep?"

"Oh, honey. You're feeling really rough, aren't you?" Her mom sat down on the bed and began stroking her hair, just the way she'd done when Lauren was little.

Lauren closed her eyes and sighed contentedly. Her pounding head and nausea was worth it for this moment. She was asleep within seconds.

EIGHT

"So, what do you think of the new pastor at church?"

Jason looked up from his textbook and chewed. His mom was staring down at the latest issue of *The Economist* and he couldn't see her face. He considered the question. Was she saying she liked the new pastor? Or not?

He swallowed and took another mouthful of salmon and new potatoes to buy himself some time. He hadn't even really taken in Pastor Davis at first. It was mildly interesting when Tiffany told him it was Lauren's dad, but Jason had spent most of church service figuring out when to fit in basketball practice, homework, seeing Tiffany, and hanging out with Calum. When that was over, he had moved on to practising three-pointers in his head. He visualized himself working his way around the court, imagined the sensation of the ball leaving his fingertips as his feet lifted off the court, hearing the ball swish through the net, just the way Coach said they should. Then he'd run over the latest drills, picturing various defense and offense moves. By the time he'd finished all that, the service was coming to an end. He'd spend the final moments avoiding thinking about sex by praying to God not to end up in Hell.

"Um, he seems ... nice?"

"Mm."

They went back to their reading, the only sound being pages turned and forks scraping against their plates. Jason had forgotten the question when his mom spoke again.

"So, he seems to be relating to the younger members."

"Pardon?"

"The pastor seems to be connecting with the younger people."

Jason remembered the young teenagers sitting in front of him that kept squirming and distracting him from his three-pointer plays in his head. He nodded slowly.

"I mean, Pastor Julian was a great guy, but he didn't really understand teenagers, you know?"

Jason chuckled nervously.

"Right?" his mom continued. "I mean, what is a sixty-seven-year-old pastor going to say to you guys about sex, huh?"

Jason inhaled his milk and choked. "Excuse me." Dammit. He really should pay attention at church.

"So, what do you think? Are you going to sign up for it?" his mom asked, overly casual in her *'This is really important so I'm not making a big deal out of it and I'm going to let you make your own decision in this matter although there is clearly only one right choice here'* way. She made a show of chasing the remaining piece of salmon around her plate.

Jason had no idea what she was talking about. Thanksgiving? They always volunteered for the Thanksgiving meal though. Helping out with Sunday School, reading children Bible stories? That wouldn't be so bad, if it got him out of the service. On the other hand, had the pastor been talking about drinking, or doing drugs? Or making a pact with the devil or something? His mom caught the salmon and popped it in her mouth. She looked at him expectantly. Jason felt himself grow warm under her scrutiny and took another drink of milk. Damn. He was such a screw up. He couldn't even spend ninety minutes in church each week paying attention to what was being said.

"Jason, I know it's a big decision. I don't expect an answer from you right now." His mom unexpectedly rescued him, smiling while simultaneously managing to look disappointed.

"Right. Okay," he nodded, keeping his expression neutral. "I'll have a think about it." He'd have to talk to Calum and Tiffany and hope that at least one of them had been listening.

Later that evening, after checking his mom was engrossed in work, Jason sat in front of his chemistry notes and sent a text to Calum.

What did new guy talk about on sunday?

wot u talking about? came back instantly.

church. signing up to something?

A few seconds passed.

Yeah, man. do it

u doin it? Whatever it was, Jason wanted company.

sure

There was a gentle tap on the door. Jason shoved his phone under his notebook.

"Hi, Mom," he called.

His mom opened the door a crack so that just her head could be seen. "Working hard?"

"Yep, chemistry."

"Ah, yes. I always struggled with chemistry at school."

Jason stole a look at his notebook, hoping Calum wouldn't message back and make the table vibrate. He smiled politely at his mom. She was still just a

59

disembodied head. Part of her 'respecting his space' was not to enter his room without his permission. She would stand with her head poking in, half in and half out of the room, talking at Jason until she wore him down enough to invite her in. It pissed him off more than if she'd just walked in whenever she felt like it.

"It's a great subject to learn, though. You get chemistry figured out, you can do anything, I say."

"Come on in, Mom."

She pushed the door wide and sat on the edge of his bed. Jason turned in his chair, hanging his arms over the back.

"Make sure you put on some extra lotion tonight. You're getting ashy."

"Sure."

"So …"

"So?" Jason tried not to sass her but was walking a fine line right now.

"Have you made a decision? About what we talked about earlier?"

"Oh." Jason was relieved. "Yes. Calum said he would too."

"You will?" His mom's face lit up. "That's great, I'm proud of you. Both you and Calum. I knew you'd do the right thing."

She leapt up from the bed and enveloped him in a hug. Jason's face was crushed against her bosom. She let go of him and stood with her arms hanging by her side while Jason stayed seated. A buzz broke the silence and they both stared at the paper on the desk, which was shaking. The vibrations stopped and Jason braced himself for the lecture on cell phones and concentration.

"I'll let you get back to your chemistry," his mom

scuttled out of the room.

What the hell had just happened there? He reached for his phone and then stopped. Was this a test? He pulled the textbook towards him, put his head down and started working through the quiz at the end of the chapter, ignoring the phone hidden under his notebook. After ten minutes Jason stretched his arms over his hand and glanced back at the door. Nothing. He pulled out his phone and read Calum's message.

Just kidding, no way

Followed by another: *life is too short*

What did that mean? He would have to talk to Calum tomorrow. His mom was in too much of a good mood for him to risk screwing it up now.

The next morning Calum was hysterical as Jason recounted the story at their lockers.

"Seriously, man, what is this thing?" Jason asked.

"You really don't know what you've agreed to, do you?" Calum wiped his eyes and another laugh threatened to erupt. Kids in the hallway were staring at them, some giggling themselves at Calum's booming laugh, and a teacher had told them to keep it down.

"No, I really don't. And you need to tell me now, because you are straight up pissing me off. Everyone's staring at me!"

"Dude, first of all – not everything is about *you*. And second of all," Calum put his hand on Jason's shoulder and paused dramatically. "You are not going to be happy about this." He shook his head.

Jason sighed.

"Okay, okay, okay. You have agreed, my friend, to a purity pledge."

"What?"

"A purity pledge."

"A purity pledge?" Jason repeated.

"You know, waiting until you get married," Calum's shoulders shook again, "before you get some lovin'!" He swayed his hips suggestively before erupting in laughter. "Does Tiffany know about this? I am guessing she doesn't." The bell rang and Calum slammed his locker door shut. "So good luck with that!"

Jason watched Calum walk down the hallway with a sinking feeling. No wonder his mom was in such a good mood this morning. She probably didn't think Jason deserved to enjoy life that much. Not that she'd even be able to remember sex – she'd been single since the divorce. Although there had been one guy, Terry, that Jason was pretty sure she'd been dating for a while when they lived in Indianapolis. At least, Terry had come over most weekends on the pretence of doing odd jobs around the house, and after a while didn't even bother bringing his toolbox. They would all eat dinner together, his mom talking and laughing the way she had when he was younger. After Jason went to bed, he would hear jazz music or a movie playing in the living room. Terry even took Jason to a Pacers game once, just the two of them. Jason had liked him, and the way he didn't make a big deal about the two of them hanging out, playing Xbox games or shooting hoops in the driveway.

Jason had known when his mom had told Terry the truth though, because afterwards Terry couldn't make eye contact. A month later, his mom told Jason that Terry wouldn't be coming over any more. Her eyes were red and she became quiet and withdrawn again. That was his fault, too. He knew his mom found it hard that his dad remarried and had another family, a chance to start over again. When Jason found out about his half-sister being born, he felt like he'd been punched in the stomach. He never let himself imagine how it must have made his mom feel. Of course she wanted him to take the pledge. Live a pure life.

So just when finally something was going right, and he had a beautiful girlfriend who was fun to be around, Jason massively screwed it up. No surprise there. He imagined smashing his head against the locker over and over. He began to count the lockers, working his way down the hall until he got to homeroom, even though it made him late.

Later that day he was still trying to decide whether to even tell Tiffany about it when she had sat down next to him in the library.

She squeezed his thigh. "Hey! Guess what I'm going to do?" she whispered.

Jason looked up from his notebook and smiled at the unexpected interruption. "What?" he mouthed, aware of the librarian's eyes on them.

"I'm going to do that purity pledge thing."

"What?"

"Shh." The librarian glared at them.

"Whatever." Tiffany glared back at the librarian. "We'll talk later," she patted his leg and stood up.

Jason watched her walk away. Her butt looked amazing in her tight jeans. Had she changed her mind about him? Was this just a polite way of dumping him? But it was a lot of trouble to go to and Tiffany didn't seem religious, even though her family went to church most weeks. Jason tried to resume studying but couldn't concentrate and followed Tiffany out. He found her in the cafeteria surrounded by a group of giggling girls poring over a magazine. Why couldn't Tiffany ever be on her own for five minutes? He shifted his bookbag onto his other shoulder and bit his lip, wondering whether it was worth interrupting them. Lauren looked up and gave him a small smile and a half wave. He smiled back at her, and Tiffany turned around and beamed as she saw him approach.

"Hi!"

"Hey, can we uh –" Jason looked at all the faces smiling up at them. He took Tiffany's hand and pulled her away from the group so they were leaning against a wall. The girls giggled and whispered to each other. It was awful.

"I was wondering, um, what you said in the library?"

"Oh, yeah!" Tiffany popped her gum. "This stupid ceremony thing. Lauren's dad is making her do it, so I said I'd do it too."

"Right. Okay. Sure. Um," Jason was baffled by Tiffany's sudden interest in religion and lack of interest in sex, which he was pretty sure she enjoyed. Didn't she? Well, obviously not.

"You know, I was thinking …" Tiffany twirled her ponytail with her fingers. Jason stared at her hair slipping round and round. He'd never be able to touch it again. "If you do it too," Tiffany said slowly, "then I bet we can spend a lot more time together, right?"

"Huh? I mean, pardon?"

"Like, our parents will trust us more. Maybe we won't even have to keep the door open when we're watching a movie at your house!" Tiffany widened her eyes suggestively.

"Oh, right!" God, he was an idiot. "That's a great

idea. I mean, if you think so. Of course I'll do it."

"Amazing! Plus, I'll get a really cute ring. We're just looking at them now," Tiffany gestured towards the table. The girls were flipping through the pages of a catalogue, pointing at different pictures. "Guys can have them too. Do you want to look?"

What the hell?

"Maybe later. I mean, with basketball and everything, I can't wear any jewelry."

"Good point. And you'll probably get my ring eventually."

"What?"

"I'm supposed to give my ring to my husband on my wedding night."

Jason's brain was going to explode. Tiffany pecked him on the cheek and ran back to join the girls at the table.

NINE

Molly put a mug down next to her mom, who was curled up in the recliner which didn't recline any more. "Here's your tea."

"Thanks, hon." Her mom wiped a tear from her eye as the credits rolled on *Home Is Where the Heart Is*.

Molly had survived an hour of watching a team of construction experts and volunteers build a home for a 'family in need' and Molly thought she would lose her mind. The tears, the drama – it was so predictable. And if there was ever a family in need, it was hers. But Molly and her mom wouldn't make good TV. Who would want to see a house built for a woman who worked at Wal-Mart and her fat kid? If Molly had several siblings with disabilities they might have a chance, but no. Her mom hadn't even managed to have more than one child.

"They really deserve that beautiful house, don't they? Those poor kids." Her mom sighed happily and sipped her tea.

Molly managed to keep her mouth shut. Just because parents didn't know how to use birth control and kept having kids and then lost their jobs – that somehow made them 'deserving?' They got a house with a pool in the backyard, table tennis in the basement and three bathrooms? Molly made straight As, worked the early shift at McDonald's, went to church every Sunday and what did *she* get? A tiny house with a roof near collapse, a bedroom that was so small she suspected it was originally a laundry room, and a bathroom she shared with her mother who felt the need to comment every time Molly got her period. (*"How are you feeling, honey? You have everything you need?"*)

"Mmm." Molly still felt bad about shouting at her. Her mom did try, really. The problem was that most of the time, she was really annoying.

"You sure you don't want some ice cream? You really don't need to diet. You're beautiful."

"I'm not hungry. I better get back to studying."

"Well, don't turn into one of these beanpoles, okay? And can you hold on a sec? I just wanted to say something."

"Um, okay." Molly sat on the couch.

Her mom turned the TV off and turned to her. "I'm really proud of you, hon, for agreeing to take part in the purity pledge. It's a great thing to commit to."

"Okay, sure." Molly stood up. Like anyone would ever be interested in having sex with Molly. She'd never even kissed anyone, so pledging her virginity really wasn't a big deal. When she was in college, and her skin cleared up, then obviously she would do what she wanted.

"But I also wanted to say, well, if anything happens, we would figure it out."

Molly sat down again. "If what happens?"

"Well, you know. We would figure it out," she repeated.

"Mom, I have literally no idea what you're talking about."

Her mom took a deep breath. "The pledge. I know you'll be making a commitment and I think that's wonderful. Of course. But if anything happens, and things *do* happen sometimes, sweetie – then I'm just saying we would take care of it. Together. And no one would ever need to know."

Molly ran the words through her head again, trying to put them into a logical order. She snorted. "Hold on, are you offering to raise a kid for me? Mom, that's hilarious. But I think people might be suspicious that your children are like, eighteen years apart. Although, it's possible. For sure." Molly considered. "That Mormon family down the street, I think their oldest and youngest are almost twenty years apart, right? Yeah, it could work. But anyway, seriously, I don't think we have to worry about that. Isn't that the whole point of the pledge?"

"No, Molly, I mean … that's not what I mean."

Her mom scraped her hair back into a bun and wrapped a scrunchie around it, which meant she was stressed. It made her cheeks look gaunt but when she had been younger, Molly's mom had been beautiful. Molly had seen a photo of her mom at seventeen and had to admit she looked stunning. Molly had possibly inherited her cheekbones but she'd never know because they were buried under layers of fat.

"Okay, Mom. Well, let me know when you want to start speaking English."

"What I'm trying to tell you, Molly, is that if anything happens, if you get pregnant, I'm just saying we could arrange for you to have – to have a –" she blinked rapidly "– a procedure. Okay? And no one would ever need to know."

"Oh my *God*, Mom."

"I know it doesn't sound like a Christian –"

"You're offering to give me an abortion?"

"Well, no, I wouldn't be the one –"

"Jesus Christ."

"And Molly, don't –"

"Wow. You obviously have no faith in me. I haven't even taken the pledge yet and you already think I'm going to mess it up?"

"No, that's not what I'm saying at all!

"That's exactly what you're saying. I can't *believe* you."

Molly stomped into her bedroom and slammed the door. She threw herself onto the bed and punched her pillow. Who were these guys her mom thought she would be sleeping with all over the place? And like she'd ask her mom to get her an abortion. Jesus *Christ*.

Molly rolled onto her back. Who would be her first time? She had hoped it would be Darryl at work, but there was no chance of that now. He had been avoiding her since the awful uniform conversation. She mentally scanned through the guys at school. Calum was cute, but had some weird stubble growing on his chin. Mr. Stein, who taught History, was definitely attractive. Molly tried to imagine him on top of her, doing ... whatever it was. But he smelled sometimes, and when he handed back their quizzes last week she'd seen dandruff on his shoulders. Pastor Davis was attractive, in a weird older guy way. What would it be like with him? She imagined he'd only ever been with his wife, but let's say things didn't work out. Or perhaps Mrs. Davis would die in some kind of accident (a quick, painless death, of course). Anyway, when Pastor Davis was ready, perhaps she could comfort him and things would progress from there ....

Molly imagined him lying in bed next to her. Mike. That was his name. She pictured Mike undressed but had to partially cover him with a bedsheet. She'd never seen a naked man from the waist down. She hadn't even seen a penis in real life, so she wasn't entirely sure how big they were in comparison to where they had to go. But it definitely looked enjoyable on TV.

There was a knock on the door. "Molly? Can I come in, please?"

"No."

"It came out all wrong, I'm sorry. I just want to –"

"Mom. Go. AWAY."

When Molly got home from school the next day, a small black box was sitting on the kitchen table. An envelope with *To M xoxo* in her mom's neat handwriting rested against it.

Molly opened the envelope and pulled out a card with a picture of a white rose on the front. Inside it read *For the ceremony. I am so proud of you as always. All my love, Mom xoxo*

She lifted the lid of the box. A silver ring with two intertwined heart cutouts rested on a black velvet cushion. Molly placed it on her left ring finger. It was kind of cute.

"Hey, honey. Do you like it?"

Molly turned and saw her mom standing in the doorway. "I do. Thanks."

"I can change it if you don't."

"No, I like it," Molly said honestly. "Thank you."

"You're welcome. I'm glad it fits. I'm looking forward to giving it to you officially this evening." Her mom made as though to hug her and then patted her shoulder instead. "I'm really proud of you for doing this. We should leave in about thirty minutes."

"What?"

"We should leave soon."

"No, I mean, what do you mean, you're giving it to

me during the ceremony?"

"Well, you know. The parent gives their child the ring. As part of the ceremony. Pastor Davis explained in that information pack he gave out."

"But it's supposed to be the fathers giving it to their daughters. I thought Pastor Davis would give it to me instead."

"Well, sometimes it's fathers. But it can be a mother. Or any 'influential adult.'" Her mom made quote marks with her fingers.

"This is the kind of thing my dad should be invited to."

"Molly. Please don't do this now." Her mom ran her hands over her face.

"I know he left us and everything, but he's still my dad. It would have been nice to at least ask him."

"Well, I don't know how to get hold of him or even where he is. So that isn't really an option, honey."

"But there's the internet. Anyone can find anyone now. You just put in the name and —"

"Molly, your father walked out. He's gone. He left us and that's that. Okay? We don't need him in our lives. Ever."

"I just —"

"No! He is not a part of your life, and he never will be." She saw Molly blinking back tears. "Oh, honey. Please. Just go get ready, okay?"

They drove to the ceremony in silence. The car radio still hadn't been fixed. As they pulled into the parking lot, Molly watched Jason Myers lope from the entryway to meet Tiffany Vanderkamp and her parents, who were getting out of their car. What the hell were *they* doing here? Everyone knew Tiffany was a total slut. Of *course* they were doing it. Unless Tiffany was like the girls Molly overheard in McDonald's a couple of weeks ago, who did 'everything but' – whatever that meant. She had been cleaning the table next to them, listening to their giggles as they talked about what they liked, what their boyfriends liked (not the same thing, apparently) and how it hurt when their boyfriends got the wrong place (*what* place?). But then the two girls had agreed they were 'waiting until marriage' so it seemed like a lot could happen before that. Molly had paused in wiping the table, wondering what exactly counted, and who decided? The girls had looked up and stared at her until Molly gave the table a final wipe, straightened the chairs and walked away, face flaming.

Molly tried to keep her face neutral as she and her mom joined the other students and parents filing into the church. In addition to Tiffany, there was about half the cheerleading squad (who were screwing half the football team – who were they kidding?) and a few other students she recognized from the grade below. An infinitesimal part of her felt sorry for Jason – he was one of only three guys there and so tall you couldn't *not* notice him. But on the other hand, he was lucky enough not to have a parent with him at all.

They walked into the Sunday School room, which Molly hadn't entered since she was about ten. The furniture had been moved so that chairs were in semi-circles of rows facing the front. Small cards printed with the evening's program were on each one. Molly headed for the back, towards Ernie Chan and his parents. Ernie looked as though he was doing homework in his head while his parents examined the program. He probably was – he was the only person at school who came close to her GPA and was going to be salutatorian. There was another boy on the other side of the room but Molly didn't know him. He looked like a total loser and possibly had special needs.

Of course, Lauren Davis was at the front of the room, crouched down talking to a blond boy who must be her little brother. She acted like she was the Virgin Mary at church but Molly guessed when her father's back was turned she was slutting around all over the place with Tiffany and co. Well, of all the people in this room, Molly, Ernie and the weird looking guy were the only people who wouldn't have any problem keeping this pledge. She was too busy studying, working and enduring the daily living hell of high school to have sex, anyway.

"I'll sit here, hon. I don't want to be all the way at the back!"

Molly turned and saw that for some reason, her mom had chosen to sit next to the Vanderkamps. Mrs. Vanderkamp looked beautiful as usual. She looked more like Tiffany's older cousin than her mother. Her sleek golden hair was pulled back into a bun and she was wearing a sequined black dress that glittered in the candlelight. Silver earrings shaped like teardrops dangled elegantly from her ear lobes. She stared vacantly into the distance while Mr. Vanderkamp, dressed in a business suit, was tapping away at his phone. See? *That's* what parents should be like – they should just sit there and look normal and not talk. All the other moms were in heels and nice dresses, but Molly's mom was wearing flat shoes, the same black pants she'd worn to work and a long-sleeved t-shirt. Molly felt bad for thinking it, but she looked like white trash. Which, if Molly was being really harsh, is what she was – a college dropout with an illegitimate child.

Well, Molly wasn't going to let that happen to her. She was going to finish her chemical engineering degree and then work for a cosmetic company and make loads of money. Then she'd have a stylist, get a personal trainer and look like Mrs. Vanderkamp and get her husband to stick around. Maybe she'd have children, but she wasn't entirely sure she liked the idea of something alien growing inside her.

"Evening!" her mom greeted the Vanderkamps.

Mrs. Vanderkamp started in her seat. "Hi," she smiled vaguely. Molly strongly suspected she couldn't remember their names even though they'd been attending the same church for about ten years.

"Well, hey, how you doing, Deidre?" Mr. Vanderkamp looked up from his Blackberry. "You ready for the big show?" he asked Molly.

Molly shrugged and looked at the floor. "Sure."

"You don't look too happy to be here," he said jovially.

"Oh, she's fine." Molly's mom laughed. "She's just a little upset it's me giving her the ring during the ceremony and not … someone else."

"Well, no big deal. It doesn't really matter who gives who what, right? I mean, Celia here is giving Jason his ring, and I don't think the poor kid even wants one. I mean, what's a guy his age supposed to do with a piece of jewelry, huh? The important thing is that we're all here in this together, supporting our kids. Right?"

Molly's mom pulled her scrunchie out of her frizzy, graying hair and fluffed it before tucking it behind her ears. "Well, exactly. That's exactly what I think, too, John." She nodded earnestly.

Oh my God. Was she *flirting*?

"I better go up there, I guess."

Her mom stood up and leaned towards her. "I won't hug you now, honey, I won't embarrass you. But I'm really proud of you," she whispered, twisting her hands round and round, bracelets jangling, like a maniacal psychiatric patient.

"Your bag's sticking out," Molly hissed through gritted teeth. Her mom's hideous Wal-Mart smock was peeking out of the oversized bag squeezed under her chair. She bent down, muttering to herself, and Molly joined the semi-circle of students forming in front of the lectern.

Molly gazed at Pastor Davis who was standing at the lectern looking at some notes. It was all a load of crap, but it was nice that he believed it. She wouldn't mind if her husband was religious. Molly realized she was slouching and straightened up, pulling her shoulders back. She hoped her mom appreciated it (*"Stand up straight, honey. Stop slouching and be proud of who you are!"*). Pastor Davis suddenly looked up, right at Molly. She stared back at him and licked her lips. She'd seen women do that in movies and it looked sexy. Pastor Davis blinked and glanced down at his notes. He cleared his throat. Molly was taken aback. Had she thrown him off? Had he noticed her?

TEN

"If you are a true believer and have made a commitment to purity, you have chosen a path in the opposite direction to the world's belief system and direction. *You* are the picture they would use in a dictionary for the definition of counter-culture." Lauren's dad paused and looked around the room.

Lauren was mortified. The ceremony was even worse than she had expected. They were in the room used for Sunday School but it had been completely transformed. The lights were dimmed, and candles and vases of flowers had been placed around the room, hiding stuffed toys and picture books. Her dad was preaching from a lectern, the students standing in a semi-circle in front of him. Parents sat in rows of chairs behind them. It was an appalling cross between a wedding and a seance.

A horrifying number of students from school had turned up. When her classmates discovered Tiffany and most of the other cheerleaders were taking part, kids Lauren had never spoken to asked her if they could take the pledge, too. Some of them didn't even attend the church. Now there were twenty-three students standing listening to her dad go on and on and *on* about the Devil, sin and sex. Lauren wasn't sure whether to be grateful or mad at Tiffany for making it popular. She just wanted to die. Or at least be sitting with her mom and brothers, not standing up here, right in front of her dad, feeling strangely exposed. She focused on a point just past his shoulder and listened to Tiffany chewing gum.

Tiffany was wearing a plain black, knee-length dress that she must have borrowed from her mom, and hardly any make-up. Her hair was pulled back into a sensible braid instead of bouncing around in her usual ponytail. The combination created a pale and tired appearance. She was staring at the floor, not even attempting to look interested.

"You will be a target of Satan's web, but you have the opportunity to free others who are trapped, through your lifestyle and testimony. Your *lifestyle.*" Her dad stared meaningfully at Tiffany. Lauren nudged her arm. Tiffany raised her head and gave a few small nods as though she knew exactly what 'Satan's web' was. Lauren's dad looked down at his notes and Tiffany yawned.

"Through your lifestyle and testimony you can free others who are trapped in Satan's web of deception …" he droned on.

Jason was standing opposite them. His wrists and ankles protruded from his pale blue suit but he looked incredibly attractive. His eyes were moving back and forth around the semi-circle as though he were examining everyone's shoes. Tiffany was wearing nude heels with a pointed toe, which made Lauren feel like she'd borrowed her flat black leather pumps from a five-year-old.

Lauren realized she probably looked like she was lusting after her best friend's boyfriend. She turned her attention back to her dad.

"Parents and guardians, please come up and join your child."

It was the part of the ceremony Lauren had been dreading the most. There was shuffling and scraping of chairs as the parents stood up and came towards the front of the room, crowding the already too small space.

Mr. Vanderkamp came and stood in front of Tiffany, who grinned at him. "Hey, Dad."

"Hey, yourself." Mr. Vanderkamp winked at Tiffany. "Hey, kiddo," he smiled at Lauren and stepped to the side, making a sweeping gesture with his hand towards the lectern.

Why, oh *why*, didn't Lauren have a dad like Mr. Vanderkamp? He made everything fun, and not a huge, serious deal. She dragged herself forwards to stand by her dad. From the lectern she could see expressions of embarrassment on most of the students' faces as their parents squeezed themselves next to them. Even the parents looked a little sheepish. Mrs. Vanderkamp's heel caught in the carpet and she stumbled. Jason reached out an arm to steady her, already the perfect son-in-law.

Lauren's dad cleared his throat and the murmuring in the room stopped. "Students," he said gravely, "repeat after me."

The students waited. Lauren's cheeks flamed as her dad made eye contact with each of them in turn, ensuring he had everyone's attention. It took forever.

Finally, he began to speak. "Believing that true love waits…"

"Believing that true loves waits…" murmured Lauren.

"I make this commitment …"

"I make this commitment …" the group mumbled after him, as if humoring him.

"and pray God will empower me …"

"and pray God will empower me …"

"to be a person of truth and wisdom …"

"to be a person of truth and wisdom …"

"I make this commitment to God, my family and friends …"

"I make this commitment to God, my family and friends…" Lauren thought about her mom and brothers.

"… and if God wills, to my future mate and children." Her dad nodded.

"… and if God wills, to my future mate and children."

Tiffany popped her gum.

Lauren's dad frowned. "Now parents, please place the ring on your child's finger and repeat after me." He picked up the ring that was in a box resting on the lectern and gripped Lauren's left hand with his. He slid the ring onto her finger until it dug into her skin.

"Accepting God's plan for a parent and believing that true love waits …" he paused for the parents to repeat after him. The saving grace was that he had to look down at his notes for the script and couldn't look at Lauren. His grip on her hand was firm, as though he could sense her wanting to snatch her arm away.

Lauren studied the ring her parents had bought her as her dad talked through the script. A delicate key crossed through a heart cut-out, with two smaller solid hearts on each side. It was set within a 14Kt gold band. Her name and the date of the ceremony were engraved inside. She had told her mom not to spend so much, but her mom had been carried away and said she deserved something special for this. Lauren tried to feel grateful, but she'd rather have had the money for makeup or clothes.

Finally, her dad finished the parents' pledge and

released her hand. "Students, you have chosen to wear a ring as a physical, visible symbol of this pledge. On your wedding night you are to give this ring to your spouse. And all of you will no doubt remember this night and celebrate your accomplishment, which will stand as a holy act of worship and commitment to God's incredible and perfect plan …"

Lauren prayed she would not be thinking about the purity pledge on her wedding night. She wanted no thoughts about her parents whatsoever on her wedding night. And now everyone in the room was literally thinking about sex because of her dad. Would they all be thinking about him on their wedding nights? It was disgusting.

To her relief, the interminable ceremony finally finished, but no one knew what to do with themselves. The students and parents stood in the semi-circle, looking at her dad for guidance as he shuffled his notes and picked up his Bible. Finally, Lauren's mom started clapping and the others joined in. The parents and students turned around self-consciously and started drifting towards their families and picking up their belongings. Lauren walked back over to Tiffany.

"Let me just grab your coat and then we can go," Mr. Vanderkamp said, heading back to his seat.

Jason joined Lauren and Tiffany. "You look great," he said to Tiffany. "Both of you," he added kindly.

"I hate this dress. My mom made me wear it. I look like an Amish person," Tiffany huffed. Jason and Lauren laughed. "You look really handsome in that suit, though." Tiffany touched his arm and Jason looked sweetly pleased.

Tiffany's parents walked towards them and Mrs. Vanderkamp stumbled slightly and caught hold of her husband's arm.

"God!" Tiffany muttered.

"These heels!" Mrs. Vanderkamp said breathlessly. "Hi, Lauren. How are you?" They were such a glamorous couple, they didn't look like parents at all.

"I'm good, thanks, Mrs. Vanderkamp. You look beautiful. How are you?"

"Well, aren't you sweet. You're the first person to tell me that today." She looked at her husband pointedly.

Lauren tried to imagine her dad's reaction if her mom had embarrassed him in public but couldn't. Her mom would never, in a million years, do that. Maybe Lauren should arrange for her mom to spend some time with Mrs. Vanderkamp.

Mr. Vanderkamp was silent as he held open his wife's coat and she slipped her arms into it. He helped Tiffany into her jacket and then looked up at Jason. "Well done, son." Mr. Vanderkamp shook Jason's hand vigorously. "Shame your mom couldn't be here."

"Is she okay?" Lauren asked.

"She got called into work at the last minute, so she drove there after dropping me off."

"Huh. Some kind of accounting emergency? The numbers getting all out of hand?" Mr. Vanderkamp laughed and looked around the group. Tiffany shook her head in mock exasperation.

Jason chuckled to make up for it. "I guess so," he said graciously.

"Lauren, you want to come to dinner with us?" Tiffany asked.

"My treat, Lauren," Mr. Vanderkamp said quickly.

"I'm sorry, I'd love to but we're having a family meal." Lauren would have given anything to exchange families right then.

"Well, just the four of us then," Mr. Vanderkamp smiled.

"I think I'll pass. I'm not that hungry," Mrs. Vanderkamp said. Tiffany was right – her mom never ate.

"Oh, come on. Let's celebrate." Mr. Vanderkamp said, his smile becoming fixed. "You promised, remember?"

"I'm not hungry. You all go without me." Mrs. Vanderkamp bared her perfect teeth at her husband.

"Well, we can't, sweetheart. Because we'll have the car. Just come with us, have a starter." Mr. Vanderkamp looked impatient.

"Are you sure your mom isn't here, Jason?" Mrs. Vanderkamp looked around the room as though Jason's mom would suddenly make an appearance. "You could all go with her, and I'll drive myself back."

"Mom, Ms. Myers is *obviously* not here. I think we would *see* her," Tiffany hissed.

Mr. Vanderkamp coughed and patted his pockets, making a show of looking for his car keys. Lauren tried not to smile. Tiffany had a point. The room was a sea of white faces, except for Jason, the Spencer family, and the Chans.

Mrs. Vanderkamp yawned. "I'm just a little tired. Why don't you drop me off at the house?"

Mr. Vanderkamp clenched his jaw. "For God's sake, Celia. Just come and eat some goddamn dinner."

Lauren looked at the floor. Jason's feet looked enormous next to Tiffany's.

"You can't *make* me eat dinner, John. If I'm not hungry, I'm. *Not. Hungry.*"

"Fine, Mom. Whatever. We'll drop you off. Let's go," Tiffany marched towards the door. "I don't care if you're there, anyway."

Jason and Lauren exchanged looks and followed her into the vestibule.

"Hey, you okay?" Jason touched Tiffany's elbow. "Let's forget dinner. It's fine. Your dad can just drop me off at home," he offered. Other families walked past them towards the exit.

"No! My dad came home early from work especially for this. I want us to eat together."

"Okay, sure. Of course," Jason agreed.

"I wish you could come," Tiffany said to Lauren. "Are you going to have to sit around and talk about virginity for the rest of the evening?"

Lauren laughed properly for the first time that day. "I hope not. I better go back in. Thanks so much for being here tonight."

"No problem. It makes our lives easier anyway, doesn't it?" Tiffany grabbed Jason's hand. He nodded and shrugged. Lauren wasn't entirely sure what that meant or whether Jason was glad he was a part of it or not.

Mrs. Vanderkamp walked past them and flung the entrance door open so hard it banged against the wall and came back to almost hit her in the face. She pushed it again and strode into the parking lot.

Mr. Vanderkamp wandered up in conversation with a pretty woman with curly black hair. The smart girl from school, Molly, was trailing behind them, scowling. Molly and the woman had the same startling green eyes and light freckles over their nose and cheeks, so it must be her mom but otherwise it was hard to tell they were related. Molly was full figured, with straight brown hair that hung in a curtain over her face most of the time. Her mom was tall and slim, her posture straight. She chuckled at something Mr. Vanderkamp said and tucked a curl of hair behind her ear.

"See you later, Deirdre. Well done, Molly!" Tiffany's dad called after them as they walked out. He gave Tiffany a hug. "Come on, let's go. Your mom's tired. We'll drop her off and it'll be just the three of us, huh?"

"Sure. It'll be more fun anyway," Tiffany smiled at him. "See ya later, then," she said to Lauren.

Jason gave Lauren a small wave. "See you tomorrow."

"See you around, kiddo," Mr. Vanderkamp said.

Lauren watched them walk away, and felt lonelier than ever as she turned back to her parents and brothers.

October
2007

"For if we sin wilfully after that we have received the knowledge of the truth, there remaineth no more sacrifice for sins,
But a certain fearful looking for of judgment and fiery indignation, which shall devour the adversaries."

HEBREWS 10:26-27

ELEVEN

Tiffany shivered as they watched the band march onto the field. Jason unzipped his jacket and slung his arm over her shoulder so it enveloped her.

"Aww, sweet. Look at that!" Calum teased from behind him.

Tiffany rolled her eyes and pushed closer against Jason, making his left side feel like it had a hot water bottle. The metal bleachers felt cold and hard through his jeans. Tiffany must be so uncomfortable with her exposed legs.

Jason turned around to Calum. "Shut up, man – if you weren't so damn ugly maybe you'd get a girl too."

"Burn!" the guys surrounding them whooped and hollered.

"Jason," Tiffany squealed and slapped his arm. "Don't be mean." But she pushed closer to him and Jason grinned. Her glitter hairspray smelled weird but he liked that he'd have sparkles on his sleeve afterwards.

"Ooh! Being in lurve has you acting all cocky now, huh? You think you Mister Love now," Calum laughed. Jason wasn't sure if he was annoyed but enjoyed feeling like he could get away with anything with Tiffany by his side, a warm bubble of the two of them inside his coat with the rest of the world outside. He looked at her legs, which were covered in goosebumps.

"You sure you don't want to put on your tracksuit?"

"Nah, there's no point. We'll be back on soon." Tiffany grabbed his right hand and put it on her bare thigh. "There, that'll keep me warm. Hey, where's your ring?"

Jason's ring was in his bedroom, at the back of a drawer, in its box. He'd taken it off as soon as he'd returned home from dinner with the Vanderkamps after the ceremony.

"I just – it doesn't feel right," he muttered. It felt like a flashing neon sign calling God's attention whenever he wore it. Especially since he and Tiffany were still having sex when they got the opportunity.

"You're so cute," Tiffany squeezed his hand, and the small diamonds on her ring glinted under the stadium lights. "It's all bullshit, but there's no point in not wearing something pretty." On the other side of Tiffany, Lauren kept her eyes fixed on the marching band performing on the field. Tiffany turned to her. "You okay? The guys being nice to you?"

Jason couldn't hear Lauren's response. He had tried to make conversation in the first half but it had been more difficult than he'd expected. They'd both ended up paying a lot of attention to the game. For some reason, Lauren kept asking him questions about moving. Jason hated lying to people anyway, but ever since the purity pledge, he felt guilty around Lauren. The ceremony had meant something to her. Every time she twisted her purity ring around her finger, he was reminded of what a terrible Christian he was. He had deceived his mom, Mr. and Mrs. Vanderkamp and God – in church.

"Gotta go, babe, we're back on," Tiffany jumped up and blew kisses, for him or Lauren he wasn't sure. They watched her bounce down the steps and into the huddle of cheerleaders on the field.

"I'm going to get a drink, want something?" Calum asked.

"No, man, I'm good."

"I wasn't talking to you, I was talking to Lauren."

"Oh." Lauren looked up at him. "Um, no thanks. I'm okay."

"You sure? Hot chocolate or something? It is cold."

Jason grinned and raised his eyebrows at Calum who was definitely avoiding eye contact with him.

"Well, yes. Hot chocolate would be great. Thanks." Lauren smiled and Calum made his way down the bleachers.

Jason tried to think of something to say. Lauren brushed some hair out of her face and watched the cheerleaders, Tiffany bouncing and shouting behind the squad captain. Just when Jason decided to ask her about the History homework, Lauren started talking.

"I can't believe she does all those moves, you know? The back flips and stuff."

"It's crazy, right?" Jason said proudly, although Lauren would look cute in the uniform too. She'd be on the bottom of the pyramid, keeping it stable. "You ever want to be a cheerleader?"

"Oh, no way," Lauren laughed. "My parents didn't even let me consider it."

"Really? Why's that?" They clapped along with the rest of the crowd as the players made their way back onto the field and Jason shifted closer to hear her answer.

"Well, the uniforms, for a start. I'd never be allowed to wear something like that. And the makeup. And just, well – you know. Everyone's ..." Lauren turned to look at him. "Everyone's watching them. And that isn't, well." She played with her ring. "I guess my parents would say it isn't ladylike."

"Wow, they sound pretty strict."

"That's an understatement," Lauren nodded. "I was lucky I even got to come to the game this evening."

"But, you wear ... I mean," Jason felt himself get hot. Lauren wore some low-cut tops and short shorts.

As though she could read his mind, Lauren flushed and looked back at the field. "Tiffany lets me borrow her clothes and I change in the car, sometimes. To help me, you know, not look like the daughter of a preacher."

Jason grinned. "Oh, right. My mom's really strict too. Not about clothes, well – a little about clothes. But about everything else."

"That must be hard, being an only child. All the pressure on you, huh?"

"Yep."

Where the hell was Calum? How long did it take to buy a drink? Jason turned back to the field. A whistle blew and the players huddled together, eleven on each team.

"And Tiffany mentioned you're really good at basketball. Are you going to play at college? That would be amazing."

"No. I just play for fun."

"'Scuse me, 'scuse me. Coming through," Calum made his way along the row, carefully holding two polystyrene cups. He handed a cup to Lauren who accepted it with a shy smile. He sat down where Tiffany had been, wedging his large frame between

Lauren and Jason. "So. What did you guys talk about? Me, right?"

Lauren laughed. "Er, no. Sorry. We were just talking about, um. Just stuff. Families and college and stuff."

Jason stood. "I changed my mind. I'm getting a drink."

Jason knew he was being rude as he made his way out of the stands. But Lauren was a reminder of why he hated meeting new people – the endless questions, assumptions. Why did people want to know everything? They felt like they could ask anything. Nothing was private.

Jason stomped past the concession stand and left the stadium. He jogged past the grunge kids smoking weed in a huddle by the bike racks and ran towards the baseball storage shed. The ringing in his ears was getting louder and black spots clouded his vision. He might not make it in time. He could hardly see. He stumbled the last few yards, heading towards the gap between the back of the shed and the wall. He rested his back against the shed and put his hands on his legs, staring at the ground. He took a long, deep breath and looked at the grass in front of him, trying to ignore the shrill tone that was threatening to split his head in two. A glimpse of white appeared and he shook his head to rid it of the image.

The grass. Look at the grass.

Breathe.

In and out. In and out.

The muddy ground morphed into white tiles for a moment and then he was staring at grass again. The ringing noise muffled a roar from the bleachers.

There was a sudden *CRACK!*

Jason gasped and sank down to the ground. The cheering from the crowd was drowned out by the ringing in his ears.

A firework celebrating the first touchdown lit up the sky but he didn't see it.

His face was buried in his arms and he was rocking back and forth, back and forth.

TWELVE

"What is the main purpose of the first paragraph?" Lauren was laying on Tiffany's bed, her legs propped up against the wall. She read carefully from the paper she was holding. "A, to describe a culture. B, to criticize a tradition. C, to question a suggestion. Or D, to analyze a reaction?"

"I have no frickin clue, babe." Tiffany was on the floor doing sit ups, her face appearing above the side of the bed every two seconds.

"Come on, you're not even trying."

"What is the point ..." Tiffany went up and down "of you not being grounded ..." up and down "... if we're just going to do this?"

"You asked me to help you study. Not watch you work out." Although truthfully, Lauren was happy anywhere that wasn't her house.

Tiffany sat up, her cheeks pink. "I didn't think it was going to be so boring, though. I thought we'd do, like, thirty minutes and then have fun."

"First of all, we've been studying less than twenty minutes. Second of all, this might be the difference between you getting into the college you want – or not. SAT scores are really important, Tiff." Lauren didn't want to have to remind her, but Tiffany's grades were pretty bad so the SAT might be her salvation.

"Well, sorry for not being a genius like you and getting it perfect last year," Tiffany huffed, going back to her sit ups.

"I'm not a genius, I just studied. It gets easier to figure out the answers the more practice tests you take, honest."

Tiffany ignored her and kept sitting up and down, making huffing noises.

"I think you've done enough sit ups now, anyway."

"I'm getting fat."

"Don't be dumb, you look amazing." Lauren said automatically. "So which one is it? A, B, C or D?"

"I can't even remember the question. Who cares?" Tiffany bounced up onto her feet. "Okay. That must have been, like, a thousand calories for sure. Do you want a drink?"

"No, thanks."

"I promise I'll make it weaker than last time."

Lauren shook her head. "No, really. Never again, thank you. So what college are you applying to, anyway? Do you want to go to the same place as Jason?" She rolled onto her stomach and watched Tiffany walk over to her dresser.

"Obviously. Although I don't know where he's going yet. But if we have to do the long-distance thing, that's fine, too. We'll make it work." Tiffany sprayed deodorant under her arms. She squirted perfume all around her neck and head and looked at Lauren in the mirror. "Where are you going?"

"I'm putting in an early application to Tellson."

"Where?"

"Tellson College.

"Where's that?"

"Iowa. It's a Christian college."

"Why?" Tiffany turned to face her.

"It's where my parents went."

"So?"

Lauren opened and closed her mouth. She had worn her first Tellson College t-shirt when she was seven. Her parents had met there when they had a class together, and her mom was always saying what an amazing place it was, but she couldn't remember what her mom had majored in. Lauren had never considered going anywhere else. "The campus is pretty. And my friend Shelby is going there, too."

Tiffany turned back to her dresser and started rearranging her makeup and perfume bottles. "Well, great. You and Shelby can have a lot of fun reading the Bible together."

Lauren hadn't spoken to Shelby in over a month.

"It would be more fun to go wherever you're going," Lauren admitted.

Tiffany grinned. "Yes, it would." She grabbed her laptop from her desk and flipped it open, sitting down next to Lauren. They spent the next two hours doing virtual campus tours, discussing bedding and posters and whether or not they should join a sorority. Deciding where to go based on her major didn't seem to occur to Tiffany ("I can major in anything, it won't make a difference to my career anyway!") and Lauren pictured herself on large campuses, with student bars and tailgating parties. Instead of a pretty, close-knit community, Tellson College now seemed small and dull.

At home that evening, Lauren read over what she had written for her Tellson admission essay for the fiftieth time. She had half a sentence.

I want to go to Tellson because

She sighed and tapped her fingers against the keyboard. She had commandeered the computer from her brothers for the evening to work on her college application but had wasted the last thirty minutes comparing photos of Tellson with different college websites. The Tellson students all looked the same, wearing oversized sweatshirts and huge smiles in the tree-lined quad, arms around each other, or sitting with books and laughing (but not too much!) over steaming mugs in the cafeteria. The students in the photos at other colleges ("*normal* colleges, with *normal* people" as Tiffany said) were wearing tank tops, funky hats and lounging on bleachers in front of cute guys practising football. They just looked like they were having so much more *fun*.

Lauren twisted her purity ring around her finger. She could write about taking the pledge in her essay. It was the only Christian thing she'd done lately.

Michael ran into the room and threw his arms around her neck. "Are you done yet?"

"No, I'm not even close, go away," Lauren shrugged out of his arms. Michael peered over her shoulder.

"It's my turn," Adam rushed in. "I get the computer next, not him! Hey, what are you looking at?"

"You guys. Go *away*."

"Who are those people in those photos?"

Lauren closed the website and clicked back onto her document. "No one."

"Boys, leave your sister alone." Lauren's mom stood at the doorway.

"She's not even doing anything, she's just looking at stupid photos," Adam said. "Look, there's nothing even on that page."

"Adam. Michael. Downstairs. Now."

The boys looked at each other and left the room, grumbling.

Her mom shook her head. "I told them to leave you in peace. How's it going?"

"Can't they use Dad's computer?"

"He's got all that confidential information on it, and all his sermons. Goodness knows what the boys would end up accidentally deleting."

She stood behind Lauren and rubbed her back. "Ah, I see you haven't got far, huh?"

"I was thinking about writing about the pledge?"

"That's a great idea. Or, write about your father?"

"Maybe. Like what kind of thing?"

"Well, how thanks to Tellson, he became a pastor, a husband and a father. And now you're inspired to go there. They'll love that. Sometimes they even find a little extra money to offer scholarships to children of alumni." Her mom squeezed her shoulders. "But the purity pledge is a great topic, too." She went to leave. "I can read over it, when you're done."

"I was thinking of maybe applying to a couple other places as well, though." Lauren blurted. "Just to, you know, cover all bases."

Her mom turned. "Well, your grades and SATs are good, honey. And if you didn't get accepted, you have plenty of time to apply somewhere else. But don't worry, I know you'll get in. Just like us." She winked and closed the door behind her.

Lauren typed.

I want to go to Tellson because my father

Her hands hovered over the keyboard. She was suddenly craving one of Tiffany's vodka and Diet Cokes.

THIRTEEN

Molly headed for a table in the far corner of the library and sat down. In here, the teasing scent of food from the cafeteria didn't reach her. She pulled a copy of *Brave New World*, a notebook and a pen out of her bookbag. She jotted down ideas for the English Lit essay assignment and considered the list before her. What would Ms. Nelson's reaction be if Molly wrote about the benefits of all babies being conceived in test tubes? And what was so bad about being created in a lab, anyway? No one would ever have to wonder why their parents weren't together. Or who their father was. Or whether their mother was hiding something. Ms. Nelson would probably give her extra credit for being satirical.

Molly put a question mark next to 'test tube babies' and moved on to soma, the pill the characters took to block out negative emotions. She copied out the line '*Christianity without tears – that's what soma is*' in her notebook. It would make a good opening quote for an essay juxtaposing the role of Christianity today with soma in the novel. She chewed the end of her pen. Could she ask Pastor Davis for his favorite Bible verses about the importance of suffering and self-denial for a virtuous life?

Molly pulled off her purity ring and closed her eyes. As she put it back on, she imagined Pastor Davis standing in front of her, holding her hand, sliding the ring onto her finger. How he'd keep hold of her hand afterwards, looking at her and really *seeing* her. Why hadn't she insisted on Pastor Davis being the one to give her the ring during the ceremony instead of her mom?

Molly's stomach growled and she opened her eyes. If Molly took a soma right now, she wouldn't be thinking about the brown paper bag containing her sandwich, juice box, and apple in her locker. She'd eaten the granola bar and potato chips between classes. Her mom packed way too much in her lunch bag even though she knew Molly was trying to be healthy. It was like she *wanted* Molly to stay fat so she could appear even skinnier. Molly's stomach contracted again. Perhaps she could pull out just the slices of tomato from her sandwich and eat them before her appointment with the guidance counselor.

Twenty minutes later, Molly knocked on Ms. Cox's door. The taste of the cream cheese and tomato sandwich lingered in her mouth, a reminder of her complete lack of self-control.

"Come in," a cheerful voice called.

"Hi, Ms. Cox." Molly pushed the door open and sat down in the chair in front of the desk, putting her bookbag on her lap to hide her stomach.

"Hi, pumpkin." Ms. Cox pushed a bowl of candy towards her.

"No, thanks."

Ms. Cox raised her eyebrows and grabbed a handful of M&Ms for herself. Ms. Cox was so enormous Molly felt almost slim around her. She wore billowing dresses covered in luminous flowers, bright pink lipstick, enormous hoop earrings and didn't seem to notice she was the size of a pickup truck. Molly was never sure whether to admire her or feel embarrassed for her.

"So, my lovely girl. I've done some research. Here's a list of the best colleges in the country for chemical engineering." She pulled a piece of paper from the file on her desk with a flourish and presented it to Molly with plump fingers.

Molly scanned the paper. "MIT? *Princeton?*" Molly placed it on the desk. "I can't afford any of those places."

"I've done some research and you'd be surprised. You're eligible for plenty of financial aid, you're on track to be valedictorian, and you're a female planning to study a STEM subject. You could get a lot in scholarships." She pushed the list back.

"Really?" Underneath the name of each college was a bullet pointed list of financial aid packages and cost of living estimates. Molly felt like Ms. Cox's pet project for the year, although she didn't mind as much as she thought she would.

"You really think I could go somewhere like MIT?"

"My girl, everything is worth a try. Reach for the moon and at least you'll fall among the stars, right?"

Molly picked up the list again. If she got enough financial aid maybe she wouldn't even have to work part-time – she could go to the gym instead. In a couple of years she'd come back to visit her mom, and her old classmates would see her shopping at the mall and not even recognise her. Maybe one of *them* would be working there, finding her a pair of size 6 jeans to try on.

"Should I apply for all of them?"

"Well, it would be good if you could apply for at least a few. I know it's a lot of paperwork, but I can help if you get stuck."

"Isn't there a fee for each application?"

"Almost all of them have a fee waiver request section on their forms, I've marked it on there."

She had an answer for everything. Her research was impressive. Molly's stomach rumbled and Ms. Cox pushed the candy bowl towards her again. Molly took one and started chewing, scanning the list again before she realized what she was doing. "Dammit," Molly muttered.

"Molly, you are the brightest student this school has had for years. I *know* you have an amazing future ahead of you and I will do whatever it takes to make that happen. *Whatever* it takes. Okay?"

Molly gave silent thanks for the hundredth time that Ernie Chan got an A- in Biology the previous year. He used to be the one always going into Ms. Cox's office, and now it was her. She thought about what it would sound like to say she was graduating from MIT or Princeton. Watching her grandma's face scrunch up skeptically as she told her she was going to Massachusetts for college. "Oh, it'll probably be too far for you to come for graduation. Don't worry about it," Molly would tell her. Molly could invite her dad instead, and her mom wouldn't be able to do anything about it. By then, she would have tracked him down. When he saw that Molly was smart, successful and pretty – well, who wouldn't want that for a daughter?

"Okay, Ms. C. Let's do it." Molly nodded.

"That's my girl. Take this list with you, and try and submit early applications for at least five. You think that's doable?"

"Yes. Definitely."

"Great. Oh, and Molly? You know the one thing that'll really help your admission essays stand out?"

"Please don't say sports. You know I can't play sports."

"You and me both, girlfriend. You and me both!" Ms. Cox burst out laughing, and Molly watched her arms jiggle, fascinated that she didn't even try to cover them up. "Oh, my. No, don't worry about that. But colleges *love* it if you've helped the community, or have some volunteering experience you can talk about. You do anything like that at the moment?"

Molly looked at Ms. Cox despondently. "This is pointless. I don't have time for that. I don't ever do anything like that."

"No big deal, sweetie pie. You don't need to be doing something big. Just, I don't know, help out at your local girl scouts, or church or some such, okay? Just a little something you can give a good spin when you write your admission essays. Something to talk about if you get an interview for a scholarship, darling. That's all."

Ms. Cox was irrepressible.

"I guess I could see if I could help out at Sunday School or something."

"There you go. Here, you want more candy before you go? Gotta keep your energy up!"

Molly shook her head and rose from the chair, her hunger pangs gone. Now she'd have a reason to talk to Pastor Davis.

November
2007

"Hast thou found honey? eat so much as is sufficient for thee, lest thou be filled therewith, and vomit it."

PROVERBS 25:16

FOURTEEN

"Lemme see," Michael reached for the centerpiece but Adam grabbed the plush turkey toy from the center of the table and held it above his head.

"Come and get it then."

"Give it here," Michael danced helplessly around him, reaching his arms up. "Give it, please!"

Adam lowered the toy then snatched it away just as Michael's hand was within touching distance.

"Come get it," Adam said gleefully. "Come on!"

"Laaaaurrrreeennnn! Help me," Michael pleaded, jumping up and down.

Lauren rolled her eyes and swerved past Michael's flailing arms, concentrating on the stack of plates she was carrying.

"Adam, don't be mean. Just give it to him." She put the plates on the table and went back into the kitchen to get knives and forks.

"What's going on in there?" her mom asked, stirring a pan on the stove.

"Just the usual," Lauren reassured her. She counted out the silverware and looked at her mom more closely. "Are you ok? You look tired."

"Oh, I'm fine, just a little worn out." Her mom smiled and raised the spoon to her lips to test the sauce. "Mmm, just right." She turned off the heat under the pan, and opened the oven door to check the turkey. The scent of cooked meat filled the room as she pierced it with a meat thermometer. "This is finished, so hopefully we'll be eating in about fifteen minutes." She pulled the turkey out of the oven and placed it on the counter.

Lauren studied her, noticing that her usually glossy hair was lackluster and limp and her face was pale. She hadn't spent a lot of time with her mom in the past few weeks but now that she was really looking, Lauren saw how wan and drained she was.

"I hope your dad gets back soon," her mom frowned at the clock on the wall. "I don't want to be putting this back in."

Lauren was happy for her dad to never come home. She'd enjoyed being in the kitchen that day, listening to the radio and making pastry while her mom supervised the boys peeling potatoes. But she had been so focused on creating the perfect pies she hadn't seen that her mom looked exhausted.

"Come sit with me," Her mom perched on a stool at the breakfast bar and patted the seat next to her.

Lauren laid down the knives and forks with a sense of doom. Her mom was getting sick and she hadn't noticed – just like with Adam. She and her parents hadn't known what was wrong with him at first; he was just over-tired and crying a lot. Lauren, eight years old at the time, had decided he was an irritating toddler and began to hate him for the constant whining and attention he got. Two doctor's visits later he was in intensive care, with tubes and monitors snaking from his tiny body.

Lauren had spent several years thinking it was her fault for wishing he hadn't been born. She was still mortified by her younger self's jealousy, and had never told anyone how she'd felt at the time. But she was older now, and she'd learned her lesson. If her mom was sick she'd do whatever it took to get her through whatever lay ahead over the next few months. Her eyes welled with tears as she watched her mom struggle for words.

Lauren wished she could freeze this moment, the moment before knowing, pretending her mom was still fine and nothing bad was going to happen. She stood up and flung her arms around her, breathing in her magnolia perfume.

"I love you, Mom." Lauren sniffed.

"Well, hey, I love you too, honey." Her mom laughed and squeezed her. She leaned back, examining Lauren's face.

"What are –"

"Are you –"

They spoke at the same time, Lauren blinking back tears. Her mom reached over to place a loose strand of hair behind Lauren's ear. "You go first."

Lauren took a deep breath and plunged in, like ripping off a Band-Aid.

"Mom, are you – are you sick?"

"What?" her mom laughed again. "No, I'm fine." She saw the tears welling up in Lauren's eyes and her laughter died away. "Really, I'm okay, honey."

"I just, you look tired and, and I just thought maybe it was like with Adam –" Lauren's voice cracked.

"Oh sweetie, I know I've been a little tired lately, but honestly I'm fine. I'm not sick, I promise." She squeezed Lauren's hands. "I wanted to talk to you about something else."

"Oh." Lauren felt faint with relief. "Sure." She waited, wondering if she had offended her by saying she looked tired.

"Honey, what is going on with you and your father?"

"What?" The question caught her completely off guard.

"You and your dad. What's happening?"

Lauren's stomach twisted into a knot. Although she and her father had barely spoken since she'd come home late on the first day of school, she thought she'd managed to avoid him in a subtle way so that no one else would notice. They exchanged basic civilities, but otherwise hardly interacted with each other. Dinners were dominated by Adam and Michael chattering and bickering, and Lauren spent half her evenings at Tiffany's anyway. The rest of the time she was in her bedroom studying and working on college applications.

When her dad's time was taken up with work meetings, Bible study groups, and visiting church goers, Lauren would help her mom cook or watch a movie with her and the boys. Whenever she needed permission to do something – go to the mall or attend a football game – she'd choose a time her dad wasn't home and ask her mom, who would then relay the request to her dad when Lauren wasn't home. She realized now she had managed to avoid being in a room alone with him, and therefore any kind of embarrassing conversation with him. But it hadn't occurred to her that she'd put her mom in an awkward situation as the go-between for her and her father. She felt awful as she realized this was the reason for the dark circles under her mom's eyes.

"I'm sorry, I just, I ..." Lauren rubbed her face. "We don't ... He just doesn't understand what it's like to be a teenager."

"I know he can be strict sometimes but we were both teenagers once, believe it or not," her mom smiled at her. "It's normal to feel like your parents don't understand you, but we do, hon, more than you think."

"I just ..." Lauren struggled. "I want to wear makeup and look nice but he said – he thinks, that –" Lauren felt her cheeks redden.

"You're beautiful Lauren, and you don't need to wear make up. There's so much pressure on girls now to look older and sexy."

Lauren blushed even more and she began to align the knives and forks on the counter. She'd never heard her mom say 'sexy' before.

"God created you, and you're perfect. Your father and I love you just as you are. You don't need to try and be someone else." She paused. "And you don't want people looking at you thinking that you're someone else, do you?"

"Yes. I mean, no. I just ... I don't know, Mom." She hoped her mom wouldn't notice the mascara she was wearing.

"I know teenagers don't always get along with their parents, but I think it's really important for you to connect with your father. Soon you'll be off to college." She touched Lauren's arm. "Oh my Lord, I can't believe my little girl is going to college."

Lauren pressed her fingertips onto the ends of the forks, the tines pricking her skin. "I know." Of course her mom didn't understand – other than a slick of Vaseline if her lips were dry, her mom's face was free from embellishment at all times.

"You don't want to miss this opportunity to spend as much time together as you can."

"Right." Lauren watched her fingers turn white where the forks were jabbing into them.

"Great. And now you'll have a chance to, because guess what?"

Lauren looked up.

"There's a father-daughter dance at the church!"

Three forks clattered onto the floor. "Huh?"

"Oh, hon. These'll need to be washed now," her mom got off the stool and knelt down on the floor. "Can you get some clean ones out of the drawer?" She picked up the forks.

Lauren didn't move. "What?"

"Just grab some more out of the drawer."

"I mean, what did you say about a dance?"

"A father-daughter dance." She stood up and opened the dishwasher. "I don't think you've done one of those since you were about eight years old. It was so cute, you were all dressed up and you loved it. Remember?"

"Yeah, sure."

She didn't remember, although a photo from the evening was hanging on the staircase wall. She had worn a puffy sky-blue dress, a tiara and a huge smile. The photo showed her grasping her dad's hand, who was wearing a dark suit with a tie that perfectly matched her dress. Her mother must have chosen it. They were both looking not at the camera but just beyond it, at whoever had been taking the photo – her mom, Lauren guessed. She couldn't believe she'd ever been that happy to hang out with her dad but it was around the time Adam had been in the hospital. Lauren had managed to block out most things from that era.

"Um ..." Lauren watched her mom get more forks out of the drawer. "I guess I, I don't know if it's a good idea. I mean, you know, some kids don't even have dads at home. I don't want them to feel left out."

"That's sweet of you, but this kind of thing has always been open to father figures, remember? So the girls can bring anyone – you know, a 'male relative or role model' as they say." Her mom handed her the silverware. "Try not to drop these, we don't have any more clean ones."

Lauren clutched the forks in her hand. "Right. Well, it sounds good, but I'm not sure I can make it that day. Tiffany and I are going to this thing we've arranged."

Her mom looked at her like she was deranged. "How do you know you're busy? I haven't even told you the date yet."

"Oh, right." Lauren felt herself blushing. "When is it? Oh – I smell something. Is the sauce burning?" She rushed over to the stove and awkwardly stirred the pan with her left hand, still holding onto the forks in her right hand.

"I turned the heat off, it's fine. What are you –"

The side door to the garage opened and Lauren's dad strode in, carrying a large plastic crate. "Sorry I'm late, but something sure smells good in here." He put the box down on the counter with a grunt as though he'd been carrying boulders around. Lauren bit her tongue.

He walked over to his wife and kissed her cheek. "Hope you haven't been working too hard."

"Hi, how did it go?"

"Good, thanks – just got a few leftovers to take to the foodbank later."

He glanced over at Lauren at the stove. "Good to see you helping out around here for a change."

Lauren set down the wooden spoon and clenched her jaw.

"She's been a great help," her mom reassured him. "And we were just talking about the dance at the church."

Lauren walked past them into the now empty dining room. Her brothers often disappeared when her dad was home.

"Lauren, come here," her dad shouted.

She considered pretending she hadn't heard him, but after the conversation with her mom it would be too obvious. She walked back into the kitchen, ready to be yelled at.

"You forgot these." He handed her the knives.

"Oh, thanks." She avoided touching his hand as she took them.

"Wait a minute, honey," her mom stopped her on her way out. "The dance, what date is it?" she asked Lauren's dad.

Lauren felt her stomach knot.

"I can't remember off the top of my head," her dad shrugged. "I'll check later."

"Well, good. Because I was just saying to Lauren you two need to spend more time together. She'll be leaving soon."

Lauren's dad made a noncommittal grunt.

Her mom opened the oven door, checking on the yams and casserole. "We'll be eating in about five minutes. Lauren, can you let the boys know?"

"Sure."

Lauren went back into the dining room and quickly finished setting the table. She headed towards the stairs but then hesitated for a second and returned to the dining room. She could hear the murmur of her parents talking in the kitchen. She moved closer, standing by the swing door, straining to hear over the clatter of dishes and pans.

"... you to get on," she caught her mother saying.

"I just think she's a little old for something like that now," her father's voice was easy to hear, its low register always carrying in church and the house.

"... college ... everything changing ..." Her mom's voice was harder to pick up. Lauren strained forwards to listen but it was just a mumble.

"...not force things," her dad's voice became louder and Lauren shrank back as the door opened, nearly hitting her head. Her dad stared down at her, steam rising into his face from the dish of green bean casserole he was holding in his oven-gloved hands.

"I was just coming to tell Mom, that, er, tell her that the boys said they'll be down in a minute."

"Uh huh." He placed the dish on the table and glanced at her.

Lauren felt her face redden. She was a terrible liar. "I'll go wash my hands."

Lauren rushed up to Adam's room where the boys appeared to have made up and were both sprawled on the floor.

"Saaave meeeee, gobble! Gobble!" Adam called to her, halfway under his bed.

Lauren stood in the doorway. "What are you doing? Dinner's ready."

"We're turkeys. Sacrificed for Thanksgiving!" Michael grinned excitedly then enacted a slow, painful death with choking noises. He lolled his tongue out as he flung an arm towards Lauren.

"You are so dumb," she said, grinning. "You guys need to wash up and get downstairs."

Adam lay on the floor immobile, eyes staring up at the ceiling. "I'm dead. I can't move."

"Seriously, come downstairs."

Michael copied Adam so that they lay like two corpses sprawled on the carpet, their shoulders shaking with the effort of not bursting into laughter as they tried to stay motionless. Lauren looked at them, wondering how two boys could be so maddening and sweet simultaneously. Thinking about leaving them behind when she went to college brought a lump to her throat. She swallowed to clear it – it still felt like forever away.

"The food's ready and Dad's in a bad mood," she warned.

The boys jumped up as if electrified and pushed past her, scrambling down the stairs.

"Me first."

"No, me."

"Ow, wait!"

Lauren waited a few moments before following, relieved they were in a particularly boisterous mood today. Maybe it would make her mom forget about their conversation.

In the dining room Adam and Michael were already seated opposite each other, gazing longingly at the spread before them. Her mom was making her way around the table with a box of matches, lighting small candles nestled between dishes of mashed potatoes, cranberry sauce and cornbread. The roast turkey was in the center of the table but it was way too much food for the five of them. This was the first year that Thanksgiving didn't involve aunts, uncles, cousins and at least one set of grandparents spread across two tables.

Lauren felt a wave of resentment at her father and his decision to move to another state. Instead of being surrounded by family for Thanksgiving, this was just another dinner to get through – exactly the same as all their other meals but with a ridiculous amount of food.

Her dad walked in from the kitchen holding a carving knife. For a split second Lauren imagined grabbing it and plunging it into his stomach.

She cleared her throat, trying to focus on how grateful she was for her mom not being sick. "This looks amazing, Mom." Lauren sat down next to Adam, nudging him.

"What was that –"

Lauren kicked him under the table.

"Ow, oh. Yeah, Mom, it looks great," Adam echoed, giving Lauren a kick back. Lauren raised her eyebrows. Adam looked across the table. "Michael, aren't you going to say how good it looks?"

"I was just about to," Michael raised his voice. "Mom, I was just *about* to say how good it looks. And I was going to say thank you!"

"Michael, don't whine." Lauren's dad sat down at the head of the table and Lauren wanted to smash the potatoes in his face.

Her mom sat next to Michael and patted his arm. "I know, sweetie, you're very good at saying thank you." She glanced at her husband who was aligning his knife and fork so they were equidistant from his plate. "And you are most welcome," she said loudly. Michael grinned.

There was a pause as Michael eyed the cornbread and Adam held his stomach dramatically. Lauren twisted the cloth napkin in her lap.

"Now, let us pray," Lauren's dad said.

He reached out his arms and the family held hands around the table, Lauren stretching her arm across the food to reach Michael's small hand. As her dad led them through the prayer, Lauren noticed the toy turkey was returned to its rightful place near Michael's plate but was missing part of a fabric wing. She raised her eyebrows at Michael but his eyes were screwed shut as he concentrated on their father's words. It was sweet. Lauren used to pray like that, really believing everything her dad was saying. She gave his fingers a gentle squeeze and closed her eyes, enjoying the warmth of her brothers' hands in hers. *Please God, don't make me go to this dance. I know there's a lot more important things for You to worry about but just this one thing would be great. And please keep my mom and my brothers healthy and safe. Amen.*

"Amen," her dad said.

"Amen," the family repeated. They released hands and Lauren's dad began to carve the turkey. Her mom asked him what his plans were for the sermon on Sunday. Michael grabbed a piece of bread and Adam started piling his plate with green beans, yams, and potatoes.

"Come on, sis. Are you hungry?" Adam held an enormous spoonful of mash potatoes over Lauren's plate.

"Thanks," she said, not hungry at all. He let the potatoes plop down.

Michael giggled. "That sounded like a –"

"*Michael,*" Lauren, Adam and their mom interrupted him at the same time.

"Like a what?" Her dad paused in his carving, a vein in his forehead pulsing dangerously.

Michael fidgeted in his chair. "Um. I don't remember."

Lauren released the breath she'd been holding and

spooned food onto her plate. She ate mechanically, nodding her head to feign interest in the right places as her brothers talked about school projects and her dad spoke about Christmas activities at church. After what felt like forever, their plates were emptied of food but the serving dishes were still half full. The turkey could have fed another family all over again.

"I guess I over-estimated how much we needed," her mom said with a sad smile. Lauren's heart went out to her. It was the first time her mom had cooked Thanksgiving dinner for such a small group.

"But," her mom rolled her shoulders back, "now I don't have to worry about cooking for a couple of days. So I'm thankful for that."

"Is it time? Is it time?" Michael jiggled up and down.

"Yes, why not?" her mom grinned, a bit of color in her cheeks now, so she didn't look as tired as she had earlier.

Oh no, please let's not do this.

"Me first!"

Her dad raised his eyebrows.

"I mean, me first *please*. I've been practising."

"Sure, hon. Go ahead." Her mom handed him the toy turkey.

Michael clutched the toy in his hands. "This Thanksgiving, I am thankful for my mom, my dad, my sister and most of the time my brother."

Lauren let out a little huff of laughter and turned it into a cough.

"I'm thankful for my friends Ben and Toby and sometimes for my teacher Miss Evans."

Lauren could see Adam pressing his lips together, struggling to restrain himself.

"I'm thankful for my bike, some of my books, and definitely for my Legos. And for my Hot Wheels car. And for my –"

Lauren met her mom's eyes across the table as Michael continued his recitation of his possessions. Adam sighed loudly and pretended to look at a watch although he wasn't wearing one. Lauren's dad was staring out the window, seemingly not paying attention to how very long it was taking.

"Okay, Michael, honey," her mom interrupted. "That's such a wonderful long list of things. But it would be good if you could pick your last thing and then maybe write down the rest?" her mom suggested.

"Oh," Michael looked downcast.

"Dessert's waiting," Lauren pointed out.

"Okay, I'll write down the rest." Michael handed the turkey across the table to Adam, who cleared this throat loudly.

"I give thanks for not growing old and dying just now," Adam smirked.

"Adam," Lauren's mom said.

"Sorry. Sorry, buddy," he said to Michael.

"For what?" Michael asked.

Lauren wanted to bottle Michael's innocence up and carry it with her everywhere.

"Okay, anyway," Adam continued. "I am thankful for my health and my family's health. I'm thankful for this awesome meal and my mom and sister for making it. I'm thankful for Skype so I can still talk to Billy even though he lives really far away."

Lauren's dad cleared his throat and Adam paused.

"Um ... I'm thankful for not being a turkey. And, you know, everything Michael said." He handed the toy to Lauren.

Lauren held the battered turkey and bit her lip, regretting not thinking ahead. "Um, I'm thankful for my friends and family, near and far." She waited a moment, but there was no response from her dad. "I'm thankful I have a good education and get to go to college. Um." She felt as though she should say something else but the pause stretched out so long it became uncomfortable. She handed the turkey to her mom across the table.

"I'm thankful for my beautiful children who bring me joy every day." She looked at each of them and smiled. Michael was staring at the table with a frown. Please God, don't let him be sick from the amount of food he'd consumed.

"I'm thankful for my husband for working so hard and giving us this home and food on the table. I'm thankful for all my family for being my strength and support through good times and the more challenging times," her mom's voice shook and she cleared her throat. She spoke on the phone to her sister every day since they'd moved, but Lauren knew it wasn't the same as being able to meet up for dinner or dropping in for coffee. "And I'm so very, very thankful that I have a happy announcement to share with you."

Lauren turned her attention from Michael and focused on her mom. Were they moving back? Maybe her parents had realized it had all been a mistake and they would go home? She'd miss Tiffany, but that was about it. Her mom's smile was huge and out of the corner of her eye, Lauren saw Adam sit up as well – he must be thinking the same. They stared expectantly.

"I'm pregnant," Her mom announced, smiling widely.

What?" Lauren was sure she'd misheard. "You're

what?"

"What's that?" Michael asked.

"I'm pregnant. I'm going to have a baby," she glanced over at Lauren's dad. "*We're* going to have a baby," she corrected herself.

A pause stretched out for several seconds.

"For how long?" Michael wondered.

Even her dad cracked a smile then but neither of her parents answered him. It was as though they were waiting for Adam or Lauren to respond, but Lauren was speechless. Finally, Adam spoke.

"Where?"

"What honey?" her mom frowned.

"Where?" Adam asked. "Where will a baby go in this house? We barely have enough room here, where's a baby gonna go?" he was almost shouting. "Because I am *not* sharing a room."

It was clearly not the response her mom had been expecting and she opened her mouth and closed it and then tried again. "But, Adam, Lauren's room will be free when she starts college in the fall," she pointed out.

"How long?" Michael repeated.

"This is why I've not been feeling so good lately, it's made me a little tired." Lauren's mom said.

"I can't believe this," Adam muttered, his cheeks bright red.

Lauren felt dizzy.

"But for how *long?*" Michael kicked his feet against the table.

"It's forever, you idiot," Adam snapped. "Because things keep getting worse instead of better."

"Adam," Lauren's dad glared at him. "That's *enough*."

Her mom put her hand over her mouth and blinked several times. Adam stood up and grabbed his and Lauren's plates, throwing their knives and forks on top with a clatter. He stormed into the kitchen, followed by the sound of plates banging onto the counter.

"I'll go and –" her mom pushed back her chair.

"No. Leave him." her dad instructed.

"Forever, Mom?" Michael looked up at her. "We're getting a baby forever?"

"I'll help," Lauren gathered together the rest of the plates, balancing them precariously on top of the mashed potato serving dish. She padded from the room, leaving her mother explaining to Michael that babies grew up eventually. Her father was staring at the turkey carcass, his jaw tight.

Adam was standing at the sink breathing heavily, his fists clenched.

"Hey, are you okay?" Lauren added her load to the dishes already in the sink.

"I can't believe them," he turned to her. "It's *gross*. Like three kids aren't enough?"

Lauren didn't know what to say. She wasn't sure how she felt herself – but she knew they hadn't responded to the news the way they should have. "It is weird," she admitted. "Mom's right though, my room will be free in a few months. And it's all yours – if you want it." Out of the three children, Lauren had the biggest room in the house, another concession to her being yanked away ahead of her senior year.

"Whatever." Adam shrugged and opened the dishwasher.

"Look, I think Mom's upset."

"I would be too, if I was married to Dad." Adam started rinsing the plates and stacking them inside.

"Well, I think we should congratulate her – that's what people are supposed to do, right?"

Adam straightened and looked at her. "*Congratulate* her? For letting him, letting him –" he couldn't bring himself to say it.

Lauren agreed it was nauseating, literally, thinking about her parents like that. She couldn't shake the idea of how very disgusting it was to think of her parents doing anything, despite knowing it was a normal part of marriage. One day she presumably would get married and start a family herself but she just couldn't imagine it.

"At least don't take it out on Michael, okay? It's not his fault."

Adam looked sheepish. "Yeah, I know. I was mean."

"Come on, let's get dessert out."

Adam gathered bowls and spoons and Lauren removed the foil covering the two pies she had baked earlier. They had come out perfectly, the crusts lightly brown and the fillings firm but not overcooked. But what was the point?

"They look great," Adam commented, overcompensating for his bad mood. His compliments for her baking usually consisted of wolfing everything down and then asking for more. "And at least this year there'll be leftovers."

"Yep, that's true, I guess."

Lauren opened the door with her hip, balancing the desserts on her arm and carrying the whipped cream. Adam followed, holding onto the stack of bowls. The room was silent, except for her mom stacking the rest of the dishes up. Her dad watched Michael attempt origami on his napkin. Lauren felt peculiarly self-conscious as she started to slice the pies.

"Those look great, honey," her mom filled the silence.

"Thanks," Lauren kept her eyes down as she placed slices into the bowls Adam held out.

Their father cleared his throat.

"Hey, Michael," Adam said, "sorry about earlier. I shouldn't have called you a name. You want some extra whipped cream?"

"Yes, please." Michael grinned as Adam squirted an overly generous amount of cream onto his pumpkin pie.

"And Mom, I'm sorry. I think – you know, it's –" he handed her a bowl. "It's cool, having a – a, having another brother or sister. It'll be, it'll be great."

"Thanks, hon. I know it came as a bit of a surprise," she smiled at him.

Adam passed their dad a bowl and then took his own, into which Lauren had placed an enormous slice of blueberry pie. He squirted a healthy dollop of cream onto it, and Lauren could sense his impatience at waiting to begin eating. Lauren gave herself a sliver of pumpkin pie, despite no longer having an appetite. As soon as her father reached for his spoon, the rest of the family picked up their spoons in unison and began to eat.

Lauren felt like she was in a Hallmark Thanksgiving movie that had gone wrong.

FIFTEEN

Jason picked up the phone. "Hello?"

"Hey, bud!"

"Hi, Dad," Jason said.

"Happy belated Thanksgiving!"

"You too."

"You do your usual?"

"Yes, we did. Served about eighty people."

"Wow, eighty? That must have been tiring, huh? Well done. I'm proud of you, son,"

There was a pause. Jason pulled a carton of orange juice out of the fridge and filled a glass. "Well, it wasn't exactly my idea, you know. The church and the pastor organize it."

"But still. It's a good thing. Helping your community."

Jason took a swig of juice. He and his mom always volunteered at the church where they were living. His mom said it was the Christian thing to do, but it was so they could avoid thinking about other Thanksgiving dinners, when they were a proper family. Yesterday his mom had spent the whole day in the church kitchen, her head bent over an enormous pot of soup, so he knew she must be feeling particularly bad this year.

"So, you still doing good at school?"

"I don't know. I'm at a 3.6 right now for this semester. So I need to do better." Jason sat at the kitchen table, which was covered by his textbook, notepad and highlighter pens.

"Well, 3.6 is really good, Jay. Surely you don't need the grades as much as the practice, huh? I hope you're getting your practice in?"

"Dad, I'm not playing ball in college. I told you."

"Nonsense. Why waste your talent? It doesn't make any sense. You scared of failure? Or success?"

Jason sighed. Since his dad had married Margie, he talked like a low-cost motivational speaker. "I just want to focus on my grades. Playing ball is for fun."

"Fun. Huh. Well, I guess you can reconsider when you get to college. How many points in your last game? What's the coach got you working on? What are you aiming for? What's your goal? Because if you don't know where you want to go, you're not going to get there, right?"

"I can send you my training plan," Jason offered. He used to do this twice a year, and his dad would call and message him several times a week to make sure he was keeping up with it. But since his half-sister arrived, his dad had better things to worry about and only managed the appearance of caring four times a year.

"No need, bud – I know you know what you're doing. You just keep doing it, you'll be great."

"Right."

There was another silence. It seemed like the less often he and his dad spoke, the less they had to say to each other. It was weird, because they should have more to catch up on.

"So ... how was your Thanksgiving?" Jason asked.

"Oh, it was good," his dad said. "And the weather is good today, so we walked on the beach before breakfast. You should come out here, come visit."

"I've gotta be here. Got my training, my studying."

"California has basketball courts, and there's

libraries here you could use. I'll make sure you get some peace and quiet for your studying. You could do your runs on the beach. That'd be a nice change, huh? From all that snow?"

Jason wondered if he'd run this invitation past Margie. He was sure the last thing she wanted was 6' 4" of clumsiness sprawling across her Indian cushions and knocking over her incense burners.

"Millicent's four now, she's getting big. You see that photo I sent you?"

"Yes, she's cute." Jason felt a lump forming in his throat.

"She misses you, she'd like to see you."

Jason doubted that. Millicent had screamed her head off the last time he saw her.

"*I'd* like to see you, bud," his dad's voice softened.

"I, I don't know. I don't want to leave Mom on her own. Not at Christmas."

His dad exhaled heavily down the phone. "Well, yeah. That's true. You think she'll ever start dating again?"

"I have no idea. Maybe." Jason had wondered this himself, but couldn't imagine his mom ever being with anyone. His mom was so ... together. She had her work and she didn't need anything else, as she had made perfectly clear, ever since Terry was out of the picture.

"But she's an adult, she can look after herself, right? And what's she going to do next year, when you're not around, huh?"

Jason squeezed his eyes shut tight and took a deep breath, held it, then exhaled.

"Where is she now? Let me talk to her."

"She's at work. Today's her busiest day."

"Oh, I always forget that. Margie doesn't believe in Black Friday so I just forget it's happening."

Jason gritted his teeth. Another thing he could add to the list of things Margie didn't 'believe' in, including eating meat, sugary drinks and negative energy.

"So what are you doing today, huh?"

"I'm practising, studying." Jason heard how dull he sounded. "I'm going to go see Tiffany later."

"Oh, you're still seeing her. Well, that's good, bud. Maybe I should come visit you soon, huh? I can meet her."

"No, no, it's okay. You're busy, don't come all the way out here. You don't want to leave Margie and Millicent." Jason rubbed the back of his neck. "Maybe I will come and see you. Maybe … maybe spring break?"

"Spring break? That'd be great. And tell your mom she doesn't need to worry about the flight, I'll take care of that."

"I mean, I'll try and see you, but I need to check and –"

"Oh, hey. Look who's here! Millie wants to say hello."

"Dad, I don't –"

"Hello." The voice was small and high.

"Oh, hi. Hi, Millicent. How are you doing?"

"Hello."

"Hi."

"Hello."

"Hi. Millie, listen, can you put Dad back on the –"

"Guess what I did?"

"I don't know, what did you do?"

"I took my dolly on the beach today."

"That's nice of you. Did she like the beach?"

"Yes." Millie said. "She was scared of the water though."

Jason struggled to swallow. "Yeah. The water can be scary sometimes."

"Yes. I didn't mind though."

Jason cleared his throat. "You're very brave."

"Yes," she said.

There was a rustle on the line and his dad cleared his throat. "Ha! She's shy, but she soon warms up," his dad said. "She's better in person."

"Dad, I have to go, sorry. Someone's at the door."

"Hey, wait a minute, let's make a plan for –"

Jason hung up and wiped his eyes. He went into the living room and did push ups until his tears stopped falling onto the carpet.

Jason was surprised to see Tiffany already seated when he walked into Steak'n'Shake. It was nearly full, with other customers surrounded by shopping bags and coats. Tiffany looked tiny sitting in the large booth, wearing her black jacket with a fluffy hood.

"Wow, you're early. What's the occasion?" He leaned down to give her a kiss on the cheek and sat opposite her. Tiffany smiled at him, her cheeks flushed. She looked even prettier than usual with the fur of her hood framing her face.

"Hey, you. I missed seeing you yesterday," she smiled at him.

He reached for her hand. It fit neatly into his but felt moist. "Aren't you hot in that?"

"Yeah, I guess."

"So ... take it off then? I mean, if you want to."

She pulled her hand away to wriggle out of the coat, giving him the opportunity to admire the cleavage straining against her v-neck blue sweater.

"You look great."

"Thanks, but I'm getting kind of fat."

"No you're not," he protested, although she was right. Her belly was curving over her jeans. "That's what Thanksgiving's all about, right? Eating too much."

She took a deep breath. Damn, he shouldn't have said that.

"You look really good, seriously." He reached across the table to take her hand again. "Why don't we go back to my place after this, and watch a movie, or something? My mom's working late today."

Tiffany twirled a strand of hair around her finger and took a deep breath. "There's something I want to talk to you about," she said slowly.

"We can talk at home," Jason squeezed her nail-bitten fingers. "And other stuff …"

"Well, that's kind of it. Um, the thing is, my period's late."

Jason grinned. "Cool. Let's go back to mine then."

"No, Jason … I mean, um. Well …"

"Hi, my name is Mabel, welcome to Steak'n'Shake, how you doing today?" A rotund waitress appeared holding a pen over a notepad.

"Er, can we have a minute?" Tiffany asked.

"Sure," the waitress turned away.

"Wait, sorry, can I get a strawberry shake?" Tiffany asked.

Jason stared at her. He had been to Steak'n'Shake probably twenty-two times with Tiffany, and she had literally never ordered a shake. It was Diet Coke or sparkling water and a salad. Always. His knees jiggled up and down. Was she going to dump him?

"Sure, sweetie." The waitress looked at him. "How about you?"

"Nothing yet. Thanks."

Tiffany waited until the waitress was out of earshot and took a deep breath.

"So, what I wanted to say, was –" she bit her lip and Jason's heart felt like it was breaking.

"It's okay. Whatever it is, it's okay." He reached over and caressed her cheek, savoring the last moment he'd be able to touch her, realizing he was blinking back tears.

"I'm pregnant?" Tiffany said, more as a question than a statement.

Jason dropped her hand. "You're what?"

"I'm pregnant. My period was late, and I took a test, and it was positive, and, and …" Tiffany looked up at him and beamed. "Jason, we're having a baby." She reached for his hand and he snatched his arm away.

He stared at her in disbelief. "*What?*"

"I'm pregnant," she said quietly. "*We're* pregnant."

"No, we are not. No. You cannot do this to me. You'll have to get rid of it. This is *not* happening," Jason whispered vehemently, feeling his erection rapidly disappear.

Tiffany stared at him, a small frown creasing her perfect eyebrows. "But, haven't you seen *Juno*?" she asked. "It's fine in the end."

The waitress returned, balancing the milkshake on a tray.

Jason grabbed his coat, retrieved his wallet and threw a twenty dollar bill on the table. He stood up, pushed past the waitress and walked towards the door, the other diners glancing up at him.

"You okay, sweetie?" he heard the waitress ask

Tiffany.

He didn't care. He crunched thirty-six steps over the snow to the car. On the way out he passed two black cars, a red one, three white ones, a grey one, two blue ones and two silver minivans.

Jason sat in the car on the driveway, running through his options of who he could talk to about the weirdness of the situation. His mom was clearly out of the question. As much as she liked to remind him that he could talk to her about 'anything' they both knew that was bullshit – he wouldn't be seeing Dr. Schaffer if that was true. He knew Dr. Schaffer had to keep things confidential but he would probably have a heart attack. There was Calum, but he'd just make awful jokes.

Jason thumped the steering wheel with his fist. He missed his grandma. She had loved him unconditionally. Even when his mom said he was too old for cuddles, his grandma would curl up next to him and push her soft, wrinkly cheek against his. Her long, skinny arms would wrap around him and she would hug him so tight he thought his ribs would crack. He would inhale the scent of her old lady perfume mixed with cigarette smoke and feel safe and loved. And she would tell him, too, all the time: "I love you, Jason." She didn't just say it when he made honor roll or won a track trophy, she would just say it constantly. For no reason at all.

Maybe that was why Jason liked being around Tiffany so much. Her perfume, almost overpowering in her attempt to drown out the smell of cigarettes, made him want to lay next to her forever. That had been the first thing Jason had ever noticed about

Tiffany, over a year ago. He had been walking off the basketball court after team tryouts at his new school. Deep in conversation with one of the players, Calum, about what to expect from the coach, Jason had been vaguely aware of a gaggle of chattering, energetic cheerleaders making their way onto the court in his peripheral vision. He had caught a scent that was so familiar he had turned his head, expecting to see his grandma right there behind him, even though she'd died a few months earlier. Instead, he had seen a blonde ponytail bouncing on top of a petite figure. A pair of slim, tanned legs was skipping onto the court and Jason had been mesmerized. As though she had sensed him watching her, Tiffany had turned her head and her warm, brown eyes met his.

"Dude, don't be a perv," Calum had punched him in the arm. Jason had grinned and turned to do a slow jog off the court.

"Who was *that?*" he had heard Tiffany asking the other girls. It had been the first time in months Jason had felt happy.

But now it was a mess. After all these weeks of being her boyfriend, and her making him laugh so much, and never telling him he needed to try harder, or do better. He had just been such a dick to her. He had ruined everything, like he always did.

The living room curtains parted and his mom's face peered into the darkness. He sighed and opened the car door. He made his way into the house, stomping the snow off his shoes.

His mom was hovering in the hallway. "Was your drive okay? People at work were getting worried about ice, so we carpooled back a little early."

"It was fine. Thanks for the car today." Jason

looked into the living room and saw a glass of red wine next to the *Financial Times* on the coffee table. Another Friday night on her own. "Shall I make dinner?"

"I thought you ate with Tiffany?"

"No. No…" He unlaced his shoes and pulled them off. "I met up with Tiffany to end things. We broke up. I want to concentrate on studying and playing ball, you know?"

"Oh." His mom rarely looked surprised but he had managed it this time. "Well. That's really sensible of you. Well done." She watched him take off his coat and hang it up. "I know it must have been hard, but I'm sure it's the right decision.

Jason wasn't sure at all, but he couldn't live with himself if he ruined his mom's life any more than he already had.

SIXTEEN

"How long is Grandma going to be here?" Molly whispered as she passed her mom in the hallway.

"Shh." Her mom glanced towards her closed bedroom door.

Molly widened her eyes meaningfully. Her mom couldn't even go into her own bedroom without knocking when her grandmother was staying. She slept on the couch, which meant Molly being stuck in her bedroom after 10 p.m. when her mom went to bed.

"I need more space to study."

"Molly, shh! She'll be gone in a couple of days." Her mom walked into the bathroom and closed the door.

Molly sighed and headed to the kitchen, hoping a glass of water would get rid of her headache.

"What were you two whispering about?" Her grandma shuffled in wearing a robe and slippers.

"I was just saying how much studying I have to do," Molly said.

"Well, if you didn't keep working at that burger place you'd have more time."

Molly raised her eyebrows. "Are *you* going to cover my room and board next year?"

Her grandma opened the fridge, apparently deaf. "You want me to fix you up some pancakes?"

"No."

"You can't go to work on an empty stomach."

"You don't think I should go to work at all," Molly muttered to her back, filling a glass from the faucet.

Her grandmother turned around. "What was that?"

"Nothing." Molly gulped down her water.

Her grandma squinted at her. "Hmm. So you're not eating breakfast?"

"No."

She shut the fridge door. "Well, I suppose that's not a bad thing. You know what they say, a moment on the lips." She reached for a mug from the cabinet and poured herself a cup of coffee.

What a bitch. No wonder her mom was so skinny, growing up with someone who said crap like that. "I've changed my mind. I will have some pancakes," Molly said. "Please."

"Huh. Well, okay. I thought you didn't want any."

"Now I do."

"Do you have time?" Her grandmother looked at the clock on the wall.

"Oh, *God*. Forget it."

Molly stomped out of the kitchen and collided with her mom. "Are you ready to go?" Molly demanded.

"Can I at least finish my coffee?" her mom asked. "And I thought you didn't have to be at work until 10."

"They just called and asked me to come in early."

Her mom raised her eyebrows.

"Grandma's driving me crazy," Molly whispered. "Just drop me off early, please?" Her stomach growled loudly.

"Well, it sounds like you need some breakfast first."

"Oh my God. Why is everyone *obsessed* with breakfast?"

"Well, do you want it or not?" her grandma called from the kitchen, her hearing suddenly perfect.

"No!" Molly shouted. "God."

Her mom blinked. "Hon, are you on your period?"

135

"Don't take the Lord's name in vain!" came from the kitchen.

"*Christ* almighty." Molly elbowed past her mom. "Just tell me when you're ready to go." She stormed into her bedroom and slammed her door.

Molly searched the fridge for leftovers. All she'd eaten at work had been a salad without dressing, even though food was free in her lunch break. She was starving but there didn't seem to be anything low calorie and appealing. She ignored the murmur of conversation over a sitcom rerun coming from the living room until she heard her name. She closed the refrigerator door quietly and stood by the side of the archway leading to the living room, hidden from view.

"Well, she's a teenager," her mom said.

"That's no excuse," Her grandmother's voice was confident and firm.

"You know what? She studies hard, she never has a day off school, she works in a fast food restaurant while her friends are probably at the movies or shopping and, once a month, if she has more hormones than normal, I think she's entitled to be in a bad mood, okay?"

Molly leaned closer. She'd never heard her mom speak to her grandmother like that. Maybe she really did remember what being a teenager was like.

"Hmph. Exactly."

"Exactly, what?"

"Hormones. You said it yourself. You better keep that girl in line, Dee."

"Mother, honestly. Give her some credit. She's going to be valedictorian. She wouldn't do anything stupid."

"Well, I thought that about you. And look where we are now."

Molly frowned. There was a long silence, and then, "Goodnight, Mother."

Molly jumped away from the wall as her mom walked into the kitchen.

She started when she saw Molly standing by the fridge. Her cheeks were flushed and her eyes bright with tears. "How long have you been there?"

"I just – I'm just getting a drink, okay? Jeez."

Molly pulled a carton of orange juice out of the fridge but remembered how many calories it had. She put it back and reached for the milk, and realized she didn't actually know how many calories were in it. Was orange juice better because it was fruit? Or was milk better because it had less sugar? She'd have to look it up.

"Can you close the fridge door while you're making your mind up?"

Molly shut the door. "I can't, I just can't decide. You know?"

Her mom sniffed. "Yes. I do. You want some herbal tea? I'm about to make some."

Molly considered. Zero calories, she was pretty sure. "Yes, please."

"I'll take some, too," The voice came from the living room.

Molly and her mom looked at each other. Molly shook her head and her mom let out a snort of laughter.

The sound of her grandma's suitcase being rolled down the hallway woke Molly up. She lay in bed, ignoring her rumbling stomach, cheered by the thought of her grandmother leaving. It had been a long, painful three days. Her grandma's snide remarks and her mother's lack of backbone had made studying almost impossible. Although her mom had stuck up for herself last night. That had been weird; her mom had always made herself sound like the perfect student, but perhaps she'd been a rebel after all? Molly tried to imagine her mom being an interesting person.

"Molly!" Her grandmother's squawk and a loud rapping at the door interrupted her musings.

"Coming," Molly yelled. She dragged herself out of bed and found her grandmother and mom in the living room.

"There you are. I thought maybe you'd sleep through me leaving." The disapproval was palpable.

Molly took a deep breath. "Of course not."

"Well." Her grandma surveyed her crumpled t-shirt and pajama pants. "I guess you're not coming with us to the airport, then?"

"Mother, I told you, she needs to study and I'm going straight to work after dropping you off," Molly's mom came to her rescue.

"She looks like she's about to just turn around and go back to sleep to me."

"I won't." Molly yawned.

"She won't." Her mom glared at Molly. "I'm working late tonight, but there's plenty of leftovers. Don't work too hard, okay?"

"Yep."

"Hmm. Well, I guess this is goodbye then," her grandma's face wrinkled as though she'd tasted something bitter.

Molly walked over and dutifully wrapped her arms around her grandma. It was like hugging a scarecrow.

"Bye, Grandma."

"Behave yourself. Keep studying." Spindly arms encircled Molly's shoulder blades.

"Okay." Molly pulled away and avoided eye contact.

"Well. Shall we go?" Molly's mom jangled her car keys.

"I'll see you at Christmas, then. Stay out of trouble." Her grandma strode out of the room, leaving her suitcase. Molly's mom picked it up and followed, her lips pursed.

Molly walked into the living room and stood by the window. She watched the car reverse down the driveway and onto the street. She leaned her forehead against the windowpane, following the car's journey to the stop sign at the end of the street until it turned right and disappeared from view. Finally. Now she could start fasting which, according to research, was going to be much more effective, and apparently easier, than reducing her caloric intake. It was hardly surprising she hadn't lost any weight when she'd been so unscientific in her approach to weight loss. But at least now she could put her knowledge into action. It was unfortunate she could only avoid eating entirely when her mom wasn't around pestering her. So, a twenty-four hour fast officially started now. Molly slapped her stomach. *Screw you, fat cells.*

That night Molly couldn't focus on the equations in front of her. They floated around on the page as her stomach made loud growls. Her third can of Diet Coke wasn't suppressing the hunger pangs. For the past two hours, ever since her mom had gone to bed, Molly had thought of nothing but food ... Hot, steaming steak pie with mashed potatoes and gravy. Burgers with fries accompanied by thick chocolate milkshakes. Apple pie smothered in smooth vanilla ice cream. She groaned and rested her head on her algebra book.

Molly's stomach grumbled again. She had never, in all her life, felt hunger like this before. There was a stabbing pain behind her right eye, her stomach seemed to be devouring itself and she felt dizzy. She would be able to concentrate properly if her belly wasn't making so much noise. Maybe just one miniscule snack and then she could get back to studying. After all, so far today she'd had zero calories. Anything under one hundred hardly counted – she'd probably burnt that many just walking around the house.

Molly lifted her head and laid down her pencil. She padded into the kitchen and opened a cabinet door. A family-sized bag of potato chips sat amongst boxes of cupcakes, brownies and bags of M&Ms. Her mom had stocked up on everything on sale at Wal-mart. Molly narrowed her eyes at the selection in front of her. She pulled the bag of potato chips out of the cupboard and sat down at the kitchen table. Opening the bag carefully – perhaps she could reseal it? – Molly delicately selected a small potato chip and placed it in her mouth. *Bliss*. Her mouth tingled with saltiness as the chip cracked into small, hard pieces on her tongue. The jagged edges pressed deliciously painfully against the top of her mouth. She closed her eyes and sucked until every morsel had dissolved. Molly sighed. She opened her eyes and looked at the bag longingly. She would never be thin if she didn't have some self-control. She pressed the edges of the top of the bag but it didn't reseal, so she folded it over and placed it back in the cupboard.

As she walked back to her bedroom, Molly was salivating. Her stomach felt even emptier than it had before. Sitting at her desk, Molly could still smell the salt on her fingers as she reached for her pencil. She slowly licked them and thought about the bag sitting in the dark cupboard. It was stupid to open a whole bag for one chip. Her mom would say it was wasting food. Maybe she could have a few more, just to make it worthwhile, and start fasting properly tomorrow.

Half an hour later, Molly had finished the bag of potato chips, as well as a box of cupcakes, two boxes of brownies and half a bag of M&Ms. It was the first time in days she felt truly relaxed. Her eyes drooped. She slouched down in a chair at the table and stretched out her legs, resting her palms on her distended stomach. Her hands moved up and down with each breath. After several minutes, Molly became aware of her dry throat. She pulled herself up from the chair and went to the sink, filling a tall glass with water. She swallowed it in several gulps and refilled the glass. This time she drank more slowly, savouring the sensation of the cool liquid sliding down her throat. As she rested the glass on the countertop, Molly was overcome by a wave of nausea. She felt the M&Ms rise up into her throat. Swallowing them back down, she stood by the sink uncertainly. She felt another wave come and this time the chocolate made it as far as the back of her mouth. Her stomach gurgled menacingly as she gulped it back down. She had devoured countless potato chips and brownies as well. It was over a week's worth of snacks, and she had eaten almost all of it in less than an hour on the first day of fasting. What a repulsive pig. No wonder she was so fat and disgusting.

A wave of shame washed over her and there was no stopping the vomit that spewed out of her and into the kitchen sink. She gripped the edge of the countertop and retched repeatedly until it seemed there was nothing left inside her. Molly wiped her mouth with shaking hands. She stared into the sink at the pungent chunks of food and wrinkled her face. She ran the faucet, washing away most of the vomit. She rinsed her mouth a few times and spat into the sink. Grabbing paper towels, she wiped down the inside and edges of the sink. She gathered together the empty boxes and wrappers and pulled the garbage bin out. She shoved the trash down into the bottom of the bin and piled the other waste on top. She surveyed the kitchen and spotted crumbs on the table and under her chair. She swept up with the dustpan and brush, the back of her throat burning and a sour taste in her mouth. She'd have to hope her mom didn't notice in the morning. Tomorrow night she could tell her she took the snacks into school for science club. Molly did a final check to ensure all traces of her binge were erased and returned to her equations.

December
2007

"Lo, children are an heritage of the Lord: and the fruit of the womb is his reward."

Psalm 127:3

SEVENTEEN

Lauren gave the Vanderkamps' front door a couple of knocks and pushed it open without waiting for an answer. She jumped when she saw Mrs. Vanderkamp making her way down the stairs. She was wearing a huge black bathrobe, even though it was late afternoon. Her face was strangely free from makeup and her hair was stringy, hanging limply around her face. It was like seeing her naked.

"I'm so sorry, I just thought I'd go ahead and come in. I didn't want Tiffany having to come down the stairs."

"It's fine, darling. Come in." Mrs. Vanderkamp said dreamily, already floating towards the kitchen.

Lauren looked around. It was nice their cleaner had a vacation but the house was a mess. Mrs. Vanderkamp might attempt to tidy up a little, given she didn't even go to work. Lauren wondered whether it would be rude if she offered to vacuum. Probably.

She made her way upstairs and knocked on Tiffany's door.

"Come in." Tiffany was lying on her bed under her comforter, reading a book.

"Hi, how are you doing?" Lauren put Tiffany's homework down on the bed and walked around the room, resisting the urge to tidy up the clothes and magazines scattered everywhere. "How's the ankle? Maybe you should get an X-ray. It seems to be taking a really long time to heal."

Tiffany had been off school for three weeks, since she'd slipped on ice and sprained her ankle. The time off probably had something to do with Tiffany and Jason breaking up, seeing as Tiffany was quiet and wasn't even limping all the time. It didn't make sense – Jason looked miserable and Tiffany clearly wasn't happy about it, but neither would tell her what happened. Lauren felt slightly traitorous still sitting next to Jason in History and talking to him, but she wasn't sure who had dumped who, and surely they would get back together, anyway? Lauren herself felt bereft without Tiffany around at school, and struggled to find something to talk to the other girls about at lunch. They were still nice to her, but if she wasn't Tiffany's friend they probably wouldn't be speaking to her at all. Lauren couldn't wait for her to come back.

"It's better. I'll probably go back to school next week." Tiffany put the book down.

"What are you reading?" Lauren had never seen Tiffany read a book by choice.

Tiffany held the book up. "*Wicked Pleasures*. It's my mom's. I've just finished it. Here, you can borrow it." She threw the book at Lauren.

Lauren caught it and looked at the cover. Black fluffy handcuffs rested on red silk sheets. "Oh, my God, Tiffany. What's it about?"

"Just read it. You're going to need to know this stuff at some point." Tiffany sounded impatient, not jokey the way she usually did when she referenced Lauren's inexperience.

"Won't your mom mind?"

"She won't notice, trust me."

Lauren shoved the book in her bag, out of sight. "Thanks. So, I have good news – the father-daughter dance isn't happening. The church committee didn't think it was a good idea, with so many single parents." Tiffany was shuffling through the homework on the bed. "So I don't have to endure *that* hell."

"Right. That's good."

"Are you okay? Do you want to do a makeover or something?" Lauren walked over to the dresser and held up a brush and blusher. She didn't know how people got over breakups – she'd never experienced one – but Tiffany hadn't updated her Facebook photo for weeks. It was weird.

Tiffany got out of bed and joined Lauren at the dresser. She didn't limp at all. "Maybe."

Lauren frowned as Tiffany picked desolately through the makeup. Tiffany had gained a few pounds. Maybe she was comfort eating. Or one of those people that put on weight as soon as they stopped working out. Her stomach was swollen beneath her sweater and her fingers were puffy around her purity ring.

"I need to tell you something," Tiffany said, playing with an almost empty perfume bottle.

Lauren realized she knew exactly what was coming. *Please don't say it, please don't say it, please don't –*

"I'm pregnant."

Lauren waited a moment but Tiffany kept spinning the perfume bottle around.

"Are you sure?"

Tiffany pulled her sweater down against the swell of her stomach and raised her eyebrows. God, Lauren was so naive. How many other people around her were pregnant that she hadn't noticed yet? "Weren't you and Jason, you know, careful?"

"God, Lauren. Obviously not enough. What does it matter?" Tiffany's eyes filled with tears and she sat on her bed. "This is why Jason broke up with me."

"Oh, Tiff. I'm so sorry." Lauren sat down next to her and rubbed her back. She frantically tried to think of what to say next while Tiffany cried. "I can't believe Jason would do that to you. He's so nice."

Lauren could never let her parents find out about this. It proved her dad's point that guys were only ever after one thing and would abandon you when they got it unless you were married. Tiffany sniffed. Her face was red and blotchy, and her eyes were swollen. It was probably a good thing Jason couldn't see her now. Lauren felt cruel and reached for a box of tissues. She pulled out a bunch and handed them to Tiffany, who blew her nose noisily.

"So, um. What are you going to do?"

"I'm thinking adoption."

"Oh." Lauren kept rubbing her back. "Are you sure? I mean, it's a pretty big thing."

"Well, I have been thinking about keeping it. But I don't know. Something in between would be good. So I could still be the mother and see the baby, but not have it *all* the time, you know? Like an open adoption."

"So you're not going to, um … I mean, you're not —"

"What?" Tiffany looked at her.

"Tiffany, having a baby is really hard. I watched my mom do it and, I just — I mean, do you still have, you know — the other option?"

Tiffany stared. "You mean, am I thinking about getting rid of mine and Jason's baby? No, I'm not."

"But what about school, and cheerleading and —"

"I'm not going to kill my baby. I would have thought you of all people would understand that." She put her hands on her belly. "It's a *life*."

"Sorry, I just —"

"Get out."
"Tiffany, I –"
"Get *out*."
"But –"
"*Fuck off.*"

Lauren picked up her bag and walked out of the room. Halfway down the stairs she turned and went back up and knocked on Tiffany's closed door. There was no response and it was probably for the best. Lauren wasn't even sure what she wanted to say anyway.

EIGHTEEN

Jason sat in History, ears ringing, his legs jiggling under the desk.

It was happening again.

Every time he'd walked down the hallway today there were whispers and stares. Not from *everyone*, but definitely from the cheerleaders. Even Lauren was ignoring him, concentrating on her notes, her face hidden behind her hair.

Jason missed Tiffany like crazy. She was still off school so he couldn't even see her. She'd said she hurt her ankle but it was to recover from getting rid of the baby. He wasn't sure how long it took, but wondered if in a haze of pain and anger Tiffany had posted things about him on Facebook. And she had photos of him – maybe she'd posted one? *This is the asshole who made me kill my baby.*

People would see it. Wonder what kind of person he was. Lauren would definitely see it, and look him up and find out what happened and –

His desk scraped on the floor as his legs bounced it up and down. A few students turned and stared.

"Sorry," he muttered.

He counted five pages of lines of his legal pad until he reached one hundred and seventy. He took a deep breath and rested his hands on his thighs. He was overreacting and being paranoid. That's what happened during times of stress. His brain kicked into overdrive. He remembered the art therapist who had taught him that. She was nice and had long curly hair that would brush against his shoulder as she looked at his pictures. He would sit and draw and color and she would say "tell me about that." Every single time. To the point where it got very irritating. Sometimes his pictures hadn't meant anything at all, they were just a child's drawings. When Jason had realized he would have to explain absolutely everything he ever drew, or wrote, or said, he started sketching different versions of a basketball court.

But at least the therapist had taught him how to take himself someplace else instead of counting. Jason closed his eyes and thought of an empty basketball court, the lines shining under a sheen of wax. His white sneakers positioned just behind the free throw line. He imagined bouncing the ball steadily, building up a rhythm, before gripping the pebbled rubber, feeling the friction against his fingertips, focusing on the net. He breathed in the smell of dusty synthetic leather before releasing the ball through the air, where it swooshed neatly through the net.

The ringing subsided and his heart rate returned to normal. When he opened his eyes he had no idea what Mr. Craven was talking about. Lauren was looking at him curiously but turned away as soon he caught her eye.

Jason would hate it if she knew. Lauren was so perfect. No, not perfect. Pure. She wore her purity ring every day, not just when it matched her other jewelry, and Jason could imagine her giving it to her future husband.

The bell rang and the students made their way out. Some of them were definitely staring at him.

"Hey, Lauren?"

"Hey."

"Is, er, is Tiffany ok?"

"I don't know." Lauren looked embarrassed. "Maybe you should give her a call?"

Jason already knew he should call her. Every day he planned to go and see her, or at least call. But the day would pass in a blur and then he'd plan to do it first thing the next day. Then that day would pass by too while he composed and deleted messages. Now – somehow – three weeks had passed and she was still off, which couldn't be right. Could it?

Maybe something had gone wrong with the procedure.

Maybe she was in pain, and really couldn't walk.

What if it had messed up her insides and she couldn't have children again? And it was *his* fault. *He* made her do that. He'd *walked out* and left her alone in a diner. What kind of person did that?

The shame of it made Jason hate himself more than he ever thought possible.

"I'm not sure if, um, if she wants to talk to me," he admitted.

"Well, she doesn't want to talk to me either." Lauren said. "We had an argument." She seemed about to say something else but then walked out of the classroom.

She knew. She definitely knew. Part of Jason wanted to chase after her, find out what was on the tip of her tongue. Another part wanted to put it off as long as possible.

As Jason followed her, he heard someone hiss *"him!"*

Jason went into the disabled bathroom next to the teachers' staffroom and pulled out his cell phone. He sent his mom a message.

I think we need to move

The phone rang a few seconds later.

"What's happened?" his mom asked.

"I think Lauren Davis knows. Tiffany's friend. You know, Pastor Davis's daughter. She lived in Iowa last year, but before that, I don't know. And she might have just found out anyway. The internet, and —"

"What has she said?"

"She keeps staring at me."

"But what exactly has she said?"

"I —" Jason rubbed his head. "It's just, everyone's looking at me. They *know*." Jason felt a hysterical sob rise up in him. He ran his index finger along the indentations between the wall bricks and swallowed. "Can you ask for a transfer?"

"Jason, you just have a few months left before graduation. Unless you're absolutely sure, then …" his mom sighed. "My boss said I'm running out of transfer options. He told me in my last review I'm almost too ambitious. So just hang in there, okay? Lauren is allowed to look at you. Maybe Tiffany has been talking to her because she's still upset about breaking up. Who knows. But don't jump to any conclusions. Okay?"

Jason wanted to burst into tears. "Okay. Sure."

"We'll talk later. You're going to practice, right?"

"Yes."

"Good. You need to take your mind off this. I'm sure it's nothing."

Jason used to hate moving. When he was ten, the most upsetting thing about his parents' separation was having to move just two years after they had last moved. He had known he would miss living with his dad, but he had agreed with them when they said they needed time apart. He had hated the silent meals and low arguments when his parents thought he was asleep. The worst part had been saying goodbye to Winston. Dogs weren't allowed in the apartment they had moved to and his mom had to work full-time anyway. Jason had cried for weeks.

He had eventually settled into his new school, and made a couple of friends, Matt and Shaun. They had come over to play soccer and basketball in the apartment complex playground, leaving his mom working quietly inside. Jason had gone to see the nice art therapist every week. Sometimes, he slept all the way through the night.

But almost a year later, as he was eating his cereal one Saturday morning, his mom had said, "We're moving. I got offered a promotion at work."

"But I like it here. Can't we stay?"

"Well, things change. It's a good opportunity. I'm sorry, though. I know moving isn't fun." She had opened her arms for a hug.

"But you *promised*. You said this would be the last time!" Jason had stomped to his room and slammed the door. He had picked up *Harry Potter and the Chamber of Secrets* from his bedside table and thrown it onto the floor. It had landed face down with a satisfying thud. He had lifted the book to throw it again. Pages 323-341 were bent back and he hadn't finished reading it. Jason had run his palms over each page, trying to smooth out the creases. It was pointless though. He had ruined it.

He had realized he ruined everything. He should have been happy his mom was getting a promotion. They needed the money because they were living in a single-income household (Matt had gleefully told him that was the reason why Matt wore Nike Air Maxes and Jason wore sneakers from Target). And Jason had understood they were living in a single-income household because his parents were divorced. And his parents were divorced because of him.

He had opened the door and gone into the kitchen. His mom had been standing at the sink, washing the dishes. "Sorry," he had said.

"It's okay." She hadn't hugged him, or even turned around.

They had moved to Texas, and their apartment was bigger. It had a balcony, as well as a play area with a full-sized basketball court. Jason practiced alone whenever the silence of their home became overwhelming. They had joined a church, and started staying after the service for doughnuts and coffee. The churchgoers had been kind and friendly, and no one ever asked about Jason's dad, which was nice.

But after just three months, a woman had approached them before the service. "Excuse me, but didn't you live in Oakland?"

Jason had grinned and looked at his mom. He had felt bad she didn't have any friends, and now here was someone who knew her!

The woman hadn't waited for an answer. "You went to Elevate Life Church? I went there with my brother a few times. You've lost weight, haven't you? You look fantastic." She looked at Jason. "And this is your little boy, all grown up."

Jason had held out his hand, as his mom had taught him. "Nice to meet you, I'm –"

His mom had gripped his shoulder and pulled him back. "Sorry, no. You must have us confused with someone else."

Jason had looked at her, frowning.

"No, I'm sure it's you. Your husband is –" the woman had lifted a hand to her mouth and stepped back. "Sorry. You're right. I'm sorry. I got confused."

Jason's mom had gripped his shoulder and smiled tightly, guiding him to a row at the back. The woman had hurried away, and whispered something to the man next to her as she sat down a few rows in front of them. The man had glanced back at them six times before they left. His mom had stared at the hymnbook while Jason had spent the service counting the man's glances. Was the reason they had moved before because someone had found out the truth?

Maybe his mom just hadn't told him. Maybe this happened all the time, and she was trying to protect him.

They had left as soon as the service was finished, skipping the coffee and doughnuts. His mom had contacted the landlord and her boss the next day.

They hadn't gone back to church again and Jason had spent the next week researching. He had looked up the population of Oakland, and the population of the town they lived in, and had tried to calculate the likelihood of running into someone who knew them even if they were in a different state. He had asked his math teacher about it, who had enthusiastically explained the concept of six degrees of separation.

Jason had been horrified to learn that no matter where you went, or what you did, people were *at most* six connections away from someone who knew them. And what they'd done.

And then he had realized why they moved so often. And why his mom always took short-term rentals. His mom's boss had told her she was the most flexible, ambitious accountant they'd ever had but he knew she must worry they'd find out, start wondering. They'd been in their current house for over a year, the longest they'd lived anywhere in the past decade.

Jason started counting wall-bricks from the lower left hand corner, stopping only when the bell rang for his next class. He'd missed lunch entirely.

After school, when Jason walked into the locker room to change for basketball practice the other guys all stopped talking. Calum stared at him and shook his head.

"Hey, guys."

A couple of his teammates mumbled greetings. Calum ignored him and slammed his locker shut so hard it bounced back open. Calum slammed it again. Damn.

They knew.

They definitely knew.

Calum had made it clear he thought Jason was an asshole for not going to see Tiffany while she recovered from her sprained ankle but he hadn't ever ignored him before. He had shouted at Jason though, saying even if they were broken up, not calling or visiting her when she was in pain made him look like a total dick. Jason had silently agreed with everything Calum said and been unable to defend himself because the truth was even worse.

Jason opened his locker and pulled off his shirt.

The other guys left the room in a huddle, a few glancing backwards. Well, Calum could always be counted on to say the truth. Jason didn't even need to go to practice. If everyone knew, then that was that. A sense of relief washed over him. The thing he'd feared for so long had finally happened. It was too late in the year to transfer schools, but he could do home schooling and he was old enough to teach himself now. His mom wouldn't have to move, or take any time off work, or get a tutor, like when he was younger. Obviously basketball season wouldn't happen, but that was fine. He was never going to play it at college anyway.

Jason wondered whether to put on his t-shirt for practice or not. He needed to get this over with. He couldn't take any more whispers or glances.

"Everything okay?" he asked Calum.

"*Everything okay?*" Calum mimicked. "No. It's not." He laced up his sneakers and stood. "When were you going to tell me? All this crap about Tiffany's ankle. And dumping her. I thought you were better than that, man." Calum shoved him in the shoulder.

"What?"

Calum shoved him again, harder. Jason stumbled backwards, almost falling against the lockers.

Calum leaned towards him. "You get a girl pregnant then you leave her? I *never* thought you would be that kind of guy." He clenched his fists.

Jason flinched. "I, she's, she's pregnant?"

"Yes. What is wrong with you?"

"I, I thought –"

Calum frowned at him. "You didn't know? Jeez, man. Half the school knows."

"What? How?"

"Man, you have got to get a Facebook account."

"She put it on Facebook?"

Coach strode in. "Guys, you gonna gossip or practice? We got our first game on Friday, and you're just standing around chatting? Myers, get changed and do fifty push-ups for being late!" He shook his head and headed out to the gym.

"On my way, Coach," Calum called. "You have got to sort your life out, man." He patted Jason on the shoulder and ran out.

Jason stood, half naked, in the empty locker room.

He was screwed.

Any hope Jason had of the pregnancy being a bad dream, and things somehow magically working themselves out, were destroyed the next day.

Tiffany returned to school wearing a tight pink shirt that showed off her bump. She was wearing less makeup than usual but her skin was flawless. Her hair was thick and glossy, and the extra weight on her face gave her sweet dimples every time she smiled. She looked stunning.

Everyone lost their minds.

Girls were gushing over her, asking whether she wanted a boy or a girl, and her favorite names. Guys leapt up to offer her a seat when she walked into classrooms and carried her bag between classes (while looking everywhere but at her very impressive chest).

Jason was pissed off with himself as he stood in the line for food. Why hadn't he called her? Why had he waited so long? Tiffany made pregnancy look like the most natural thing in the world – and it was. What was so bad about having a baby with someone you loved? And he did love Tiffany, he realized as he saw her chatting with her friends in the cafeteria, studiously ignoring him. And as Calum had pointed out, it would be an incredibly cute baby unless it had the misfortune of inheriting Jason's lanky limbs. But every time Jason thought it through, it ended with him having a conversation with his mom, and he couldn't let that happen.

"Hey." Calum came and stood next to him.

"Hey."

"You still haven't talked to her, have you?"

The conversations of the students standing in front and behind them stopped. "Can we not discuss this right now?" Jason muttered.

"Okay, sure. Let's be the only people in the school *not* talking about it." They shuffled along as the line moved forward. "Has Ms. Cox called you into her office yet?"

Jason turned to look at him, panicked. "No, why? What's happened?"

"You are a fool. What do you think? Although I guess it won't be to give you condoms because it is too late for that."

"Shh."

Calum lowered his voice. "You know Ms. Cox is going to call your mom, right?"

"This is going to destroy her. I can't let her find out."

"Well, she'll find out some day, won't she? It may as well be now. Maybe she'll even be happy to be a grandma? Hey, where are you going?"

"I'm not hungry anymore."

Jason left the cafeteria and headed into the bathroom. He went into a stall and leaned his head on the door. Every option he ran through was terrible, but

Calum was right. Why had he acted like such an asshole? Tiffany had his baby inside her. He should be supporting her, not making her feel bad about it. He needed to be a better man than this. He pulled out his cell phone and tapped a message.

Im sorry. really miss u. Can we talk?

He held the phone in his hand for ten minutes.

Nothing.

It was way too little, way too late. He banged his head against the door. It felt good.

He did it again, and again.

How hard would he have to do it to lose consciousness? How long were people in comas? He just needed about six months. One really hard knock should do it.

He moved his head back. His phone buzzed.

Ok. in libry

Jason opened the door and headed to the library to find Tiffany. It was time to man up.

Jason found Tiffany in a study room, doodling in a notebook. She didn't look up when he came in and shut the glass door behind him.

Jason sat in the empty chair next to her. "I'm sorry for how I reacted."

Tiffany colored in a circle.

"I was just surprised. *Really* surprised," he added. "But I am sorry. So sorry. And I want you to know I'll be here for you. And the baby." The words sounded scripted, like a bad film.

She put the pen down and picked at a mark on the table.

"I love you," he tried. He reached for her hand.

Her closed fist unfurled in his. "Really?"

"Of course." Jason really did. How could he not have her in his life? She was funny, laid back, kind, never hassled him.

"What are you thinking about right now?"

"I was just thinking about how amazing you are," Jason answered honestly.

A small smile formed on Tiffany's face. Jason knew somehow they would work things out. He would make it work out.

As they walked down the hallway together, Jason didn't care about the looks and whispers that followed. They reached Biology and Jason handed Tiffany's book bag to her. "I'll see you later?"

She nodded and smiled. Jason walked to Trigonometry, feeling lighter than he had for weeks. Until he saw Ms. Cox waiting outside his classroom.

"Mr. Myers." She tilted her head. "We need to talk. Come with me."

Jason followed her large frame down the hallway, her turquoise dress billowing behind her. Everyone loved Ms. Cox, but he was terrified. Was he going to find his mom sitting in her office? He struggled to breathe. He wasn't ready for this. There were 164 floor tiles on the way.

Her office was mercifully empty and Jason sat down.

Ms. Cox settled into her chair and regarded him. "So, let's talk."

Ms. Cox knew he'd had sex. Jason didn't know what to say. "Are you going to tell my mom?"

"I think that's your job, don't you? If you can get someone pregnant, then it seems to me you're perfectly capable of talking."

Jason nodded. How on earth was he going to tell his mom?

"Also, I'm not legally allowed," Ms. Cox continued. "Unless a minor is at risk of harm, I can't break confidentiality."

Jason could move in with his dad, take Tiffany with him and call his mom from California. It was the coward's way, but seemed by far the most appealing option.

Ms. Cox sighed loudly. "But I can help you tell your mom, if you'd like me to be there?"

"Really?"

She pushed a bowl of candy towards him. "I know this must be tough for you and Tiffany. There's no reason to make things worse. How do you think your mother will react?"

Jason shook his head. He had absolutely no idea what his mom would do. But he would find out soon enough.

"Do you want me to call her in? Because it seems to me people are finding out pretty fast. And trust me, it's better she finds out from you than someone else."

"I know. I'll tell her tonight."

"Okay. Come see me tomorrow? Let me know how it went?"

"Sure." Jason felt sick.

"Mom."

"Yes?"

"Tiffany's pregnant."

"Wow. Good thing you got out when you did. What a shame she's so young."

"What? I mean, pardon?"

"But you'll meet someone else, too. One day.

Although obviously the purity pledge didn't mean much to her. But let that be a lesson to you."

"Mom?"

"Mm?"

"The baby's mine."

NINETEEN

Molly froze in the stall at the end of the bathroom as she heard quick footsteps. Couldn't she have a spare moment to herself, *ever*? She straightened up and took her fingers out of her mouth, waiting for whoever it was to do her business and get the hell out. But to her surprise, Molly heard the unmistakable sound of retching, followed by a splash and then a sniff.

Jesus Christ, is that what *she* sounded like when she was being sick? It was repulsive. Molly waited, puzzled. Finally, she heard another sniff and another retch. For the love of God. Molly was hardly likely to be the only girl in the school who threw up, but it was annoying that this bitch had managed to find the one bathroom in the entire school not overrun by girls gossiping, crying, smoking, drinking or applying makeup. Molly only had ten minutes until Advanced Algebra.

In spite of herself, Molly couldn't help admiring how quickly her bathroom companion had managed to bring up her lunch. She rubbed her eyes, feeling exhausted. She had been in the stall too long now to casually flush and walk out. She would just have to wait. Molly let her eyes run over the graffiti. *Jenni + Brian 4eva. TAV is a whore. Mrs Clements sucks cock.* Why couldn't anyone write anything useful? Like *Tips on How to Vomit.* That was the kind of stuff that was really needed. She felt a sudden wave of solidarity with her mysterious cohort, who now seemed to be struggling to finish what she'd started as well.

Molly pulled a black marker pen out of her book bag, crossing out extraneous apostrophes and correcting spelling errors. After a few minutes she relaxed enough to ram her fingers down the back of her throat. There were footsteps and a shadow fell under the door. Dammit. Molly yanked her hand away but it was too late. With a loud belch, the last remnants of her lunch flew out of her mouth and into the toilet.

"Hey, are you okay?" a voice asked.

"I'm fine. Just, I felt a little sick." Molly flushed the toilet and hoped the girl would leave but she seemed to be waiting.

Molly took a deep breath and opened the door.

"Oh." Tiffany Vanderkamp looked just as surprised as Molly felt. "Here, do you want some?" Tiffany held out a bottle of water. "I don't have a cold or anything."

"Thanks." The water soothed Molly's sore throat and she drank half of it. Tiffany looked flushed and had a sheen of sweat on her forehead. "Are *you* okay?"

"Yeah. Comes with the territory I guess." Tiffany smiled and patted her rounded stomach.

Jesus Christ. Tiffany Vanderkamp was *pregnant*.

What on earth? How was she dumb enough to get pregnant? And why was she still wearing her purity ring?

Molly handed the bottle back. "Thanks."

"Sure." Tiffany ran some water from the faucet and splashed her face. "I get sick, like, three times a day. I don't mind so much but it makes me get all sweaty." She patted her face with paper towels and pulled lip gloss from her bag.

"Well, you still look really good." Molly washed her hands at the sink, not knowing what else to do with herself.

"Thank you." Tiffany swiped gloss over her lips. "You still working in McDonald's?"

"Yeah." Molly was stupidly pleased Tiffany remembered.

"You're like, really good at math and science and stuff, aren't you?"

"Um, yeah."

Tiffany grabbed her arm. "This is amazing. I'm so glad we're talking properly!"

"You are?"

"I'm finding it hard to concentrate, you know – baby brain? I'd love some help, if you wouldn't mind?"

"Um, sure." Tiffany would probably forget the conversation as soon as she left the bathroom, but it was nice to be asked, anyway.

"What's your number? I'll call you."

Molly rooted around in her bag for pen and paper but Tiffany pulled out her cell phone. Of *course* she had a cell phone. Molly was going to have to give her home phone because that's all she had. God. Well, Tiffany would never call anyway. Molly recited her number while Tiffany tapped it into her phone.

The bell rang and Tiffany gave Molly an unexpected hug. "We have to look out for each other now, right?" she whispered in her ear.

As she watched her leave the bathroom, Molly understood the very enormous conclusion Tiffany had jumped to.

To Molly's surprise, Tiffany called her that evening and asked if she could help her study. They arranged to meet in a study room in the library at lunchtime the next day. Molly wondered if it was some kind of setup, but Tiffany was there when she arrived. A closed Statistics textbook, a notebook covered in doodles and several pens and pencils were scattered across the table. Tiffany's bump was hidden, which was a relief. Her stomach was the same size as Molly's.

Molly sat down opposite her. "So, what do you need help with?"

"The statistics test next week. I failed the last two." Tiffany twirled her ponytail around in her fingers. "And Biology isn't going great. And probably English as well." She considered it. "And History."

"That's a lot of stuff." Molly put her bag on the table and pulled the Statistics textbook towards her.

"But you're good at everything, right?"

"I guess."

"I need to get better grades for my college application."

"You haven't applied anywhere yet?" Molly was horrified.

"I applied to one college," Tiffany shrugged, "but I probably won't get in."

"What's your SAT score? That usually helps applications, and of course you'll be able to say you – uh. You can explain on your application form, you know." Molly didn't know how to say it without actually saying it. "Extenuating circumstances."

Tiffany grinned. "You sound like Ms. Cox."

"Let's get to work. We only have 45 minutes."

Half an hour later, Molly understood how Tiffany got pregnant. Her grasp of conditional probability was non-existent but Molly learned it in her freshman year. She considered using the likelihood of pregnancy per sexual encounter to explain how it worked but Tiffany was already in tears of frustration.

"Sorry, it's the hormones, you know?"

Molly didn't know but nodded her head understandingly.

"It's none of my business, but have you decided what you're going to do?"

"It depends which college gives me the best scholarship."

"I mean, with the baby. Are you going to keep it?" Tiffany wiped her face.

"Oh. I'm not ..." Molly did not expect to feel embarrassed by *not* being a knocked-up high schooler. "I'm not pregnant."

Tiffany's gaze flicked towards Molly's stomach. "I thought, I mean, you're ..." She shifted in her chair. "You were puking."

Molly pulled her notebook onto her lap, covering her lard. "I was just feeling sick. That's all."

"Oh. Are you better now?"

"Yes, thanks. But it's fine if you don't want to study together anymore. I get it."

"Why wouldn't I want to study with you?"

Because I'm a fat, ugly loser.

"I don't know."

"If *you're* okay with it, I'd really like to study with you. You're smarter than anyone I know. And I just hate all this math stuff. It's so dumb. What's the point of understanding all this stuff?"

"To get into college, I guess."

"But what's the point of college, even?"

"To get a good job." *And not work in Wal-Mart wearing a vest for the rest of your life.*

"Well, I don't want a job where I have to sit around figuring out what the chances are of pulling a blue marble out of a bag. Who even *does* that?"

"What do you want to do?"

"I'm going to be on TV. And people don't care if you've been to college for that."

"So why go to college at all, then?"

"My parents. They're going to freak out if I don't get in somewhere. And they're already kind of mad about the baby."

"Oh, right. Well, we have about ten minutes. Maybe we should move on to Biology?" Molly's stomach growled and she coughed to cover it. Tutoring Tiffany was a helpful distraction.

"I think I'm too tired. And you sound hungry, you should eat." Tiffany slammed her notebook shut. "The test is on Monday. Maybe you could come over this weekend. Saturday?"

Tiffany Vanderkamp was inviting her to her house!

"I'm working," Molly admitted. "But I could come over after that?"

Tiffany reached over and squeezed her hand. "Yes. It'll be fun."

Molly would have to figure out a plan to get home from work, change and shower, and get herself back to Tiffany's house. There was no way she was inviting her over to her own disgusting house. She'd have to ask her mom for a ride and beg her to stay in the car.

But she was going to Tiffany Vanderkamp's house!

January
2008

"And he said, That which cometh out of the man, that defileth the man."

MARK 7:20

TWENTY

Lauren lay on her bed, staring at the ceiling. Should she call Tiffany and apologize? Or send her a text? Or a Facebook message? Somehow Jason had managed to fix things and now everything was completely fine with the two of them. But even if Tiffany did forgive her, they wouldn't be able to spend any time together because her parents would see Tiffany was pregnant. There was no way her dad would let her spend time with someone who had blatantly broken the purity pledge. And it was probably too late anyway. Tiffany wouldn't want to speak to her now – it had been over a month since their fight. A tear ran down her face as the usual train of thought circled round and round in Lauren's mind.

It had been the worst month of Lauren's life. She had become exactly what she'd feared when she started her senior year – the outcast. She had stopped sitting with the other girls at lunch, unsure what Tiffany had told them about their argument. She went to the library instead, working her way through assignments. Sometimes she saw Tiffany studying with Molly, but they both ignored her. If Lauren didn't have Jason to exchange a few polite words with in History, she would spend her entire school day not speaking at all. At first she had checked Facebook constantly, but stopped when she saw her number of 'friends' dwindle away to just two, and she wasn't entirely sure who they were. Now she had no idea what was happening with Tiffany or anyone else.

She spent her evenings and weekends shut in her room studying to avoid her father. For the first time in her life, she was getting straight A's. Her mom had been thrilled and then worried. ("You don't have to study so hard, Lauren. You'll get into Tellson, I'm sure!")

Lauren had finished her History essay Friday evening and now had a whole Saturday stretching ahead of her with nothing to do, surrounded by the bare walls of her room. The only decoration she'd been allowed on her bedroom walls was a plain wooden cross. She wanted to stab her father through the heart with it, like killing a vampire. If he hadn't forced her to move, she'd still be in her old school, with her friends.

She could call Shelby, catch up with her. She rolled onto her stomach and reached under her bed for the scrapbook Shelby had given her before she left Iowa. She hadn't even looked at it since August, she'd been so caught up with her new life. She stretched her arm under her bed and pulled the album towards her. She picked it up and saw she was holding *Wicked Pleasures*. Lauren had forgotten she had hidden it under her bed the day Tiffany gave it to her.

She flipped through the pages, words that weren't in any of the books on her bookshelf catching her eye. She tucked the book between the pages of her history text so it looked like she was studying if anyone barged in and turned to the first page.

An hour later, there was a knock. Lauren rested the books against her stomach.

"Hey, honey. Do you want to help the boys decorate some cupcakes?" her mom pushed open the door. "Are you okay? Your face is all flushed. Are you sick?" She came over to Lauren and touched her forehead. "I think you need to take a break. You're spending too much time studying up here. Maybe you can go for a walk, get some air."

"You know what, you're right." Lauren placed the books onto the bed, face down. Her mind was cluttered with images of people doing things she hadn't even realized were possible.

She made her way downstairs into the kitchen, finding Michael and Adam endearingly concentrating on piling edible decorations on top of their cupcakes.

"These look great, guys. Wow, I think you have enough icing on that one, Michael."

"You do one, then Mommy can be the judge and pick the best one!"

"Okay." Lauren gripped the sticky tube of icing in her hands and squeezed firmly. As the cream cheese frosting oozed out, she wondered if this is how Alessandra, the woman in *Wicked Pleasures*, would hold her lover's penis. And that would ooze stuff out too –

"Why is your face all red?" Michael was watching her.

"Yeah, it is." Adam agreed. "Are you sick? Don't infect our cupcakes with your germs."

"Ew. Lauren's got cooties," Michael giggled.

"It's just – it's warm in here." Lauren handed the icing tube to Adam. "Here. I'm going for a walk."

"It's, like, minus ten degrees out."

"Do you want to build a snowman?" Lauren asked.

"Yes." Michael licked his frosting-covered fingers.

Lauren felt nauseous. "Okay, get wrapped up then. Come on, I'll help you."

Lauren fussed over finding Michael's snowsuit and

boots. She needed to get these images out of her head – she was disgusting herself.

The next day Lauren simultaneously hoped for and dreaded that Tiffany would be at church. If she was there, then Lauren would definitely apologise. Even if Tiffany got mad at her again, at least she would have tried.

Lauren swivelled in her seat at the front every few minutes as the church began to fill up, the parishioners chatting to each other. Usually her mom was in the midst of the crowd, greeting people and handing out programs, but today she said she wanted to rest her back and sat down.

"Who are you looking for, honey?" her mom asked.

"No one. Just stretching."

"Do you know why the Vanderkamps haven't been coming lately?" Her mom rested her hands on her bump. "I don't think I've seen them since before Christmas."

"I'm not sure." Lauren flicked through the hymn book.

Her mom put her arm around her. "You can talk to me about anything. You know that, right? Whatever happened with you and Tiffany, it seems like you really miss her."

"I don't know, Mom. It's pretty bad."

"'For if ye forgive men their trespasses, your heavenly Father will also forgive you.' You know that verse."

"Matthew, 6:14." Lauren looked at her mom. "Do you really believe that anything can be forgiven?"

"Of course. That's what being a Christian *is*."

Lauren watched her father make his way towards

the pulpit. The congregation started to settle in their seats, ready for the sermon.

"Do you think Dad believes it too?"

"I know he does. He wouldn't be able to do his job otherwise. Look at all these people here." Her mom lowered her voice. "Do you think they've never made mistakes? That they don't have any regrets?" Lauren looked at all the people milling around and settling into the pews. "Your father forgives them all, and so does the Heavenly Father. So whatever it is, Lauren, it can't be unforgivable. Nothing is."

That evening Lauren told her mom everything. Well, almost everything. Her mom was filled with concern for Tiffany ("That poor girl!") and anger at Jason ("What was he *thinking*?"). Her mom assumed their argument had been over Tiffany breaking the purity pledge and Lauren had to let her think that. How could she tell her that she suggested Tiffany have an abortion? Her mom would be horrified. Lauren herself wasn't sure why she had suggested it. Even worse was that as her mom's belly kept growing, Lauren had images in her head of her mom falling down the stairs, or being in a car accident, that somehow caused her to lose the baby. What was wrong with her? Lauren felt even worse about her argument with Tiffany. She was about to call her when Adam ran into her room.

"Dad wants to talk to you. Can I use the computer?"

"I guess."

"Thanks, you're the best sister ever!" Adam was already pulling up his favorite game.

Lauren made her way to the study and knocked.

"Come."

She pushed open the door and sat down. It was so stupid the way her dad had his study set up, so he could peer over the top of his computer at people coming in. There was even a chair in front of his desk, like she was sitting in front of the school principal. It was their house, for God's sake, why did he have to make it seem so formal?

"Adam said you wanted to talk to me?" She sat in the chair, twisting her ring around her finger.

"Yes. I understand you aren't speaking to Tiffany Vanderkamp now? Because of her ..." Lauren stared at her hands. Her dad cleared his throat. "... condition."

She wasn't sure whether it was a statement or a question.

"And your grades are very good."

Lauren waited for the criticism.

"This is what happens when you live a righteous life, Lauren, as a woman of God. And you're providing a good example to your brothers. Well done."

Lauren couldn't remember the last time her dad had said that to her. It was like receiving a hug from someone you had thought was going to attack you.

"Thank you." She felt strangely embarrassed.

"But you need to reach out to Tiffany. She's made a mistake, a grave mistake, yes. But the Vanderkamps are still welcome at our church. Remember Ephesians 4:32!"

Lauren jumped. What was it? "Be kind and forgiving to one another?"

"'Even as God for Christ's sake hath forgiven you,'" he finished.

"I was thinking about calling Tiffany, seeing how she's doing?"

"Good. Jesus forgave the immoral woman and we can do the same. The church family is there to support both her and her parents through this difficult time."

"You're right. I'll call her tonight. I've been worried about her," she admitted. "Thanks, Dad." It was the best conversation they'd had in months. Lauren got up and was almost out of the study when her dad called her back.

"Lauren? Why don't you see if the Vanderkamps want to come to the Valentine's Day auction? That would be a great way to welcome them back to church. I think they'd really enjoy it."

"Oh. Sure." Lauren closed the door. God, she was such an idiot. Of course her dad was willing to forgive the Vanderkamps with their enormous house and wallets.

Well, screw him.

She wouldn't call Tiffany.

TWENTY-ONE

"We are on an unprecedented winning streak," Coach said. "Let's nail these guys!"

Calum mouthed the words along with him and grinned at Jason. Jason curved his lips but couldn't bring himself to laugh along. The boys crowded together, piling their fists on top of each other in the center of the huddle. "Let's Go BULLDOGS!" They high-fived each other and ran out onto the court. The home crowd erupted into yells, led by the cheerleaders waving green and gold pom poms and placards.

"Hey, Jase. Focus on the game, huh?" Calum slapped his back as they ran out. "Don't mess it up."

Unlikely. Jason's mom and Tiffany were both attending the game. They hadn't spoken to each other since a very tense Christmas Eve when Tiffany revealed she hadn't decided whether to keep the baby or let her cousin adopt it. His mom did the silent, lip biting, rapid blinking thing. She managed to ask about the cousin and say how sad it was that the couple couldn't have their own children. Then she had added that it would be good if one bad decision didn't ruin Jason and Tiffany's lives (Too late for *that*, Jason had thought). Tiffany had burst into tears, accused his mom of making her own grandchild sound like a mistake and stormed out. Jason had followed Tiffany and comforted her, all the while hoping – no, *praying* – that she would come to her senses and the adoption would happen.

As he ran onto the court, he saw Tiffany sitting in her usual place in front of the cheerleaders. It was strange to see her dressed in regular clothes and not the cheering outfit at the games, but she had dressed in white, green and gold and put glitter on her cheeks and a ribbon in her hair. She gave him a small wave and blew kisses. Jason lined up with the other players for the national anthem and noticed Lauren and her brothers sitting near where his mom usually sat. His mom was sitting ridiculously far back, in the upper corner of the stands. Usually she sat in the center middle row for his games with the other basketball parents. She would have to get over this thing with Tiffany at some point but at least he didn't have to worry about a confrontation at the game.

As the music started, he closed his eyes and ran through offense play strategies. By the time the anthem ended, he was focused on nothing but shaking off his defender and getting the ball through the net.

He only heard the slap of the ball as it was caught and passed, the squeak of shoes on the floor, the shouts of his teammates. When the final whistle blew, Jason was disappointed. He wanted the game to go on forever, even with the sweat dripping off his face, his aching back and sore knees.

"An undefeated season. Well done, guys. But we have a lot of room for improvement," Coach shouted over the crowd cheering and clapping as they huddled, panting, in the center of the court. "Get under the scoreboard. Team photo for the school newspaper."

The boys found another burst of energy, and ran across the court, self-conscious in front of the crowd now the game was over. Jason stood at the back. He saw his mom watching as the photographer yelled instructions for them to pose together. Calum grinned and pointed up at the scoreboard above their heads with a few of the guys. As the photographer shouted "Smile!" and the camera flashed a few times, Jason looked down. The cheerleaders joined for the second photo while Tiffany stayed on the bench, looking small and lonely, her hands rubbing her stomach.

Maybe she should have gotten rid of the baby. She'd have her old life back if she had. But things would never be the same for her now, and her senior year was ruined. Because of him.

"You coming out with us?" Calum asked as he towelled off in the locker room. "Or are you still under house arrest?"

"Still under house arrest."

"I don't get it. I mean, I know your mom is mad but it's already happened, right?"

"She thinks it's a slippery slope, I guess. If I hang out with *you*, who knows what'll happen." Jason shook his head. "It's my own fault, anyway."

Calum shook his head. "It takes two to tango, and Tiffany's parents are letting her come out. It's only Steak'n'Shake, not some drug den we're going to."

"If you want to have that conversation with my mother, go ahead."

"Fair point. I think I'd rather live." Calum grinned. "You're eighteen next week. Then you can do what you want."

"And get kicked out of the house? No, thanks. Have fun tonight, and look after Tiff for me, huh?"

He slung his bag over his shoulder and walked outside. His mom was standing outside the gym, head buried in her scarf. "Why are you waiting out here? It's freezing." His mom always chose suffering over comfort.

"I'm fine. Let's go."

They shuffled across the icy ground to the car. She unlocked the doors and got in the car, blasting the heating.

"The other guys are going out this evening. Just for some food." Jason pulled the ice scraper out of the passenger side. He let the idea hang in the air as he scraped the windshield, glancing at his mom through the glass. She adjusted the heating, turned on the radio and rubbed her hands together.

He got back into the car.

"Thank you," she said. Classical music was playing. He hated classical music.

"You're welcome."

The doors to the gym swung open and they watched his teammates and a few cheerleaders leave, splitting off into groups of three and four to make their way to the restaurant. Tiffany was holding Calum's arm so she didn't slip.

"That was our highest scoring game of the season." Jason didn't mention he'd scored the most points – the announcer had said it twice at the end of the game.

His mom reversed out of the space and drove slowly towards the parking lot exit, the car occasionally sliding on patches of ice. Jason pursed his lips. He'd be punished forever.

When they pulled into the garage his mom finally spoke. "Today at work, we had a meeting with a new client. When I walked into the room, he asked me for a coffee with milk, two sugars."

Jason was baffled.

His mom turned off the radio. "I'm a senior accountant at one of the largest retail companies in the Midwest. And people assume I'm just there to make the coffee. Do you know how many times I've stood in front of people who are looking over my shoulder, waiting for the meeting to start? How many times I've watched people do a double take when I say that *I'm* the one chairing the meeting?"

"I, I didn't realize. I'm sorry."

"I don't want you to be sorry, Jason. Sorry is not helpful. Do you know what it's going to be like when I tell my colleagues that I'm about to be a grandmother? And the father of this illegitimate child is my teenage son, who hasn't finished high school yet?" She blinked rapidly.

"But I, Tiffany's cousin, they –"

"Have you even met them?"

"No, but –"

"You think this white couple is going to want –" she stopped. "You think you can make a mistake and then just hand it over to someone else to deal with?" Her voice was getting louder. She never shouted. Ever. "Because you couldn't keep it in your pants, a baby is being brought into this world that doesn't even have a home. And you think you can just walk away from it?"

"No, of course not. We'll get married then. I'm not going to leave her."

"And then what? You drop out of school and get some job that barely pays the bills?"

"So what do you want me to do, Mom? Keeping the baby is wrong, and giving it to her cousin is wrong. Getting married and getting a job is wrong, and not getting married is wrong. What am I supposed to do?" His voice broke. "I *know* I messed up. If I could go back in time and do things differently, trust me, I would. If I could go back and undo things, I swear to God, I would give anything for that." Tears streamed down his face. "*Anything.*"

His mom looked away from him. Jason wished she would squeeze him, like when he was young. She'd been bigger then, and her hugs were like being squished inside a warm pillow. She'd cover his head in loud kisses, "mwah, mwah, mwah!", her plump arms holding him tight as he giggled and pretended to try and escape.

She was a completely different person now. His dad had been able to leave and start over – but Jason couldn't. And neither could his mom as long as Jason was around, his presence a constant reminder.

She closed her eyes and sucked her teeth, exhaling loudly. She pulled the keys out of the ignition. "Do you need an extra appointment with Dr. Schaffer?"

Jason wiped his face with his sleeve. "Maybe."

She nodded. "Okay. I'll call him." She left Jason sitting in the car.

TWENTY-TWO

Molly collected more soup cans from the pile on the table in the middle of the store room. The other volunteers, four older ladies, were emptying donated grocery bags and her job was to stack the food onto the shelves. They were relieved not to do the heavy lifting, and Molly enjoyed listening to their conversations about relatives. She pretended they were her grandmothers and great-aunts – infinitely preferable to the miserable bitch she had as a grandmother, who hadn't even bothered to stay with them for Christmas.

Molly had mistakenly thought the food pantry would give her more contact with Pastor Davis than volunteering in the nursery, the only other option. But other than the occasional "Good evening, ladies," as he walked past to the kitchen, she never saw him. The work was dull, but it definitely burned more calories than tutoring Tiffany or reading a book. And Molly could now work a two-hour shift without the muscles in her legs and arms protesting the next day. The first morning after volunteering when she'd woken up aching she had excitedly looked in the mirror, expecting the effects of manual labor to be apparent. But she had looked exactly the same – fat and gross.

"Molly, sweetheart. Do you want a cookie?" Margaret stood up from her chair and pulled a tupperware container out of her bag.

"No, thanks." Molly smiled and took off her flannel

shirt. The room felt stuffy but the others were wearing sweaters or cardigans.

"You've been working so hard, take a break," Margaret waved the container at her. "They're peanut butter."

Molly restrained herself from snatching the container away and devouring every single one. "No, thank you, Margaret. I'm going to get some water, though."

Apparently water kept hunger pangs away. She wouldn't let herself undo all the lifting and carrying by consuming at least 250 calories for a stupid cookie.

Molly walked into the kitchen and filled her water bottle up from the faucet. She gulped it down, lifting her hair off her sweaty neck with her other hand.

"Molly, right?"

She jumped, spilling water down her tank top. She turned and saw Pastor Davis smiling in the doorway. He was wearing khaki pants and a navy blue sweater over a white collared shirt. It made his eyes look so blue.

"Hi, yes. Molly. I mean, yes, I'm Molly." She looked down at her soaked chest. When she looked up, Pastor Davis was looking at it as well. Her cheeks burned with embarrassment. Why had she taken off her shirt? Had she shaved her armpits? She couldn't remember.

"Let's get that cleaned up." Pastor Davis opened a drawer and pulled out a dishtowel. She kept her upper arms clamped to her sides as she lifted her hand, expecting him to give her the towel to dry off. Instead he raised his arms over Molly's head and draped the towel around her neck. His hands brushed against the damp fabric of her top.

"How are you enjoying it?"

"Wh – what?"

"Working in the food pantry. How are you enjoying it?"

"Oh. Um, yes." She turned back to the sink to refill her bottle so he couldn't see her red face. "I mean, you know. It's kind of, monotonous. But it's great to help other people," she said hurriedly. "I'm glad I'm doing it."

"Are you good at organizing things?"

"I've put all the food in order of expiration date. That's what Margaret said to do. Was that right? I can change it."

"How would you like to help out with the Valentine's Day fundraiser?"

"Um, sure."

He tilted his head. "Don't you want to find out what you'd be doing first? Maybe it won't be as much fun as the food pantry." He raised an eyebrow.

"Well, yes." She laughed uncertainly. "What is it?"

"Labelling things up, keeping track of who donated what, and then how much the items sell for at the auction. Does that sound interesting?"

"Definitely. Yes."

He stepped towards her. Their chests were almost touching.

"Better than hanging out with the old ladies in the pantry, huh?" he whispered. He turned and left.

Molly shivered. She had goose pimples all over her arms.

Margaret had dropped Molly off at Tiffany's house for a study session, and had marvelled at Molly's fortune in having a friend with such a beautiful home. Molly herself still couldn't believe she was here, sitting on Tiffany Vanderkamp's bed (which was *huge*. And she'd obviously made the most of it).

She put her pen down and studied Tiffany, who was laying on the other end of the bed, drinking a smoothie and reading *Cosmopolitan*. "Um, can I ask you something?"

"If it's another question about plant or animals cells I'm going to kill myself."

"No, don't worry. I've written up flashcards of the stuff you'll probably get asked on the test." She handed the cards to Tiffany. "I was wondering, what do you think of the pastor at church?"

"Who? Lauren's dad you mean?"

"Mm-hmm." Molly tried to sound casual.

"I don't know." Tiffany waved her hand dismissively and took a sip of her smoothie. It looked deliciously creamy and Molly wondered if she should have accepted one when it was offered. Tiffany flipped through more pages of the magazine. "It doesn't really matter, anyway. We don't go anymore."

"Why not?"

"My mom doesn't like getting up early. She said we should both get extra sleep instead." Tiffany patted her stomach.

"Oh. Right." Molly was astounded at Tiffany's naivety. Of course Mrs. Vanderkamp wouldn't want to take her pregnant daughter to church after she'd participated in the purity pledge.

"Lauren thinks he's a dick though."

"I guess most people think that about their dads, huh?"

Tiffany shook her head. "No. I like my dad. Don't you?"

Molly twirled the pen in her fingers. "I don't have a dad."

Tiffany snorted. "Everyone *has* a dad. He just doesn't live with you, right?"

"He left before I was born. So, no. I literally don't have a dad. Although I guess biologically I do."

Tiffany threw the magazine on the floor and leaned forward. "Oh my God, Molly. That's so sad." She patted Molly's foot. "Do you want to know him?"

"I guess. But my mom hates him and says he doesn't deserve us. So …"

"Bullshit. Everyone makes mistakes. Jason wasn't super enthusiastic about the baby at first, but he'll be a great dad. What if your dad changed his mind, and really wants to meet you, and your mom hasn't told you?"

Molly frowned.

"I bet there's like, a stack of letters and unopened gifts somewhere. He's probably been looking for you for years. I saw a show about that once. It was awful. The guy missed so much of his daughter's life."

"Maybe," Molly said doubtfully.

"Well, even if he hasn't, he'll be excited to find out he has a daughter, right? And you're going to be valedictorian." Tiffany gasped. "Oh my God, you can invite him to graduation! But don't tell him you're valedictorian. And then when he's there he'll be all happy to meet you, and then even *more* excited when he sees that you are totally the smartest person at school. It'll be like a movie!" Tiffany sat up and reached for her laptop. "What's his name?"

"I don't know."

"Find out his name and I'm sure we can look him up. You can find *anyone* on the internet." She typed a few words painstakingly slowly and clicked. "Look. It says here all you need is his full name and the state he lives in."

"What if he doesn't want to meet me, though?"

"He's your *dad*, Molly. Of course he wants to meet you." Tiffany tapped busily at the keyboard, more animated than she'd been all afternoon. "He just doesn't know it yet," she added cheerfully.

February
2008

"He that worketh deceit shall not dwell within my house: he that telleth lies shall not tarry in my sight."

PSALM 101:7

TWENTY-THREE

Lauren lay in the darkness in the silent house, the dim glow from the nightlight in the hallway illuminating the crack under her door. *Wicked Pleasures* was like a magnet. It tugged at her attention all the time, especially when she tried to sleep. Scenes came unbidden into her mind when she was watching cartoons with Michael, or cooking with her mom. Every night when she turned off her bedside lamp she'd see a flash of Alessandra's hands being held down or glimpse Kane's naked buttocks as he straddled her. It was simultaneously repulsive and compelling, like the time she was riding her bike and saw a cat that had been run over. She couldn't not look, even as she saw things she never wanted to see. She had even circled back so she could ride past it again.

She let out a sigh for the sake of hearing a noise. She only had three hours before she had to get up. Maybe reading would make her sleepy. She reached to turn on her bedside light. A shadow interrupted the sliver of light under her door. She froze, holding her breath. Was it her mom? Or one of the boys getting thirsty? She should check, see if they were okay. The shadow retreated and Lauren pulled her hand away from the light. She was shaking.

"Morning, Mom." Lauren walked into the kitchen. "How did you sleep last night?"

"Good, honey. Thank you. That pregnancy pillow

is really helping. My back feels so much better now." Her mom set cereal boxes out on the table and looked at Lauren. "Maybe Tiffany would appreciate something like that?" She was looking more like herself now she was in her second trimester but Lauren hated her stomach. It didn't look endearing, like Tiffany's bump. It just looked disgusting.

"Sure." Lauren poured herself a glass of orange juice and Michael burst into the room.

"Can I check the mail? Can I?" Michael ran around the table. He had definitely had a full night's sleep.

"I'm not sure it's arrived yet, sweetie." Lauren's mom smiled and sat at the table.

"It has, it has. I saw it!"

"Okay, put your shoes on."

Michael ran out of the kitchen and bumped into Adam, who rolled his eyes and sat at the table. He launched into a detailed description of the volcano his science class was going to create that day, while Lauren stifled yawns.

Her dad walked into the kitchen and her mom got up to pour him a coffee. Surely her dad was capable of pouring his own coffee, and didn't need her pregnant mother to do it? He didn't look tired, either. Perhaps she'd dreamt last night. Michael ran into the room, saw their dad leaning against the counter, and ran back out to take his shoes off at the door. He re-entered frowning at the mail in his hands.

"This one is for you." Michael handed a clothing catalogue to her mom.

"Thank you, well done, sweetie."

"And this one, is for you!" Michael handed a large, thick white envelope to Lauren and climbed onto his chair.

They all looked at the envelope in Lauren's hand.

"What's that? Looks important." Her mom poured milk over Michael's cereal.

Lauren bit her lip.

"Open it, open it!" Michael was thrilled.

"I'll wait until later." Lauren put it under her bowl casually, covering the state university logo in the corner. She ate a spoonful of cereal which tasted like mush.

"It looks big. I'm sure it's good news," her mom said.

"It's from college, right? This means I get your room soon." Adam grinned.

"Open it," her father ordered.

Lauren moved her bowl and opened the envelope. She pulled out a letter and booklet covered in scarlet red coloring. Her eyes flickered over the page.

We are pleased to inform you...

"Well?" her mom asked.

Her family was staring at her.

Adam squinted. "I thought Tellson colors were blue."

Lauren had never wanted to kill Adam before. "Yes. This is from another college."

"Pardon?"

"Where?"

"Why?"

They all spoke at once. Lauren's cheeks were flaming.

"I just wanted a backup. Just in case."

"You didn't tell us," her dad said. "That's something you should have discussed with us."

"It was just a ..." Lauren paused. "A last minute decision."

"Your father's right, that's a big thing to do. I had

no idea you were so worried you wouldn't get in. And how did you even pay the application fee, honey?"

"Tiffany and I put in early applications together, so her mom paid for both." Technically, Tiffany had retrieved her mom's checkbook from her purse, written out two checks and forged her signature while Lauren had watched, horrified. "It was just... easier."

"Oh, we must pay them back." Her mom got up and reached for her bag. "I'm so embarrassed, when was this? To think all this time we owed the Vanderkamps money." She sat down and began writing a check.

"Sorry," Lauren said. Tiffany had been so casual Lauren had forgotten all about it.

"How much was it? Her first name is Celia, isn't it?"

Lauren nodded. "I think it was $55."

Her dad slammed his mug down on the countertop. "So you thought it was acceptable not only to make a major decision like this but also to spend our money? Without speaking with us first?"

Her brothers focused on their cereal.

"I, no. I just –"

"We'll talk about this later." Her dad marched out.

Adam smiled at her sympathetically.

Her mom got up and picked up a cloth. She wiped up the spilled coffee. "Make sure you give that check to Tiffany today. Yes?"

Lauren nodded, already dreading coming home that evening.

Lauren approached Tiffany during Earth Science when they were supposed to be labelling a topographic map with their partners. She hoped the hum of the room would hide their conversation. Tiffany was handing colorful pieces of laminated paper to her lab partner while he carefully placed them against small peaks and troughs.

"Hi. How are you?"

Tiffany crossed her legs. "Fine." Her bump was smaller than Lauren's mom's but impossible to ignore. It seemed like Tiffany hadn't even considered maternity clothes.

Tiffany's lab partner, Daniel Costa, pretended to be engrossed in checking the textbook.

"My mom wrote a check to pay your mom back. For that college application." Lauren handed an envelope to her, which included a note of apology she'd spent half an hour agonising over.

"Okay." Tiffany stuffed it in her backpack without looking at it.

"Well, anyway. I hope you're okay?"

Tiffany shrugged.

"Um, did you get your mail today?"

"Not yet."

"I got a letter. Confirming I got in."

"Congratulations." Tiffany looked bored.

Lauren looked down. "My dad was really mad," she said softly.

"Wait, he was mad because you got *accepted*? That doesn't make any sense."

Daniel wasn't pretending to work any more and looked at Lauren as well, eyebrows raised.

"Because it's not Tellson," Lauren explained.

"So he's still a dick, then?"

Daniel let out a hoot of laughter and the girls looked at him. He leaned over the map, his neck red. Lauren and Tiffany exchanged glances and Tiffany rolled her eyes. It was almost like before and Lauren blinked back tears.

"Hey," Tiffany touched her arm. "Are *you* okay?"

"I think my dad's going to kill me when he finds out I didn't apply to Tellson."

"But there's still time to submit the application, right? I mean, if you do it, like, today?"

"Yes."

"But you don't *want* to go there?"

"No."

"Then don't." Tiffany shrugged.

Lauren couldn't believe she was feeling envious of a pregnant teenager but everything was so straightforward for her.

"Okay, class. Let's see how you're getting on." The teacher clapped his hands and Lauren scurried back to her desk.

"Sorry," she whispered to her lab partner, Shannon McGuire, who had neatly but incorrectly finished labelling their map.

Lauren was testing Michael on his spelling, distracting herself from her dad's arrival home. She was dreading listening to the Bible verses that would be pulled out (*A false witness shall be punished, and a liar shall be caught ... The Lord detests lying lips, but he delights in people who are trustworthy ...*).

Her cell phone chimed, making her jump. Tiffany had sent her a message:

I didn't get in :(

"Michael, how about you write those words out and then I'll check them in a minute, okay, buddy?" She rubbed his head and went into her room, closed the door and called Tiffany. "Hey."

Tiffany sniffed. "This sucks. Now I have to apply

all over again. And do the stupid SATs again."

"I can help you study if you want? I'm sure you can apply again. Or call them or something? Maybe talk to Ms. Cox?"

Tiffany blew her nose. "Whatever. Maybe it's a sign, anyway."

"What kind of sign?"

"Maybe I shouldn't go to college."

"Do you, do you want me to come over? We can talk about it, and I can help you figure out a plan?" Lauren's heart pounded. She felt like she was asking someone out on a date. "If you want me to, that is. It's fine if you —"

"Sure, whenever. Just let yourself in."

It was like the last two months had never happened. Lauren was elated.

Lauren's mom had reluctantly agreed she could go to Tiffany's if she promised to be back by dinner, before her dad came home. Lauren knocked and let herself in. She stood in the living room doorway where the TV was playing to an empty room, astounded by how laidback Tiffany's parents were. The blinds were pulled down but Lauren could see mugs and crumb-covered plates littering the coffee table. Blankets and magazines were strewn across the two sofas and there was a musty smell. If her dad arrived home to this he'd be apoplectic. Lauren made her way up to Tiffany's room, stepping over a white fluffy sock on the stairs, wondering when Maria was next due to come. She knocked on Tiffany's door and pushed it open.

Tiffany was sitting at her desk, tapping at her laptop. "Good, you're here. Now you can help me."

"Sure. Are you working on a new application?"

Lauren had expected to find her inconsolable.

"What? No. I'm done with that. I'm going to do something better." Tiffany paused dramatically. Lauren waited, pleased that Tiffany hadn't lost her dramatic flair. "I'm going to be on *16 and Pregnant*," Tiffany announced.

"What? Oh my God."

"I know. So I'll get spotted by a talent agent. I probably won't even need to finish high school. So the whole college thing doesn't really matter."

"Wait, so you're going to be on it? When did you apply? When did you find out? Oh, wow, Tiffany!"

"I haven't been told I'm on it yet," Tiffany admitted. "I'm just doing the application form now. So you can help me." She gasped. "You can be on it, too."

"What?"

"As my best friend. You'll totally be on it!"

Lauren was thrilled and horrified. "Um, I don't know. I don't think it's a great idea. For me, I mean," she quickly clarified. "But, for you, I – I … Wow."

"Come and look at what I've written so far. What do you think?" Tiffany stood up and gestured for Lauren to take her place.

"Um. I thought – are you sixteen?" Lauren sat down.

"Not, like, technically."

"What if they check? I mean, you're a senior."

"Wow. Are you seriously not even supporting me with this now?"

"Of course. I just –" Lauren pursed her lips together. "Yes. Absolutely." She turned her attention to the screen. "So, what are you trying to say?"

For the next hour, they composed a few paragraphs explaining why Tiffany wanted to take part. Tiffany eventually agreed to let Lauren type that having sex so young was a 'mistake.' Lauren had to admit the fact Tiffany hadn't made her mind up about what to do when the baby arrived would be compelling watching for viewers and a 'life changing journey.' Lauren took multiple photos of Tiffany and they also attached a couple of her cheerleading.

Tiffany couldn't find any digital photos of Jason. "I really think I should attach one. It'll definitely help, he's so cute."

"It says 'time is of the essence' and to email them as soon as possible on the website though. I think we should just send it in." Lauren suggested.

"Hmm." Tiffany chewed her nail. "Okay. Let's do it. Just send it."

Lauren clicked and the email disappeared from the screen.

Tiffany squealed. "This is so exciting!"

Lauren smiled. "I better go now, but I was wondering… do your parents want to come to the Valentine's Day auction thing at church?"

"Probably not." Tiffany screwed up her face and Lauren realized how very lame it sounded.

She felt despair snaking inside her at the thought of going home. "My dad was hoping they'd be there. He's really pissed off with me. I think this might help?"

"My dad works all the time lately, every evening and weekend. It sucks." Tiffany considered. "But Jason's still not allowed to see me during the week. So maybe me and my dad could go to the auction together and then out to dinner or something. That might be fun."

"That would be amazing. Thank you." Lauren hugged her, Tiffany's firm rounded belly still a surprise as it pressed against hers.

TWENTY-FOUR

By Saturday afternoon, Molly had been through every single drawer and cupboard at home and still hadn't found her birth certificate. It was really pissing her off. She ran her fingers across the clothes in her mom's closet, wondering if she'd fit into any. The door from the garage slammed shut.

"Hi, Moll, I'm home!"

Molly marched into the hallway where her mom was unwinding her scarf and stamping snow from her shoes.

"Where's my birth certificate?"

Her mom froze for a moment. "I'm not sure. I'll have a look later. What do you need it for?"

"A scholarship application."

"Right. Can I see it?"

"I'm perfectly capable of filling in a form, Mom. I just need my birth certificate."

Molly's mom hung up her coat. "I'll have a look later. Can you just give me some time to relax? I had a long day. Someone on my team got injured moving stock." She shook her head. "I had to fill in all the paperwork and arrange cover. We're waiting to hear how long he's going to be off, poor guy."

It was so annoying when her mom tried to make her job sound important. How hard could it be telling people to put stuff on shelves? "Whatever."

"Molly."

Molly raised her eyebrows.

"Just give me a break, please?"

Molly exhaled loudly. "*Whatever.*" She slammed her bedroom door.

An hour later, Molly emerged from her room to find her mom putting her coat back on. She had changed into a v-necked, fitted green sweater, her hair twisted up into a french knot. Silver hoops dangled from her ears.

Molly peered at her. "Are you wearing *make-up*?"

"I'm going out with the girls. There's some leftovers in the freezer you can have for dinner."

Molly stared at her. A car hooted outside.

"That's Megan. See you later." She walked out the front door, closing it with more force than completely necessary.

What a bitch. Molly had spent the whole afternoon alone and now her mom was making her spend her whole evening by herself too. And where was her birth certificate?

Molly had spent hours going through every single room in the house as soon as she got back from work. She should have been studying, catching up on the time she spent volunteering at church and helping Tiffany. Although it had definitely been almost like exercise, squatting down to open drawers and pulling boxes out from under her mom's bed. She could *feel* herself getting slimmer. She went into her mom's bedroom and looked in the full-length mirror. She looked fat. As usual. Damn it. She needed to burn more calories.

Molly put on her sneakers and went into the garage to find the old jump rope she used to play with. As she scanned the shelves lining the garage, rubbing her arms to keep warm, she realized she hadn't thought to look in here for her birth certificate. Several cardboard boxes were stored on the shelves, some of them labelled but most of them not. She lifted the stepladder off its hook on the wall and climbed up to the first box. She lifted the lid and saw a jumble of screws, nails, a screwdriver and a drill. She closed it and moved on, going methodically along the shelves. When she came across a box with any kind of paperwork, she went through it.

The evening wore on and the garage became icy-cold. Molly could see her breath. She really wanted a hot chocolate. With marshmallows. And chocolate sauce squeezed on top. She pressed her lips together and opened another lid, seeing a tangle of nails, picture wire, and hammers. She was about to put the lid back when she glimpsed a small, rectangular box. She took the box down and sat on a step of the ladder. She fished out the carton. It was a packet of cigarettes. What on earth? Molly opened it, and saw it was half empty. So all those lighters her mom had weren't just for candles then. She scowled. Her mom acted like she was such a damn saint. She shook her head and replaced the lid. She climbed the ladder to put it back and saw a box file at the back of the shelf, invisible from the ground. She pulled it towards her and opened it. On the top was something about the mortgage for the house. She leafed through each document, reading the titles on the top. The mortgage and deed to the house. A will. Some bank stuff. And finally! *Certificate of Birth*.

The thick paper was smaller than she expected. She studied it.

It didn't make any sense. There was her name, her

place of birth, and the date. But next to *Child of,* it just said Deidre Calderwood. And next to *Birthplace of Father* there was a blank space.

What was going on? Was it some kind of mistake? She went through the rest of the box, wondering if there was a second, original version. Perhaps her mom hated her dad so much she got another copy, removing his name from it? But there wasn't. Molly's hands were tinted blue with cold and she struggled to put the ladder back. She checked that the shelves looked the way they had before and went into her bedroom with the paper. She couldn't stop studying the blank space where her father's name should be.

It took only five minutes to figure out the reason her mom hadn't listed her dad's name on the certificate – her mom had slept with so many men she didn't even know who Molly's father was.

The next morning Molly studied her mom from the kitchen doorway. She was sitting at the table, reading the paper and eating toast, still in her robe. Molly tried to imagine her at nineteen, drinking and smoking in crowded bars. She must have had a fake ID. And worn slutty dresses. And gone home with random men. Molly understood the theory, but couldn't seem to apply it to the person in front of her. It was like a bizarre quantum physics thought experiment.

"Mom? Are we leaving soon?"

"I thought we might skip today." Her mom yawned.

"Why?"

"I felt like sleeping in."

"But, we can't skip. The fundraiser is Thursday night. I have to be there."

Her mom closed her eyes for a moment. "Can you ask Margaret for a ride?" There was a packet of Tylenol next to her plate.

"Are you hungover?"

Her mom pressed her fingers to the bridge of her nose. "Molly, I'm just not feeling great today, okay? Call Margaret. I'm going back to bed." She stood up holding her mug and shuffled past Molly down the hall.

For God's sake.

"Mom?" Molly watched her carefully. "Don't worry about the birth certificate. I didn't need it after all."

Her mom stopped. "Okay." She didn't turn around.

On Thursday evening, Molly placed the final item for the auction on the long trestle table set up at the back of the fellowship hall. She had put some bidding slips and envelopes next to it. Thank God her mom had dropped Molly off early on her way to work. Molly could barely stand to look at her, and she certainly didn't need her hypocrisy at a church event. This whole 'your father left us' bullshit. Now her grandma's comments at Thanksgiving made sense.

She blinked away tears and walked backwards a few steps to check all the items and their labels were clearly visible.

"Oh!" She bumped into a solid mass behind her.

"Careful now." Pastor Mike smiled at her, his blue eyes crinkling around the edges.

"Sorry, I didn't hear you come in." It was hard to believe someone old enough to be her father could be this attractive.

"This looks great." He placed an arm around her

shoulder. "And set up over an hour early."

Molly took a deep breath, smelling his cologne and savoring the weight of his arm across her neck. "Thanks."

They looked at the fruit baskets, bath sets and restaurant vouchers spread before them. Molly had spread everything out, alternating the lowest value items equidistant from the highest value items so people wouldn't crowd around any one area. She had neatly handwritten descriptions and drawn a little heart in the corner of each label with a red marker. She had put several pots of pens on the table so no one would have to struggle to find something to write with.

The table looked amazing. Molly felt her neck and shoulder grow warm and itchy against the fabric of Pastor Mike's sweater. If they turned their faces towards each other right now, their lips would be approximately seven inches apart. She was pleased the fundraiser was actually on the 14th, so they could spend some of Valentine's Day together.

He squeezed the top of her arm. "It's a shame there's not a tablecloth on here. It looks a little … messy."

"Oh. I can get one."

"No, it's okay."

"No, no. It's fine. You're right." Molly nodded. "A tablecloth would look so much better. I want it to look perfect."

God, she was so stupid. Why hadn't she thought of that? She blinked rapidly.

"And you're going to keep track of all the bids that come in?"

"Yes, sure."

"Good girl. I knew I could count on you."

The sound of people talking and laughing drifted in. He dropped his hand from her shoulder and moved towards the door. Volunteers wheeled in a large trolley stacked with folded tables and chairs and began setting up the room.

Molly rushed into the kitchen to get two white tablecloths and went back into the hall. She did sections of the table at a time, removing the items, laying out the tablecloth and then replacing it all on top. She tried to be efficient but not move so fast she became sweaty. As more people filed in and helped with setup, the room became a buzz of activity and several volunteers complimented her table layout. Molly was almost enjoying herself and glanced at Pastor Mike regularly, catching his eye a few times. She was pleased she had worn her mom's sweater even though it was tight. It looked pretty good if she remembered to hold her stomach in.

When the event officially began and people started putting their silent bids into the shoebox, Molly knew she was doing something genuinely useful for Pastor Mike. She had colored coded and numbered all the slips so that she could quickly establish the winning bid for each item while he was giving the speech during dinner. She tidied the table as people picked up the different offerings and replenished pens from a packet hidden under the tablecloth as it seemed like every other person walked away with one. Some items were more popular than others but Molly couldn't wait to calculate how much money they'd made at the end of the evening.

"Hi, Moll." Tiffany wandered up to the table and sniffed a bottle of hand lotion. "Ugh. No wonder people are giving this stuff away."

"Hi, I didn't expect to see you here. We still on for lunchtime tomorrow?"

Tiffany shrugged. "I don't know. I don't really think I need to study any more."

"Really?"

"That sweater really brings out your eyes." Tiffany picked up an unbranded makeup set wrapped in cellophane and wrinkled her nose. "God. I guess this is where Christmas gifts come to die."

Molly was offended. "There's some good stuff here."

Tiffany looked up and down the length of the table. "I can't see any. You should wear green more often."

Mr. Vanderkamp came up holding a paper cup of coffee. "See anything you like?" he asked Tiffany.

"Definitely not. It's the graveyard of Christmas gifts."

Mr. Vanderkamp let out a bellow of laughter and Tiffany grinned. Molly was insanely embarrassed that Mr. Vanderkamp was standing next to his pregnant daughter. What did they say when they were at home together? Maybe they just didn't mention it. Perhaps he pretended his daughter was still a virgin, imagining she had stuck to the purity pledge.

Pastor Mike joined them. "Great to see you both here. How are you doing?" He reached his hand out to Mr. Vanderkamp, barely glancing at Tiffany. Molly was pleased. Tiffany looked really pretty this evening in a clingy purple dress, but it was weird how much her stomach stuck out.

Mr. Vanderkamp held up his coffee and Blackberry. "Sorry, hands kind of full here."

"No problem. So, you like the look of anything here?"

"We're not sure. Still looking, you know?"

"Well, better get a few bids in fast then. And make them high, there's competition."

"I don't know about that." Mr. Vanderkamp looked pointedly at all the slips still on the table.

Pastor Mike worked the muscles in his jaw. Molly wanted to cup his face in her hands, feel his stubble scratching her palms.

"Well, you know how important this fundraiser is for the work we do. So we'd appreciate anything and everything."

Molly scanned the table, trying to find something that would interest them. "How about these?" She held up the restaurant vouchers. "Or – or this?" She picked up a scented candle and holder set.

"Oh no, nothing that smells. This one's become sensitive to everything." Mr. Vanderkamp nudged Tiffany with his elbow, spilling some of his coffee. Tiffany nodded and widened her eyes in a *What can you do?* look.

Good grief. Pastor Mike was looking at them the same way Molly felt.

Mr. Vanderkamp's phone rang and he answered, turning away.

Tiffany sighed. "God, I hate that stupid phone. I'm going to say hi to Lauren." She headed towards Lauren, who was holding a baby while the mother wiped the face of a crying toddler.

"I better go and check on the food," Pastor Mike said.

Molly nodded and straightened up. "I've got everything under control here."

Mr. Vanderkamp didn't come back to put any bids in. He and Tiffany didn't even stay to eat. And they should really be trying to get on the right side of God, all things considered.

Pastor Mike announced who had made the winning bid for each item from the slips Molly had made. The room clapped and laughed while the winners walked up to claim their prizes. Molly did a final check of her list of all the winning bids, and wrote down the total amount raised on a spare piece of paper. She considered adding 'xo' but someone else might see it and so she drew a smiley face instead.

"And now, let's find out just how much we've made from your generosity this evening!" Pastor Mike walked over to Molly and she handed him the paper. He examined it and looked up at Molly. "Is this definitely right? Did you check it?" he hissed.

"Three times," Molly nodded. He was speechless. If they were alone, he would probably hug her.

He turned back to the crowd. "We'll have confirmation of the total amount raised at Sunday Service. But thank you all so much." Molly looked at him. The total she had given him was absolutely correct. "I know it's a difficult time for everyone so I do appreciate everything you gave. And thanks, of course, to the volunteers who made this wonderful food we're lucky enough to be enjoying and everyone who helped set up."

People clapped and smiled. He forgot to thank her, but that was fine. Molly didn't want everyone staring at her anyway.

Molly packed up and returned the tablecloths to the kitchen, hoping to see Pastor Mike on her way. There was no sign of him helping anyone and his family seemed to have gone home already. She decided to slip the list under his office door. When she arrived at his office his door was slightly ajar. He was sitting at his desk, looking at the computer. She knocked.

"Ah. Come in. Did you find the error?"

"No. The total was right. I know it seems like a lot, but it really is."

"Show me the list. It can't be right."

He scooted his chair over so Molly went to stand next to him. She placed the handwritten list of items and their winning bids on the desk. He leaned towards it, some of the hairs on his head brushing against her sleeve. She was acutely aware of his face next to the rise and fall of her chest. Could he hear her heart beating? She stared at the numbers.

"You didn't use a calculator."

"I didn't need to."

"'When pride comes, then comes disgrace.'" He opened a drawer and took out a calculator. "'But with humility comes wisdom.'" He placed a hand on her lower back and looked up at her.

Molly held her breath.

"Maybe you should familiarize yourself with Proverbs 11:2."

He removed his hand and tapped the lines of numbers into the calculator. Molly exhaled and waited.

Pastor Mike sat back and pressed the total key. They looked at the figure. It matched the one written on Molly's list.

He slammed his fist down on the desk. Molly jumped.

"I – what's wrong?"

"This isn't even half of what we were supposed to make."

"What? But, it's over five hundred dollars."

"You think you're so clever, don't you?"

"No, I just —"

"This doesn't even cover a month of bills."

Molly blinked.

He shook his head. "I told you to tidy up that table. It was a mess. No wonder the bids were so low."

"I —" Molly's lower lip quivered like a child's.

He stood up.

Molly stepped back. "I did, I thought I — I'm sorry …"

"Hey, hey. It's okay. Come here." He opened his arms.

Molly leaned against him, tears running down her face. She sniffed and he rubbed her back. He didn't even mind that she was getting tears and mucus on his sweater.

"Molly, are you here?"

Goddammit.

They broke apart and Margaret came into the room. "We're all finished up, you ready to go? Oh, sweetie. You okay? You look upset."

"I'm fine," Molly wiped her face. "I just, I —"

"She's just upset we didn't make more." Pastor Davis patted Molly on the back and smiled at Margaret. "But like I told her, everyone did a great job. It's just sometimes these things don't go to plan."

TWENTY-FIVE

Jason let himself in the front door, wincing as he took off his coat. His hip was still sore from last Friday's game. The player guarding him had crashed into him attempting to steal the ball, and sent him flying onto the floor. The foul resulted in three extra points and winning the game so it had been worth it, but today's practice had been intense.

"Hey, Mom? Do we have any painkillers?" Jason went into the living room. The TV was on but his mom wasn't there.

A news anchor was speaking: "Little information is available at the moment, but what we do know is that this shooting is reminiscent of last year's Virginia Tech massacre."

A banner on the bottom of the screen scrolled *Breaking news: Shooting on university campus, fatalities confirmed* as the anchor continued. The shot went to a video of a student crying as she spoke to a reporter. Jason's heart pounded. He rushed to turn off the TV.

"Hi. Did you call?" His mom came into the room, carrying a laundry basket.

Jason swallowed. "No. I mean, I was just saying I'm back. I'm going to do some studying before dinner."

"Sure." She reached the remote to turn the TV back on. Jason forced himself to walk from the room at a normal pace.

It was nearly midnight when Jason leaned back against

his headboard and checked his phone for the twelfth time. Tiffany said she didn't mind not seeing him on Valentine's Day but maybe she'd changed her mind. She hadn't responded to any of his messages. He should have at least sent her flowers but he couldn't even do that without asking his mom for her credit card.

This was the worst Valentine's Day he could remember. Even the silent auction at church would have been preferable to the silent meal he'd shared with his mom earlier. Valentine's Day used to be one of his favorite days, and his mom was the one who had made it so much fun. The family would have a Valentine's Hunt, similar to Easter, but instead of eggs they'd find chocolates and Love Heart candies taped to little notes. On each note his mom had written something she loved about them – each one different. Now Jason couldn't remember what any of the notes said and regretted not saving them all. He had just expected the notes to be there, year after year.

Jason had considered doing something similar for Tiffany, but the logistics were too difficult. He realized how long it must have taken his mom to write each one and hide them all. He wasn't allowed to go out on weekdays, anyway. He had a brief image of still being grounded at 22, telling his four-year old child he couldn't see him today because Grandma wouldn't let him.

Jason knew he wouldn't fall asleep for hours although he was shattered. He picked up his notebook and studied the plays for the game tomorrow night. They were still on a winning streak, the longest in ten years. They had a real shot at making state finals this year. He hated how Coach Wilkins kept reminding them.

On Friday night the boys slapped Jason's back as he limped towards the locker room.

"One step closer to State!" Calum pulled him into a hug, twisting Jason's side.

Jason bit his lip to stop himself crying out and shoved Calum away. "Get off, man."

Calum grinned and slapped the top of the doorway as he went into the locker room.

"Myers!"

Jason turned and saw Coach in the hallway, looking annoyed despite their win.

"You need to ice that hip, straight away."

"It's not so bad."

"You're my highest scoring player, and I – the team – need you for Sectionals. I think you should sit out next week's game."

"What?"

Coach folded his arms. "I don't want a martyr. I want you taking care of yourself and telling me when it gets painful. You need to rest up."

"But –"

"No buts. I'll bring you some ice. Take a cold shower."

Jason watched him walk away and shook his head. Now it would be his fault if the team didn't get through to Sectionals next week.

The next day Tiffany snuggled against Jason as they laid on her bed, a movie they weren't watching playing on her laptop. He had told his mom he was getting in extra basketball practice with Calum, who had taken pity on Jason and Tiffany not having any time alone with each other. Calum had picked up Jason, had a chat with his mom about what drills they were going to do, and then dropped him off at Tiffany's house. He had even promised to give him a ride home later. That was a real friend. Jason promised to repay the favor someday but doubted Calum would ever need it.

Jason buried his face in Tiffany's hair which was pulled up into a messy bun and breathed in her scent. He kind of missed the smell of cigarettes she used to have mixed in with her perfume and shampoo. "I hate not being able to see you more often." He rubbed her arms, enjoying the sensation of the pink velour top she was wearing.

"I know. Honestly, I don't know why your mom thinks grounding you is going to make a difference. But you're here now. Let's make the most of it." She kissed his cheek. "Especially when you think about stuff like that college shooting. It's so sad. What if something like that happened at our school? I can't imagine."

"Let's not talk about that."

"You're right. We should get a photo. Today is our belated Valentine's Day." She picked up her phone and turned it around, taking a few photos of them.

"Just for your wall, right?" Jason asked between clicks.

"I'm sure one of these will be good." Tiffany leaned her head against his shoulder and checked the images. "Look, I love this one, it's so cute. I'm totally putting it on my Facebook page."

"Tiff, please don't."

"You've got to get with it. You're, like, the only person I know that doesn't have Facebook."

"I just, I think it's weird."

"*You're* weird. You're my boyfriend and I want to

show you off. Is that so bad?"

"No, but –"

"Are you embarrassed?" Tiffany leaned on her elbow and propped her head up with her hand.

"Of course not. I just don't like having my photo taken. You know that." Jason rubbed his eyes. He was so tired.

"Well, at the moment I'm looking like I got knocked up by some random guy."

Jason sat up and rested his arms on his knees. "Who thinks that?"

"Well, right now? No one. But when I get on that show, everyone's going to think that I'm some kind of stupid ho if you're not around."

"What show?"

"Didn't I tell you? I applied to be on *16 and Pregnant*. So you're going to have to get used to being on camera, babe." She squeezed his leg. "It's my big break!"

"Hold on, what?"

"I haven't heard back yet, but I'm sure they'll choose me."

"Isn't it called *16 and Pregnant?*" Jason emphasized the number. "I mean, you're supposed to be sixteen, right?"

"I don't think they really care. I mean, I think who looks good on camera and what makes a good story is way more important, right? And we make a great story."

"We do?"

"Yes. God, Jason. I don't know what's wrong with you sometimes."

Shit.

"I just," Jason pressed his palms against his eyes, "I don't think it's a good idea." She wouldn't get on the show. Would she? His heart was racing.

"Why? Are you embarrassed?" Tiffany pulled back from him. "Do I embarrass you in some way?"

"No!" Jason took a breath and exhaled. Tiffany's quilt cover was patterned with tiny colored polka dots. It was huge, so there must be at least a couple hundred. He started with the red ones.

"Well?" Tiffany demanded. "Why, then? Why can't you be supportive?"

The doorbell sounded.

"I'll get that." Jason jumped up with relief. Mrs. Vanderkamp wouldn't make it to the door any time soon. He'd never met anyone who spent so much time gazing out windows and taking naps.

"Whoever it is can let themselves in."

"Calum must be early. I'll go down." Jason jogged down the stairs. His hip seemed to be better today but his knee had a little twinge. He opened the door and thought he was hallucinating.

His mom was standing on the doorstep. "So now you're lying, too. Get in the car."

"What are you doing here?"

"Get in the car."

"Mom –"

"We're not discussing this."

"You can't tell him what to do. He's eighteen." Tiffany was halfway down the stairs. From below, her belly looked even bigger.

"You," his mom pointed her finger at Tiffany and shook her head. "*You* don't get to talk to me."

"Excuse me? You're at *my* house. And I'll talk to whoever I want."

Jason's head went back and forth like an umpire at a tennis match.

"This is not *your* house, little girl. And I am here for my son," his mom said through clenched teeth. She looked at Jason. "Get in the car."

Tiffany came down the stairs and stood in front of Jason. She looked up at his mom and crossed her arms. "Actually, Jason is staying here. Permanently."

Jason's head snapped to her. What the hell was she talking about?

"Oh, right." His mom scoffed. "Why, so you can play house?"

"No, so he's treated like an adult. Which he is. He's eighteen and you treat him like a little kid."

Jesus Christ.

His mom stepped forward. "I am just trying to stop my son from destroying his future. I am doing what is best for my child. You've already done enough to try to ruin his life."

"What's best for him? You are such a selfish bitch. You're doing what's best for *you*. He can't go anywhere or do anything. He's miserable."

"You know, at some point, you're going to understand what being a mother is. I sincerely hope, for your child's sake, that day comes soon."

Tiffany narrowed her eyes and tilted her head. "Well, I already know I'll be a better mother than *you*, that's for damn sure."

The slap was so loud the noise reverberated in Jason's ears.

"*Mom!*"

Tiffany held her hand to her cheek which was already turning red. His mom gazed at her, open-mouthed, looking as shocked as Jason felt. After a few moments she turned and got into her car, starting the engine. Tiffany shut the door, still holding her cheek.

"I'm so sorry. Are you okay?" Jason tilted Tiffany's chin up. "Let me get you some ice."

"Has she hit you before?"

"What? No, never." The idea was ludicrous.

"You know, I could call the police, press charges."

"Please, please don't." Jason thought he was going to pass out, even though Tiffany was the one who should be fainting. "Come on, let's put something on that."

They went into the kitchen and Jason found a bag of frozen peas. Tiffany held it to her face while Jason rested his hand on her knee. For once, she seemed to have very little to say.

"Who was that at the door?" Mrs. Vanderkamp walked into the kitchen.

"Jason's moving in with us, is that okay?"

Jason stared at Tiffany. "Wha–"

"Oh. Well, sure. If you want to, hon." Mrs. Vanderkamp patted his back. "That'll be nice." She poured herself a glass of orange juice and left, apparently not noticing Tiffany holding the peas.

"You're serious?" Jason asked Tiffany.

"Why not? You can't live with your mom. She's insane. Just stay here."

What if Tiffany got onto the show? There was no way of avoiding it if he was living in her house. "I can't. Tiffany, I can't just –"

"Why not? I meant it. And my mom doesn't mind."

"But, I mean, what about your dad? I really don't think this is a good idea."

Tiffany put down the peas. Her cheek was a blotchy red. "Dad moved out." Tears ran down her face. "He and mom are getting divorced. Please, Jase. I need you. Don't leave."

March
2008

"Behold, I was shapen in iniquity; and in sin did my mother conceive me."

PSALM 51:5

TWENTY-SIX

Lauren carried two mugs of chamomile tea upstairs. It was supposed to be good for pregnancy and sleeping so hopefully would benefit her and Tiffany, even if it smelled gross.

Tiffany was walking around her bedroom, her cell phone held to her ear. "But you received my application, right? You saw the photo?" Tiffany waved at her to sit down and held a finger up.

Lauren sat on the bed while Tiffany listened to whoever was talking at the end of the phone. Tiffany's room was a tidal wave of chaos although the rest of the house was tidier since Jason had moved in. She wanted to know what the guest room, now Jason's room, looked like but the door was shut whenever she walked past. She still couldn't believe he had moved in with Tiffany.

"But I was sixteen when I *got* pregnant." Tiffany said to her phone. "Do you want to see more photos? I can send them. And Jason's hot. Like, really hot. I can send a photo of him?"

There was a pause and then Tiffany threw her phone on the floor. It bounced off the stained carpet. "Stupid bitch!" She sat down at her desk and wiped tears away.

"Who was that?"

"Like, what does the exact age matter, anyway?"

Tiffany rubbed her belly and stuck out her lower lip. She looked like Michael had when he was an angry toddler. Lauren looked around for a box of tissues but couldn't see one.

"What happened?"

Tiffany used her sleeve to wipe her face. "*16 and Pregnant* don't want me."

"I'm so sorry." Thank God there wouldn't be a camera crew around.

"This sucks."

"Do you want to watch a movie or something?"

"I want a drink, and you're having one, too." She stomped down the stairs, Lauren following. In the kitchen Tiffany poured two Diet Cokes into glasses, added a slosh of vodka and handed one to Lauren. "Don't tell Jason."

"I'm not sure that's good for –"

Tiffany shot her a look.

"Where's your mom?" Lauren whispered.

"Out, finally. Seeing some divorce lawyer. And Jason's always at stupid practice." Tiffany looked as though she was about to burst into tears again and took a long swallow of her drink. She made a face and took another sip. "This is gross. You can have mine as well." She handed her glass to Lauren and retrieved a tub of ice cream from the freezer.

They went into the living room and put *Knocked Up* in the DVD player, settling themselves on either end of one of the sofas. They draped a blanket over their legs. Lauren politely sipped her drink. In the movie version of her life, she'd move in with Tiffany as well. The movie was funny and as the vodka took effect, Lauren felt relaxed for the first time in months.

She woke up to a cushion being shoved onto her face. Tiffany was standing over her and the credits were rolling.

"Sorry hanging out with me is so boring."

"Sorry, I'm just tired."

"You and Jason are always tired. It's not great for my self-esteem."

"I just, I'm not sleeping well lately." Lauren rubbed her face. It wasn't exactly that she wasn't sleeping. It was the weird, exhausting dreams she had every time she fell asleep. Sexual dreams. It was like Lauren had made up an erotic book in her head and was one of the characters in it. And she kept seeing the same scene, and having the same dream, over and over – a man getting into bed with her and ... *doing* things. She knew Tiffany would be thrilled if she told her, but Lauren didn't enjoy it. She'd wake up, heart pounding, and feel sick and ashamed of her own imagination.

"You should take something," Tiffany suggested. "My mom has stuff that helps her sleep. You could try that?"

"What kind of stuff?"

"Some kind of prescription."

"I don't know." Lauren yawned and stretched. "I don't think people are supposed to take other people's medicines?"

"God, Lauren. It's not anything weird. It's from a doctor. Come on, I'll show you." Tiffany pulled Lauren's hand to help her off the sofa and they headed upstairs.

Lauren had never been in Mrs. Vanderkamp's room before. She was amazed to find it even messier than Tiffany's room. The carpet was cream, the bed linen and curtains were white, and towels, clothes, make up, lotions, robes and magazines were littered around the room. Lauren loved it. This was exactly how she'd have her room when she was an adult.

"Does Maria not come over any more?" Lauren asked cautiously.

"We let her go. Anyway, Jason keeps cleaning up. He's weird like that." Tiffany went into the master bath, where Mrs. Vanderkamp's toiletries were scattered across the right side of the bathroom counter. "I think they're in here."

They went through each drawer but they didn't find anything other than cotton balls, tampons and facecloths. The left side of the counter was empty, and so were all the drawers. Did Mrs. Vanderkamp expect her husband to move back in? Lauren had been shocked when Tiffany told her he'd left. Marriage was supposed to be for life.

Tiffany blinked at the empty spaces, took a deep breath and went back into the bedroom. She sat on the side of the enormous bed and pulled open the drawers in the bedside table.

Lauren felt like a burglar. "Let's just leave it, it's not that big of a deal."

"They're here. She moved them." Tiffany pulled out a handful of prescription bottles.

"That's a lot of medication. Is your mom okay?"

"She's just a drama queen. And I think she has a crush on her doctor." Tiffany read the labels on a few of them. "I think it might be this one."

Lauren stared into Mrs. Vanderkamp's drawer, fascinated by its contents. Her mom's bedside table had nothing but a Bible, Kleenex and Vaseline for her chapped lips. "What's that?"

"You've never seen one of these before?" Tiffany reached into the drawer. "Here, want to hold it?"

"It's heavy." The gun rested in her hand, cold, smooth and solid. "I didn't know guns came in pink."

"She didn't want anything 'manly' but I don't even know if she knows how to use it, so it's kind of pointless. Anyway, I think it's these ones." Tiffany handed a bottle to Lauren and took the handgun back. "Just take the whole thing. She won't even notice." She put the gun back in the drawer and threw the other bottles on top. Lauren rattled the tiny pills. She didn't plan on taking any but it was nice to know they were there.

"Why does your mom have a gun?" Lauren asked as they walked to Tiffany's room.

"Some people tried to break in here when I was little, so my dad got it for her when he was working away all the time. She could never remember the alarm codes. Now listen, with those pills." Tiffany turned to her. "Just take one, before you want to sleep, okay? Don't take them during the day."

"Okay. But, wait. I need to drive home and I've been drinking." Lauren was horrified.

"Yeah, and then you had a two-hour nap. You're fine, trust me." Tiffany shook her head. "God, you're adorable."

"What if I get pulled over?"

"Lauren, chill. Jesus, no wonder you don't sleep."

Lauren bit her lip. "Okay, I guess. I better go, but thanks for these." Lauren put the bottle in her book bag and pulled out *Wicked Pleasures*. "Here's the book back, by the way."

"Did you enjoy it? Do you want another one?"

"I don't know. It was weird." Lauren went red. "And you know what, it's a blessing you didn't get onto *16 and Pregnant* anyway. All the girls end up looking stupid on it and the guys look like assholes. You're so much better than that. And so is Jason."

Tiffany hugged her. "Now leave before I start crying again."

"See you tomorrow."

Lauren drove home extra carefully, arriving three minutes before her dad got home.

"Honey, be careful. You're cutting it awfully close," her mom said as they heard her dad's car pull into the drive.

"I know. Sorry. Tiffany was upset about something." Lauren dropped a fork and two knives as she set the table. Was she still slightly drunk?

"Has she made a decision? About the baby?"

Lauren shook her head. Her mom didn't even know Jason was living at the Vanderkamp home. She was almost relieved when her dad walked into the kitchen, ending the chance of any further conversation about them. Her dad had been so judgemental about Mr. Vanderkamp leaving the family home, so her mom wisely avoided discussing them in front of him any more.

As she waited to fall asleep that night, Lauren regretted giving *Wicked Pleasures* back to Tiffany. Or at least she should have accepted Tiffany's offer of another book. Reading someone else's thoughts on sex would be better than being stuck with her own overactive imagination. What was wrong with her that she couldn't stop thinking about it? She plumped up her pillow and thought about the pills in her book bag. They looked like aspirin. And they were a prescription. She turned on the bedside lamp and pulled her bag towards her, finding the bottle. Before she could change her mind, she unscrewed the cap, placed a tablet on her tongue and swallowed it with water.

She woke up to her mom shaking her.

"Lauren, wake up. You slept through your alarm."

Lauren blinked and stretched. "Okay, thanks."

"Are you sick?"

"No." She yawned. "I feel really good."

It had been the best night's sleep Lauren had experienced in months. She really needed to listen to Tiffany more often.

TWENTY-SEVEN

Jason lay back on the bed and winced as he pressed an ice pack against his side. He wanted to sprawl across one of the enormous sofas in the living room and watch TV but still felt like a temporary guest. Mrs. V ("call me Celia, hon. Or Mom!" Tiffany had rolled her eyes) told him to make himself at home and stay as long as he wanted but Jason was pretty sure this didn't extend to her seeing his pants pulled down so he could ice his hip. Jason kept the guest room neat and clean, and tried to tidy the rest of the house when Tiffany and Mrs. V weren't around. They seemed to accept without question that used plates made their way to the dishwasher and dirty clothes ended up in the laundry room, and he felt calmer with things in their proper place.

Thank goodness *16 and Pregnant* wasn't happening. Jason was already living in an episode of *The Jerry Springer Show*, and hoped to God Tiffany wouldn't realize and apply to be on that next. He still couldn't believe his mom had hit Tiffany. Occasionally, there were a few blissful moments where he would forget, and then – he'd see his mom's hand making contact with Tiffany's cheek, he'd hear the loud *thwack!* of it, feel Tiffany's face burning hot – all over again. He'd remember he hadn't spoken to his mom for almost a month.

How had so much time passed? Jason had returned home a couple days after the incident to pick up some things when he knew his mom was at work. At the time, he hadn't stopped to think what that evening would be like for her – arriving home and seeing half his clothes gone, his desk empty of textbooks and highlighters, his toothbrush gone from the bathroom. On top of that, she must have worried about Tiffany calling the police and pressing charges against her. The thought of his mom, anxious and alone, was unbearable.

Jason had thrown himself into studying, extra practice sessions with the team, and exercises to heal his sore knee and hip. He tried to help Tiffany feel as comfortable as possible, rubbing her feet and back, and borrowing her mom's car to go to the store to buy ice cream and hot chocolate. Sometimes Jason would drive past his house, checking the lights were on in the living room. At least then he'd know his mom had made it home safely that day. A couple of times he'd finished Tiffany's assignments for her while she dozed on the bed. At least he could look after someone and not mess it up too much. But he was on borrowed time – in June he would graduate, the baby would arrive, and then what? He needed to look into scholarships and ask his dad how much he might be able to contribute because he couldn't assume his mom would pay for college any more. And he still wasn't sure what Tiffany wanted to do about the baby. If she kept it, should he even go to college? Whenever he let himself think too much about anything, his ears would start ringing and he'd feel dizzy. He couldn't even remember what sleep felt like.

He put the ice pack down and opened the top drawer of the dresser. Four black t-shirts. Two blue. Three white. Jason took deep breaths, slowing down his heart rate.

His cell phone lit up, his dad's seventh attempt at calling him today. He rubbed his eyes and pressed accept.

"Hi, Dad."

"Hey, buddy, finally. I was starting to get a little worried there."

"Sorry, just been really busy, you know."

"Well, sure, sure. I'm calling to wish you luck tonight. I know you guys are going to nail it. I can't believe you didn't tell me you're playing at the state arena."

"It's not a big deal."

"Not a big deal? Best team your school's had in a decade, right? As soon as you win the game tonight, I'm booking a flight for the finals next weekend."

"No, Dad, really. Don't."

"I know you decided not to do college ball, and I'm hoping you change your mind on that, but this might be my last chance to see you play."

"Really. It doesn't matter. It's just a game."

"Huh. That's what your mom said."

Jason frowned. What had she told him?

"I don't want to distract you ahead of tonight, but I want to come visit anyway. You and I need to have a conversation. Face to face."

Jason picked up the damp ice pack and walked into the kitchen. "I have to go, Dad, sorry. I'll call you tomorrow."

He put the ice pack in the freezer, unloaded the dishwasher and wiped down the already clean countertops. He went back to the guest room and packed a gym bag of clothes, shoes, water bottles and snacks ready for Calum to pick him up. He did visualization techniques and stretches listening to music on his headphones. He was either nervous about tonight, or about his entire life being a mess. Tiffany was already at the school with the cheerleaders making pom poms and signs to hand out to supporters at the game. She was thrilled the team might make it to State Finals. Jason wanted to fast forward his life to July and beyond so it was all over. But he also wanted time to stop so he could stay exactly where he was – alone in this quiet, clean generic guest room – forever. The doorbell rang and Jason grabbed his bag.

Calum was bouncing on his feet on the doorstep. "Here we go, man. Here we go." He slapped Jason's shoulder and they walked to the car.

"I'm going to just listen to my music. Get into the zone, you know?"

"You do you." Calum nodded. "You okay?"

"Yeah. Great." Jason put on his headphones and turned up the volume.

Jason removed his headphones for a brief warm-up in the school gym, Coach's talk, and put them back on for the bus journey from the school to the arena. The bus was quiet, most of the other players listening to music or staring out the window, the intensity of the evening hitting home for all of them.

When the team jogged out onto the arena floor, the shock of being in such a large space, seeing the enormous scoreboards and advertisements, gave the evening a sense of unreality. Spectators were further away, and the other team's players seemed smaller. The team had practiced so much, for so long, the same plays and drills over and over, that when the game began Jason knew exactly where everyone was without needing to look. The ball slapped into his hands reassuringly as he caught passes, leaving a breeze of air as it left his hands for the net.

The team's plays were better than during practice and they only fouled once. Jason didn't feel any pain – everything was working exactly as it should. Coach nodded his head, occasionally yelling encouragement and plays. The cheers were enjoyably deafening as they reached half-time and were eleven points ahead. In the locker room Coach warned them about complacency and they went into the third quarter using their most aggressive tactics. They could afford a foul or two. During a time out called by the other team, fear crept in as they huddled around Coach.

Could they really make State? His dad would fly in. There'd be cameras and reporters, people watching on TV. The results would be reported in the newspapers and on the local news channels. The piercing ringing started and Jason couldn't hear what Coach Wilkins was saying. He leaned forwards with his hands on his knees, inhaling deeply through his nose. In front of him was a jumble of shoes, socks and legs. Most of his teammates' socks were white, but Calum's were green and two other guys had black ones. Should he do socks first? Or shoes? And why did his teammates all tie their shoelaces differently? He couldn't keep track of how many –

The whistle blew.

"Pull it together," Jason whispered to himself. "Come on. Pull it together."

They jogged back into place, resuming play.

Jason ran down to the defensive end of the court, blocked a goal and stole the ball to wild cheers. He saw a gap and dribbled the ball, passed to Calum who passed it back to him as Jason dodged another player. He jumped up to catch the ball and had a clear shot at another three-pointer. This would put them on the tipping point of a sure victory. Jason lined up the shot, the one he'd been practicing for years. He balanced the ball on the fingertips of his right hand, steadied it with his left, and rose onto his tiptoes.

He heard Coach calling his name.

Repeatedly.

Loudly.

Telling him to get on guard.

What? What was happening?

Was he on the wrong end of the court? Was he at the opposing team's basket? Was that why it was so empty? He turned to find Coach, confused. What was happening? He saw Calum frowning and shouting. Behind him Coach waved his arms frantically, his mouth moving. Jason couldn't figure out where he was supposed to be or what he was supposed to be doing. It was like he was underwater. His limbs were heavy and slow. He saw people's lips creating shapes, he heard muffled distant noises, but he couldn't make out any actual words. He looked at the ball he was holding, unsure what he was supposed to do with it.

He watched it snatched away by another pair of hands.

The opposing team's player had simply grabbed the ball, and Jason had been powerless to stop him. They stared at each other in disbelief until the other player came to his senses, dribbled the ball and passed to his teammate who aimed for the basket at the far end of the court. The ball swooshed through the net. Three points. Jason's hearing returned. Half the crowd was groaning while the other half was cheering and foot stomping.

"Myers, FOCUS! *What are you doing?*" Coach screamed over the noise.

"I don't, I ...." Jason's feet finally started receiving messages from his brain and he jogged over to Coach.

"Is it your hip? Are you injured? We need a substitution!" Coach called a time out.

Jason was substituted for a sophomore player, who looked terrified. Jason panted and wiped his face as he sat on the bench, bewildered. Why had Coach distracted him at such a crucial point? The game resumed and it was as though two new teams were on the court. Jason's team fumbled passes and missed shots. The other team played with confidence and fluency, rapidly clocking up points. Jason watched the scoreboard with a sinking heart.

"Are you okay, Myers?" Coach squatted in front of him. "I need you back in there, but not if you're in pain and can't focus."

"I can do it." Jason nodded. "I swear. I'm fine."

"Okay. Good man."

Jason went back on at the start of the fourth quarter, but his teammates weren't following the usual maneuvers. Instead of passing to Jason when he indicated he was free, they started making up plays. Defense passed the ball back and forth too long, and when they did pass it was to Calum. Coach was flushed and sweating, shouting instructions that were ignored. Their supporters were groaning and yelling. The team made more mistakes and fouls until the score was tied. In the final five minutes of the game, Jason didn't touch the ball – his team didn't trust him any more.

They lost, by nine points.

The other players jumped around and hugged each

other when the final buzzer sounded. Jason's teammates lined up and shook hands with the other team. The player who had grabbed the ball from Jason smiled sympathetically at him. Jason wanted to burst into tears. The boys made their way down the corridor towards the locker room while the other team stayed on court to celebrate and have photos.

Jason slowed down to walk beside Calum. "I don't know what happened out there." Calum didn't look at him. "I mean, Coach was calling my name before that shot. I would have had that. I don't know why he distracted me."

Calum stopped. "What are you talking about?"

"Coach distracted me."

"No, he didn't. We set you up for the easiest shot of the game, and you didn't take it. I don't know what happened there, man, but you –" Calum pursed his lips and closed his eyes for a moment. He took a deep breath and looked at Jason. "You know what, I don't know what happened. But, it's unfortunate it was in the third quarter of State Semifinals, you know what I'm saying?"

He walked into the locker room and Jason followed, head bowed. Coach gave a speech about it taking a whole team to play a game and how far they'd come. He talked about lessons learned for next year, how strong the team would be and thanked them for all their work. No one mentioned Jason's screw up, which made it worse. Jason wondered whether he should say anything but couldn't think of what would make it better. There was nothing.

The bus ride back to school was silent. Jason sat across the aisle from Calum. Calum's head was turned so far to the window Jason couldn't see his expression but noticed he wiped his face several times. Jason wanted to cry too, but if he started, he'd never stop.

The bus arrived at the high school and they shuffled off into the dimly lit parking lot. Jason held his bag and looked for Tiffany, hoping he could ride home with her instead of Calum.

"Hi, honey." Jason turned to see his mom.

"Oh. Hi." Another thing to feel guilty about. Great.

"Your afro's growing out."

"I've not made it to the barbers."

"It looks good. I was just going to see if you wanted a ride. To the Vanderkamps', or anywhere else."

"We lost."

"I know."

"How?"

"I've never missed one of your games."

"I don't know what happened out there." Jason shook his head. "I thought – I, I don't know what I thought." He stared at the ground.

"Oh, baby boy." She hadn't called him that for years. Jason lifted his head and saw she was crying. "The other coach *was* calling your name. Your old name. It's not your fault, okay?" She opened her arms. "Come here."

Jason leaned into her arms. They cried together for the first time in years.

TWENTY-EIGHT

Molly stood in the shower letting the hot water run over her. She had just thrown up her dinner and was tired of being sick. Her throat was raw, her eyes bloodshot and her stomach muscles felt like she'd done a hundred crunches. Worst of all, she was still fat. It didn't make any sense. If most food wasn't staying inside her, why wasn't she thinner by now?

Molly scrubbed her hair with shampoo, rubbing until her fingernails scratched her scalp. She hated her hair, always lank and greasy. Maybe if her mom bought decent shampoo, her hair would have half a chance of looking better but of course they had the cheapest of everything. She rinsed her hair and smeared conditioner over her head, even though it was pointless. She balanced on one leg, resting her foot on the side of the bath and picked up the shaving cream. It squirted out with a satisfying belch. It wasn't warm enough to wear shorts or dresses but it was nice to imagine Pastor Mike running his hand over her smooth skin.

She covered her leg with the cream and traced the razor through it, methodically working her way from left to right. She imagined digging the razor in further, creating tracks of blood on her leg instead of pale, dull skin. The image was strangely appealing. Molly shook her head and ran her hand over her leg to check for missed stubble. She switched legs, using more cream and creating the same white trails up to her knees. She paused with the razor at the bottom of her thigh and pushed the blade down into her skin. Nothing happened. She pressed more firmly. Nothing. The safety razors her mom bought really were safe.

Molly angrily jerked the razor away and gasped at the sharp pain. A thin, bright red line appeared above her knee. A blob of water hit the cut and blood streamed out, watery red swirls making their way down her leg, snaking along the white bath and disappearing into the drain. Molly wiped the cut with her hand and blood rushed out. What the hell was she doing? God. Why would anyone do this to themselves? She rubbed shower gel everywhere, her leg stinging even more, rinsed out the conditioner and turned off the shower. She pressed toilet paper to the cut, lifting it up every few seconds to see if the bleeding had stopped, which took forever. Molly towelled herself dry. The last thing she needed was her mom bitching about stained towels. She pulled on her pajamas, opened the bathroom door and walked straight into her mom.

"Jesus!" Molly yelped.

"Hon, you okay? You were in there a while."

"Yes, Mom. God." Molly felt the cut throbbing.

"Okay. And don't take the Lord's name in vain, now," her mom smiled and winked.

Molly raised her eyebrows and waited. Her mom stepped around her and went into the bathroom, closing the door. Molly shook her head and huffed. She went into her room to start working on her English essay. It was going to be a late night. The essay was due tomorrow and she only had a few handwritten notes so far. Between McDonald's, tutoring Tiffany and helping Pastor Mike with the church administration, she was struggling to keep up with her school work.

Molly sat down at her desk and the fabric of her flannel pajamas pressed against the cut. She felt wide awake, typing up her notes and transforming them into coherent paragraphs. She was vaguely aware of the dull throb of her leg but after forty minutes the essay was finished. She moved on to studying her Advanced Algebra, preparing for Tuesday's test. The equations made sense now, and she managed to get all the practice questions correct except one. As she reworked the incorrect equation she pressed her hand against her thigh, playing with the soreness. It had been two hours since she'd thought about being fat and ugly.

The next morning Molly turned off her alarm and wondered why her thigh was hurting. She swung her feet onto the floor and pulled down her pyjama pants. The sharp red line above her knee was a surprise. It was impressive how something so small could sting. She got dressed and washed her face. As she moved around getting ready, sometimes the cut hurt and sometimes it didn't. She rubbed her finger over her jeans as she drank her coffee in the kitchen.

She had made a decision. Today would be the day she confronted her mom about her dad. Or rather, the fact her mom had no idea who her dad was. Her mom walked into the kitchen, pulling her hair up into a bun.

"Morning, hon. Did you get that essay done?"

"Have I ever missed a deadline?"

Her mom sucked her teeth. "Molly, enough sass, please." She sliced a bagel and put it in the toaster. "Are you eating breakfast?"

"I already ate."

Her mom glanced at the empty sink. "What did you have?"

"There's no point in using a plate. It's just another thing to wash."

"Hmm."

"What time do you finish work today?"

"Four."

"And then you'll come home?"

"Yes." Her mom poured coffee and looked at her. "Why? Do you want to do something? We could have a movie night? I'll get a DVD from work. There's some on sale. We could even order a pizza. Let's make it nice, hon." She smiled. "We won't be able to do this much longer."

Thank God.

The bagel popped up. Her mom opened the cabinet door for a plate and then closed it. "You know what, you have a point. Why use a plate?" She picked up the bagel and took a bite, holding it aloft as she chewed.

God, she was so annoying.

"How was school?" Her mom smiled widely as she carried bags into the kitchen where Molly was doing her homework.

"Fine."

School had been really weird. Everyone had been subdued, even the teachers. The announcement by the principal at the beginning of the day said how well the basketball team had played at the weekend. Molly knew nothing about sports, but even she understood that couldn't possibly be true given that they'd lost. At lunchtime Tiffany hadn't wanted to talk about the game, or been able to focus on anything. Molly had wondered why she was bothering tutoring her. She needed to concentrate on her own studying.

Molly waited for her mom to finish unpacking the

bags, tapping her pen against her notebook. She felt sweaty and nervous, which was moronic because Molly didn't have anything to be ashamed of. Her mom was the one that should be feeling nervous, but now she was just standing there holding an envelope. She still had had the same big stupid smile since she'd walked in.

Molly cleared her throat and licked her lips. She'd wipe that grin off her face. She had spent most of school going through the speech in her head. She was going to demand to know who her dad was. When her mom couldn't tell her (and obviously, she wouldn't be able to) she was going to tell her mom she knew everything. And how long had her mom expected to keep Molly's own birth certificate from her? She must think Molly was retarded. And she should stop being such a hypocrite. Someone like her shouldn't be going to church, offering to help out, giggling in front of Mr. Vanderkamp. Molly had seen the way she looked at him. It was disgusting.

And what had she really been doing when she went out last month? Had she even met up with her friends? Molly thought back to her mom sitting at the table in her robe the next day, looking hungover. She had probably slept with someone. Molly glared at her.

"I brought in the mail." She handed the envelope to Molly. "I think it's really good news."

The envelope was thick and heavy, and had a black and red logo in the corner.

"Oh my God." It was from the college Molly dreamed of going to. But what if she didn't get in? Or worse, if she got in but didn't get the scholarship she needed to actually go?

"I'm sure it's good news. Look how big that envelope is." Her mom gave her a hug from behind.

"Open it, sweetie."

Molly wriggled out of her arms and tore open the envelope, her hands shaking. Her mom stood behind her, reading over her shoulder.

We are pleased to inform you ...

Her mom squealed and squeezed her, giving her a loud kiss on the cheek. "Oh, sweet Lord, thank you."

"Mom, shh! Let me read." Molly scanned down the page.

"Oh, my God. I'm so proud of you, all that hard work. Oh, my. It just goes to show, you can do anything you want. Anything at all. My little girl is going to one of the best colleges in the entire country. In the world!"

"Mom, stop. I'm not going." Molly put the documents down on the table. She'd seen everything she needed.

"What?" Her mom sat down next to her, her beaming face flushed.

"They gave me a partial scholarship. Even with the financial aid, it only covers some of the costs." Molly pushed the palm of her hand against her thigh. "I'll have to go somewhere else."

"No. No, my girl. You are going there. That's where you want to go, and they want to have you, and we're going to make this work." Her mom nodded. "You send back that acceptance form."

"How? How can I *ever* afford to go there?"

"I've been putting money aside. I've saved up a few thousand dollars. Enough to cover a couple years' living expenses. And there's the house. I can refinance." She rubbed Molly's arm. "We will make this work. Don't you worry about that."

"What?" Molly was stunned. All this time they'd

been eating cheap food, buying ugly clothes, never going on vacations, and the whole time there had been money sitting there? "What do you mean?"

Her mom nodded. "I've made sure you could go to any college you wanted. Anywhere. Do whatever you want to do. Get the best possible job you can."

"You mean, be the opposite of you?"

"Well." Her mom pressed her hand to her chest, her martyr's stance. "I guess that's one way of looking at it. But of course I want you to do well. And I have the savings to make that happen."

"I don't want your money."

Her mom reached for Molly's hand. "Oh, honey. It's all for you. Everything I've done was for you. Of course you should take it."

"No. I don't want *your* money. I don't want money that's come from some slut that doesn't even know who my dad is."

Her mom sat back and held her hand over her mouth.

"I found my birth certificate. So I know you've lied to me my entire life." Molly's voice was measured. "And how have you even saved all this money anyway? Thousands of dollars? From doing what you do best, I guess. Whoring around, right?"

"Molly!" her mom gasped. "I –"

"Oh, just fuck off, Mom. Fuck. Off."

Molly walked to her bedroom feeling strangely calm. She didn't even bother slamming the door when she closed it.

Her mom would be sitting at the kitchen table for hours now, clutching a mug of tea with her slender hands. Molly could go back in there any time. Apologize. Eat pizza and watch a movie.

But she didn't want to.

April
2008

"For the flesh lusteth against the Spirit, and the Spirit against the flesh: and these are contrary the one to the other: so that ye cannot do the things that ye would."

Galatians 5:17

TWENTY-NINE

Lauren and Tiffany were sitting next to each other on the sofa in Tiffany's living room. Lauren carefully balanced a peanut M&M on Tiffany's stomach. They waited. It rolled off, bounced on a cushion and landed on the rug.

"You breathed, that's cheating."

"No, the baby kicked. That's not my fault. Drink!"

They picked up their glasses and swallowed.

"My turn. This is definitely going to balance." Tiffany put the candy on her stomach.

"You're totally holding your breath. I can tell."

"No, I'm not," Tiffany said in a strangulated voice.

They giggled and the M&M fell onto the floor.

Lauren finished her vodka and Diet Coke. "I need a refill. You want one?"

Tiffany held up her half-full glass of milk and shook her head. "You might want to slow down. You're driving later, right?"

"Yeah, in like, two hours."

"Well. Maybe we should just watch the movie now." Tiffany reached for the remote control and *Juno* started.

Lauren glared at her. Now who was the prairie girl? They hardly ever had Tiffany's house to themselves. Even though Jason had moved back in with his mom he came over all the time, bringing groceries and cleaning, even spending the night sometimes. He was nice to hang out with, but Lauren and Tiffany had an unspoken agreement to let Jason think they didn't drink. Lauren had been desperate for the last three days for Jason and Mrs. Vanderkamp to go out so she could search Tiffany's house. She'd run out of sleeping pills and her weird, erotic dreams had turned into nightmares, so vivid that sometimes she wasn't sure if she had been awake or asleep. Every morning she woke up feeling exhausted and defiled, and was on edge for the rest of the day.

Tiffany moved around and propped another cushion behind her back.

"Should I get your pillow from upstairs? Would that make you more comfortable?" Lauren asked.

"It's okay. I'm good." Tiffany rested a bowl of popcorn on her stomach and picked at it.

"No, I'll go."

Lauren jogged up the stairs, passed Tiffany's room and opened the door to Mrs. Vanderkamp's room. She stepped over clothes and empty glasses and went to the bedside table. Jason still never came in here to tidy up, like it was some kind of sacred space. It was cute. Lauren pulled open the bedside table drawer and bottles of pills rolled around. She picked up each one, reading the labels. She found the same prescription as before, but it only had a few pills in it.

"Damn," she whispered.

Would Mrs. Vanderkamp notice if it was gone? She must be taking these regularly. But the last few nights had been awful. Lauren came to the Vanderkamps' every day but Mrs. Vanderkamp was always around until today, when she had finally gone out for a meeting with a lawyer. This was her only chance. She put the bottle in the pocket of her hoodie and looked at the other pills again. There were a couple of bottles with pills that looked almost the same as the ones she had, so she took one of those as well. She could look on the internet to find out what it was, and Mrs. Vanderkamp probably didn't even know it was there.

Lauren ran her finger over the gun. How would it feel to fire it? If an intruder came in while Mrs. Vanderkamp was sleeping, wearing one of her floaty nightgowns, half naked and vulnerable in the darkness ... would she really have the time and the nerve to open the drawer, pull it out and defend herself? Or would it be too late by the time she realized what was going on? Would the intruder climb on top of her and –

Lauren slammed the drawer closed and headed downstairs. She slipped the bottles into her bag by the door before sitting back down on the sofa.

"So, where's the pillow?" Popcorn spilled out of Tiffany's mouth.

"Oh. I forgot."

"Seriously, you *are* drunk. Jeez. What were you doing up there?"

"Bathroom." Lauren jumped back up, her face burning. "I'll get it now, sorry."

"Hey, I meant to ask. Are you sleeping better? Do you want more of those pills?"

"No. Thanks. But, um ... do you have another book?"

"Book?"

"You know, like *Wicked Pleasures*?" Lauren felt guilty just saying the title.

Tiffany raised her eyebrows and grinned. "So you enjoyed it, huh? My mom has the whole series. She hides them under her bed. Help yourself."

Lauren ran upstairs and went back into Mrs. Vanderkamp's room. She found another book from the series – *Sinful Pleasures* – and remembered Tiffany's maternity pillow on the way back down. Lauren put the book in her bag and gave Tiffany the pillow.

"Thanks. My dad would say you're a dark horse, you know that?" Tiffany threw a piece of popcorn at her and leaned against the pillow. "You know, I'm thinking of keeping the baby."

"Well, sure. You should do whatever you want." Lauren turned to watch the film. Tiffany had changed her mind twenty times over the past few weeks. By Monday, she'd want to go for adoption again. Lauren was impatient to go home, read and get a proper night's sleep.

On Friday night, Lauren ran out of the sleeping pills and tried one of the different ones. She slipped into sleep almost immediately and didn't have any dreams at all. She woke up surprised to hear her mom knocking on the door. It was still dark outside.

Her mom opened the door. "Lauren, honey. We're leaving soon," she whispered.

Lauren yawned. "Okay. I'm up, I'm up."

She went to the bathroom and shuffled into the kitchen, still tired despite her heavy sleep. She was stuck baby-sitting her brothers while her parents went to visit her grandmother who was in hospital recovering from a fall. Her mom looked as exhausted as Lauren felt.

Lauren squeezed her. "Give Grandma this hug from me, okay?"

"I will." Tears welled up in mom's eyes. "I just thank the Lord I can still get on a plane. If this had happened in a week's time I wouldn't even be allowed to fly."

Her dad came into the kitchen and looked at Lauren. She folded her arms over her chest, painfully aware of the thin fabric of her pajamas.

"You're up, finally." He turned to her mom. "Okay, let's go."

Her mom kissed Lauren's cheek. "If you need anything at all, you just call me. Straight away, okay?" She gave Lauren another hug and went into the garage.

Her dad followed and turned at the door. "We'll be calling. To make sure everything's okay. No friends over. Got it?"

Lauren nodded. "We'll be here." *Studying the Bible all weekend* she was tempted to add. She couldn't wait for him to be gone.

He closed the door and Lauren went back upstairs and got into bed. She expected to fall asleep instantly but felt too jittery. In the end she reached for *Sinful Pleasures* and read until the boys woke up.

Lauren hadn't noticed how annoying Michael and Adam were before. At breakfast they bickered over how much cereal they each had in their bowls, who was pouring the milk, and who got the last drop of orange juice. Lauren couldn't believe she had a whole day with them stretching ahead of her. Watching them eat their cereal, milk spilling everywhere, made her feel nauseous.

"Okay, guys. What will make you stop arguing?"

"Playing on the computer!" Michael yelled. Lauren's head throbbed.

"Yeah, that would work," Adam agreed.

"That's not an option. I need the computer to do homework." Lauren also wanted privacy so she could sleep. Or keep reading.

"We can use Dad's then," Adam said mischievously.

"No." Lauren pictured her dad's dark study. Could she get comfortable enough on the rug on the floor to have a nap? "Okay, look. Use my computer, and I'll use Dad's. But do *not* tell him, okay?"

"Can we have a snack?"

"You literally just ate breakfast."

"I'm hungry," Michael whined, making Lauren's headache worse.

"Eat whatever you the hell you want, I really don't care."

They gaped at her.

"What?" Lauren asked. "You guys need to chill. So, are you using my computer or not?" They pelted upstairs and Lauren followed to get her book bag. "You guys behave okay? And don't bother me. Find stuff in the pantry for lunch."

"Can we eat ice cream?"

"Sure. Whatever."

"Thanks, sis."

"You're the best!"

Lauren carried her bookbag downstairs and opened the door to her dad's study. Light peeked around the cracks between the blind and the window. The room was dim and quiet when she closed the door. Even though her dad wasn't in the same state any more, it felt as though he was somehow watching her. Screw him. She refused to let it creep her out.

Lauren left the blinds pulled down and sat at the desk. It was so dumb and typical of her dad to bar the rest of his family from his study. A whole room just for him when he already had an office at church, and Adam and Michael were stuck sharing with each other.

And then he stood at the pulpit on Sundays preaching generosity. What a hypocrite. Lauren could feel her pulse rate increasing as she thought of his selfishness. He probably hadn't even read any of the books lining the shelves behind the desk.

"Fuck you, Dad," Lauren muttered. She reached into her book bag and got out her notes on *The Crucible*.

She turned on the computer and pulled up a blank document. The cursor flashed accusingly at her. She drummed her fingers on the table. Her hand looked naked without her purity ring. What was the point of this? The whole assignment was so stupid. So some girls became hysterical, talked a load of crap and got someone in trouble three hundred years ago. So what?

She had planned to write about mass hysteria but perhaps she should make the topic of the paper Reverend Parris's hypocrisy. She could print an extra copy and leave it lying around for her dad to find.

Although why should she waste her Saturday writing about some fictitious reverend when she had a hypocritical pastor for a father in reality? Lauren picked up the photo of her family on the desk. The church had held a picnic to celebrate Adam's remission and raise money for the children's hospital ward. They had all worn orange and white tops. Michael was a cheerful toddler and her mom was holding him in her lap, beaming. Her Dad was sitting on one side of her mom and had curved his lips into a smile but as usual it didn't reach his eyes. Lauren was in her 'quiet phase' as her mom had called it, and sat on her mom's other side, her hair falling over her face. She had her arm around Adam and a small frown as though she couldn't quite believe Adam was in remission. Her biggest fear, even though he'd now been healthy for so long, was that he would get sick again. She still had nightmares about it now, alongside her other weird dreams.

She turned the photo around to stop herself throwing it against the wall and looked back at the screen. The cursor was waiting for her. Lauren looked around the room and sighed. Her leg jiggled under the desk. What if there was some kind of problem, and her parents didn't get on the plane? Her mom could feel sick, or the flight might be cancelled. What if they were on their way back right now? Her dad would fling open the study door. He'd be furious and –

Lauren rubbed her eyes and sighed. Why couldn't she just calm down? Maybe half a pill would help her relax enough to concentrate and get some work done. She had slept so well after taking one last night. She and the boys should have some fun together while her parents were away, and she'd apologize to them for being irritable. They could play board games and stay up late watching movies. Lauren left the study and listened at the bottom of the stairs to see if any arguments had erupted. She heard the boys talking in relatively calm voices and got a glass of water from the kitchen and returned to the study. She closed the door, sat down at the desk and reached for the bottle in her bag. She snapped a tablet in half and swallowed it. She turned on the desk lamp and flipped through *The Crucible*, looking for a paragraph to demonstrate the Reverend's piety to start her essay. She ended up getting engrossed in the book, noticing elements she hadn't picked up on before. It was actually a pretty good story. There was a knock on the door.

"Hi," Adam stuck his head around. "Do you want some food?"

Lauren realized her headache was gone. "No, thanks."

"Are you sure? You didn't eat much breakfast."

"That's so sweet of you, Adam. I'm okay. Do you need any help?"

"No, we're just making Pop-Tarts."

"Cool." Lauren felt a rush of affection for her brother. "I really love you, you know that?"

"Um, sure. Thanks. You too," he mumbled. He shut the door and then opened it. "Are you okay?"

"I'm great. Thanks."

"Do you want the blinds open?"

"Not really," she shrugged.

"Okay." He looked at the desk. "Why did you turn that photo around?"

"Because I really hate looking at Dad's face sometimes."

Adam stared at her. "Are you sure you're okay?"

"Never better."

"Can we play outside after lunch?"

"Sure, why not?"

"Thanks." He shut the door again.

Lauren felt fuzzy. Like after a vodka and Diet Coke, but better. Calmer. Like being wrapped up in a soft blanket. Amazing what a difference half a little pill could make.

She stretched her arms over her head, luxuriating in the silence. She could type anything, really. She was a good student. She wrote decent essays. She would just start typing, and the essay would write itself. She tapped at the keys, making a few spelling mistakes but the spell checker picked them up so she kept going. Lauren wrote a stream of consciousness, her second skim reading of the book giving her clarity and insights she hadn't had before. She clicked onto the internet to look up the history of Salem, where *The Crucible* was set. Her fingers slipped on the keys. The search engine page changed to a list of websites. Lauren frowned. She scanned the screen, trying to figure out how to return to the previous page.

Her attention was caught by the website addresses. Some were obviously websites dedicated to popular scripture verses and fundraising ideas. But others ... she squinted. They had names similar to the titles of the books under Mrs. Vanderkamp's bed.

She clicked on one. A web page came up with images. A man and woman doing some of the things described in *Wicked Pleasures*. And more.

A lot more.

She had no idea people did these things to each other. She closed the page down, her hand shaking on the mouse. The list was still there on the screen. She clicked another link, and a video started playing.

It was revolting. *Way* grosser than she'd imagined. When she read the books she had imagined it to be – not romantic, exactly, but sexy. Not like *this*. The expressions on their faces weren't like people who were in love.

Lauren closed the page and looked at the list. She just couldn't help herself.

She clicked onto another link, and another. If she'd had any food in her stomach she would have been sick. This one had pictures of young girls.

THIRTY

Jason carried Tiffany's book bag into the house and kissed her on the cheek. "I'll give you a call later." He turned to go.

"Can we talk real quick?" Tiffany clung onto his arm.

"I have to go but I'll call you."

"Where are you going?"

"I promised Calum I'd help him with something."

"He can wait a few minutes, right?"

"I really, just, I don't have time."

"Five minutes! Jeez. What's more important, Calum or the baby?"

Jason felt a lurch of fear. "Is everything okay? Is the baby okay?"

Tiffany walked into the living room and lowered herself onto the sofa. "Yes, the baby is fine. Sit down for a minute."

Jason glanced at his watch.

"Jeez, Jason. It doesn't matter if you're late sometimes."

Jason sat next to her and took her hand. "Sorry." He tried not to think of Dr. Schaffer waiting for him, Penny checking the voicemail messages. "Go ahead."

"So. I've been thinking. A lot. And," Tiffany took a deep breath, "I've decided. I want to keep the baby."

"What?"

"I've looked at loads of stuff online, and I know I can do this. I want to be a mom. I'm keeping the baby." She squeezed Jason's hand and smiled.

"But I just sent my acceptance back. To college."

"What does that have to do with anything?"

"I, I mean, I – you, what about you?"

"God, you sound like my dad. I can go to college in a few years. You're kind of hurting my hand, babe."

"Sorry. Sorry." Jason released her hand. "I'm just ... I was not expecting this." He pressed his lips together. "It's fine, though." He nodded. "I'll just write to them and let them know. It's just college, right? I mean, lots of people don't go to college."

"Jason, this isn't about college. *You* can still go. But I'm not. Your mom was right. You shouldn't change all your life plans because of a mistake. And anway, it's not a mistake to me. Four more years of studying sounds pretty terrible anyway. And I'm excited about being a mom." Tiffany beamed.

"No, I'm not going to leave you."

"Jason, go to college. You have it all planned out. So go."

Jason rubbed his head. "But, where will you live?"

"Here. There's plenty of room. And my mom said she'd help. She told me last night she *wants* me and the baby to live here. And you can come stay on weekends and vacations."

Jason shook his head. "This isn't a safe place for a baby."

"What are you talking about? It's a house."

He picked something up from the carpet. "Right. Okay. What is this, then?"

Tiffany peered at it. "A peanut M&M?"

"Exactly. Just lying around on the floor." He held it in front of her. "This is a choking hazard. Plus a potential allergen."

"You know the baby isn't here, yet, right?"

Jason stood up and pointed at the hallway. "Those stairs right there? If a child fell down those, it would crack its head open on the floor."

"That's horrible. Don't say stuff like that."

"I'm just pointing out, you haven't thought this through. Look at these." He walked over to the window and held up the cord for the blinds. "Did you know children get their necks twisted up in these until they can't breathe? They get strangled from these."

"What the hell, Jason. I'm not going to let my kid die, okay? Why are you being such an asshole?"

"You can't look after a baby, Tiffany. And your mom isn't going to help – she can't even get herself dressed. She wouldn't even notice a baby in the house at all, let alone help out."

"Oh my God. So I'm going to be a bad mom, is that it?"

"No. I'm not – I'm just saying, I –"

Tiffany's eyes filled with tears. "You really think I can't do this, huh? You're so perfect, you think you know everything. You get the perfect frigging grades, you're the perfect son, you're the perfect boyfriend – everyone thinks you're so fucking great!" Tears ran down her face. "But I know you've never wanted this baby, ruining your perfect life. I get that. It's fine. So don't worry about it. I'll do it by myself." She cupped her hands around her belly. "Me and the baby will be totally fine without you, believe it or not. So you can fuck off." She heaved herself off the sofa and went to the door, holding it open pointedly.

Jason strode into Dr. Schaffer's office. He was shaking. "Tiffany changed her mind and thinks we should keep the baby and I know it's a stupid idea. And I think, I think she just broke up with me."

Dr. Schaffer leaned back in his chair. "Have a seat."

Jason sat and looked around, reassured to find almost everything the same as usual. The pen holder, the clock, the desk. The Kleenex box was different. Dr. Schaffer's beard looked scraggly. Jason wanted to tidy it up.

"Jason?" Dr. Schaffer prompted.

"She wants me to live with her when I'm not at college. And thinks that she can just have the baby. At home. And look after it."

"Okay."

"And it's, it's just, I mean, it's a terrible idea. She can't – we can't – we can't be parents."

Dr. Schaffer tilted his head. "And what are your reasons for thinking that?"

"It's *insane*." Jason paced around the room. "We're eighteen. We just can't be parents, we'd be terrible."

"There are many people who become parents at that age, and some of them are very good at it." Dr. Schaffer leaned forward and rested his elbows on his desk, clasping his hands together. "I'm wondering why you think you wouldn't be."

"Well, I –" Jason sat in the chair. "Seriously? You think I should drop out of school, go work at a gas station and just be a dad and never leave this place?"

"No. I'm not saying that at all." Dr. Schaffer's tone was annoyingly reasonable. "I'm just curious to know what your reasons are for thinking you wouldn't be a good father."

Jason clenched his jaw. "I just know I won't."

"But you can't give me a reason?"

"It's going to sound stupid."

Dr. Schaffer shrugged. "Try me."

"Babies are ... messy."

Dr. Schaffer nodded.

"I don't just mean the puke and the, the poop. I mean, they don't understand schedules. And routines."

Dr. Schaffer waited.

"Babies just, they just do whatever they feel like. They need feeding at random times. They cry in the middle of the night. They just pick stuff up – anything – and put it in their mouths." Jason's knee jiggled up and down.

"So you're saying they're unpredictable."

Jason nodded. "Exactly."

He waited for Dr. Schaffer to laugh but he just inclined his head in agreement. "Go on."

"And then they grow up. Obviously. Start crawling and walking. You have to watch them all the time. You can't relax even for a minute."

"And then?"

"And then, they get even older and –" Jason stopped.

"And?"

Stop asking questions, you asshole. And figure your beard out. "I don't know." Jason looked at the clock.

"We have plenty of time. I want to know what's on your mind, Jason. What are you afraid of?"

"I don't know what you mean. I've just told you. There isn't anything else."

Dr. Schaffer sighed and lifted his glasses up to rub his face. He looked as tired as Jason felt. He put his glasses back on. "I'm going to challenge you on this. I think you remember."

Considering mental health professionals were supposed to know about crazy people, Jason was surprised none of his psychiatrists had said this to him before.

Of course he remembered. He remembered it like it was yesterday. He remembered the day (Wednesday), what he was wearing (new black Nike shorts and a blue t-shirt), what Jasmine was wearing (her favourite bright pink sundress with matching hair clips), and the smell of dinner cooking (beef casserole).

"I don't. I don't remember."

Dr. Schaffer and Jason stared at each other. Jason broke eye contact first, checking the clock again.

"Would you like me to refer you to a counselor? There are people who specialize in –"

"No."

"– young parents. It would be covered under your insurance plan."

"No, thank you. It's fine. I just came to get my prescription."

Dr. Schaffer waited.

Jason jiggled his knee.

"Sleeping okay?"

"Yep."

"Well, I'm writing your prescription for one month. I want to see you again next month. If you change your mind about the counseling you can call. Any time. And I'll arrange it."

On the way home Jason drove so slowly the car behind started blaring their horn. His vision went fuzzy and his ears were ringing. He pulled into a grocery store parking lot. There were eight shopping carts in the cart corral. They needed straightening up. A shopper came along and shoved a cart into the corral, making it even messier. Jason closed his eyes and breathed. The cars were impossible to keep track of – shoppers kept coming and going before he could get to final numbers. He practiced his breathing and visualization techniques until his hands stopped shaking. He wanted to call Tiffany, she always made him feel better, but he'd messed that up again.

What was he going to do? If he stuck to his plan, and left her and the baby behind, what kind of man did that make him? But if he stayed, eventually, somehow, she would find out. And then she wouldn't want him to be in the baby's life anyway. It was hopeless.

The store security guard passed by his car twice, peering at him suspiciously. Jason left and drove home. At least his mom was a little easier to talk to now, but he still hadn't told her his long-term plan. When he arrived at the house his mom was chopping vegetables. A glass of red wine and a half empty bottle were on the countertop.

"Mom? Can we talk?"

"Your dad called me at work today. He's coming to graduation, and said there's absolutely no way he's going to miss it." Jason's mom sighed. "I told him that you'd changed your last name. He wasn't too happy about it." She took a drink. "I let him think it was my feminist principles."

"You didn't have to do that."

She picked up the knife. "It's okay. I think it made him wish Millie was a boy though. Said stuff about the family name dying off, all that. Anyway, it's done. So you need to make sure you get him a ticket for graduation."

"Okay. Thanks, Mom."

Jason held it together until he reached his bedroom. He cried so hard he had to muffle his sobs with his pillow. Was there anyone's life that he hadn't ruined? His girlfriend, his best friend, his parents.

At least now he knew what he needed to do. And he would be doing them all a huge favor. They'd see that eventually.

THIRTY-ONE

Molly's mom watched her get in the car. "Why are you wearing that?"

Molly clicked her seatbelt on and looked out the windshield at the driveway. Her long-sleeved t-shirt hid her arms, which were covered in cuts. She'd put another t-shirt on top because layering made people look thinner.

"It's really warm today. Do you need long sleeves? And *two* layers?"

"The Vanderkamps have air conditioning that actually works."

"You know, I'm doing you a favor here." Her mom glared at her. "You could show some appreciation. It's not exactly on my way to the store." She started the car. "And I'm surprised Tiffany doesn't have a car she can use."

"She's *pregnant*." Molly had no idea what being pregnant had to do with not being able to drive. She didn't understand why Tiffany didn't have a car anymore either. And she needed to write her AP English Lit paper but Tiffany had called her crying.

"I know what being pregnant is like. And I was still capable of driving."

"If you hate taking me places so much, why don't you spend some of your savings on a car for me? Then you won't need to be reminded of my existence."

"Molly. Can you stop being such a –" She stopped the car on the driveway. "I don't hate taking you places. I know you're mad at me. I've said sorry a hundred times about your birth certificate. I don't know how to make it up to you. But it will not do you any good to know your father. I wish you could understand. And maybe when you're older, you will."

"Right. Because I'm just a dumb little kid. I still don't believe you, anyway. If you knew who he was, you'd have put his name on it even if he was a total asshole."

Her mom opened her mouth to respond and then thought better of it. Her hands gripped the steering wheel so tightly they turned white. They drove to Tiffany's house in silence, Molly looking forward to whatever crisis Tiffany was having.

When Molly arrived, Mrs. Vanderkamp opened the door, yawning. She was wearing sweats, but they were soft knitted grey sweats which made her look like a Lands End model. If Molly wore them she'd look like a slob.

"Come in, sweetie. I need some caffeine." Mrs. Vanderkamp looked at the car. "Does your mom want to come in for a coffee?"

"No, she has to go."

"That's a shame." Mrs. Vanderkamp waved at her mom and closed the door. "I'm glad you're here. Tiffany is so upset, and I'm hoping she doesn't change her mind about keeping the baby."

"Really?" Molly was surprised. She'd been prepared to tell Tiffany how terrible her own life was growing up after being conceived as a mistake. She thought adoption sounded great – if her mom had given her up for adoption she'd be living with amazing parents who truly wanted her, probably in a huge house.

"Oh, absolutely. She needs to stay here. With the baby." Mrs. Vanderkamp nodded. "She's in her room."

Molly went upstairs and found Tiffany sitting on her bed with her laptop, surrounded by crumpled tissues. "Hi," she closed the bedroom door behind her. "What's wrong?"

Tiffany sniffed. "Jason thinks this house will kill the baby."

"What? That's weird." Molly sat down on the bed and pushed the box of tissues towards Tiffany. "This is an amazing house for a baby. I would love to grow up somewhere like this. And have someone like you as a mom. Your baby is so lucky."

Tiffany blew her nose. "Do you really think so?" She looked at her hopefully.

"Yes. You're going to be a great mom." Molly sincerely believed Tiffany couldn't be any worse than her own mother. At least the baby would grow up knowing who its parents were.

"Thanks. That's sweet." Tiffany gave her a small smile.

"Can I ask you something? I know you're mad at him and stuff, but are you still going to put Jason's name on the birth certificate?"

"Of course. I have to, right? He's the dad."

"Right."

"Hey, that reminds me. Did you ever find your birth certificate? We need to hurry up if we want to invite your dad to graduation."

Molly scratched at her arm. She hadn't told anyone what she'd discovered, not even Pastor Mike. And he had told her she could tell him anything. He had whispered it in her ear as he had hugged her goodbye at the church office last week.

"No. I changed my mind. Maybe, maybe he doesn't want to be part of my life."

Tiffany rubbed her belly. "Jeez. You could at least try. I still don't understand why you don't ask your mom. Or what about, I don't know, you mentioned your grandma, right? Ask her. She should know who your mom was dating." She looked sad. "I wonder what things will be like for my baby. What if Jason doesn't want anything to do with it? Maybe I shouldn't put his name down. He doesn't deserve it if he's not going to support me."

"No, you definitely should. No matter what. It's horrible not knowing who your father is."

"Well, then. You should find out who your dad is. Now here, help me pick out baby names." Tiffany pulled at Molly's arm, causing her to gasp. "You okay?"

Molly blinked back tears. "Yes, just really happy you've decided to keep the baby. It's great. You'll be great."

Tiffany tilted her head. "You really need to find your dad, you know?"

Molly nodded. "I know."

On Saturday when her mom was at work, Molly called her grandma.

"Hi. It's me." There was no response. "Molly."

"Oh. Well. Hi."

"I wanted to ask you something. When Mom told you she was pregnant with me, what did she say?"

The silence stretched out for so long Molly thought she'd been disconnected. "Hello?"

"I can't remember. Why are you asking about that?"

"I just want to know. Like, was she happy about it?"

"Well, she certainly wanted to keep you."

"Really? Did she talk about ... her boyfriend, or ..."

"How's school?"

"Fine. So did you ever meet Mom's boyfriend?"

"You hear about that college you wanted to go to yet?"

"Yep. I got in." Molly twisted the phone cord around her index finger.

"So you'll be moving. Living – where is it again?"

"Massachusetts."

"Hmm. All the way on the east coast. Well, you be careful."

"Of what?" Molly's finger turned purple.

"You focus on studying when you're there. Don't ... well. Just focus on studying."

"I can't just study." God, her grandma was so dumb. "I'll have to work as well. I can't afford it otherwise."

"I don't mean work. I mean – behave yourself."

"Right. Okay. Do you want to clarify what that means?"

Molly's finger turned from purple to white as she waited.

"Ask your mother. I have to go now."

"Are you coming to graduation? I'm valedictorian."

"We'll see. Okay? I have to go. Take care."

There was a click.

What a bitch. Molly was her only grandchild and she didn't give a damn. Molly put the receiver down and let the phone cord unravel, replaying the conversation in her head. Her finger tingled as the blood rushed back in, turning back to purple and then pink.

Her grandma had changed the subject as soon as

she brought up her mom's boyfriend. Obviously, Molly was right. Again. She looked at the clock, checked the church volunteer schedule pinned on the noticeboard by the fridge and picked up the phone again.

Molly knocked on the church office door and went in. Pastor Mike was at his desk, scribbling something on a pad of paper.

"Molly. What are you doing here?"

"Um. I just, I just wanted to see if you needed any help? With anything?"

He frowned. "No. Did we say you'd come in today?"

"No, no. I just, I just thought I'd come by."

"Right. Is your mother with you?"

"No, just me. Margaret gave me a ride and picked up some stuff for the food bank." She shuffled her feet and gripped her arms, feeling the raw cuts she'd made while she waited for Margaret to arrive.

"Is everything okay?"

Molly opened her mouth to speak but nothing came out except a whimper. Pastor Mike got up and walked around the desk. He led her to the small sofa and they sat together, his arm around her.

"Come on, talk to me. Whatever it is, it can't be that bad, huh?" He rubbed her back.

Molly leaned against him. He slid his hands down her arms until he was holding her hands in his. He ran his thumb over her ring, pressing it into her skin. Molly sniffed, and felt her breathing quicken. Not because she was upset, but because something had shifted in the air between them. His fingers played with the cuff of her plaid shirt.

"Why do you wear all these clothes when you have such a nice figure, huh?" He lifted the edge of her sleeve.

Part of Molly wanted to pull her arm away. Another part of her hoped he'd see everything. She remained motionless. His thumb moved slowly up her bare skin lifting the fabric until he came to a red line marking the inside of her arm.

"What's this?" he murmured.

Molly waited as he unbuttoned her cuff and pushed her sleeve up to her elbow, one hand still holding hers. They stared at the red lines criss-crossing her arm. A couple were still spotting blood. Molly lifted her gaze and looked at him defiantly. Waiting for him to call her a freak. Reject her.

"Let's get this cleaned up." He stood up and got the first aid box from a shelf and clicked it open. He kneeled on the floor in front of her and rubbed antiseptic on her arm and then a soothing cream. "How about your other arm?"

Molly nodded and he unbuttoned her other sleeve and applied the same treatment. "Best to just give these air, let them heal. Are there any more?"

Molly hesitated.

"Where?"

Molly pointed at her thighs. Pastor Mike looked up at her. "Stand up," he instructed softly.

Molly stood, not sure if her legs would hold her. "You're not … going to tell anyone, are you?" Molly whispered.

Pastor Mike unbuttoned her jeans and pulled the zip down. "Don't worry." He tugged at her jeans. "It's our secret," he breathed.

May
2008

"Trust ye not in a friend, put ye not confidence in a guide: keep the doors of thy mouth from her that lieth in thy bosom."

MICAH 7:5

THIRTY-TWO

Lauren chewed her cornflakes cereal and watched her dad struggling with the coffee machine. Her mom was in the bath, and he had no idea how to put the filter in or fill it up with water. She narrowed her eyes. So he could run a church, but couldn't even make a cup of coffee. He acted like the ideal father and husband, but sat at his desk looking at pornography.

Lauren spent a lot of time observing her dad and considering options lately. She could print out his search history and mail it to the church secretary or associate pastor, but then her dad would know Lauren had accessed the computer in his study. She could show her mom, but then her mom would be upset and embarrassed. Her mom had probably never seen images like that in her life. She probably didn't even know they existed in the world. If Adam was a little older, she might confide in him. But he was still young, and innocent. She had started to tell Tiffany a couple of days ago, but then Tiffany announced she was definitely keeping the baby and asked Lauren to be her birth partner because she didn't want Jason to be there. Lauren had almost burst out laughing for some reason. She had agreed, even though being around when someone gave birth sounded gross. By the time the baby arrived, Tiffany would probably be back with Jason anyway and he could do it.

Lauren had thought about telling Ms. Cox, the guidance counselor. But tell her what? Maybe lots of people looked at this stuff. There seemed to be loads of webpages, so maybe *she* was the one who was disturbed, thinking that her dad was weird. And who would Ms. Cox tell – her mom? Or the police? And if her dad was arrested, and lost his job, then what? Lauren's mom had never worked. She'd be raising her brothers, plus the baby, on her own. Lauren would have to get a job and help out instead of going to college. It would be Lauren's fault her dad went to prison. He might not even get arrested. Maybe it would just be a fine or something. When Lauren considered all the options, none of which were truly viable, it made her head hurt.

Thank God for the pills she was taking. She needed two just to fall asleep at night. If she tried to go to bed without them, she had hallucinations. She would hear hissing in her ear, feel cold, scaly snakes sliding over her skin. It was like a huge boa constrictor had curled itself around her body, crushing her, and she would jolt up, sweating. When she did fall asleep, her dreams were so vivid, colliding with the pictures her mind created when she read the books, and the images that she had seen on her dad's computer, she couldn't tell what she had read, or seen or dreamed.

Lauren had even, a couple of times, had a small flash of – what?

She knew that her dad used to come into her room in the evenings to say prayers before bed because her mom told her. But she couldn't actually remember it happening. Tiffany had so many happy memories of her dad and Lauren didn't have any. Good or bad. She just couldn't recall anything at all about him from when she was younger.

Looking at her dad now, unable to do the most simple

task, the pill she'd taken thirty minutes ago kicking in, Lauren wondered why she had ever found him so terrifying. He had a secret porn collection and couldn't even make a coffee. Her dad sighed with frustration as he tried to figure out where to pour the water in. He wouldn't ask for help. He never asked for help. It was pathetic really. Lauren was glad he couldn't drink his coffee. Served him right for treating his wife like a slave. She smiled to herself.

"Lauren?"

She jumped as Adam patted her arm.

"Are you okay?" he whispered.

"Mm-hmm. Yep." She nodded at him and went back to staring at her dad.

Her mom shuffled into the kitchen rubbing her back. "I think the bath helped. I'm sorry, honey. I should have set that up for you." She waddled over to the counter and took over, lifting the lid of the reservoir and pouring water in.

"That would have been good. Set me back about twenty minutes."

"I'm so sorry. I'll bring it to your study. And make you some toast. Okay?"

"Mom, you should be resting."

Her dad gave Lauren a look that could kill as he walked out of the kitchen.

"I've rested. I'm fine now, Lauren." She flapped her arms around. "Now, have you all had enough? Do you want some french toast?"

"Thanks, Mom." Adam finished off his cereal.

Lauren didn't pray any more but if she did she would ask God to ensure she never ended up like her mother – a maid and baby machine to a perverted man that didn't appreciate her.

When the family was eating dinner that evening, Lauren's mom cleared her throat. "We have something special to tell you guys."

Lauren and Adam looked at each other. At least her mom couldn't announce being pregnant again.

"I had another scan yesterday, and the baby is healthy and well. And," she paused, "you're going to have a sister. We're having a little girl."

"Yuck." Michael said. "Girls are gross."

Adam nodded. "That's – nice."

Lauren curved her lips. "That's great, Mom."

"You've been waiting years for this, Lauren, remember?" Her mom laughed and started talking about how Lauren used to pretend her dolls were her little sisters. Lauren pushed her food around her plate until she saw her dad glaring at her. She started to eat, although she'd completely lost her appetite.

When she went to bed that night there were only three pills left. How had she gone through so many? She couldn't remember how many were left in Mrs. Vanderkamp's drawer. She sent Tiffany a text message, arranging to go over to her house the next day. Lauren fell asleep, wondering what her baby sister would be like.

"Oh my God. Lauren, wake up!"

Lauren blinked in the bright overhead light. Her mom was sitting on her bed, gripping her shoulders. Michael was standing in the middle of the room crying. Adam had his arms around him and was looking at Lauren with wide eyes. Her dad was standing in the doorway.

"What's happening?"

Her mom wiped her forehead. "You're all sweaty. You must be sick."

"Boys. Go to bed. Now," her father commanded.

"What's going on?" Lauren squinted.

The boys shuffled out of the room, Adam steering Michael by the shoulders. Her dad followed them.

"You must have been having a bad dream. My goodness. I don't know what's going on this evening. Michael had a nightmare. He said he tried to get in bed with you but then you started yelling and hit him and scared him even more."

"What?"

"Poor thing was petrified. He started screaming and woke us up." Her mom picked at her fingernails. "You know what your father's like before a sermon. He needs to get up in about four hours. Oh, dear. This is so unfortunate."

"Oh my gosh. Mom, I'm so sorry." Lauren rubbed her eyes. She couldn't remember anything.

"It's not your fault, don't be silly. Maybe you're both coming down with something. Or it was that lasagne we had for dinner. Let me go check on Michael and then I'll come back to you, okay?"

Lauren nodded, tired and confused. Her mom heaved herself off the bed and switched off the overhead light as she left the room. Lauren shivered. Her skin was cold and clammy. She tried to remember what happened. She vaguely remembered having her nightmare with the snake, feeling like it was really there.

Her mom came back into her room, carrying a glass of water. "I'm making Michael some warm milk. Do you want any?"

"No, thanks. I'm sorry. Tell him I'm really sorry."

"He knows, sweetie. It's fine. Shall I leave the door

open?"

"No, close it please."

Her mom shut the door softly. Lauren reached for the bottle and took the last two pills. As she slipped into sleep, she heard a hissing whisper in her ear and felt a hand slither across her torso. She jerked awake with a gasp and sat up, breathing heavily.

It wasn't a dream she kept having. It was a memory.

The hand was her dad's. And the hissing was his voice whispering "this is our secret."

Lauren buried her face in her pillow and muffled a scream, her heart thudding. Her baby sister would never be safe. She would have to do something.

THIRTY-THREE

Jason and Calum were playing one-on-one on Calum's driveway, using the basketball net above the garage. Their shirts were stuck to their backs and sweat ran down their faces. With two weeks of school left, they had no homework this evening and Calum was in a jovial mood, looking forward to the summer ahead of him. Jason tried not to think of the empty days and sleepless nights laying in wait for him. Tiffany would have the baby in a month, and he had no idea what he was supposed to do before he left for college – visit every week? Or every day? Stay for an hour? Or a few hours and help out? Babysit, while she went out? Jason still hoped she'd change her mind again and go for adoption. He'd contacted his college to see if he could arrive early but the dorms wouldn't be open so he was stuck here. He hated summers. No schedules, no focus, nothing. He'd applied for a job in a department store at the mall but they weren't going to give him many hours so he was thinking about taking a second job. He just had to get through the next twelve weeks and then he'd be in another state, anonymous.

Calum threw the ball to Jason. "So, you and little T together? Or broken up again? Cause I can't keep up."

Jason grinned ruefully and bounced the ball a few times. "Yeah, I know. We're, well. It's kind of complicated. And she's not so little any more." Jason aimed at the net. It swished through without touching the rim. Was Calum thinking the same thing as him? He could have just done that at the semi-finals – it was so simple.

Calum jogged to catch the ball, did a layup and passed the ball back to Jason. It was about the size of Tiffany's bump. It was weird to think there was a tiny person inside her. He had rested his hand on her stomach and felt it kicking, like a little alien creature trying to break out. She'd done a pregnancy photoshoot, half naked, for her newly created Myspace page and posted the photos on Facebook as well. The baby hadn't even arrived, and she'd already said she wanted a photo of him shirtless, holding the baby in his arms like the famous poster of the male model and baby. Jason didn't understand her obsession with putting photos and intimate details of her life out there for strangers to look at. She had random people scrutinizing her webpages, asking when the baby was due, commenting how beautiful she looked. And more bizarrely, she interacted with them all – answering their questions and posting smiley faces and hearts in response.

They could never be together as a couple. Jason would send her money and make sure she and the baby were looked after, but he just couldn't be a part of their lives in the way Tiffany wanted.

"We're doing this birthing class together." He passed the ball back to Calum. "It's ... weird. We're the youngest people there."

"I'd hope so. Any younger would be disturbing. So you're going to watch the baby come out of her –" Calum aimed for the net and missed. "Urgh. It's putting me off my game."

Jason shrugged. "Of course I'll be there."

"Do the crime, do the time, huh?"

"Don't be a dick, man."

"You want to grab some pizza?"

Jason caught the ball and held it under his arm. "I have to go. Tiff and I are ... practicing breathing stuff. For the birth."

"You're a terrible liar."

"Huh?"

"So you're telling me if I drive past Tiffany's house in thirty minutes I'm going to see your car parked outside?"

"Yes." Jason bounced the ball a few times. "Well, no. We might go out."

"What is this thing you do on a Tuesday?" Calum pulled up his t-shirt to wipe his face. "It's always a Tuesday. Every month. You make stuff up about seeing Tiffany, doing something with your mom. You don't have to tell me what it is, if it's some private thing. Whatever, man. But don't lie to me."

"I'm not lying." Jason threw the ball at him, hard.

Calum caught the ball. "Bullshit."

"What does it matter what I'm doing?"

"You've been lying to me all year. That matters. And you're in this weird on-off thing with the girl you got pregnant. *That* matters. I'm saying *man up*." He slammed the ball down and caught it. "I don't know what's going on with you, but you need to figure your life out. You really like that girl. I thought you and T were in it for the long haul. But when she needs you the most, you bail." He did a layup, caught the rebound and tucked the ball under his arm.

Jason looked up to avoid Calum's gaze. A single cloud drifted across the vast blue sky. What would Calum say if he knew the truth? He already thought Jason was an asshole but if he knew everything, he'd never speak to Jason again.

Jason shook his head. "What is your deal? You're being paranoid."

"And you're being an asshole." Calum turned and headed into the house, slamming the door.

Maybe it was better this way. Jason was going to move, change his identity again – hopefully for the final time. He wouldn't be able to stay in touch with Calum and Tiffany anyway.

On the drive to Dr. Schaffer's office Jason counted sixteen gray cars, twenty-four black, twenty-three white and lost track of the other ones.

Dr. Schaffer smiled. "How is Tiffany?"

"Big."

"Keeping the baby?"

"Yep."

"And how are you?"

"Everyone thinks I'm an asshole. So, you know. Fine."

"What makes you think people think that?"

"Because it's true." Jason spoke loudly to cover the ringing noise.

Dr. Schaffer knitted his eyebrows. "I'm concerned about your mood. And you have a pattern of your symptoms getting more severe in the summer."

Jason studied the carpet. A small fleck of dirt sullied a few tufts. Had he brought that in with him? Did he forget to wipe his shoes on the mat?

"We also need to put a plan in place for you at college. Have you disclosed your diagnosis to them?"

Jason shook his head.

"Your mom said they have an excellent counseling service for students. Get in touch with them, and I'll transfer your files over. Of course, you can still come and see me during vacation times.

"Don't worry about transferring the files. I don't think I need it."

Dr. Schaffer continued as though Jason hadn't spoken. "I also want you to see a cognitive behavioral therapist over the summer, to support you in coming up with coping strategies and symptom management. You can see the same one as before, but if you want someone else, I've got a list of names."

"No, it's okay." He jiggled his leg. "Honestly, I'm better now."

"We need to ensure you have a plan in place, and that you attend regular appointments at college." Dr. Schaffer laid down his pen. "It's nothing to be ashamed of and the appointments will be completely confidential."

Jason sat on his hands to stop himself from taking a Kleenex and scrubbing the dirt off the carpet.

"Jason. You don't seem to understand. This isn't optional. You have a condition that requires ongoing treatment."

"I don't want to go to college and have it be like this."

"Be like what?"

"I don't want to be the weird kid that has to lie about what I'm doing every time I go for an appointment." Jason wrapped his arms around himself. "And – and every time I see my therapist on campus they're going to look at me, and, and –" his voice caught in a sob "they're going to know what I did."

"And what did you do?" Dr. Schaffer asked softly.

"I killed my sister," Jason wept. "I killed my little

sister and I ruined my parents' lives."

Jason had spent so long pretending he couldn't remember and never talking about it, that there were fleeting moments he put what he'd done out of his mind. But at some point, every single day since he was eight years old, he would remember. And on long, hot, empty summer days, the memory nagged at him constantly, until he succumbed to counting every step he took, every line on a page, every car that passed. He had to keep going until he reached a calm, soothing one hundred. Or one thousand. On the worst days, the memory would hit him viscerally, making him gasp and sink to his knees. On those days, nothing helped. He'd curl up in bed and pretend to have a migraine. He would lay in the dark, reliving the moment over and over and over again as his eight-year-old self.

It had been too hot to play outside. His best friend had been away at camp so Jason had been stuck with his little sister. Playing hide and seek in the cool air conditioning of the house had been enjoyable for both of them and there hadn't been any arguments or tears so far. Jasmine had been good at finding small hiding places but her giggles had given her away. Jason had started drawing out his searches, acting as though he was finding it increasingly difficult to find her, otherwise he'd end up stuck hiding for ages, feeling his legs stiffening and back aching while Jasmine wandered around, genuinely baffled as to where he could be. He'd have to reveal himself with a cough or a sniff and she'd be thrilled at her discovery.

Jason had known Jasmine was hiding in the cabinet under the sink in his parents' master bathroom when he had seen the door bounce shut as he had walked in.

He had wondered how long she could stay curled up amongst old mouthwash and bleach, her pigtails squashed down and her dress covered in dust.

"Not in here, I guess!" he had announced, and had left his parents' bedroom.

He had been halfway down the stairs when he had decided to open the cabinet door and pretend to miss her. He had grinned, imagining her stifled laughs. He had walked back into the bathroom and had been startled to see Jasmine standing in front of the sink.

"Look what I found." She had held out a dark, shiny object in both hands. "It's *heavy*," she had warned as she handed it to him.

And thus the defining juncture of his life happened.

How could any psychiatrist think a person could forget a moment like that? All his decisions, all his mistakes – each one its own, irreversible blunder – that had ruined his family's lives. Of *course* he couldn't forget.

First mistake: Making the game last longer, instead of just opening the door and saying "Found you!" to a giggling Jasmine when he walked into the bathroom. Which had left enough time for his sister to get bored and start running her small fingers over each object in the cabinet.

Second mistake: To grab the gun away from her in a burst of excitement, and pretend to shoot her. "Bang, bang!" he'd shouted, and pulled the trigger. "You're dead!"

Third mistake: He'd laughed. The force of the recoil had made him stumble backwards but he had assumed Jasmine was pretending when she dropped to the floor. He had been so busy admiring her acting skills – her small wheezing breaths! – he hadn't seen the blood creeping out the back of her dress. She had lay staring at the ceiling, mouth partly open, as though she was about to burst out giggling. Jasmine had always been so dramatic, flinging herself onto her bed in tears after an argument or throwing her arms around their mom when she baked chocolate chip cookies ("You're the best mommy in the world. I love you so much!"). When Jason had seen her fall backwards and collapse with a small wheeze, he had thought she was just being … dramatic.

He hadn't tried to stop the bleeding.

He hadn't held her, while she must have been in excruciating pain, and told her how much he loved having her around no matter how much she drove him crazy sometimes.

He hadn't said he was sorry for wiping out her entire, young life and everything she could have become, in one indelible, moronic moment.

He had simply stood there, wondering why his ears were ringing, waiting for her to sit back up and chuckle.

So when his mom had come running into the bathroom, followed by Winston barking hysterically, and discovered her five-year-old daughter dying on the floor, she had found her son standing over her, doing nothing – *nothing* – to help her. Just watching her die and *laughing*.

Jason waited for Dr. Schaffer to end the appointment early, and tell him that he didn't need to come any more. That their work was finished. Or that Dr. Schaffer didn't work with murderers.

"And you've not told anyone else you remember?" Dr. Schaffer asked.

Jason shook his head. "I just want to forget about it. Please don't tell my mom."

"I won't tell your mother, that's your decision. But this is an important step forward, Jason. Now we can get down to work, and I can refer you for better support. There's EMDR, which is effective with healing traumatic childhood memories and there's also trauma-focused talk therapy…" Dr. Schaffer went on listing options and scribbling notes in Jason's file.

But Jason knew Dr. Schaffer was lying. Nothing would help him.

It didn't matter what therapy there was. Or how often Jason was on the honor roll, or how many points he scored on the basketball court. It didn't matter whether he pretended he couldn't remember anything before the age of nine. And it didn't make any difference how often he moved towns, changed his name, and tried to start over.

Jason couldn't fool himself.

He would always be a fuckup, and there was nothing he could do about it.

THIRTY-FOUR

Molly ignored her mom sitting at the kitchen table and tore open the envelope with her name on it. A welcome pack spilled out with fliers about welcome week activities, accommodation, and dining hall options. Her mom was opening up another large envelope. Jesus. Even Molly's mail wasn't private any more. God, she couldn't wait to leave.

"Is that for me?"

"No, it's for me, hon."

"Are you sure? It looks like college stuff."

Her mom took a breath. "Yes. It is college stuff."

"So then, it's for me."

"No, it's not." Her mom pulled out the stack of pages, read the first one and smiled. "I got accepted. I'm starting college as well, in the fall."

"What?"

"I applied to the local community college and I'm in."

"Okkaaayyy." Molly rubbed her arms.

Her mom turned to the next page and studied it for a moment. "Oh, thank you, Lord." She held up the paper and looked at Molly. "They're offering me a great financial aid package. I may not even need to take out a loan. Wow. Oh, hon, God is good. We'll both be in college together!"

"Right. Whatever." Molly's stomach growled. She turned to the sink to fill up a glass of water.

"You know, how about a 'congratulations'? That

would be nice."

"Okay, fine. *Congratulations*. And try not to fuck it up this time."

"Excuse me?"

Molly turned to her. "I said, try not to fuck it up. Maybe a little less partying this time around."

"Don't you dare speak to me like that! And watch your language." Her mom had two bright pink spots on her cheeks. "I studied my ass off and worked hard. I was a really good student."

"Really good at sleeping around too, I guess." Molly muttered.

"You have got to let this go."

Molly shook her head in disbelief.

"I know who your father is, okay?"

"Then tell me."

Her mom let out a huff of air and pressed her lips together.

Molly exploded. "How come *you* get to decide whether I know my dad or not? Okay, so maybe he was an asshole but so what? People change. What if he's nicer now? I mean, Jason is being horrible to Tiffany right now, but she's still putting his name on the birth certificate. And whoever my dad is, he deserves to know his daughter. And I deserve to have a dad. And it's *your fault* I don't! Because you were sleeping around all over the place. And *you don't know!*"

"Molly. For the last time." Her mom spoke through gritted teeth. "I know who your dad is and I chose not to put his name on the birth certificate. You have *got* to get over this."

"I DON'T BELIEVE YOU. STOP LYING!" Molly smashed her glass on the floor.

Her mom stood up. "You want to know the truth?

I didn't put his name on your birth certificate because I didn't want a rapist to have any rights to you."

"What?"

"I was raped when I was nineteen, and I got pregnant. I was at a party, and I drank too much. I felt sick and this guy said he'd look after me and –" She shook her head, her voice choked. "It doesn't matter now." A tear rolled down her cheek and dropped onto her t-shirt. "The point is, I found out that rapists have parental rights and there was no way I was ever going to let that man have anything to do with you. So I left the father's name blank. Okay?" Her fists were clenched and she was shaking.

Molly felt like she'd been hit by a car.

Her mom took a breath and continued. "I went back home and my mother told me to get rid of the baby. But I knew no matter what happened, I wanted to keep you. So I had to leave college, otherwise the guy who did it would see I was pregnant. And I had to leave home because my mom kicked me out for keeping you. But some people in the church offered to help out, and I decided that you and I were going to just work it out together." She raised her chin defiantly and wiped her eyes. "And that's the reason there's no name on the birth certificate."

"So, so you're saying – I'm *worse* than a mistake?"

"What? No, honey, no." She stepped towards Molly and trod in water and shards of glass.

"Don't touch me." Molly reared back against the sink.

"I didn't mean to tell you like this, but –"

"You've lied to me my whole life. I'm ... I never should have happened. Grandma was right. You should have got rid of me."

"No! Honey, you're the best thing that —"

Molly stepped across the glass and went into the living room. She picked up the phone and called Margaret's number. She cleared her throat. "Hi, Margaret. I was wondering, can you do me a huge favor? I've got to help out at the church, it's urgent, and my mom's stuck at work. Can you give me a ride?"

Her mom followed. "Molly, what are you doing? Stay here, let's talk about this. Please."

Molly ignored her and spoke into the phone. "Great, I'll see you soon." She hung up and turned to her mom. "Leave. Me. Alone."

"But, what are you even doing? What are you going to do at the church?"

"Helping with the accounts," Molly lied.

"Shouldn't there be an accountant who does that?"

"That's the whole fricking point. I'm helping prepare things for the accountant." Molly was instantly annoyed at how long her sentence was. "And you know what? It's none of your business what I do. Not anymore."

Molly went outside and sat on the porch step, waiting for Margaret to arrive. The sun blazed down, making her sweat in her black pants and long sleeved shirt. Her mom peered anxiously out the window at her until Margaret's car pulled up, but left her alone.

Molly felt the need to be with Mike like an addict craving a drug. He looked at her like she was the most important person in the world when they were together, not a mistake that should never even have existed. He was the one person she could count on to make her feel better, help her piece together an understanding of the bomb that had just exploded.

Molly made small talk with Margaret, plastering a smile on her face for the duration of the journey. When she stepped out of the car she was relieved to see Mike's car in its usual place and the secretary's car gone.

Molly went into the bathroom first, wiping the sweat from her face and splashing water under her arms. She studied her face in the mirror. Half her DNA came from her father. So he was the reason her skin burned in the sun, instead of turning a deep tan like her mom's. Did her father have the exact shade of pale skin as hers? Or even lighter?

Was his hair flat and greasy?

Did he have problems with his weight?

Was his complexion spotted with acne?

Did her mom see a rapist every time she looked at Molly?

Molly pulled a pair of scissors out of her bookbag and rolled up her sleeve. She dug the blade into her arm and tore at her disgusting, repulsive skin.

Why had her mom let that happen to her? She dragged the blade across her arm again.

Why hadn't she been more careful? Another tear on her skin.

Why hadn't she taken her grandmother's advice, just gotten rid of Molly when she had the chance? She could have finished her degree, got a good job, and be living a totally different life. She was so stupid. So, so dumb.

Molly ripped at her arm until all she could feel and think about was the searing pain. She stopped crying and her breathing returned to normal. She wiped the scissors with a paper towel, put them back in her bag and pulled down her sleeve. She pulled open the door, wincing as her bag hit her arm, and walked to the church office, an oasis of comfort in an awful day.

Thirty minutes later Mike pulled up Molly's panties and patted her bottom.

Molly took a deep breath. "I love you."

Mike didn't hear her and turned towards the desk.

"I –" Molly fumbled with the zip and button on her jeans. "When I go to college, how will we see each other?"

Mike picked up his cell phone and pressed buttons. "Hmm?"

"I said, when I go to college. How will it work?"

"How will what work?" He kept his attention focused on the phone screen.

"This. Us." Molly waved a hand at the church office, the sofa they spent so much time on.

"What?" Mike raised his head and looked at her.

"Well, I mean ... you know. I'll be in Massachusetts but I'll come back as much as I can." Molly was only planning on coming back to see him. She could stay in a motel nearby. Or perhaps even sleep in the office, on the sofa.

"Don't be silly." He walked to the other side of the desk and sat on the office chair.

"What?"

"Don't make this into something it isn't." He turned on the computer monitor.

"What do you mean?" Molly stood in front of him.

Mike sighed loudly. "Nothing will happen. There isn't an 'us'".

"But ..." Molly twisted her ring around her finger.

"You had a tough time. I gave you what you wanted." He studied the screen.

Molly opened her mouth and closed it. The things they did – it was what *he* wanted, surely? She wasn't even sure she enjoyed it. "But, I thought, I thought you –" She changed tack. "You're the first person I …. I broke the purity pledge for you."

Mike leaned back in his chair and looked at her. "Now you're being foolish. You haven't broken the purity pledge. I thought you were smarter than this."

"But we –"

"We what? We haven't had sex." He spoke like he was explaining a story to a child at Sunday School. "Molly, let's remember. You came into my office, throwing yourself at me."

Molly's face flushed with heat.

"I gave you some comfort when you were going through a tough time. You're graduating next month, you're valedictorian. You've got a bright future ahead. Just see it for what it was, hm?"

"I –"

The office phone rang and Mike picked it up. "Hello, Pastor Mike Davis here." There was a pause. "Oh, yes. Certainly, now's a great time. One moment, please." He covered the telephone speaker with his hand and looked at Molly. "Is there anything else?"

Molly stared at him mutely.

"Close the door on your way out." Mike turned away and spoke into the phone. "Go ahead."

Molly picked up her bookbag and shut the door quietly behind her. She stood in the hallway and heard the faint sound of his voice and then a chuckle of laughter.

Molly had replayed the scene over and over in her head for days, and every time she wanted to die. She rubbed her nail into a scratch on the desk, waiting for Ms. Nelson to hand back the final essay project.

"Here you go." Ms. Nelson smiled sympathetically as she handed Molly a slim folder.

Molly flipped it open and saw a 'B'. "This isn't mi–" Molly stopped. Her name was at the top of the title page.

She studied it. Her name and essay title. And a large, red B.

Ms. Nelson must have made an error, put someone else's mark at the top of her paper. Molly flipped to the final page where the teacher had made handwritten comments:

While good, this is not to your usual standard. Unfortunately, you also failed to fully answer the question posed and did not list two of the sources you cited in your references.

Molly flipped through her folder back to the original assignment. She read the assignment question again. She read her concluding paragraph. Damn it. Ms. Nelson was right. She hadn't properly answered the question. The paper didn't merit an A. It didn't even warrant a B. Ms. Nelson probably just felt sorry for her.

She'd received a B on the quiz last week as well, when she'd stupidly studied the wrong chapter. Molly did some calculations. The essay was 40% of the final grade. She'd received a B on the test worth 20% last week. No matter what she did now, she couldn't possibly get an A or keep her 4.0 GPA.

Molly glanced over at Ernie Chan. If he had received an A, and other than his single A- he always received As, then that was it. He would be valedictorian, and Molly wouldn't. She clutched at her arms, thinking about the scissors in her bag.

Molly didn't have her perfect GPA. She didn't have Pastor Mike. She didn't have proper parents. She had nothing.

And that was as it should be, really. Because she shouldn't have ever existed anyway.

June
2008

"And if thy hand offend thee, cut it off: it is better for thee to enter into life maimed, than having two hands to go into hell, into the fire that never shall be quenched:"

MARK 9:43

THIRTY-FIVE

Lauren pulled into Molly's driveway, white, pink and blue balloons bobbing around in the back seat, and beeped the horn. Molly opened the door, yelled something to whoever was in the house, and slammed it behind her. She was carrying a large shopping bag and inexplicably wearing a long black dress with spaghetti straps over a long-sleeved black t-shirt. It wasn't hot yet, but the temperature was forecast to be in the 90s by noon. Lauren was wearing a flowered summer dress with short sleeves.

"Hi," Molly got in the car and shoved the bag at her feet.

"You can put that in the back if you want."

"No, it's okay. I don't want to pop any of the balloons."

Lauren backed out of the driveway.

"Careful!" Molly shouted.

"What?" Lauren braked.

"You nearly hit the mailbox."

"Sorry." Maybe the second pill had been a mistake. Lauren could probably drive from her house to Tiffany's with her eyes closed, she'd done it so many times, but she'd never been to Molly's house before. The driveway was narrow and the houses were crowded closer together.

"What's in the bag?" she asked as she set off again to distract Molly from scrutinizing her driving.

"Some decorations for brunch, and my robe and

stuff."

"Aren't you going back home before the ceremony?"

"No."

Thank God Lauren wouldn't have to give her a ride home. The day was turning out better than she could have planned. Lauren turned on the radio to fill the silence. She and Molly had never spent any time together – it seemed like when one of them was with Tiffany, the other wasn't.

Lauren glanced at Molly's left hand. Molly still wore her purity ring, too. What did it mean to her? Was she really planning to wait? Probably. Molly was salutatorian, attended church every week and volunteered as well. She was perfect. Molly didn't know how lucky she was, that it was just her and her mom at home. No one else to worry about.

What would Molly think if she knew the truth about Lauren's father? If Lauren showed her what she'd seen on her dad's computer?

"Are your parents coming today?" Molly asked.

"Of course." The car bumped against a curb as Lauren veered off the road.

"Jesus." Molly clutched the armrest.

"Sorry."

Lauren returned her attention to driving, although it was like watching herself in a movie. She felt detached from everything that she was doing but managed to drive to Tiffany's house without any further incidents.

She parked in the driveway and pulled the balloons out of the back of the car. Molly carried her bag, sweating in the heat, and tapped quietly on the door. Mrs. Vanderkamp opened it, wearing a white linen dress that complemented her slim frame.

"Come in, girls," she said in an exaggerated whisper. "She's still in bed," she pointed at the stairs and put her fingers on her lips. They went into the kitchen which had bowls, flour, and utensils strewn across every surface. "I'm trying to make pancakes, but …" she gestured helplessly.

Lauren looked at the chaos, overcome by a wave of nostalgia. "I can make them," she offered. "I make them for my brothers all the time."

"Oh, would you?" Mrs. Vanderkamp grabbed her and kissed her on the cheek. "You're a doll. Now, let's get the dining room decorated." Mrs. Vanderkamp threw an arm around Molly and guided her into the dining room.

Lauren wiped the countertops down, gathered together the ingredients and found a clean bowl. She mixed the pancake batter and listened to Mrs. Vanderkamp exclaiming over the decorations Molly had made and deciding where to place them. She put the oven on low, and started pouring the batter onto the frying pan, creating perfectly round pancakes. While they cooked and she waited to pile them up in the oven to stay warm, she found fresh berries in the fridge and put them in a bowl. She pulled out orange juice, cranberry juice, sparkling water and glasses. She wanted to make this perfect for her friend. Now it was all going so smoothly, Lauren felt bizarrely calm.

Mrs. Vanderkamp scurried in and gasped. "Look at you! We've been busy too. Come see what we've done." She was like an overexcited child. She went into the dining room and Lauren picked up the juice cartons and followed her.

Banners with small pink pacifiers were hanging from

the ceiling light and stretching to the four corners of the room. Pale blue confetti in the shape of graduation caps was scattered over the table and the pink, white and blue balloons were tied to the backs of the six chairs.

"Wow, this looks great." Lauren felt like she was complimenting her little brothers but Mrs. Vanderkamp looked pleased and Molly managed a small smile. "The pancakes are done. When do you think Tiffany will wake up?"

"Lauren? Is that you?" Tiffany walked into the dining room, squinting in the bright sunlight flooding the room. She wore an oversized t-shirt, glasses and her hair was sticking up.

"Surprise!" Mrs. Vanderkamp shouted.

"Happy graduation day slash baby shower," Molly added.

Tiffany lifted her glasses up to rub her eyes. "What's happening?"

"I didn't know you wear glasses. You look cute." Lauren was overwhelmed with emotion. It was so endearing that Tiffany had hid wearing glasses from her. "And surprise," she remembered to say.

Tiffany looked around the room, taking it in. She burst into tears.

"What's wrong?" Mrs. Vanderkamp put her arm around her. "Did we wake you up?"

"I love it!" Tiffany sobbed and laughed. "It's perfect. Let me get my phone. And put my contact lenses in. And make myself look ready."

"I'll fry up some bacon, sweetie," Mrs. Vanderkamp offered. "Go get yourself ready."

"Did you check with the other guy what he'll be talking about? Otherwise you might say the same stuff." Mrs.

Vanderkamp took another drink of orange juice.

"Um, no. I haven't." Molly was sitting with her elbows on the table, squeezing her upper arms with her hands.

"So in a way, being salutatorian is better! Because you get to give your speech first." Mrs. Vanderkamp looked pleased with herself. "If he repeats anything, then it just sounds like he's copying you."

Molly nodded. "I guess."

Lauren looked at the clock. They'd been waiting forty-five minutes. She should have gone upstairs when Molly and Mrs. Vanderkamp were decorating. The bacon had been put in the oven to keep warm and Mrs. Vanderkamp seemed perfectly happy to sit and wait, sipping at her juice. Lauren was craving another pill, thinking about what lay ahead of her.

"I'll go help her finish up," Lauren stood up.

"Sure, hon. No rush though." Mrs. Vanderkamp nodded.

Lauren ran up the stairs, her heart thudding in her ears. As she passed Tiffany's door, it opened and Tiffany came out. Damn. Lauren had almost made it.

"You're ready?"

"Can you help me do my hair?"

"You look great. Come on, we're hungry."

"This is going on my webpages."

"Okay, okay." Lauren went into Tiffany's room and stood behind the desk chair.

Tiffany lowered herself onto it with a grunt. "Urgh. I feel disgusting today."

"You look beautiful." Lauren stroked her hair and picked up the curling irons that were heating on the dresser. She divided Tiffany's hair into sections and began wrapping it around the metal. Tiffany's hair was soft and smooth in her hands, each curl giving a satisfying bounce as she released it from the grip of the tongs. This was the kind of thing she imagined doing for her baby sister.

"Are you okay?" Tiffany was studying her in the mirror.

Lauren glanced at her. "I'm great."

"Lately you seem –" Tiffany hesitated. "Distracted, I guess?"

"I'm good. Thank you, by the way."

"For what?"

"Being an amazing friend." Lauren blinked back tears.

"Are you sure you're okay?"

"I'm fine. I just wanted to say thank you properly. At the beginning of the year, when I moved here and didn't know anyone, you were a good friend to me. And I just want you to know that I really, really appreciate that." Lauren cleared her throat and fluffed Tiffany's hair. "Okay, all done."

"I'm supposed to be the emotional one with all the hormones." Tiffany reached back and squeezed Lauren's hand. "I can do your hair after brunch?" Tiffany offered. "Do all your makeup and everything?"

"It's okay, I have to get back home and get ready for the ceremony and stuff. But, you could do Molly's?"

"Good idea. I'll make sure she looks amazing for her speech." Tiffany nodded and heaved herself out of the chair. She clasped Lauren's hand as they walked downstairs and Lauren felt giddy at the thought of confiding in her, telling Tiffany what she was about to do. But it was selfish. Tiffany had enough to think about, and Lauren couldn't let anyone know in case someone tried to stop her. No matter what, Lauren needed to see things through to the end.

THIRTY-SIX

"How on earth can it take someone as pretty as Tiffany so incredibly long to get ready?" Mrs. Vanderkamp shook her head in mock incredulity.

Molly smiled politely.

Mike had thought Molly was pretty. The first person other than her mom to say it. The only other person to say it. Ever. *I hope you know how beautiful you are*, he'd said, running his fingers over the cuts and scars on her thighs during those astounding, delicious weeks she'd had with him. And in those moments, it hadn't mattered that Molly didn't know her dad, or that she was fat, or that she suspected Tiffany was just friends with her because she did her homework for her. Molly had felt, for the first time since she could remember, like she mattered. She swallowed and picked at a scab through her sleeve.

You're a silly teenager ... You threw yourself at me.

His words didn't stop echoing in her head.

How could she have thought that someone like him would ever be interested in someone like her? The shame of it filled her very being. It followed her around, stalking her when she was writing notes in class, taking a customer's order, listening to Tiffany blathering on about the baby. Any kind of infinitesimal abatement – just a few milliseconds – at any point over the last month would have been something to cling onto. To think that maybe, at some point, she might feel better. But Molly felt the same as she had since her mom had told her the truth – she shouldn't be here.

The logistical complications associated with ending one's life were, as it turned out, remarkably challenging. Personal and web-based research brought up impediments to every method Molly considered. An overdose required complete control over her gag reflex which, after months of throwing up, was nonexistent. The slitting of wrists required a significant amount of time alone in the bath and – as it turned out when she finally had the house to herself for a few hours – the will-power to cut her veins more deeply than she could manage. Molly had read that hanging took longer than expected and included involuntary defecation, a protruding tongue and a slow asphyxiation. It sounded deeply disturbing. Besides, without the technical knowledge to get the knot right, it wouldn't even work. She couldn't bear the thought of anyone finding her like that (although that didn't make any sense, because she wouldn't even know). She had no car to drive off a bridge or into a tree and she'd probably chicken out of that anyway. Molly had only one viable option and by the time she figured it out, it was almost too late. She was such a fucking idiot.

Today was the first day Molly had woken up looking forward to the future. As long as she didn't think of Mike, it wasn't too bad. In a few hours she'd have peace. A lovely, blank unconsciousness. She imagined Tiffany later today. What she might put on her Myspace and Facebook pages. It would, actually, be the best gift Molly could give her – something truly dramatic to write about. And while there was absolutely no way she could face seeing Mike at graduation today it was satisfying to know he'd be there when it happened. Perhaps he'd even see it for himself. Then he'd realize it wasn't just a stupid crush. Then he'd be sorry.

Tiffany and Lauren walked into the dining room. Tiffany's face was framed by soft curls and she was wearing a short, pale blue maternity shift dress that contrasted with her tanned skin.

Mrs. Vanderkamp clapped her hands. "I can't believe my baby is graduating. And having a baby!"

Molly couldn't believe how weird the Vanderkamps were. She and Lauren went into the kitchen and brought back the food. Tiffany took photos of the table, the decorations and balloons. She took a few selfies and then took a photo of the pancakes when they were laid out on the table.

"Can you take some of me?" Tiffany handed her phone to Lauren. "Make sure you get the decorations in."

"Who are these for, again?" Molly watched Lauren take photos of Tiffany standing, sitting, and pretending to eat.

"You sound like Jason. They're for Myspace and Facebook." Tiffany said, finally picking up a fork to eat.

"Right." Molly chewed small pieces of the pancakes slowly. Even though it didn't matter how much she ate any more, her stomach was churning.

"You know what would look amazing with that dress?" Lauren asked. "Those dangly earrings with the little hearts. Don't you think, Molly?"

"Um, sure." Like earrings mattered.

"I'll get them." Lauren stood up.

"Oh, I thought these looked good. You know, simple." Tiffany touched the small pearls at her lobes.

"They do, totally. I was just thinking, those other

ones will look … even more amazing. I'll get them, let's see."

"No, it's okay, I don't think –"

Lauren left the dining room.

"Aww. Everyone is being so sweet." Tiffany picked up a piece of bacon. "You know what? Maybe I should go all out. I was going more for the natural look. But maybe I should be doing the smokey eye look."

Mrs. Vanderkamp nodded and topped up her orange juice. "Maybe, hon."

Tiffany turned to Molly. "Can you ask Lauren to bring down my makeup as well?"

"Sure." Molly walked through the kitchen, into the hallway and up the stairs into Tiffany's room. But Lauren wasn't there. Molly took her last look around Tiffany's room, wondering for the millionth time how her life might have been different if she'd been adopted. If she'd grown up in a huge house with an enormous bedroom with fairy lights, a queen-sized bed and a wardrobe full of designer clothes. And parents that really cared about her. That had wanted her, *chosen* her.

Molly went back into the hall and collided with Lauren who was coming from Mrs. Vanderkamp's room. Lauren gave a yelp of surprise and dropped her bookbag. Something slipped out and thudded onto the carpet.

"God. You scared me." Lauren bent down and picked it up, shoving it into her bag.

"What the hell?"

Lauren zipped her bag closed and looked at her. "Don't say anything. Please."

"Is that a gun?"

"No. I mean, yes, but it isn't mine. I –"

Lauren glanced over the banister and pushed Molly into Tiffany's room. She closed the door and leaned towards her. "Tiffany asked me to take it out of the house for her. It's her mom's," she whispered.

"What? Why?"

"She, she said her mom's been depressed. She's worried about her. That she might, you know – do something."

Molly thought about Mrs. Vanderkamp chattering happily away, excited about her grandchild arriving. "Really? She doesn't seem like the kind of person who would do that."

"Well. You know. The divorce and stuff. Just, don't say anything, okay? Don't say you saw me."

"Okay, sure. Whatever." Goddammit. If only Molly had known about the gun. "What are you going to do with it?"

"I'll keep it safe."

"I can look after it, if you want?"

"No. She asked me. You're not even supposed to know."

"I won't tell anyone, I promise." Lauren clutched her bag closer. Molly gave up. "Anyway, Tiffany wants all her makeup. She asked me to let you know."

Lauren nodded. "Sure, no problem."

She gathered together Tiffany's makeup and Molly picked up her jewelery box. They went downstairs and rejoined Tiffany and her mom at the dining table. Molly felt almost jubilant as she looked at the wall clock above Tiffany's head. In three hours, it would be over.

THIRTY-SEVEN

Jason's dad poured more maple syrup onto his breakfast. "Don't tell Margie." He took a bite of his pancakes and groaned. "God, I forgot how much I miss IHOP."

Jason picked at his food. "So you had a good flight?"

"Yep, it was fine."

They chewed in silence for a minute. It would have been better if his mom had joined them. The conversation was even more stilted than it would have been if she'd been there. Although every time Millie's name came up, Jason thought about Jasmine, which would probably have been the same for his mom. What were his parents going to talk about when they were seated next to each other at the graduation? His mom would probably spend the whole time on her Blackberry anyway.

"So, how are things with you and Tiffany?"

"Um."

"Will I get to meet her later?"

"I don't know."

"I would like to meet the mother of my grandchild."

Jason played with the pancakes. "It's, I mean – we're not really, you know. Talking. So…"

"Son, help me understand what's going on here. Please."

"I'm going to be away at college. So it doesn't make

sense to –"

"But you'll be back during vacations, right? And college is only four years. It may seem like a long time now, but it'll fly by. You need to start building a foundation, being a father. From day one. You don't want to miss those years. And *I* don't want to miss those years, my first grandchild." He took a drink of his coffee. "I'll come visit more. I realize now, I should have been doing that all along. I'm sorry about that."

"Actually, Dad. Um. The thing is, I've been accepted at a college in London. So I'm going to go there."

"What?" His dad's fork clattered onto the plate. "You're moving to London?"

"Yes."

"In *England*?"

"Yes."

"You're abandoning your child, and the mother of your child, to go to England? When there's literally hundreds of colleges here?"

"Dad, I –"

"What does Tiffany have to say about this?"

Jason stared miserably at his half-eaten breakfast.

"Or does she hate you so much she's happy about it?"

"She doesn't know."

"God almighty, Jason!"

The other diners turned to look at them. Jason slouched down in his seat.

"What about your mother? She must have tried to talk you out of this?"

Jason's mom was currently investigating a transfer into the German office of her company.

"Hold on, was this her idea? What is she doing?

She's got you changing your name and now this? It's like she's trying to –" he wiped his face with his napkin and threw it on the table. "I've lost my appetite. We can go when you're finished."

"The ceremony doesn't start for another hour."

"I'll read my book." He signalled for the bill.

Jason was relieved they had driven separately as he drove the short distance to the high school, his dad following him. Jason wondered what he could say to make his dad hate him less but really, there wasn't anything. He had already cost his dad a daughter and a marriage. His dad should have just stayed in California and not even come today.

The parking lot was almost empty and they got spaces near the doors designated as the guest entrance. Jason got out of his car, picked up his gown and cap off the back seat and waited until his dad rolled down the window.

"You coming in?"

"No, I'll read for a while, give Margie a call."

"Okay. Well, I'll see you later."

His dad nodded, jaw clenched, and didn't look at him. Jason walked around the building towards the entrance marked for graduates and sat under a tree in the shade, his robe and cap on his lap. The air was heavy with humidity. He did his breathing exercises and closed his eyes. He smelled the freshly cut grass. He felt the dry ground beneath his fingers. He opened his eyes and looked up at the white clouds – and was hit by the memory of a long-ago picnic. A park somewhere, laying on grass near a lake. Jasmine was laying with her head next to his, and they were both transfixed by the clouds scudding across a bright blue sky. They had giggled as they described the shapes they saw, each one more fantastical than the last. A bear. A unicorn. A troll. They had laughed so much their parents, who had been sitting on a picnic blanket nearby, his mom's head in his dad's lap, had come over to see what was so funny.

"Look, Daddy. A rhinoceros!" Jasmine had yelled. His mom and dad had laid down to see what they saw and caught the giggles as well, until all of them were laughing and shouting out the names of animals, their four heads in the center making a perfect X. It had been a few days before –

Jason rubbed his eyes. Did his dad have all these memories? Or had he made new ones? No wonder his dad was pissed off with him. Jason was incapable of not disappointing people. His parents. Tiffany. Calum. He could never make things right but at least he could try not to ruin anyone else's life. He got up, went into the school, and counted the lockers in the hallway. He walked up and down, up and down, counting, worrying he'd missed one even though he already knew exactly how many lockers there were in the hallway (one hundred twelve). Counting. Over and over, ignoring his classmates in their suits and dresses who passed him. Calum walked in.

Jason stopped. "Hi. Listen, I –"

Calum pushed past him.

As Jason walked down the hallway on his twelfth round, he saw Tiffany and Molly approach through the window of the door. Tiffany was wearing heavy makeup and a short blue dress and was holding her stomach. Molly had both their gowns draped over one arm and their caps in the other, but looked like she was in another world, staring up at the roof of the gymnasium. Molly was dressed all in black and looked different, somehow. Older. He opened the door for them and held it as they walked past. Neither thanked him.

"Hey, Tiff? My dad wants to meet you."

"Well, whatever."

Molly whispered something in her ear and Tiffany paused. She chewed her gum and considered something. "You know what? It's his grandchild, so I guess so."

"Thanks. I know I haven't –"

"Just shut it, Jason. Okay? I want my child to have all the grandparents possible in his or her life to make up for a shitty father. So yes, I will meet your dad."

Jason stopped talking as instructed and they made their way down the hallway, pausing in front of the full-length mirror that had been propped against the wall at the entrance to the gymnasium. Tiffany leaned towards it, removed a fleck of mascara under her eye, and fluffed her curls. She took her gown and cap from Molly and put them on. Molly was just standing there, motionless.

"Are you nervous about your speech?" Jason was so glad he didn't have to be up there, in front of all those people.

"Of course she's not. It'll be perfect, won't it?" Tiffany said. "And doesn't she look gorgeous? Here, let me do this for you." Tiffany took the cap from Molly and pinned it to her hair, Molly squatting slightly so Tiffany could reach. "Now wobble your head around like this, we need to check it won't fall." Tiffany demonstrated, the tassel on her cap swaying.

Molly shook her head a little and her cap stayed in place. "Thanks." She gave Tiffany a hug. "You're a great friend," she said in a choking voice.

Molly was right. And Tiffany would be an amazing mother as well. Why had Jason said all those awful things to her?

"Jeez, Molly. Why is everyone crying today? Come on, we're in the way. Put your gown on and let's graduate!"

The three of them moved to the side as a trail of students filed past, some stopping in front of the mirror. Jason shrugged himself into his gown and balanced his cap on his head. They went into the gymnasium which was filling up with students and their families. Jason saw his parents standing to the side and ignoring each other. His mom was studying the program intently and his dad was looking around at the gymnasium. At least they weren't arguing. A few people were glancing at them curiously. As Jason, Tiffany and Molly approached them he saw someone's mother nodding to herself, as if Jason's coloring made his mom's dark skin next to his dad's pale skin acceptable.

"Hey, Dad. This is Tiffany."

Tiffany held out her hand. "Nice to meet you, Mr. Myers."

"It's Williams. Ben Williams."

Tiffany scrunched her face up. She looked at Jason then back at Jason's dad. "What?"

"Ask her," he tilted his head in the direction of Jason's mom and pursed his lips. "Good to meet you too, maybe we can do lunch while I'm here?"

"Dad. She's about to have a baby, she's kind of busy."

"No, it sounds great. Thank you." Tiffany smiled up at Jason's dad. "Do you all want a family photo?" Tiffany offered. Jason's mom and dad looked at each other. "Come on, your son's graduating."

"Sure."

"Why not."

Jason stood between his parents.

"You're going to have to move closer, I can't get you all in," Tiffany instructed, holding up her phone. His parents shuffled nearer to Jason. It was the closest the three of them had been in years. "And now can you try and look like you're happy to be here?"

Jason forced a smile to his face.

"Say cheese!"

Jason and his parents stood silently among the buzz of the gymnasium. Calum and some of his classmates were watching them. What if someone had overheard his dad saying his last name was Williams? What if they went home, and entered 'Williams family' and 'California' into a search engine? What if –

"Hmm." Tiffany reviewed the photos. "Maybe I should take a few more."

"It's fine."

"I'm sure they're great."

"Let's go to our seats." Jason and his parents talked over each other.

"You're not all smiling at the same time. I'm not sure any of these are very good." Tiffany said. "No offense."

Jason tugged at his cap and looked at his parents. "You should probably sit down, it'll start soon."

"You're right, let's go," his mom shoved his dad away and they headed towards their seats.

"I guess hating photos runs in the family." Tiffany said. "You have a different last name from your dad?"

"It's not a big deal." Jason glanced at Molly standing awkwardly next to her. "I'll explain later. Why don't you sit down, you look ..." Tiffany looked terrible "... tired."

"Like you care. Anyway, I'm looking for Lauren. Have you seen her?"

"No. I'm sure she's around. And I do care, okay?"

"She's not here. And she's not texting me. But I wanted to get a photo of me, Lauren and Molly, in our graduation stuff together. You should take it. You're tall. But hold the phone high up in the air, ok? We don't need extra chins, right, Moll?"

"Right."

Jason nodded, feeling exhausted. "Sure." As long as he wasn't in it, fine. He scanned the crowd, looking past the mothers already dabbing their eyes with tissues and fathers wiping sweat from their foreheads and younger siblings stifling yawns. He couldn't find Lauren in the midst of all the other graduates wearing the same caps and gowns.

Tiffany tapped at her cell phone and held it to her ear then shook her head. "No answer. Maybe she left her phone at home." She bit her lip and tapped the phone. "She's been acting weird lately. How did you think she seemed today?" She turned to Molly.

Molly started as Tiffany touched her arm. "Huh?"

"Lauren. Did you think she was being weird earlier?"

"Oh. Um, she was just doing that thing you asked."

"What thing?"

Molly raised her eyebrows. "She told me not to say anything, but that thing you asked her to do."

"Omigod, Molly. I have no idea what you're talking about." Tiffany put her hands on the small of her back and rubbed.

"The gun," Molly whispered.

"*What?*"

"What?"

Tiffany and Jason spoke simultaneously.

"She knew you were worried so she took it home," Molly said.

"You have a gun in your house?" Why the hell hadn't he known this?

Tiffany looked baffled. "I didn't ask her to take it home. Why would I do that?"

Jason's heart was pounding.

"God, I have no idea what's going on but I need to sit down. This air conditioning isn't working." Tiffany staggered over to the nearest chair. Ms. Cox walked over and sat next to her, fanning herself and Tiffany with a program.

Jason gripped Molly's arm. "Tiffany has, has a *gun* in her house?" He thought he was going to pass out.

"Well, not any more."

"Molly. Can you tell me exactly what happened? *Exactly?*"

Molly shrugged and he wanted to shake her. "I guess it doesn't matter that much now. I ran into Lauren coming out of Mrs. Vanderkamp's room and –" she lowered her voice "– a gun fell out of her bag. She said she was taking it home for safekeeping. But she said Tiffany said not to tell anyone."

"Where are her brothers?"

"I don't know. Her family's not here yet. But … it's weird." Molly scratched at the sleeves of her gown. "Tiffany just said that she didn't ask Lauren to take it, right?"

They looked at Tiffany on the bench, who was now drinking out of a bottle of water. Ms. Cox was rubbing her back.

"We need to go. Now." Jason turned and walked towards the door. The ringing noise was back, intense.

"But –"

Jason turned back. "Come on!"

"Fucking hell," Molly muttered.

She followed him and they pushed their way against a wave of students chattering in the hallway. Jason picked up speed as they rounded the corner into an empty corridor which led to the parking lot. Molly had to run to keep up with him.

As they left the exit and ran towards the car, they passed a man and two women, one carrying a toddler, rushing towards the doors. A rumble of thunder sounded in the distance.

"Ceremony's starting soon, kids," someone's father or uncle called after them. Jason and Molly ignored him, their gowns billowing behind them as they ran.

THIRTY-EIGHT

Lauren shoved her bookbag under her bed. Her mom shuffled in and sat on her bed with a groan. "Oh, it's warm today. I hope it rains soon, get us some fresh air. You should probably get changed, sweetie."

"Right." Lauren opened her closet door and pretended to consider her dresses. "Mom? I really love you. And the boys. And the baby. I want you to know that." She spoke to her clothes.

"Come here, darling." Her mom opened her arms. Lauren turned and sank into them. "Are you okay, honey?"

Lauren wiped her eyes. "Yes, just – emotional. Graduation. You know."

"I know it was hard moving right before your senior year but you did so well. I'm so proud of you."

"Thanks, Mom." She rested a hand on her mom's belly and felt the baby move. Like she was saying thank you in advance. "I was thinking, it would be nice for me and dad to drive to the ceremony together, spend some time with each other. You and the boys could go to the school separately. Maybe you could take them to McDonald's first or something?"

"Yes, that's a great idea." She kissed Lauren's cheek and hugged her. "I'm really pleased you're trying to make things better with your father. And the boys can wear themselves out in the play area before the ceremony. They'll be happy about that."

She tried to stand up, but Lauren kept holding her, not wanting to let go.

Her mom laughed and lifted up Lauren's chin. "You are the best big sister, you know that?"

"I know."

Lauren opened her bag and pulled out the gun as soon as she heard her mom and brothers leave the house. She had checked the pistol had the magazine in it when she was at the Vanderkamps' house. The weight of it felt reassuring, not awkward and heavy like the first time she'd held it. She had looked on the internet to find out how to check what type of gun it was, if it was loaded, and how to disengage the safety. She'd watched the videos over and over, concerned she might forget on the day, but it was surprisingly simple. She unloaded and reloaded the magazine and checked the safety. She held the pistol in both hands and pointed it at the mirror. The gun trembled at her reflection.

Lauren rested the gun on her bed and opened her bag again to take out a bottle. There were three pills left. She placed one on her tongue and remembered how she'd almost hit Molly's mailbox. She removed it and put it back in the bottle. She could take them all afterwards. She might only have one shot, and she had to get it right.

She picked up the gun and sat on the floor, staring at her cell phone lying on the carpet. She'd wait until she was sure her mom was on the way to the high school with the boys before doing it. She couldn't risk her forgetting something and coming back for some reason. She squeezed her eyes shut, needing to block out her mom and brothers. She couldn't think about them. What it would be like when the police told them what had happened. It was for the best, and she just needed to focus.

She looked at her phone and opened a message from Tiffany. She hit delete. The phone buzzed with a call and she rejected it. She felt jittery and edgy. Screw it. She took a pill and waited.

The message from her mom arrived more quickly than Lauren had expected.

On way now. Love u xo

She hit reply.

Us too! See you there xoxo

Lauren pulled her purity ring off her finger and held the gun in her hands. She was ready to do what needed to be done.

Lauren entered her dad's study without knocking.

"What are you doing?" Her dad was sitting at his desk wearing a suit and tie. He was too surprised to be angry. "Why aren't you ready to go?"

Lauren stood just inside the doorway. "I thought I'd give you back this ring, *Dad*," she spat out the last word venomously. "Seeing as it's total bullshit." She threw her purity ring at him. It ricocheted off the bookcase behind his head.

"Lauren! How dare you –" her dad stopped, his mouth open. "Is that –" He let out a disbelieving laugh. "What is that? A toy?"

"No. No, it's not a toy." Lauren aimed at the gun at him.

She waited. Like all those times he'd stared at her in silence, making her question herself, wondering what she'd done wrong, what she'd said. How she'd sinned. What was going to happen to her.

Now he had to wait, and wonder. Lauren looked down at him. All the times she'd been too frightened to come in here, ask his permission to go to Tiffany's or go to a football game. Now, he was scared of her.

"It's – I don't know what you're doing, but it's your graduation day. We'll talk later. We should –"

"We're not going anywhere."

"Lauren, I – honey." He never called her that. Lauren's arms were beginning to ache, but she couldn't lower the gun now. He might think she wasn't serious. "Honey, whatever this is about, let's go to graduation and –"

"Bullshit, Dad. *Bullshit*. You know what this is about." Her hands shook.

"I don't know what Molly told you, but –"

"What?"

"That girl has some serious problems. She needs some help." In spite of the chilled air in the room, hairs were sticking to his forehead with sweat.

"What the hell are you talking about?"

"She, she came into my office, and she –"

"Molly? What have you done to her? This is about *me*."

Her dad raised his hand, leaving a damp outline of a palm on his desk. "What – I don't –"

"Don't you dare tell me you don't know what I'm talking about. Don't you *dare*. I remember everything. I can't let it happen again. I'm going to make sure my little sister stays pure. Just like you preached during the purity pledge, right?"

He stood and stretched out his arms, imploringly. "Lauren," he pleaded.

She shut her eyes to the sight of his hands reaching for her and pulled the trigger.

The gunshot wasn't as loud as Lauren expected. She opened her eyes.

Shit.

She hadn't realized it would be so easy to miss. Her dad was sitting, stunned, staring at her with his mouth open. The bullet must have hit the books behind his head. He looked like he'd just shit his pants. Lauren felt a hysterical giggle bubbling inside her.

"Lauren, please don't do this," her dad gasped. "Please." A trickle of sweat travelled from his temple to his cheek. She studied his forehead thoughtfully. If she didn't get the placement of the next bullet just right, she was screwed.

"Please, I don't …" he was crying now. It was very distracting. "I don't know what's wrong with me." He pressed his palms together as though in prayer. "I'll get help. I'll see someone. I don't know why I – why I …" he raised his hands helplessly.

He did look very, very scared. If he went to someone, and she kept the gun, just in case, and he promised not to hurt her sister – was this enough? But then, what had he done to Molly? She lowered the gun, struggling to think. She needed another pill.

"Please, forgive me. I'm sorry. Forgive me."

Forgive him? *Forgive* him? It was a shame he'd asked for that.

How could she forgive those nights of sneaking into her room while her mom was at the hospital with Adam?

On the pretense of comforting her.

And at first, he had. He had cuddled Lauren and stroked her hair until her crying subsided and tiredness washed over her. She had been slipping into sleep when his hands had started creeping across her body, places where they shouldn't have gone. She had jolted awake, confused and then terrified, and had tried to squirm away. But he had held her down and touched her and –

Lauren shook her head. He thought that was forgivable?

While he stood in church and preached chastity and honoring your parents?

While he pretended to write sermons when he was sitting in his office looking at porn?

While he placed a ring on her finger and told her to stay pure for her future husband?

"I was a child. A little girl. How could you?" Tears ran down her face.

"But I didn't – I thought you…"

"What? What did you think?"

"You didn't say anything." He slammed his palms down on the desk. "You just let me – you could have said something. And you didn't."

"SHUT UP."

Lauren raised the gun and stepped closer, determined not to miss this time. Her dad reached towards her and she pulled the trigger as thunder cracked overhead.

THIRTY-NINE

Jason swerved into the driveway. He got out of the car, ran up to the house and knocked on the front door. He put his ear to it but there was a crash of thunder and he couldn't hear anything from inside.

Molly was behind him. "She's probably on her way to the ceremony. We should go back."

"We need to get in there. Find the gun. Before something happens."

"But –"

Jason tried the handle and the front door opened. He stepped into the hallway and looked into the room on the right. Lauren was standing in front of a desk and bookcase. He came to stand next to her and saw Mr. Davis sitting behind the desk. His mouth was open, his hands resting on the arms of the chair. Half of his forehead and his right eye were missing. The books behind him were splattered deep red with speckles of white.

Behind him, Molly gasped.

Jason looked at Lauren, who had both hands wrapped around the grip of a gun and was staring at Mr. Davis. What the hell had just happened?

"Lauren, give me the gun. Now."

Lauren blinked and moved her mouth but didn't speak.

"Lauren." Jason gently took the gun out of her hands. He put it down on the desk carefully, pointing away from them.

Lauren looked at him. "You're not supposed to be here."

"Are you okay? What happened?" Jason asked.

"I'm keeping my baby sister safe. My pledge was to make sure she has a pure life. So that's what I've done."

"You killed him," Molly said, her eyes wide.

"You need to leave," Lauren said. "Act like you were never here. I'll call the police now, they may be on their way already. It was loud, wasn't it? I didn't think it would be that loud." Lauren let out a noise that was between a giggle and a sob.

She reminded Jason of Tiffany when he'd seen her drinking once.

"Are you drunk?" he asked, pointlessly.

"One of you will need to be Tiffany's birthing partner." Lauren swayed. Her legs crumpled under her and she sat down heavily on the floor.

"You did this on purpose?" Molly asked.

Lauren nodded.

"What did he do?" Molly crouched down in front of Lauren.

"He did stuff to me. When I was little. Now he can't do those things to anyone else," Lauren said, softly.

"What do you mean? You mean, like …"

"Take a look. It's on his computer. Photos. Videos. With kids. You know."

"Oh my God." Molly put her hands over her mouth and retched.

Jason looked at Lauren's dad sitting behind the desk. His remaining eye was staring ahead, as though he was expecting someone to walk in. A Bible and yellow legal pad were next to the keyboard. A framed photo faced him. It didn't look real. More like a movie set with a talented makeup artist. He half expected Mr.

Davis to start admonishing them for being in his office. Just five minutes ago, he'd been alive. On Sunday, Jason had listened to him give a sermon.

Jason couldn't make things fit together. He'd known something terrible was going to happen, but this wasn't the scene he'd been expecting. And he'd arrived too late to stop it.

Molly put her arm around Lauren's shoulder. "Oh, Lauren. I'm so sorry." Mascara streaked her cheeks as she cried, but Lauren was strangely calm.

What had Lauren been through to have to do this?

And what about Jason's unborn baby, cocooned safely in Tiffany's belly? The moment that baby was born, anything – literally *anything* – could happen. Accidents. Illness. Abuse. How on earth could someone like Jason even attempt to keep a child safe?

How many books were lined up on the shelves? He started counting.

Lauren shrugged herself out from under Molly's arm and turned to face her. "Can you let my mom know that she shouldn't come visit me in prison? And make sure she doesn't come inside the house. I don't want her to see this."

Jason had to start counting from the beginning.

"You won't go to prison," Molly interrupted. "When the police get here, just explain everything he did. He's a pedophile. He was, I mean. He deserved this. You did the right thing."

Lauren laughed bitterly. "I shot him. I killed him. Of course I'll go to prison."

"Jason, tell her. It's self-defense, right?"

Jason stopped counting again. "It doesn't matter. Whatever the reason, this is going to follow her around. This is going to destroy her life." How could he describe what Lauren's future would be like? Molly could never understand. "Everyone, every single person she ever meets, will know her as the girl who shot her dad."

"God, Jason." Molly stood up. "What is wrong with you?" she whispered frantically in his ear. "She needs our help. Her dad is a pervert. He deserved it."

"Trust me," he said softly. "She'll carry it around with her forever. Her life is ruined."

They looked at Lauren, who was hugging herself and shivering.

"Then what are we supposed to do?" Molly asked.

"Make it look like suicide?" Jason suggested.

Molly considered it and shook her head. "They'll check for gunshot residue. It's all over Lauren and won't be on him. We need to get him to shoot it. Or she could say he attacked her, and she was defending herself? Dammit. That won't work."

"Why not?"

"She took the gun from Tiffany's house this morning. That makes it premeditated." Molly bit her nails.

Jason inhaled and let out a long breath. If he could spare Lauren the hell of his own life, he needed to do whatever it took. "Pull it together," he whispered to himself. He looked at Molly. "I'll say that I asked her to take the gun home with her. That I didn't want it in Tiffany's house."

"Why would you do that?"

"To keep the baby safe. My psychiatrist will back it up."

"You're seeing a psych– oh God, it doesn't matter. So, we need to get him to shoot the gun." Molly blinked back tears. "Hopefully they won't check

Lauren's clothes. Or mine. And your fingerprints are on it." She pulled her graduation robe over her fingers and picked up the gun. She rubbed at it with the fabric, her hands shaking. "After I, you know. When it's done, I'll put our robes in the car. They probably won't check there."

"I'll do it," Jason said. If the police figured out they tried to cover up what really happened, it should be Jason who paid the price.

"Are you sure?"

Jason nodded. He imitated Molly, covering his hands with his graduation robe, and took the gun from her. He walked around the desk. He couldn't believe what he was about to do, but this was everything he deserved.

"He's right-handed," Molly said, wiping tears away. "Make sure you put it in his right hand."

Jason cried out when he lifted the pastor's hand. It was still warm. He wrapped the lifeless fingers around the gun, placing the index finger on the trigger, and covered it with his own. He hesitated.

"Just do it, quickly," Molly said. "Aim at the floor."

Before Jason could change his mind, he closed his eyes and fired. The feel of the recoil was exactly how he remembered. He stumbled backwards, his ears ringing.

When he opened his eyes, Molly was standing in front of him. "Give me your robe and sit with Lauren."

Jason pulled off his robe and Molly carried it out of the room. When she returned a few moments later, he was still standing helplessly in the same place, black dots clouding his vision.

Molly kneeled in front of Lauren. "Lauren, listen. Tell the police Jason asked you to take the gun home with you, and your dad must have found it."

Lauren gazed at her and nodded. "I'm sorry, Molly," she whispered.

Molly looked at Jason. "I don't know if she's understanding me." She turned back to Lauren. "Say you were upstairs. You heard a gunshot, and you found your dad in here, okay?"

Lauren stared ahead and nodded again.

"Jesus." Molly put her arm around her. "We should call them now before it looks like we took too long."

Jason pulled his cell phone out of his pocket. He had eight missed calls from Tiffany, seventeen from his mom and five from his dad. They were all going to be so mad at him. He dialled 911.

"911, what's your emergency?" The operator spoke quickly.

"Someone's killed themselves." The ringing noise intensified. "I, I – I don't know the address. Someone gave me directions." He couldn't catch his breath.

"Give me the phone and sit with Lauren." Molly stood up and went into the hallway. "Hello? No, no one's in danger. But my friend – she needs help. She found the body."

Jason sank down next to Lauren. He really, really wanted to count the books but Lauren leaned against him and he couldn't stand up. He listened to Molly giving the address. He felt the soft fuzz of the carpet under his fingers, the weight of Lauren's head on his shoulder. Her hair smelled like flowers. He breathed in and out. He counted each tuft of carpeting until his fingers touched something small and round. He was holding Lauren's purity ring.

Sirens wailed and flashes of red and blue lit up the wall. Two sharp knocks, a yell – "Police!" – and the hallway and study were filled with police officers and paramedics dripping water over the carpet. He was hauled to his feet while a police officer and paramedic crouched down in front of Lauren.

Jason and Molly sat in the kitchen, waiting to be interviewed. They watched the rain falling outside the window and sipped at glasses of water a paramedic had given them. It was very tidy. Just two mugs, three plates and a plastic cup on the work surface. Two, three, one. Twelve cabinet doors, ten drawers.

"What are you doing?" Molly asked.

"I'm counting."

"Why?"

What the hell. He might as well tell her. "I have OCD. I count things when I get stressed. That's why I see a psychiatrist."

"Oh. But you seem so ... together."

Jason shook his head. "I'm not. I'm definitely not."

"I've never touched a gun before," Molly whispered.

"Shh. They might hear," Jason inclined his head towards the hallway. He leaned towards her. "You were amazing today. So calm. I don't know what I would have done if you weren't here. Thank you." Molly started crying. Jason suddenly realized the enormity of what he'd done by dragging her away from the gym. "You missed graduation. Your speech and everything. I'm sorry. I totally messed that up for you." He felt terrible.

Molly blew her nose into a paper towel. "I wasn't going to do a speech."

"Really? Well, you missed graduating. And your mom missed seeing it. I'm so sorry. I bet that was really important for her."

"It's okay. I mean, I wasn't going to do a speech because I wasn't planning on being there. Or graduating." She swallowed. "I was going to jump off the roof of the gym."

Jason had thought nothing would surprise him ever again. He let this sink in for a few moments. "Wow. Why? You're so smart and everything." Molly looked at the table and rubbed her arms. He struggled to understand. "Because you weren't valedictorian?"

"No. Well, I don't know. Partly, I guess. Although that seems kind of dumb, now. Just, I don't know." She picked at the skin around her nails. "Lots of reasons. I just – I just didn't feel like anything was ever going to get better."

They listened to the rain and the murmur of the police and investigators for a while. Jason got up and refilled Molly's glass of water and put it in front of her.

"I know that feeling." He sat down. "But, listen. You can't do that. You can't do that to your mom. Or your friends. It would just –" he buried his face in his hands. "It would just destroy them. No matter how bad life gets, you can't make things even worse by doing that. Do you promise?"

"But do you really get it? Understand what it feels like?" Her voice wobbled. "That you shouldn't even be here?"

Jason looked at her and put his hand on hers. "Yes. I really do."

FORTY

Molly left out the part about seeing Lauren take the gun in her statement to the police. It wouldn't make Molly or Mrs. Vanderkamp look good. Molly was mortified that she'd spent the whole morning with Lauren and had no idea what she'd been planning. At least the police hadn't taken away their clothes for evidence, but not everything was like CSI. Another police officer was taking Jason's statement in a separate room, but it seemed their versions of events was being accepted.

"Do your parents know where you are?" the police officer asked.

"No. It's just my mom, and um, no."

"You need to give her a call. She'll be worried."

"She was at graduation, but I don't know where she is now."

"Does she have a cell phone?"

Molly shook her head. She remembered Jason's cell phone was still in her pocket. She pulled it out and saw loads of missed calls. "This is Jason's. His parents are freaking out. Can I give this back to him so he can call them?"

The officer nodded. "We're done here, for now. Although we may be in touch to follow up."

"What will happen to Lauren?"

"We have trained specialists who will talk to her," the officer said. "They'll make her as comfortable as possible. And remember what I said – there's people you can speak to as well. You've been through a lot today."

The kind police officer had no idea.

Molly waited in the kitchen for Jason, who came in a few minutes later. "I'm sorry. I had your cell phone this whole time."

He took it and scrolled through missed calls and messages. "Oh, no."

"What is it?"

"Tiffany's in the hospital. We have to go."

They ran through the rain and got into the car. Jason opened his fist and gold glinted on his palm.

"What's that?"

"It's Lauren's. It was on the carpet. Can you look after it?" He handed it to her.

The car sprayed water across the road as Jason sped towards the hospital. Molly wondered if she was going to wake up from a delusional dream. Today should have turned out so differently. The ambulance was supposed to arrive for her, not Mike. That morning, Molly had pictured Mike standing over her broken body on the sidewalk, coming to the realization that he would never hold her again. Never run his fingers over her body. Never kiss her mouth, her scars. He would have started to comprehend how much he had messed up and he would spend the rest of his life regretting it, trying to pay penance for it.

But Mike had died having no idea at all. His brain lobes scattered across the books behind him, his face a jumbled mess. It was strange how his lips had looked the same as always, though. The lips that had –

Molly wiped away tears, glad Jason was focused on driving. She had spent the last two hours on autopilot and now what they'd seen – and what they'd done –

was finally sinking in. She couldn't stop crying and shaking. Could she have avoided this if she hadn't flirted with Mike at the purity pledge ceremony? Mike was right, she had thrown herself at him. Molly pulled off her ring and held it next to Lauren's. She hated what it represented.

Molly shoved the rings into the glove compartment as Jason pulled into the ER parking lot. They splashed across the wet asphalt and through the doors.

Jason ran up to the reception desk. "My girlfriend, my ex – I got a message that she's here. She's pregnant. I think there's something wrong."

"Are you the father of the baby?"

"Yes, her name's Tiffany Vanderkamp."

The receptionist typed something on her computer. "She's in the maternity ward. Follow the blue arrows to the second floor."

They ran along the corridors, leaving wet footprints behind. Jason cursed himself for not checking his messages sooner. Molly felt guilty for forgetting his phone was in her pocket.

Jason was too impatient to wait for an elevator, so they jogged up the stairs and through double doors leading to the maternity ward.

Jason ran up to the reception desk. "Tiffany Vanderkamp, where is she? I'm the father of the baby. Are they okay?"

Molly trailed behind, panting.

The receptionist pointed. "Room 5, at the end of the hallway."

Jason ran and Molly started to follow. "Excuse me, are you family?" the receptionist called.

"No, I'm a friend."

"I'm sorry, family only in the room. There's a room

around the corner where you can wait," the receptionist gave her a kind smile.

"What's happening? I guess you can't tell me, huh?"

"Sorry, no. But her family is here. You can talk to them, okay?"

Molly walked along the corridor and heard raised voices. She stopped and peered around the corner. Tiffany's parents were standing a couple of feet away from her, scowling at each other.

"You haven't told her yet, have you?" Mr. Vanderkamp asked.

"Of course I haven't told her, because it's not going to happen," Mrs. Vanderkamp hissed.

"It *is* going to happen. It's already happening. The realtor is coming to value it tomorrow."

"I know you don't care about me, but you can't make your daughter and your grandchild homeless," Mrs. Vanderkamp said. "What kind of person are you?"

Molly pretended to read a poster about breastfeeding and edged closer.

"I don't have a choice, Celia. I am fucked. The company is fucked. Watch the news. Pay attention for once in your goddamn life."

"Well, there's no point selling now, anyway. House prices are falling."

"Christ, Celia! That's the whole goddamn point. That's what the problem is. We have got to do this now."

"Bullshit. You've spent the last five years bragging about how much money you're making. Don't turn around and pretend you don't have any."

"The market. Is. Collapsing." Mr. Vanderkamp said flatly.

"That is not my problem."

"You're unbelievable. You wanted to know why we're getting divorced? Because of this shit."

Molly was riveted until someone grabbed her arm. "Molly! Oh my God." Molly's mom pulled her into a hug. "My baby girl. Where have you been? I've been looking all over for you. I thought maybe you'd come with Tiffany when she went into labor, but you weren't here. And then I went home and you weren't there, either. And I, I came back and –" she let go and looked at Molly. "What's going on? Why weren't you at graduation?"

Molly looked at her mom's worried face, that had been right there ever since she could remember. "Mom, I – something terrible happened. I'm sorry."

"It's okay. Whatever it is," her mom held Molly's hands, "we'll deal with it together. Are you hurt?"

Molly shook her head hopelessly. How could she even begin to explain what she'd done?

"Whatever's happened, I promise you, I will be with you the whole time." Her mom pulled her into another hug.

Molly leaned into her and let out a shuddering sigh.

"Come with me." She guided Molly into the waiting room, past Mr. and Mrs. Vanderkamp who stopped arguing and stared at them. Molly's mom shut the door behind her. The room had three sofas similar to the type in Mike's office and a couple of matching armchairs. A low coffee table was covered with magazines and leaflets about parenting and a vending machine was in the corner.

"What's happening? Is something wrong with the baby?" Molly was shaking.

Her mom sat her down on a sofa. "Tiffany went

into labor early, but she's fine. She just, you know, had a baby, which is scary. But she's good, and the baby is, too." She smiled and pulled a tissue from a box on the table to dab tears off Molly's face.

"Really? They're both okay?" Molly took a tissue to blow her nose. Her mom put her arm around her.

"They're fine. Of course, Tiffany thought she was dying, but I remember thinking that too."

"Who was with you, when you had me?"

Her mom squeezed her hand. "It was just me, hon. Me and you. And a very lovely midwife."

"So after, after –" Molly swallowed and tried again. "After all that, that stuff ... happened ... you had to give birth on your own?"

"Yes," her mom said softly. "And you know what? It was the best day of my life. It was the day I met my best friend."

Molly looked at her, confused.

"You. You had been with me, getting me through the worst time of my existence."

"But, if you hadn't – if that guy hadn't –" the words caught in Molly's throat. "That guy should never have done that to you. I shouldn't even be here."

Her mom cupped Molly's face in her hands. "Listen to me. You were the one thing that came out of it that I could turn into a positive. I decided I was pregnant for a reason, and you were mine. The day I decided to keep you was the first day I smiled in three months. I decided we would make it through, and make it through together. I have absolutely loved you, since the moment you were born. Since *before* you were born." She wiped Molly's tears away with her thumbs. "I was a victim of rape. Not a victim of pregnancy. You saved me. You were my beautiful angel sent by God to help me survive those months afterwards."

Molly stared into her mom's green eyes, mirror images of her own. "Really? You don't ever wish it had never happened, and I'd never been born?"

"My God, Molly. Is that what you think?" Her mom shook her head, her eyes filled with tears. "Because of you I learned to love. Unconditionally. I saw the beauty in life again. You were the greatest gift I've ever been given. I cannot be more grateful to have you in my life." She pulled Molly towards her again and stroked her hair. "I'm so sorry I haven't told you that enough. I thought you knew. I love you so much, and I always will."

"But, Mom. I've done some stupid things. Some really stupid things."

"Well, you know what I've learned? There's nothing, absolutely nothing, that you and I can't handle together."

Molly nodded to herself. She looked at her mom and took a breath. "I need to show you something." She began to roll up her sleeve.

FORTY-ONE

Jason ran towards the room at the end of the corridor, and stopped when he reached it. What lay behind the door? He couldn't hear anything. Surely there should be sounds – doctors and nurses in there, Tiffany talking – anything? It must be worse than he thought. Why had he left Tiffany at graduation? Why hadn't he looked after her? He braced himself and pushed open the door.

Tiffany was asleep in bed, a clump of hair stuck to her forehead. She was wearing a white hospital gown and an IV drip was attached to her arm. His mom was sitting in a chair a few feet away from the bed,

"Mom, what are you –" Jason saw a pale yellow blanket in his mom's arms.

"Want to meet your baby?" she whispered with a smile. She looked down and Jason glimpsed some pink skin amongst the folds of material.

He stood in the doorway, frozen.

"You have a daughter, and she's absolutely perfect." A tear dropped onto the blanket.

"Is Tiffany okay?"

"She's fine. Just really tired, so we're letting her rest before she needs to nurse again. Where were you? We were worried sick about you."

"I'm sorry." He didn't know how to begin to explain what had happened.

His mom sighed. "We'll talk about it later. Here, want to hold her?"

Jason walked a couple of steps into the room. He saw a round cheek and an unimaginably tiny nose. A small tuft of dark hair. He turned away and looked at Tiffany lying in the bed. She looked so fragile and exhausted, Jason thought his heart would break.

"Are you sure she's okay?" he asked softly. "She looks sick."

"She was a little dehydrated. That's what the drip's for, just some extra fluids. And giving birth is tiring. Consider yourself lucky that you'll never know how much." She paused. "She did good."

Jason looked at his mom in surprise. It was the first compliment she'd ever given Tiffany.

She stood up slowly, holding the baby. "Sit down here. I'll pass her to you."

"Oh, no. No, it's okay." Jason backed away.

"I'll show you how to hold her. It's simple." She held the baby towards him. He flinched as though the bundle was a live grenade.

"No, no. I just wanted to make sure everything was okay. I'll go now. Tiffany probably doesn't want me here anyway." He reached behind him for the door handle.

"Don't you dare walk out that door," his mom hissed. He stopped, startled. His mom leaned over the clear crib next to the bed and placed the baby in it. She came to stand in front of him. "I don't know where you've been, or what's going on, but you are not leaving this room until you have held your daughter in your arms."

"I can't." Jason whispered.

"You are her father. She needs you. And Tiffany needs you."

"No." He shook his head vehemently. "She needs

me to *not* be here."

"What are you talking about?"

"It's safer."

"What? What do you mean?"

"I'll hurt her, Mom. Maybe not today, but at some point, I'll mess things up." He looked at the floor. "It's better if I'm not in her life. For her and for everyone."

"I don't understand." His mom reached out her hand and let it drop by her side. "What do you mean, it's safer?"

Jason walked to the window and rested his hands on the ledge, determined not to look in the crib. Dusk was falling, and the lights in the parking lot were coming on. Where was Lauren now? A hospital? Did her mom and brothers know what had happened yet?

There were six cars in the first row, and eight in the second row.

Jason should have driven faster. If he had arrived sooner, he could have prevented the shooting. He could have stopped all those lives being ruined.

His mom joined him at the window and her hand covered his. "Jason. Talk to me. Please."

Five white cars. Two red. Three gray. Three black – or was one dark blue? "I just want to do everything possible to protect the baby. And that means not being around her. Ever."

"Jason, please be honest." His mom rubbed his hand. "Do you remember the accident?"

"I never forgot it," he admitted. "I just pretended."

She inhaled sharply. "Oh, God. I –"

"I'm sorry, Mom. I know there is nothing I can ever do to make it up to you, but I can at least try not to hurt anyone else." He gripped the ledge. "That's where I went today. I found out Lauren took Mrs.

Vanderkamp's handgun for some reason." His mom gasped and cupped her hand over her mouth. "I was worried about Lauren, and her brothers. I thought maybe I could stop something bad from happening. But ..." he trailed off as the blood splattered office and Pastor Davis's disfigured face came into his mind. He squeezed his eyes shut. "I just wanted to make sure no one else gets hurt."

"Please don't tell me you think what happened to Jasmine is," his mom squeezed his hand, "you don't think it's your fault, do you?"

Jason met her eyes in the reflection of the glass. "Of course it was my fault."

"No, no, no. Son." She gripped his shoulders and turned him towards her. "That accident was my fault. My fault, and your father's fault. We never should have kept a gun in the house. I'd give anything to go back, to undo that stupid, stupid decision." Tears streamed down her cheeks. "It is our fault Jasmine died. Not yours. You were a child." She shook him. "I told your father I didn't want that gun in the house. He said he'd hidden it. And you'd know the difference between a toy and a real gun. I knew it was a bad idea, but I went along with it. I've never forgiven him, and I've never forgiven myself. But I have never, not once, blamed you."

"But I shot her. *I* was holding it. No one else. And every time I think about it, I –"

"What are you guys talking about?" Tiffany croaked, making them both jump. They turned to her. "How is she?" Tiffany looked at the crib.

"She's fine, just sleeping," Jason's mom wiped her eyes.

"You're both crying. You never cry," Tiffany accused Jason. "I hope it's because you feel bad for not being here."

"I'm sorry." Jason could hear how useless those words were.

Tiffany sat up and winced. "Where were you? And Lauren? And Molly? I just gave birth on my own." She glanced at Jason's mom. "Well, not entirely on my own. But still." There were snuffling noises and then a mewl. "Oh!" Tiffany reached for the baby.

Jason's mom wheeled the crib next to the bed and placed the baby in Tiffany's arms.

"Hey, gorgeous girl. Did you have a good sleep?" Tiffany murmured. She kissed the baby on her forehead.

Jason was overwhelmed. He tried to catch his mom's eye. "Mom?" he mouthed, uselessly.

The baby started to cry, shockingly loud for such a tiny thing.

"Shh. Let's give you some food, huh?" Tiffany pulled down her hospital gown and lifted her breast towards the baby's mouth. His mom wedged a pillow in Tiffany's lap so she could rest her arm on it.

Jason turned away, stunned. He and his mom had both seen Tiffany's breast. At the same time.

"That's it," his mom said. "Give her some time to latch on."

A few seconds passed. Jason stared at the floor tiles, avoiding the scene behind him and the reflection in the glass. There were suckling noises.

"There you go, you're a natural. Jason, look how well she's doing."

He turned slowly and raised his eyes. Tiffany's nipple was thankfully hidden from view. One hand cradled the baby and with the other she was stroking the baby's cheek.

His mom placed a blanket around Tiffany's shoulders. "It'll be more comfortable when your mom brings you a maternity gown." She rubbed Tiffany's back. "You're doing so well. I struggled with nursing."

"I can't imagine you struggling with anything," Tiffany muttered.

"Oh, yes. Not with Jason, but with –" She stopped herself. "Tiffany." She sat on the bed next to her.

"Mom, don't," Jason whispered.

She ignored him. "There's something I need to tell you. About an accident that happened a long time ago."

Tiffany looked at her. "Okay."

"Mom!" Jason couldn't stop her.

"I had another child. A daughter." Tiffany opened her mouth, but his mom took a deep breath and kept going, as though a timer had been set and she had to say it all as quickly as possible. "And when she was five years old, she discovered a handgun that her dad and I thought was hidden away. She was curious about everything. So, she picked it up, and started playing with it. But she, she accidentally shot herself. And she died."

Jason's world tilted.

"God, that's awful. I'm sorry." Tiffany reached for his mom's arm, but she recoiled and kept talking.

"Jason was only eight, and he found her. It was very traumatic for him."

"Oh," Tiffany breathed. She clutched the baby to her.

Jason looked at his mom. She kept lying for him. Over and over again.

"He never spoke about it. Ever. And the doctors told us that children can forget traumatic memories. So all this time, I was hoping he didn't remember, but I just found out he does." Her voice broke. "And he spent all this time being alone with that terrible memory." His mom was looking at Tiffany and the baby, avoiding Jason completely. "I messed up. I should have kept checking in with him. So, I just want to say, whatever you do as a mother, please, don't be scared to talk to her. Okay?"

Tiffany nodded. "I'm so sorry that happened. What was her name?"

"Jasmine." His mom hadn't said Jasmine's name for years.

Jason stood helplessly by the window.

"That's a beautiful name," Tiffany said.

"I'm going to give you both some time alone." His mom stood, walked over to Jason and pulled him into a hug.

It wasn't like the warm, squishy hugs he used to get, she was bonier and more awkward now, but it was still nice. He closed his eyes and squeezed her back.

"I love you," she whispered.

"I love you, Mom. I'm sorry about today. Making you worry."

"We'll talk about that later. Spend some time with your daughter." She let him go and left the room, closing the door quietly behind her.

Tiffany had adjusted her gown and was covered again. She was studying him as though they'd just met. "Why didn't you tell me? You had a sister and I didn't even know."

"I'm sorry. I just, I find it really hard to talk about her. Every time I think about her, I –"

"Oh, Jason. Don't worry. That must have been awful. I'm sorry you had to go through that. And your parents. They must feel so guilty, all the time. I can't imagine it."

Jason opened his mouth. He needed to tell her the truth.

"Here. Hold your daughter."

He shook his head.

"Come on."

"I can't."

"You don't get to say that." Tiffany glared at him. "I was just nearly torn in half. I was terrified. And you weren't here. I thought I couldn't do it, but you know what? I did. Because I didn't have a choice. And neither do you. So come over here."

Jason stepped closer. The baby's eyelashes were fluttering as she slept. Her mouth was open in a little 'O' and a miniscule finger twitched.

"She's so tiny," he whispered.

"She didn't feel tiny on the way out. Here, sit next to me."

"I –"

"Stop being stupid and come here."

Jason did as he was told. Tiffany smelled different. Of sweat and something else he couldn't make out. Tiffany pushed a fold of the blanket away and he saw the baby's whole face for the first time. Delicate black eyelashes rested on her cheeks. She was scowling and her eyebrows were almost invisible.

"Here. Hold your arms like mine," Tiffany instructed.

Jason felt like he was going to be sick.

"Come on, Jason. I need the bathroom."

He put his arms into position and Tiffany passed him the baby. He stopped breathing and moving.

"See? It's really not hard."

Jason had expected the baby to feel like a feather but she was a solid mass. How had Tiffany carried her around in her stomach? He let himself breathe. The baby opened her eyes, let out a grunt, and slowly closed them.

"She has your eyes," Tiffany commented.

Jason held his breath again, not wanting to disturb the baby.

The door flew open and Mrs. V came in carrying an overnight bag. "You'll never guess what your father's doing!"

"Mom, what took you so long? Can you help me to the bathroom?"

Mrs. V placed the bag on the floor. "Hi, Jason. Isn't she gorgeous?" She nodded at the baby.

"Seriously, Mom. I'm going to pee myself."

"Okay, okay." Mrs. V pulled back the blankets and Tiffany swung her legs out of the bed.

Mr. V came in. "Tiffany, we need to talk."

"Not now, John," Mrs. V snapped, her arm around Tiffany's back as she guided her into the bathroom.

"I'm sorry, but this won't wait," he said.

"Dad, go away. What is wrong with everyone?"

The door was shut in his face but Mr. V talked through it, something about realtors and mortgages. Jason cradled his daughter in his arms and had to breathe again. She blinked and was suddenly gazing right at him, her deep brown eyes staring right into his soul.

She was incredibly – stunningly – beautiful.

"Hi," he whispered.

She scrunched up her face. Opened and closed her mouth. Every time he took a breath, it seemed to unsettle her. Her eyelashes were clumped together.

Should he count the clumps? Or each one? His pulse rate quickened. She squirmed.

Could she feel his heart pounding through his ribcage? Were her tiny eardrums picking it up? She would have been used to Tiffany's heartbeat all this time. He moved her away from his chest and she scowled.

He'd known his daughter for five minutes, and already he was throwing her off. Messing up her internal rhythms.

He'd never be a good dad. There weren't enough classes or books or therapy for people like him. The baby knew. She already hated being held by him. Something bad would happen to her, and it would be his fault. No matter how careful he was, or what he did to keep her safe, he would mess it up like he messed up everything. And then other people paid the price. He couldn't do that to his own daughter. To his mother. To Tiffany. They shouldn't trust him.

Mr. and Mrs. V were still arguing through the door. Jason's arms ached from trying to hold the baby without hurting her or dropping her.

"I hope you know I love you," Jason murmured. He stood up as though he was holding fragile glass. Slowly, slowly, he carried her to the crib. He placed the baby down, sweat running down his temple. "Please don't cry," he mouthed.

She didn't cry. She snuffled and wriggled her arms. She was perfect, and he'd make sure she stayed that way.

July
2008

"O God, thou knowest my foolishness; and my sins are not hid from thee."

PSALM 69:5

FORTY-TWO

"What do you think of this?" Molly's mom held up a pale blue, long-sleeved t-shirt. "It's a light fabric, so it should feel nice and cool."

Molly nodded. "Sure." She held out the heap of clothes in her arms. Her mom placed the t-shirt on top of the pile. "I need to try some of this on, it's getting heavy."

"And this one." Her mom added a forest green version of the same t-shirt onto the stack. "It'll bring out your eyes."

"Yours as well. Why don't you try it on? You haven't even chosen anything yet."

"I don't need anything, hon. We're shopping for you."

"And what would Keira say about that?" Molly raised her eyebrows. Her mom pursed her lips and they looked at each other.

"That I need to treat myself with the same love and kindness I treat others," her mom recited dutifully.

"Exactly. If you're starting college as well, you should get new clothes, too." Molly tilted her head towards a pile of short-sleeved t-shirts. "There's a green one there you could try. We could match on our first day, even if we're a thousand miles apart." Her mom's eyes filled with tears. "Please don't cry, Mom."

Her mom cried constantly since they started seeing Keira, a trainee family therapist. Keira had said it was a lifetime of pain working its way out and maybe Molly should try it some time. But Keira didn't have to go out in public with her.

"Not in Target, please. Hold it together."

"Sorry. Yes, we're treating ourselves and having fun." Her mom smiled and a tear rolled down her face. "See? I'm fine."

"Whatever." Molly shook her head and went into a changing cubicle. She set the clothes down on the bench and turned away from the mirror as she pulled off her shirt. The cuts on her arms and thighs were healing but the doctor had said some scarring would probably always be visible. Her mom had bawled, obviously, but Molly didn't mind so much. Maybe it had been the antidepressants kicking in, but the thought of wearing long sleeves for the rest of her life was fine – no one needed to see her chubby arms. And she had never walked around in short skirts or dresses anyway, so what did it matter?

Molly pulled on the green t-shirt and looked in the mirror. She pushed back her shoulders, sucked in her stomach and tried to picture herself on campus in a few weeks, striding across the quad to a Physics class. Maybe if she put on some make-up and wore this top with flared jeans, she'd look – not pretty, but not totally ugly. Tiffany would have helped her figure out how to "work the look" as she used to say, but she wasn't speaking to Molly anymore. The last time Molly had gone to see her she had told Molly to "Stop lying and fuck off, you're not my fucking friend."

Molly didn't blame her. The police and their parents might have believed the story about Mike's suicide, but Tiffany somehow knew there was more to it. Molly didn't want to reveal any secrets that weren't hers to share but hadn't been able to contact Lauren or Jason to figure out the details of what story they should concoct for Tiffany. She didn't even know what had happened to Lauren, other than "she was getting the help she needed" according to the police officer she had called, demanding to know where Lauren was. Jason had also disappeared. He and his mom hadn't attended the church memorial service for Mike, and the only reason Molly had gone was to talk to him.

Molly was fed up with her own thoughts, wishing she could go back to the evening of the purity pledge. Why – *why* – had she flirted with Mike, setting everything in motion? Molly would give anything to go back to her life before the ceremony, where she'd never spoken to him. Never needed him. Never loved him. She couldn't even talk to anyone about the horror of finding him dead, discovering the truth about what kind of man he was.

It was like she had a DVD stuck on repeat in her mind. She kept seeing Mike's eye staring ahead out of his bloody face, Lauren shivering on the floor, Jason panicking and hopeless. There wasn't even a reprieve when Molly slept. In her dreams, Mike would kneel on the floor in front of her, run his hands across her stomach and breasts, unzip her jeans. She'd tell him to stop.

Then he'd look up at her, his face a bloody pulp, half his head shot off. She'd wake up screaming and her mom would come in and hold her.

A few nights ago, her mom had sat on the floor next to the bed, holding her hand until she fell back to sleep. The next day she had asked Molly if there was anything Molly wasn't telling her about Pastor Mike. Molly had shaken her head. "It was just sad, what happened. And gross." Molly could never tell her mom the truth. What she'd done. The things she'd let Mike do.

Her mom had told Molly that bad memories eventually fade. But Molly knew they wouldn't. She stared at the door and pinched her upper arms, waiting for the endorphins to make her feel better. At least she'd helped Lauren, who had been through much worse than her. But Lauren had been a child, unable to stop it, whereas Molly had wanted it. Asked for it, even. She had deserved everything that happened.

"Are you ready to show me?" her mom called out. Molly tugged the sleeves over her wrists, unlocked the fitting room door and stepped out.

Her mom had tried on the green t-shirt as well. She smiled. "I knew that would be a great color on you. Look."

She turned Molly towards the full-length mirror on the wall at the end of the fitting room. She pulled Molly's hair back. "You should wear your hair up more, honey. Stop hiding your beautiful face."

"You look pretty, Mom. Green really suits you." Molly sniffed.

"Now who's crying?" Molly's mom let her hair down and wrapped her arms around her. Their eyes met in the mirror. "I still can't believe it. Off to college together. You and me, baby girl. We got this."

FORTY-THREE

Lauren sat in the medicine room, her arm elevated on a cushion.

"I'm just going to place this cuff on your arm, now." Stephen slid the cuff past her elbow. "Gonna inflate this, so you'll feel some pressure." He pumped the cuff, squeezing Lauren's arm until it tingled. The pressure released. "125 over 84."

Eunice noted it down in the file. "Better."

It was only last week that Lauren noticed what they were doing. She had emerged from a haze of trying various drug combinations and visits from social workers and realized that all the staff articulated what they were going to do before they touched her. Even the yoga teacher requested permission before making a gentle adjustment to her alignment. And Lauren was never alone in a room with a male staff member. Even though all the doors were left ajar or had windows anyway.

It was like they all thought Lauren was an undetonated bomb that might explode if they caught her unawares.

Maybe she was.

Lauren hovered by the reception area with Stephen, her eyes flickering from the clock to the window panels in the doors. At 2.01 p.m., her mom entered through the first set of doors, carrying Amelia against her chest in a wrap. Lauren felt the usual wave of relief as her mom signed in at the desk, even though she had come to visit almost every day since Lauren had been admitted. The only days she had missed were the day she gave birth to Amelia and the day after.

Her mom gave her a small smile through the glass. The door release clicked and her mom pushed the door and opened an arm, the other one holding onto Amelia. Lauren encircled them both, inhaling the sweet, fruity smell of Amelia's wispy hair.

"You want to go for a walk today?" Stephen asked them. Lauren nodded. "Okay, let's see what we can do. I need to get some of this off." He patted his belly. "Looks like I'm about to have a baby."

Lauren and her mom walked around the grounds, taking it in turns to hold Amelia. Stephen trailed behind them, mopping his head with a tissue. Her mom told her that she'd found a small house to rent near her sister and she would try and get Lauren transferred to a psychiatric hospital nearby. Adam was looking forward to playing basketball with his cousins. Michael was still enchanted by Amelia and impatient for her to start talking.

They lapsed into silence. As always, Lauren wanted to ask about Molly and Jason, if they were traumatized by what they'd seen. Find out why they'd made such a sacrifice for her. Discover if she could have prevented what her dad did to Molly. But she couldn't. She'd probably never know. Lauren suspected her mom had questions she was too afraid to ask, too.

Perhaps it was enough that her brothers were healthy, her mom was beginning to start a new life, and her sister was safe. Lauren shielded Amelia's delicate head from the sun as they turned back towards the hospital. It would have to be enough, for all of them.

FORTY-FOUR

"Calum stopped by again." Jason's mom stood by the car holding her purse and keys.

"I know." Jason hoisted his suitcase into the trunk of the car. He had heard Calum's car pull into the driveway and turned on the radio to drown out the sound of him knocking that morning.

"Are you sure you want to do this? You can still change your mind."

"The flight's in five hours." He took his bookbag off his shoulder and unzipped the front pocket, checking his passport and ticket for the sixteenth time.

"You could just take a vacation, and then come back. I'm sure you can get a late acceptance to –"

"Mom. I'm going." He opened the passenger door and sat inside the car, the bookbag at his feet, leaving the door open for the car to cool down.

His mom opened the driver's side and sat down, pursing her lips. She started the car and blasted the air conditioning. "You could at least say goodbye to people properly."

"Why? We never did that before. Whenever we moved, we always just left."

"That was different. And," she paused. "I didn't always handle things well. Please don't use me as your example on how to behave."

Jason pulled his door shut.

"There's time to stop by to see Tiffany and the baby."

Jason lifted his bookbag onto his lap, opened the front pocket, ran his fingers over his passport and ticket. "I don't want to be late. We should go."

She pulled her door shut and drove. It was silent except for the radio, tuned in to traffic updates. Jason counted cars as they passed, starting over again when he got to sixty.

When his mom spoke, after a tight bend at the turnoff for the airport, he jumped. "Who knows. Maybe some time somewhere completely different will help. Perhaps an English counselor will talk some sense into you. Help you face reality."

She was missing the whole point. Jason *was* facing reality. Everyone was better off without him around. He had treated Tiffany like crap. He had lied to Calum and ruined semi-finals, the most important game of Calum's life. He hadn't realized that Tiffany's parents were splitting up, although looking back it was blindingly obvious. He hadn't noticed that Calum had seen through his lies the whole time. He had deceived his mom, and God, by taking the purity pledge while knowing he wouldn't keep it.

And to add to it all, he hadn't arrived at Lauren's house in time to stop her shooting her dad. If he had driven faster, just a little, he wouldn't have been caught at a red light, and that silver minivan wouldn't have pulled out in front of them, slowing him down even more. He would have arrived in time to stop it.

Most of Jason's days were spent thinking about what would have happened if they had arrived just sixty seconds earlier. If he wasn't such a useless idiot, Mr. Davis would still be alive. Molly wouldn't have had to see someone's face shot off. Lauren might not be locked away in hospital. Her mom wouldn't be a widow. Her brothers would still have their family.

Jason couldn't stop himself counting up to sixty. Timing it on his watch. Sixty seconds made all the difference in the world – there was so much that could be done in one minute. Preparing a bowl of cereal. Getting undressed and stepping into the shower. Grabbing a gun from your little sister and killing her.

The best thing he could do for Tiffany, for the baby, and even for his mom, was to go to London and not come back. Ever.

His mom drove into the departures short-term parking garage and pulled into a space. "What's rattling around in the glove compartment? Can you check?"

Jason clicked open the glove compartment door and saw two rings, one gold and one silver, resting side by side in the compartment. Lauren's and Molly's purity rings. As though God had placed them there as a reminder that he was making the right decision.

His mom opened her door. "What is it?"

"Just some loose change." He picked up the rings and slipped them into his bag.

June 2018

"And ye shall know the truth, and the truth shall make you free."

JOHN 8:32

FORTY-FIVE

She strides through the doors and past the check-in desk, staffed by volunteers who look like older versions of the homecoming spirit squad.

"Hi, and welcome! Excuse me, you need to –" a woman calls after her, holding out a pen.

She pushes past couples giving her curious looks.

Oh my God, is that –

I didn't think she was coming!

She enters the conference room. About twenty large round tables are set for dinner but most people are milling around the middle of the room, hugging, chatting and taking selfies together. She stalks around the room, people glancing at her, whispering.

"Calum." She grabs his arm.

"Hey, look at you," He embraces her and steps back. "This is my wife, Cindy."

A pretty woman holds a hand over a swollen belly. "I love your show so much. So good to meet you."

She remembers her personal brand. "Thanks, that's so sweet. And congratulations on the little one on the way." The woman opens her mouth to respond but is interrupted. "Listen, is Jason here?"

Calum looks at her. "You're kidding, right?"

They aren't here.

She had been so sure. Absolutely positive. But – nothing.

Maybe she was wrong. Maybe there wasn't some secret. Unless …

"I'll catch up with you both later." She returns to the reception area and marches up to the desk.

"Hi. Wow. You didn't RSVP so we didn't think you'd be here, but no problem. Not sure if you remember me? Shannon? Shannon McGuire? Well, actually, now I'm Shannon Whiteside. I can get you signed in and –"

She snatches the sign-in sheet from Shannon's hand and flips the paper over, scanning the names. There! She was right. Of course she was right.

She hands the paper back. "Where's the hotel bar and restaurant?"

"Um, everything's happening here? Right through those doors?" Everything Shannon says is an anxious question.

The woman looks around and sees signs pointing to the hotel reception. She flashes a smile at Shannon. "Of course I remember you. Great to see you again."

"Really?" Shannon flushes. "I love your show. Can we get a selfie together?"

"Definitely. I'll be right back."

"Amazing. Thank you." Shannon reaches for her phone but the woman is gone.

She strides down the hallway, around a corner and through double doors. The hotel lobby is a large, beige marble space with a surprisingly ugly modern black chandelier.

Three receptionists look up and smile simultaneously. She ignores them and turns to the bar entrance.

"I'm joining a group that's already here." She walks past the young hostess without waiting for a response.

It's the first bar she's entered in seven years. It's windowless, cool and dimly lit. Her eyes need to adjust so she can peer past the large plants dotted around and into the dark corners. And there. Right there! She knew it.

Jason and Lauren are sitting together, and now he's reaching for her hand.

The soft carpet muffles her heels as she makes her way to the low table in the corner. "What are you doing?"

"Tiffany, I –" Jason pulls his hand back. His mouth opens and closes. Tiffany can feel the stare from the woman sitting opposite them but doesn't take her eyes off Jason. "What are you ... I didn't think you were coming."

"Exactly. So to clarify, you can fly back from Europe for a high school reunion but you can't be bothered to visit your own daughter? And don't even get me started on *you*." She points a manicured finger at Lauren.

Lauren blinks at her. "I almost didn't recognise you. The brunette suits you."

Tiffany glares at them. "I know what's going on here."

"What?" Lauren touches her hair nervously, which is styled in a short pixie cut, framing her face. She wears a plain royal blue wrap dress and no makeup. Back to the prairie girl look. Such a waste of her features.

"I just saw you holding hands. I figured this out years ago, so you can stop pretending now."

Lauren's eyes widen. "What, me and Jason?"

"Yes, you and Jason. I'm not an idiot. You both disappeared off the face of the earth and that's obviously not a coincidence, is it? You're not on Twitter, Instagram, Facebook or even – urgh, what's it called? – oh, whatever. The whole *world* is on something now, and –"

A waiter appears. He looks too young to work in a bar. "Can I get you anything?"

Tiffany fluffs her bun. "Club soda and lime, please."

The waiter leaves and Tiffany sits next to the woman on the small sofa opposite Jason and Lauren. The woman has to shift over to avoid Tiffany sitting on her lap. Tiffany does a double take when she realizes it's Molly. She's wearing a long-sleeved blush pink pencil dress with a tie belt that hugs her curves. Tiffany would have discouraged someone pale from wearing such a light color, but it makes her smooth, creamy skin and dark hair a feature. Molly's makeup has been expertly applied – perfect contouring, on-trend pinky nude lipstick and a touch of mascara. Blended taupe and tawny eyeshadow highlights her eyes. Maybe she did pick up a few things from the makeovers Tiffany used to give her.

"Hi, Tiffany. You look great. Very… Kardashian." Molly picks up a glass of white wine on the table and takes a large swallow.

"And you knew about them. Like you always know everything." Tiffany says.

"There's nothing to know."

"Stop fucking lying." Almost word for word, it's the same conversation Tiffany had with Molly ten years ago, the last time they saw each other. "So, how long have you all been secretly meeting up without me?" Tiffany is already imagining relaying this scenario to Daphne, her Al-Anon sponsor. A tiny part of her is thrilled to have been right all this time.

"We've not been secretly meeting up," Jason says.

"Bullshit."

"Really, we haven't. This is the first time I've seen Lauren since –"

"You need to start telling the truth. I'm here to get some answers that you owe me from ... about, oh, let's see ..." Tiffany tilts her head and pretends to count on her fingers. "Ten fucking years ago." Tiffany hasn't sworn for years, ever since her daughter Jasmine started talking. Now she seems to have reverted back to her eighteen-year-old self and can't stop. "I want to know what happened on graduation day. It was the worst day of my life. I want some answers and I want them *now*."

The waiter returns and places a lime and soda in front of Tiffany with a shaking hand. "On the house." He clears his throat. "Might I, er, get you to write something for my mom? She's a huge, huge fan." He holds out a pen and a napkin.

"Of course." Tiffany scrawls 'Sending my love!' a smiley face, a heart, several x's and o's and #talkandteawithtiffany. It takes a while. She hands them back to him and beams. "Your mom is very lucky to have you."

The waiter turns red and picks up Molly's empty glass. "Another one, ma'am?"

Molly shakes her head. "I'm leaving soon."

Tiffany grips her arm. "No, you're not," she hisses. "None of you are."

Molly looks at the waiter. "Large, please."

"Sir? Ma'am?" The waiter turns to Lauren and Jason.

"I'm good, thanks," Jason nods at the coffee in front of him.

Lauren shakes her head. "No, thank you." A cup of herbal tea in front of her is untouched.

Tiffany watches them watch the waiter walk away. She waits.

No one speaks.

Tiffany has a craving for a double vodka and Diet Coke. Maybe she should have called Daphne, or her therapist, before she barged in here.

"Well? When did you two get together?" Tiffany waves a finger at Jason and Lauren, blinking back tears. Dammit. It's only four minutes in and she's about to completely lose it. "And don't you dare fucking lie to me."

"I swear, we're not –" Jason is a terrible liar.

"My ex-best friend and my ex-boyfriend. The real reason why you never see your daughter."

This could be an extended show. Or more than one. She'll have to discuss it with her agent and the show's producer but she's already imagining possible headlines for the covers of *Us Weekly* and *People* ('*My betrayal*' or '*Pushed to the edge by ex's secrets*').

Lauren holds up her left hand, displaying a plain silver band.

"You're still a virgin? You kept the pledge?" Tiffany is stunned.

Molly splutters and coughs.

"It's my wedding ring. I'm happily married." Lauren's voice is soft. "And not to Jason."

"But you've kept your purity ring, right?"

"No." Lauren pauses. "It didn't really seem to mean anything."

"Well, I've kept mine."

"Tiffany, you weren't even a virgin when you *took* the pledge," Molly says.

"But it's kind of cool we all did something together, right? It's something to remember high school by. And each other. I thought it would be cute if we all kept ours."

Lauren and Jason pick up their cups in unison and drink. Molly picks at her nails.

"God. It's like it meant nothing to all of you." Tiffany feels tears threaten to fall and takes a breath. "And anyway, something happened. Maybe it didn't last but you both disappeared."

Lauren and Jason exchange a glance.

"*There*. See?" Tiffany turns to Molly for confirmation but Molly is looking over Tiffany's shoulder, watching the waiter arrive with her wine.

"Thank you." Molly picks up the glass.

Jason rubs his head. "I promise, I haven't seen Lauren for ten years. I came today because I was hoping she would be here. I wanted to see how she was."

"Me too," says Molly.

Lauren nods. "And I came because I was hoping they'd be here, so I could say th–" she stops. "Fill them in on things. But I'm glad you're here, Tiffany, because I wanted to apologize. I'm sorry I wasn't there for you when the baby was born."

"Well. I mean, obviously you were dealing with ..." Tiffany's unsure whether to mention Lauren's dad's suicide. Whatever she says now she'll sound like a bitch. She takes a sip of her soda and lime. "I was worried about you. When I heard what happened, I just wanted to make sure you were okay. And I couldn't get hold of you. Your cell phone was turned off. I went to your house a couple of times and it was all closed up, no one was home. And then you moved.

Without telling me. I just got there one day, and the house was empty. It was like, like you had –" Tiffany's voice is choked, "– abandoned me!"

"Not everything is about you, Tiffany," Molly raises a groomed eyebrow.

"Molly," Jason says warningly.

"What? I spent my senior year doing her homework for her."

Tiffany flinches.

"Molly."

"Well, I'm just saying."

"You don't need to be mean." Jason looks at Tiffany. "Just ignore her."

Tiffany plays with a strand of hair. "Oh, whatever. She's probably right. I have dyslexia. I was diagnosed a few years ago. I probably wouldn't even have graduated if it weren't for you all helping me with my homework. So, you know – thank you."

Molly has the decency to look ashamed. "I didn't realize. Sorry."

"I didn't get a chance to tell you. Because you all disappeared. Without telling me," Tiffany points out.

"I'm sorry," Lauren says. "I did think about you, and the baby, often. But I couldn't call you or visit. I was ... away for a while."

"Where? With Jason?"

"No." Lauren plays with the hem of her dress. "I, I was at a –"

"Don't tell her," Jason interrupts. "She'll make a show about it."

"Oh my *God*, Jason. Is that what you think of me? That I turn everything into a show?" Tiffany is rather pleased. Several people have complimented her on her resourcefulness.

"Well, don't you?"

"If the topic is relevant to my show's vision and mission, then it's something I consider."

"And what exactly is your show's 'vision and mission'?" Molly asks.

Tiffany clears her throat. "To demonstrate connection and support to single mothers choosing to live their best lives through shared experiences. Is that acceptable to you?"

"With makeovers and diet tips?"

"There's lots of different ways for women to feel good about themselves inside and out, and *Talk and Tea with Tiffany* explores all of those various paths." It's killing Tiffany not to ask Molly who did her makeup. She must have paid someone.

Molly shrugs. "It just seems kind of like a gossip show to me."

"If you watched it, you'd have seen the one about dyslexia. And how people come up with coping strategies."

That shuts her up.

"Should you be in here, Tiffany?" Jason is frowning. "You know, with your recovery and stuff?"

"Like you care. That's why you decided to hide out in here, isn't it? You thought I wouldn't come into a bar." Tiffany is triumphant as a realization hits her. "Lauren is the one you should be worried about, anyway. You were in rehab, weren't you?"

Lauren opens her mouth and closes it again.

"I know you were stealing my mom's prescription pills. But I told the police I didn't know anything when they were asking questions."

Lauren bites her lip. "Please tell your mom I'm sorry. I was addicted to them, but I shouldn't have been stealing them."

"Well, you did my mom a favor," Tiffany admits generously. "The fact she couldn't remember what medication she'd taken or when, or when she last saw her own handgun, made her realize she needed help with her addiction issues. She joined AA and NA the week after Jasmine was born."

Lauren puts her hand over her mouth. "I had no idea things were that bad for her. I'm glad she got help."

"Are you okay being here, though? Maybe it isn't a good idea for *you*." Tiffany can see the bartender preparing two martinis out of the corner of her eye. They look delicious. "We can go somewhere else."

"This is fine," Lauren reassures her.

"We just wanted somewhere quiet to talk, and catch up," Molly says.

Tiffany studies her. "You know, I have a show coming up about transformations – ugly ducklings turning into beauties. I could see if I have space for one more person." She pulls out her phone and taps in some notes for herself. When she looks up Jason and Lauren are looking at her as though she's just announced she enjoys torturing kittens. "What? It's a compliment. You know that, right?"

Molly laughs, her cheeks flushed. She looks even prettier. "Thanks, but no thanks."

"Well. You look really good. So, you know. Think about it." Tiffany fishes a small pink card out of her purse and hands it to Molly. "The number on here is for my assistant. Contact her if you change your mind."

"It's just makeup, Tiff. It's not a big deal. It's from work." Molly puts the card on the table.

"Really?" Another possible theme? *Tap into work to help your transformation*? "What do you do?"

"I work for a makeup company," Molly says.

Never, in a million years, would Tiffany have guessed that Molly's career would be based around makeup. "Like, on a beauty counter? Your mom works in a store, right?"

"No, I'm a chemical engineer. And my mom's a lawyer now." She's halfway through her glass of wine. Tiffany feels a pang of jealousy.

"A chemical engineer? At a makeup company?" Tiffany isn't sure if Molly's joking. She turns to Lauren. "What do you do?"

"I'm a social worker."

Of course she is. Tiffany can perfectly visualize Lauren with a clipboard listening to parents complain about their children. It sounds almost as boring as Jason's accounting job.

Jason clears his throat. "Look, I really can't stay too long."

"Then you better hurry up and talk." Tiffany's almost forgetting why she's here. "What the hell happened on graduation day? Why did you all leave? Well, not you," she graciously concedes to Lauren. "I get why you ... you know. Had other stuff. But still." She looks at Molly. "At least you visited a couple of times that summer, which is more than those two. But then you went away to college and literally never came back. And Lauren, I know your dad's suicide was awful, and you went to rehab and stuff, but I tried to be there for you. You didn't call me. Not once.

"I was by myself at graduation, and going into labor early was scary. My mom was drunk the whole time and arguing with my dad. I gave birth, and thought I was going to die." Tiffany flushes at her choice of words, but it's true. She had truly thought she was going to be torn in two. She takes a breath and continues. "I found out my dad was selling our home. And then the police turned up asking all sorts of questions that I had no fucking clue about. It was the worst day of my life and none of you were there. And I will never, ever forgive you for that." She turns to Jason. "Especially you. You know what? I'm happy you left. You don't deserve to be part of your daughter's life now."

Jason blinks back tears and Tiffany is glad, even though it contradicts her affirmations on forgiveness. Lauren scrabbles in her oversized bag and finds tissues, handing a few to Jason and Tiffany and keeping one to wipe her eyes. Lauren looks like she's about to say something.

"It was my fault," Molly blurts out.

"How? Don't do Jason any favors." Tiffany dabs her eyes, careful not to smear mascara.

"Jason stopped me from killing myself."

"What?"

"I was in a bad place. I had really low self-esteem and an eating disorder. And depression. Things just got worse and worse and one day, I just …" Molly shrugs, like it's no big deal. "I was planning to end things on graduation day. It sounds stupid now, but at the time it made sense. Anyway, Jason kept me safe. He drove me away from the school, where I was going to do it. That's why he wasn't there."

Tiffany realizes her mouth is open and closes it.

"I just wanted to leave it all behind me when I went to college, so I didn't come back. My mom eventually moved out east as well. We both wanted a fresh start." Molly swallows the last of her wine defiantly. "So, you shouldn't be mad at Jason. He saved my life and kept it a secret because I asked him to."

Tiffany looks at Lauren, who is staring at her tea. "You knew as well and no one told me –" She stops herself and picks up her soda water. Tiffany has built her entire career on letting go of fear and anger, and finding serenity in order to live her best life. She nibbles at the straw. She regularly posts about love and forgiveness on Facebook and Instagram and TikTok. She puts the glass down and takes a deep breath. "I mean, that sucks. I didn't know you felt that way. I'm sorry you went through that. But you could have told me at the time. I would have helped you."

Molly gives a small smile. "Thank you. I'm sorry, too, that you were by yourself when you went into labor. And I think your shows are really good for your target audience. Very contemporary."

"Thanks, Molly." Tiffany squeezes her arm and thinks she might start crying. She turns to Jason. "So, okay. I guess you're really good at keeping secrets. And I get why you weren't there for the labor. But the last ten *years*? Your mom keeps making excuses for you, and I'm sorry about what happened with your sister, I really am, but the day Jasmine was born, you took one look at her, and left." She dabs her eyes with a tissue. "Because we weren't good enough for you. And we still aren't."

Jason shakes his head. "It's not that. It was never, ever that. And I'm sorry you feel that way. I just … I just wanted what was best for the baby, and for you. You're a great mom. She's so lucky to have you."

"How is you not being here best for us? You abandoned us."

"I'd be a terrible dad, trust me."

"But you haven't even tried." Tiffany expects a show of female solidarity from Molly and Lauren but they're silent. She wants to scream.

Jason stands up. "Sorry, but I have to go."

"Me, too." Molly picks up her purse.

"You're both leaving? Together?"

"We came here together," Molly says.

"What?"

"I did a study abroad year in France, and Jason was in London. Our moms put us in touch and we visited each other and…" Molly looks at Jason, as though for confirmation. "Now we're friends." She stands. "I'm going to the restroom, okay? Then we can go."

Jason nods and sits back down in his chair, looking as though he'd rather be anywhere else. Molly squeezes past Tiffany and heads to the restroom. Her heels give her an extra couple of inches, the dress hugs her figure and her hips sway. Molly Calderwood looks *sexy*.

Tiffany studies Jason. "All this time you and Molly have been friends with each other?" She feels like she's landed in an alternate universe.

Jason stares at the floor. He knows how much Tiffany hates secrets.

"I think it's great that you have each other in Europe," Lauren chimes in unhelpfully. "It would have been so lonely there – oh! Here's my ride."

Tiffany turns and sees a petite Asian woman approach. She's wearing blue jeans, a black tank top and her glossy hair is in a neat bob. She doesn't look like a taxi driver.

"Hi. I'm sorry to interrupt but I just wanted to see if you're okay?"

"This is Priya, my wife." Lauren stands up.

"Your wife!" Tiffany has underestimated Lauren. Not quite the prairie girl after all. "I'm Tiffany. So good to meet you." She rises and gives Priya a hug. "You are welcome at my place any time."

"Oh my gosh, I know who you are. Thank you. That would be amazing. I love your shows. And your blog. And your Instagram."

Priya is adorable. Jason shakes Priya's hand and Tiffany raises her eyebrows at Lauren. "She's beautiful," Tiffany whispers.

"I know," Lauren mouths, beaming. Lauren hasn't really changed. Just when Tiffany thinks she has her figured out, she still has the capacity to surprise.

Molly comes back from the restroom, lipstick freshly applied. Lauren introduces her to Priya. "It's so good to meet you." Molly looks up at Jason. "Don't we have time to stay a little longer?"

"Sorry, we have to go," Jason says. "I'll get the bill."

"It's on me," Tiffany offers, thinking they'll have to stay for another drink. They all protest. "I insist. Really."

Jason gives Lauren a hug. "Take care of yourself." He turns to Tiffany and bends down to kiss her cheek.

Tiffany turns her head away. "Whatever. Just leave. Like you always do."

Molly pulls Tiffany into an embrace. "I know you're mad at him but he's trying," Molly whispers. Her breath smells of wine.

They walk out of the bar, Jason's tall frame sloping alongside Molly. Tiffany feels like she's watching two thieves walk off with her life savings.

"Are you heading into the reunion now?" Lauren asks. "I'm sure there's loads of people who'll want to speak to you."

"Yes, I am. We can go in together! I just need to fix my makeup."

"No, I'm not heading in there. It'll be, you know. Kind of weird. And we're driving to my brother's house, so we better make a start."

"Right. Sure." Tiffany grabs Priya's hand. "Come visit. I really mean it." She turns to Lauren. "How is your mom? And your brothers? I mean, it must have been a struggle, financially, after …"

The silence gets weird until finally Lauren shrugs. "The church raised some funds for us, so it was all – you know. They were okay, eventually. Adam finished his degree last year. Michael's still in college. My mom's working part-time. My sister's doing good at school."

Priya squeezes Lauren's shoulder and Tiffany regrets bringing it up. She hugs Lauren. "I've missed you."

"I've missed you, too. You were the best part of my senior year." When Lauren pulls away she's blinking back tears.

Priya takes her hand. "Come on, babe."

"See you both soon, I hope," Tiffany calls after them as they leave.

Tiffany stands by the table. The bar is getting busy but she has the sensation of being completely alone. The young waiter scurries past her with a tray of empty wine and cocktail glasses. For some inexplicable reason, Tiffany feels like bursting into tears. She reaches for her purse and sees that Molly left the business card on the table. Well. She can always ask Jason for her contact details. Since apparently they're friends.

At least she'll see Lauren again soon. Maybe she and Priya can be on a show (*'Under the Covers: A Celebration of Diversity and Love'*). She takes out her cell phone to give an update to Daphne before heading to the reunion.

Tiffany pauses halfway through the message.

Lauren never left her contact details, so they can't see each other again.

Same with Molly. Who pretended to like her but left the business card behind. She really does think Tiffany is stupid.

And Jason is still hiding things from her. Like he always has.

They didn't even keep their purity rings, to remember the one thing that tied them all together.

And they all just walked off and left her. Alone. Just like last time.

What's the point of all the therapy and twelve step meetings if nothing ever changes?

Tiffany puts her phone away and walks to the bar. She perches on a stool and waves at the bartender. "Vodka and Diet Coke, please. Double."

FORTY-SIX

"You think I'm a dick, don't you?"

Jason and Molly walk towards the car in the dusk, Molly's heels clicking on the concrete.

"No," Molly replies. "But I think you need to go back into therapy."

"You sound like Tiffany."

"Well, she has a point. You have unresolved issues. And your daughter is growing up without a father. I know what that's like, and it's awful."

"Yes, and I know what that's like as well, remember?"

Molly sighs and stands by the passenger door of the hire car. "Sorry. I know." She squeezes his hand. "And I don't think you're a dick at all. I just think it's really sad Jasmine is missing out on getting to know a wonderful dad." Jason shakes his head. "Seriously. Jason." She's still holding his hand. He lifts his gaze to meet hers. "You're my best friend for a reason, okay? I think you're the most amazing person I've ever met."

He smiles, waiting, but Molly doesn't make a sarcastic comment. Her eyes flicker across his face. Her lips are glossy and full. He's been noticing them all evening. He tightens his grip on her hand almost imperceptibly. She steps closer and they are inches apart. He can smell her perfume.

Molly tilts her face towards his.

Before Jason can change his mind, he dips his head and kisses her. The first one is quick – a soft experiment. The second one is firmer, lingering.

Jason has thought about doing this for years, but it's even better than he thought it would be. He pulls back, worried.

"This could completely ruin our friendship."

"Good. I'm tired of being your friend anyway." Molly wraps her arms around his waist and pulls him closer.

Jason has the unfamiliar sensation that things in his life are slotting neatly into place.

And then Molly ruins it. "Just tell her. Tell her about your sister."

"No."

"It's not fair. She deserves to know about the accident and your OCD, and why you're scared."

"She'll make a show about it. Or do an interview with some magazine. Or both." Already his heart rate is quickening, his breathing shallow.

"Give her some credit, Jason."

"And she might never let me see Jasmine again. At least this way I get to talk to her, and see her occasionally."

Molly places her hands on his shoulders. "Remind me. Who knows about what happened when you were a kid?"

"You."

"Yes. And?"

"My mom. Obviously." He clears his throat. "My dad. My psychiatrists."

"And?"

"And Lauren, as of tonight."

"Right. And out of all those people, has anyone stopped speaking to you?" Molly looks at him. If he wanted to, Jason would be able to count the gold flecks on each green iris.

"No."

"Has anyone cut you out of their life?"

"Well. No."

"All those people accept you for exactly who you are, right?"

"Right," he says, grudgingly.

"And one of those people has just kissed you, right?"

"Yes." He still can't believe it. He goes to kiss her again.

Molly holds his face in his hands. "So get back in there, and tell her the truth."

FORTY-SEVEN

"So, Tiffany thinks you were in rehab?" Priya steers the car out of the parking lot.

Lauren shrugs. "As long as I don't end up on one of her shows, I guess it doesn't matter."

"Do you think she meant it? We can go and stay with her?"

"We're not staying with her." The last thing Lauren needs is Tiffany delving into the past with Priya there.

"But it's an invitation to Tiffany Vanderkamp's house. We'd get to drink tea, and talk. With Tiffany! The girls at work are going to be so jealous when I tell them."

"You're not telling them."

"It's their favorite show."

"You're not telling them anything about meeting her."

"Why not?"

"Because if they know I went to high school with her, they'll start looking things up. They might see stuff about my dad. The news articles are still out there." Lauren thinks of the headlines Priya's co-workers would find. *Pastor's Struggles with Sin End in Tragedy* was one of the nicer ones. *Perverted Pastor Commits Suicide* was not. "It's easy for people to connect the dots. I understand why Jason went off grid."

"Things have changed. People talk about abuse a lot more now." Priya stops at a red light.

"I don't want your friends seeing a victim every time they look at me."

"You know that's not what I see, right?" Priya glances at her. "I see a beautiful, strong, brave survivor."

"I love you. But we're not going."

"Okay. Fine." Priya sighs dramatically. "Tiffany Vanderkamp invites me to her home, in LA, and I can't tell anyone."

"Correct." Lauren leans over to kiss Priya on the cheek. "Thank you for being there. Waiting for me."

"I know it was important you got to see them. And even if I can't tell anyone else, it's amazing I met Tiffany."

Lauren smiles, wishing Priya had gotten to meet the high school Tiffany with the messy bedroom and penchant for spontaneous makeovers.

The traffic light turns green and Priya drives. "And Molly and Jason. They're not together?"

"No, just friends."

"Huh."

"What?"

"Just seems like – they're more than that, that's all. Anyway, are you glad you went?"

"Yes. But it's sad." Neat, unremarkable rows of suburban houses pass by, like the one Lauren's family lived in her senior year. She wonders what secrets are happening in them. "I still can't believe what Jason told me tonight. Imagine feeling like you've destroyed your whole family just from being a little kid playing around. I had no idea he had been struggling with that all these years."

"A lot of people struggle with the past," Priya squeezes Lauren's knee. "And you're living proof they can turn out just fine."

Lauren isn't entirely sure about that, but she loves Priya for believing it. Priya is so kind, so innocent.

For the millionth time, Lauren sends a silent thank you to Molly and Jason for what they did that day, giving her the chance to have an almost normal life. Now she's thanked them in person, understood why they came to her rescue, she feels lighter.

Lauren plays with her wedding ring. It seems unfair that Molly and Jason know her better than Priya does. But Lauren has spent the last decade lying to her family, her whole marriage lying to her wife. Life might be unbearable without moments like these, when she can see herself as Priya sees her.

She doesn't ever let herself imagine Priya discovering the truth.

FORTY-EIGHT

Molly sits in the passenger seat feeling pleasantly tipsy and watches Jason walk back to the hotel. A light breeze comes through the open window. She leans her head back on the headrest and touches her lips.

She remembers when Jason had come to visit her in Paris during her study abroad year. He had entered the brasserie they had arranged to meet in and Molly had waved him over, feeling nervous. She had already started on the carafe of red wine she had ordered for them to share. They had hugged awkwardly and Jason had pulled off his scarf and coat, draping them on the back of his chair.

Molly had watched him pouring himself a glass of wine from the carafe. "Oh my God, Jason. You're wearing your purity ring? Why?"

Jason had looked sheepish. "My mom told me I should wear it the whole time I'm in college as a reminder not to get anyone else pregnant."

Molly had laughed. "I don't think it'll make a difference."

"That reminds me." Jason had reached into his coat pocket, pulled out a small envelope and passed it to Molly.

"What is this?" Molly had asked as she opened it.

"Your rings. They ended up in my car. You know, that day – that, um. I wasn't sure if you wanted them or not."

Molly had tipped the rings into her hand, giggled hysterically, and then burst into tears.

By the end of lunch they had been halfway through their second carafe of wine. Jason had been ruminating, again, on arriving at Lauren's house too late. "If I had just driven a few seconds faster … It would have changed everything, you know?"

"He was a manipulative pervert who deserved to die. The more I think about it, the better I feel that I let Lauren take the gun."

"He was a terrible person, yes. And he should have gone to prison. But Molly, if I'd just arrived sooner –"

"You think him being alive would be better? Her brothers spending the next few decades deciding whether to have him in their lives? Not knowing whether to visit him, or write to him? Loving him and feeling guilty about loving him, and knowing their father was the kind of person who –" Molly had topped up their glasses. "It's better he's not in their life at all. Lauren probably saved a whole load of girls from him, not just her little sister. She did the world a favor when she killed him, trust me." She had looked at Jason defiantly.

"What do you mean?"

"Me and Mike, we … I let him – no, wait. I didn't let him." Molly had remembered the support group she joined her sophomore year at college, and the wording they used. "He molested me. He made me do stuff I didn't want to do. It went on for weeks." She had clutched her wine glass as though it were a lifebuoy, waiting for Jason to remind her she had been eighteen at the time. An adult. Fully capable of making her own decisions, including the ability to say no.

But he had reached across the table and held her hand, and waited. So Molly had continued talking, and Jason had listened. By the third carafe of wine, they were both extremely drunk, Jason had told her about the accident with his sister, and they were both in tears.

Afterwards, they had walked along the dark streets, their arms linked to keep warm, until they arrived at a bridge over the Seine.

"You take Lauren's." Molly had handed him Lauren's ring. "Because you really need to let go of that shit about not getting there in time."

They had silently flung the three purity rings into the river, then gone to another brasserie and ordered sparkling wine they couldn't afford.

Molly had thought Jason was the only person who knew about her and Mike other than the support group she had joined and the counselor at college. Until tonight, when Lauren had told her how sorry she was for what her father did to Molly. Lauren had spent years regretting not telling someone as soon as she'd remembered being abused, wondering if she could have stopped him abusing Molly. After Lauren was discharged from hospital, she had tried to find Molly but hadn't been able to. Molly had reassured her it wouldn't have made a difference and had felt strangely guilty seeing Lauren's face flood with relief.

Molly watches a few of her former classmates making their way back to their cars. It's hard to tell in the dark, but one of them looks like Calum and a very pregnant partner. She squints. Behind him, is that Ernie Chang? She could get out of the car, say hello. But he might ask where she went on graduation day, and there would be too much explaining to do.

Molly stays motionless, hoping they don't see her. Why is everything so complex? All this time Lauren felt guilty about Molly. Jason felt guilty about Lauren, on top of what happened with his sister. Molly still feels guilty about how she treated her mom, and some of the things she said to her. And Molly envies Tiffany – perhaps now more than ever. Tiffany is the only one of them who doesn't have anything to feel guilty about.

Molly counts the number of floors in the hotel. Fourteen.

Sometimes, when Molly thinks about Mike, she looks up at the tallest building she can see and imagines herself standing on the roof.

Stepping to the edge.

The millisecond between her feet lifting off solid ground and the descent.

How it would feel to be weightless, suspended between everything she's ever known and whatever comes next.

Sometimes, she can see herself actually doing it.

But then she reminds herself of the job she loves. She pictures her mom's head bent over her law textbooks. She feels the warmth of Jason's hand over hers.

And the moment passes.

FORTY-NINE

The bartender measures the vodka into a glass and tops it up with Diet Coke. Tiffany can already feel the tingle on her tongue. The heat sliding down her throat. The delicious fuzziness in her brain. There's a slight cough. The young waiter from earlier, the one she signed the napkin for, is standing next to her.

"It's none of my business, but are you sure you want that?" He nods at the drink the bartender has placed in front of her. His face – incredibly – is redder than it was before.

"I just ordered it."

"I mean, I know." He looks like he might cry. "But I just wanted to say, you saved my mom. That's what she always says. If it weren't for you, and your show, she wouldn't have gotten help for her drinking. And she always says if you can do it, after everything you've been through, anyone can."

The bartender places a tray of cocktails in front of the waiter and he picks them up shakily. "Maybe just think about calling your sponsor?" He seems near collapse.

Tiffany turns back to the bar, expecting to hear a crash at any moment. She is mesmerized by the tiny bubbles floating to the top of her glass. Each bubble makes its own little journey, sometimes colliding with others, sometimes not. But on reaching the surface they all end up self-destructing anyway.

The glass is slippery with condensation as she lifts it.

"Tiffany?"

She turns. "What do you want?"

"I have to tell you something." Jason bites his lip. "Molly said it wasn't fair I'm keeping it from you. And she's right."

"Okaaayyy."

He sits next to her and watches the bartender walk to the other end of the bar to take an order. "I killed Jasmine."

Tiffany laughs uncertainly. "She's fine. I spoke to her a couple of hours ago. She's with my mom."

"No, I mean –" his eyes dart around, looking everywhere but at her, "– my sister, Jasmine. The story my mom told you about what happened that day. It wasn't true. Jasmine wasn't by herself, we were playing together. She found the gun, but I was the one who shot her. I didn't know – I didn't understand that the gun was …" he shakes his head and looks down. "I killed her."

"Oh my God." Tiffany puts the glass down.

"And our daughter looks so much like Jasmine did. The same name and – she's just, she's just so perfect. The day she was born, when I held her and saw how perfect she was, I made a decision." He picks up a napkin from the bar and wipes his eyes. "I'll never let myself be alone with her. I might accidentally hurt her, and I can't live with doing that again."

Tiffany's mind is spinning. Jason is finally being honest with her and it's awful.

"So …" he finally makes eye contact. "I just thought you should know the truth. Why I've always been so – you know. Well, Molly insisted I tell you. I'm sorry I'm a bad father. I know I am. But I'm trying to do what's best. Because I love her so much." He chokes up. "That's all. I'll leave now."

"No." Tiffany clutches his arm. "You're not leaving now." She pulls him over to a sofa that two people have just vacated. A large palm provides some privacy. "Sit down."

"Excuse me, ma'am. Your drink?" The bartender calls after them.

"I changed my mind. Can I get a mint tea, please?" Jason is jiggling his knee. "Make that two." She sits next to him. "I need to sit with that a moment. That's a lot to take in. How much time do you have?"

"Molly said I should take as long as I needed. As long as you needed."

"She's always been very smart. Now start over again. And tell me everything."

Twenty minutes later, Jason is finished. He's never spoken so much all at one time. Once he started talking, he didn't stop. It's the saddest story Tiffany has ever heard.

She rests her hand on top of his. "I'm so sorry you went through that, Jason. That's a terrible experience for any child. Her death wasn't your fault. You had no way of understanding what would happen."

Jason sighs. "I worry about things going wrong with Jasmine. What else might I accidentally do? I start seeing all the possible problems and I panic. And then my OCD comes back. And then it seems easier to just, I don't know, avoid her altogether."

"Please, don't avoid her. You're the only father she has. Maybe we can figure out a way of you spending time with her when I'm around, if that'll help?"

Jason's eyes are bloodshot but he is leaning back on the sofa now, and his legs are still. "Really?"

"My agent keeps telling me I should spend more time in Europe. Widen my fan base. And you can stay with us in LA any time. I have a guest room. There's plenty of space."

"And you'd be there the whole time?"

"Yes, if that's what you want. Her birthday's coming up, why don't we figure out something for that?" Tiffany sips at her tea, which is lukewarm. "You know, we could work with a therapist, or a hypnotist. We'd ease you into it. I did an episode on phobias, and it was incredible how quickly people can overcome them with the right support." She'll call her producer as soon as Jason leaves (*'Overcoming Childhood Trauma'* or perhaps *'Confronting Ex's Demons'*).

"You're not going to do a show about this, are you?"

"It helps other people when they hear about –"

"No. Absolutely not. Never." He looks terrified.

"Okay, fine."

"You have to promise. You can't tell anyone else."

Tiffany huffs. The buzz of excitement in planning a new show, meeting new people, is better than any high alcohol can give her. It's disappointing. But there are other topics, other shows. "I promise. Your secret's safe," she nods.

"Thank you." He sits back. "And, um, do you think Molly could join me, if I visit you for Jasmine's birthday?"

"Sure. I want to talk to her more anyway. I'm thinking about starting a makeup line. Maybe she can be a consultant or – oh!" A knowing smile spreads across her face. "You and Molly – you're together?"

"Um. Well. Maybe. I mean, not yet. Well, we just – I don't know."

Tiffany tilts her head. "You don't know? You can tell me, you just told me everything else."

He grins sheepishly. "No, I really don't know. But I think we're about to become something."

Tiffany waits to feel jealous. Or pissed off. Or sad. But she doesn't. All those hours of therapy have paid off. She just feels relieved that Jason has someone sensible and clever to look after him. "Of course Molly's welcome. Where is she? Come on, let's go tell her we'll all be celebrating Jasmine's birthday together."

"But the fearful, and unbelieving, and the abominable, and murderers, and whoremongers, and sorcerers, and idolaters, and all liars, shall have their part in the lake which burneth with fire and brimstone: which is the second death."

Revelation 21:8

FIFTY

Shannon McGuire (now Whiteside) watches Tiffany and Jason leave. They're so self-absorbed, they don't even notice her. It's like high school all over again.

Shannon had come into the bar looking for Tiffany and the selfie she was promised and had seen her deep in conversation with Jason Myers. Shannon had seen Jason earlier, not that he had noticed her. He and that voluptuous woman, who had ended up being Molly Calderwood of all people, had left the reunion with Lauren Davis almost as soon as Lauren had walked in.

Judge not, that ye be not judged, Shannon reminds herself.

But really, what was the point of Shannon and the rest of the committee putting so much work into setting up the reunion – months and *months* of meetings and preparation, organizing venues and decorations and menus – when some people think they can just walk off as soon as they arrive?

The problem with people like that is that ten years on, they still think they're special. Just because they all sailed through high school being perfect and popular, doing their stupid cheerleading routines and basketball games. A decade later, they *still* don't talk to people like Shannon. They just go straight back into their cliques.

Not that Shannon's surprised. She had suspected she was in a room of hypocrites and idolaters when she had taken the purity pledge. She was probably the only one who had stayed pure until her wedding night. It was hard, and she faced temptation many times, but she did it. And it was worth it, the look on her husband's face when she handed him her purity ring on their first night together as man and wife. And when Shannon and her husband go through the usual marriage ups and downs all couples experience – their arguments over the kids, and money, and where to live – she reminds herself of the sacrifices she has made and feels stronger for it. She knows she can endure, because she is a woman of God. As she has proven time and again.

Anyway, now Shannon has something better than a photo with Tiffany Vanderkamp.

She retrieves her cell phone from under the fronds of the large kentia palm that separated her armchair backing onto the sofa Tiffany and Jason were sitting on. She taps the red record button to *Off*. Jason was speaking so quietly, she didn't catch most of what he said, but she knows it's something interesting. Some kind of secret. And it's right there, ready to be shared. Maybe even sold to the highest bidder.

Shannon waves the waiter over and orders a martini. As she waits for it to arrive, she tries to remember the exact Bible verse she's thinking of. What is it now? She searches the Bible App on her phone. Ah, yes. Luke 12.3: *Therefore whatsoever ye have spoken in darkness shall be heard in the light; and that which ye have spoken in the ear in closets shall be proclaimed upon the housetops.*

Shannon puts in her headphones, finds the audio file and presses *Play*.

AUTHOR'S NOTE

Sometimes it might feel like it, but you are never alone. If you, or someone you care about, are affected by the issues in this novel, help is available.

In the UK:

Samaritans: www.samaritans.org/
      (call 116 123 for 24-hour help)
Mind: www.mind.org.uk/
BEAT: www.beateatingdisorders.org.uk/
Victim Support: www.victimsupport.org.uk/

In the USA:

988 Suicide and Crisis Lifeline: 988lifeline.org/
      (call or text 988 for 24-hour help)
Substance Abuse and Mental Health Services
      Administration: www.samhsa.gov/
National Alliance on Mental Illness: nami.org/home
NEDA: www.nationaleatingdisorders.org/

ACKNOWLEDGEMENTS

This novel began as a few short stories scribbled in a beginners' writing course in a pub. To have it published is a culmination of years of support from family, friends, teachers, Chalk the Sun, and Pen to Print.

Thank you to my parents for surrounding me with books and reading. Thank you to my mum for reading to me every night before bed – quite possibly the best thing any parent can do for a child.

Thank you to my sister Robyn for the magazines and stories you created when we were young, and for letting me complete this story in your kitchen. Thank you to my nieces, Grace and Keira, for waiting patiently (most of the time!) for me to finish it.

Thank you to Lubala Chibwe for reading the first draft and offering wonderful suggestions to improve the story. And for all the ongoing creative and moral support (prosecco, pub visits, etc.).

Emily Coakley, thank you for your generosity in proofreading the manuscript. Any remaining errors are my own and I owe you a lot of English tea.

Thank you to Kerri Gladson for your patience in answering my odd questions and helping me get the details right. And for making high school fun.

Alexia Rowley, Becky Annandale and Caroline Kenny, thank you for being there in the Balham Bowls Club where it all started – and for still being around.

All the teachers and fellow students of my writing classes over the past decade – thank you for providing ideas, feedback, and a space to explore and play. Thank you to Ian Ayris for making me consider middles, endings, and how to write with economy and clarity.

Thank you to Preetha Leela Chockalingam, my mentor, for keeping me going when it got tough and telling me to the purity pledge back in! I'm so grateful to have you on my team.

Thank you to the entire Pen to Print team for your stellar work and support, and to Arts Council England for funding them.

Most of all, thank you to Ardella Jones, my first writing teacher, for making creative writing fun, accessible and sociable. Ten years ago, when I was writing short stories about Molly, Tiffany and Jason, you said, "This could be a novel, you know." You were right, of course. I wish you were still here to see it happen and celebrate with me.

ACKNOWLEDGEMENTS

This novel began as a few short stories scribbled in a beginners' writing course in a pub. To have it published is a culmination of years of support from family, friends, teachers, Chalk the Sun, and Pen to Print.

Thank you to my parents for surrounding me with books and reading. Thank you to my mum for reading to me every night before bed – quite possibly the best thing any parent can do for a child.

Thank you to my sister Robyn for the magazines and stories you created when we were young, and for letting me complete this story in your kitchen. Thank you to my nieces, Grace and Keira, for waiting patiently (most of the time!) for me to finish it.

Thank you to Lubala Chibwe for reading the first draft and offering wonderful suggestions to improve the story. And for all the ongoing creative and moral support (prosecco, pub visits, etc.).

Emily Coakley, thank you for your generosity in proofreading the manuscript. Any remaining errors are my own and I owe you a lot of English tea.

Thank you to Kerri Gladson for your patience in answering my odd questions and helping me get the details right. And for making high school fun.

Alexia Rowley, Becky Annandale and Caroline Kenny, thank you for being there in the Balham Bowls Club where it all started – and for still being around.

All the teachers and fellow students of my writing classes over the past decade – thank you for providing ideas, feedback, and a space to explore and play. Thank you to Ian Ayris for making me consider middles, endings, and how to write with economy and clarity.

Thank you to Preetha Leela Chockalingam, my mentor, for keeping me going when it got tough and telling me to the purity pledge back in! I'm so grateful to have you on my team.

Thank you to the entire Pen to Print team for your stellar work and support, and to Arts Council England for funding them.

Most of all, thank you to Ardella Jones, my first writing teacher, for making creative writing fun, accessible and sociable. Ten years ago, when I was writing short stories about Molly, Tiffany and Jason, you said, "This could be a novel, you know." You were right, of course. I wish you were still here to see it happen and celebrate with me.

KJ Quinn was born in Wiltshire and spent her impressionable years in America's Bible Belt. She lives in London, and The Purity Pledge is her first novel.

KJ Quinn was born in Wiltshire and spent her impressionable years in America's Bible Belt. She lives in London, and The Purity Pledge is her first novel.